The Smith Dynasty of Strong Women!

Hope You Enjoy the Read!

DYNASTIES

WINDS OF FIRE
BOOK ONE

ANJU GATTANI

ANJU GATTANI

Dynasties: Book One Winds of Fire Book Club Edition Copyright © 2022 by Anjana Gattani

Art cover credit: The Kim Killiion Group

Author photo credit: Daryl O'Hare Photography

ISBN: 979-8-9866524-2-9 (ebook)

ISBN: 979-8-9866524-1-2 (trade paperback)

ISBN: 979-8-9866524-0-5 (hardback)

PRAISE FOR DYNASTIES

"Dynasties kept me captivated from the first sentence to the very end. An enticing Downton Abbey-style saga but set in India! I simply adored it and I cannot wait to read the next book in the series. "—Barbara Bos, Managing Editor, www.booksby-women.org

"Hard to believe this lush, passionate novel is the author's first. In Dynasties, Anju Gattani has created an utterly immersive reading experience—fascinating characters, evocative details, compelling dramatic turns, all set against the teeming irrepressible vibrancy of modern-day India. A bravura performance."—David Corbett, award-winning author of The Art of Character

"With stories that take us into the culture and dynasties of India, Gattani introduces us to one powerful woman's journey against all odds."—Patti Callahan Henry, NYT Bestselling author of The Secret Book of Flora Lea

"With a richly evoked sense of place and culture, Dynasties is a deeply engrossing depiction of one woman's struggle for love and independence. It will keep you turning pages until the end."—Ausma Zehanat Khan, author of A Deadly Divide

"Five Diamonds in the Pulpwood Queen TIARA, my highest mark!"—The International Pulpwood Queens and Timber Guys Book Club Reading Nation.

"The truth of this story will stay with you long after the rich imagery disappears."—USA Today Bestselling Author, Barbara Conrey

"In Dynasties, Gattani brings to life modern day India in a way never before imagined as she breathes life into the pages with her depiction of the lush tapestry of Indian society."—USA Today Bestseller Lauren Smith

"A young woman, forced into an arranged marriage, battles cruelty, deception, and secrets to find her voice in modern-day India. A compulsive read."—Barbara Claypole White, Bestselling author of The Perfect Son and The Promise Between Us

"Like all good stories the story of Sheetal conveys deeper meanings about human experiences and relationships."—Qaisra Shahra, Peace activist, author of The Holy Woman & Founder/Executive Director of Muslim Arts and Cultural Festival, UK

To my parents...
Mom, Lalita
The strength of the pen that writes.
My Dad, G. D. Daga, for
Perspective and insight.

To my husband, Vivek
The river of my life.
Vikhyat and Vishesh
My Darling golden boys.
You are my creativity and
My silent writer's voice.

PROLOGUE

The Day of the Wedding, June 15, 2003

ALL OF RAIGUN, INDIA, BUZZED IN ANTICIPATION OF THE FIVE-hundred-million-rupee wedding of the decade.

EVERYONE...BUT THE BRIDE.

1

TISANDHI (THE ARISING)

Six months earlier

SHEETAL TRUDGED UPHILL TOWARD THE BROKEN FORT AND GLANCED behind to make sure no one followed. In the valley, glass facades of skyscrapers reflected the harsh glare of the winter sun. Nearby, several tourists in brightly colored T-shirts, sunglasses and visors gazed across the city of Raigun. Others followed a self-guided trail of the historic, abandoned Hindu temple while a few trekked downhill. A man dressed in worn white pajamas and a soot-smeared vest, a basket of peanuts roped to his neck, caught her gaze and pointed to the basket.

Sheetal shook her head, continued her climb along the cracked clay path and brushed away a drop of sweat that tickled the side of her face. She needed these final moments, this final goodbye, and for the hundredth time rehearsed the words she needed to say.

She stumbled on a half-buried chunk of broken masonry and regained her balance, but not before the pink chiffon *dupatta* that draped her shoulders snagged on a thorn bush and tightened around her neck. She hastily plucked the sash from the thorns of a single white rose, then reached to untangle the cuff of her elbow-length sleeve, now caught on thorns. A prick caused her to jerk back her hand. A drop of blood glistened on her index finger. She pressed the finger to her lips, sucked hard, then rewrapped the two-meter-long dupatta around her shoulders and covered her head while praying no one recognized her.

Mama and Papa were meeting with the wedding planner to finalize details for next month's engagement ceremony, and her wedding five months after, but they would be home soon. Sheetal hurried.

The gentle gradient gave way to a section of ruins closed to the public. Broken walls and marble pillars encircled a blue idol of Lord Krishna, a flute pressed to his lips. Crumbling statues of men and women in intimate poses graced the periphery.

Help me, please, she begged the god.

Tears pressed her eyelids. This holy place, renowned for its sense of calm and assurance bestowed on worshippers, offered no peace for her today. She'd come to end an innocent friendship that had blossomed into love over the last eight months.

Her heartbeat quickened when she spotted Arvind waiting beside a crumbling pillar. He could only ever be a friend. Just a friend. Never anything more.

As she drew near him, her pulse skipped a beat. He still

stole her breath. At five feet eleven, Arvind rivaled the gods with his dark, thick hair and copper-bronze skin that gleamed in the scorching sun. Oh, how she loved the intensity of his stare, as if he could see into her soul and penetrate her thoughts.

"Did you talk to your father about us?" he asked, his voice tight with male pride.

Sheetal halted and looked past his shoulder at the broken pillars. If only he'd stop looking at her with such yearning.

"I didn't."

He stared in disbelief. "You what?"

"Papa wouldn't listen," she lied.

"Did you try?"

She looked at the idol from the corner of her eye. *Please, Krishna, help me get the words right so it doesn't hurt.* But her only answer came in the form of a sand-coated breeze from the northern Rajasthan desert.

"All you had to do was say no," Arvind said. "Simple."

Nothing was simple. "Papa. He—"

"You don't love me. It was all a game. To lead me on. To—"

She stepped toward him, intending to touch him and soothe his anger, then stopped. "I risked everything to meet you...be with you."

"To tell me you're going ahead with the wedding. And I should just stand back and watch you marry another man. Is that it?"

Sheetal bit her lower lip. This was wrong. Falling in love. Promising Arvind they would be together. Now breaking his heart. She dropped her gaze to his tattered imitation suede shoes and her heart sank. Mama was right. He could never live up to their standards.

Arvind seized her shoulders and she snapped her head up to meet his gaze. "Do you understand," his voice gentled, "how much you mean to me? How much I love you?"

Her heart fisted in her throat. She took a deep breath and clasped her fingers together to refrain from touching. No physical contact. No touches. No hugs. She had promised herself this and much more before leaving the limousine parked in the lot below.

"Love means nothing to Papa. Money, reputation, class, and status. That's all that matters." Her attention shifted to the ripped beige front pocket of his shirt, one of many things Mama had brought to her attention last week. "Papa wants me"—she swallowed—"well taken care of."

"I can't dress you as fine as this." He pressed her shoulders, ran his hands down the length of her sleeves, then caught her hands. "But I can give you a decent life. One with love."

Decent? Her chest constricted. How many times had Papa reminded her that wealth passed from generation to generation, and a family's reputation had to be maintained by preserving the family honor? How could Arvind give her a decent life when they were worlds apart? He was unpolished, she was refined. He was rugged, she was haute couture. But the biggest difference was that he was a free Hindu man and she was a Hindu woman obligated to marry to uphold the family honor. Today, she belonged to Papa. In six months, she would belong to a man of Papa's choosing.

The lines on Arvind's face softened. "I'll talk to your father."

Talk Papa into allowing her to marry him?

She shook her head. "No."

"Why?"

"Papa won't see you." There was no telling what Papa would do if Arvind spoke with him. "He doesn't even know I'm with you right now. No one does."

"Sheetal—"

"Why can't you understand? I've tried so hard to make everyone understand. They won't listen. Neither will you. They said that you...you're not fit to be my husband."

Silence hung between them.

"Is that how you feel?" he asked in a quiet voice.

She tried to pull free of his grasp, but he held fast. "It doesn't matter what I feel. Everything has to be on Papa's terms."

"What do you want?" he whispered.

No one had ever cared to ask. What did it matter what she wanted when she was a slave to Papa's wants today and a husband's tomorrow? Sheetal tightened her grip on his fingers. "It's over. Let me go."

The hurt mingled with anger in his eyes broke her heart. She freed a hand and reached for him. A gust of wind swirled through the remains of a broken dome. She slid her hand around his waist, pressed the taut muscles of his back and dragged her fingers down the thin fabric of his cotton shirt. His arms remained pressed by his sides.

She had promised herself a swift and simple goodbye. That was still best. But Arvind's expression had gone from anger to outrage. They couldn't part like this. She pressed her lips to the skin visible through the plunging V of his open shirt.

This is wrong. So wrong.

In the eight months they had been together, Sheetal had never dared such close proximity to Arvind. The custom that forbade an unmarried man and woman from being together like this also denied them the right to choose a marriage partner. She told herself to leave, afraid of what she might do and where she might touch him.

She ran a hand up his back, into his hair, and pulled his face down until they gazed into each other's eyes. The scent of his wild musk caused her to close her eyes. Arvind's mocha breath washed over her eyes, nose and lips.

She waited.

At last, he kissed her.

She tightened her grip on him and sank into his embrace.

We will never risk returning to the days of hardship and hunger, Mama's admonition rang in her head.

Papa had spent a decade toiling blood, sweat and tears to bring the family this far. As their only child, she must marry the man they had chosen, keep the alliance and secure the family's status. What right had she to throw away her family's future on love?

Sheetal squirmed, stepped from Arvind's embrace and looked up at the man she must surrender.

"Give me one chance," he said. "Trust me, I won't let you down."

She forced back tears. "I... I..." Her voice cracked. "It's too late. I can't... We can't. You must forget me."

He brushed away a tear that escaped her resolve. "Just like that? You can forget me?"

A knot tightened in her throat. Arvind's questions burned into her with the force of the sun's heat.

"Do you know how agonizing the last two months have been without you?" he asked. "I have only ever loved you. I can't live without you."

His deep voice pricked with the same quick pain as the thorn that had pierced her finger, while Mama's caution rang in her ears... *Disobey and Papa will throw you out penniless.*

She spun and ran.

"Shee-tal!" Arvind called after her.

Her name ricocheted off broken pillars and hollow domes as she pounded one foot ahead of the other.

2

THRESHOLDS

For the fifth time, Sheetal paced toward her bedroom door, then back toward her bed. This time, she glanced through the window and headed in that direction. A topiary hedge lined the stone wall that separated the front yard of her parents' ten-acre estate from the cars zooming along Rosewood Street. She halted before the window, crossed her arms and sighed at the rush hour traffic. Workers were returning home while she stood there, stalled.

Shee-tal.

Arvind's cry still haunted her, even four weeks later. Guilt clenched her heart. She should have turned back, should have assured him that her decision to end their friendship had been the only right thing to do, had been the only way they could go.

She ran her tongue over her lips. She could still taste the mocha of his breath and ached for his touch. Was the right way really the only way or could there be an alternative?

"*Sahiba*, what you look?" Preeti, her maid servant, asked.

Sheetal whirled. Preeti sat cross-legged on the floor near the bed's footboard. When had the girl entered her room?

Sheetal leaned back against the window's ledge, trying to appear relaxed. Little surprised her anymore, considering that, for the past two weeks, Preeti had become Sheetal's personal satellite.

A teenager barely four feet tall, with skin the color of mahogany and two thin plaits tied at the ends with bright red ribbons, Preeti was half Sheetal's size, and her native language, Hindi, suffered from a lack of formal education. She had served Sheetal loyally for the last six years as her personal maid, but over the last two weeks, Preeti shadowed Sheetal's every move. Clearly, her loyally had shifted.

"Are Mama and Papa back yet?" They had met with the caterers that afternoon.

"Just come. Downstairs in hall." Preeti's voice rose in pitch with excitement, "All talk your wedding about food, desserts..." Ever since the announcement of Sheetal's engagement to Rakesh, that's all anyone in the family talked about. Everyone except Sheetal.

"How long have you been here? I didn't notice you come in."

"Five minutes."

An hour ago—for the seventh time this week—Sheetal had called her best friend, Kavita, but a woman on the other end said Kavita had gone out, would return at six that evening and she'd convey Sheetal's message to call back. That was the first time someone had picked up the phone. "Maybe you should see if Mama needs help around the house," Sheetal suggested, wanting privacy when Kavita returned her call.

"Your Mama say keep you company."

More like, keep a watch.

The walls closed in and Sheetal's chest tightened. She crossed to the wooden doors on the opposite side of the room and threw them open, needing fresh air from the balcony. The breeze that raced past carried the scent of damp grass. She walked onto the balcony and halted at the railing. She had loved to walk barefoot through the grass after the gardener watered the lawn and savor the curl of grass blades beneath her feet as the damp earth moistened her toes. But ever since she'd said goodbye to Arvind, she hadn't set foot on the turf. Neither had she helped the servants' children with their homework, nor watched them practice their handwriting. Although she hoped to become a professional oil painter, she hadn't completed an oil-on-canvas since she'd parted from Arvind. Several times, she'd tried to engage in past interests, but her attention drifted to the horizon or to a wall behind her easel, and she'd find herself lost in the moment of their first and only kiss.

The phone rang and Sheetal rushed inside to pick up the receiver. "Hello?"

"Hello, Sheetal?"

"Kavita. It's been ages. I tried calling you so many times, but you didn't return my calls. Are you okay?"

Kavita, against her parents' wishes, had eloped with her college sweetheart, Gaurav, shortly after they'd graduated. The couple had severed all contacts with family and friends shortly thereafter, and no one had heard from them since.

"We had to leave. You know what my dad would have done."

Sheetal knew only too well. Kavita, Gaurav, Arvind and Sheetal had been a foursome on the college campus. Kavita incessantly complained about how her parents would never permit her to marry Gaurav because he was a Gujrati from West India, whereas Kavita came from northwestern Punjab. They were expected to marry within their social rank and caste.

"Has your family accepted—" Sheetal stopped. Though Preeti flipped through the pages of a fashion magazine, she probably would report every word to Mama. "How about we meet up somewhere? It's been so long since we caught up."

Kavita hesitated. "I'm not sure."

Maybe she was worried about being found by her parents? "Surely you can make time to meet for coffee?" Sheetal was anxious to discover how Kavita and Gaurav had accomplished their marriage feat without telling anyone—not even she and Arvind, their closest friends. Sheetal had found out when Kavita's mom called to ask if she knew of Kavita's whereabouts because she'd been missing for two days. Sheetal later heard through the college grapevine that the two had eloped.

Kavita paused. "I'll have to see."

"You must be so happy you're finally—. You got what you wanted." She cupped her hand around the receiver. "You're with Gaurav."

"It's hard to believe we're married. We had to fight to stick together."

"Sheetal?"

Sheetal whipped round to see Mama at the door. "I'll talk to you later." She returned the receiver to its cradle.

"Who were you talking to?" Mama asked.

"Nupur," she lied. If she mentioned Kavita, Mama would

start again about how Kavita had disobeyed her parents and brought shame to the family.

Marriage was not just a phase in life, but a holy sacrament binding a man and woman for life. Children were expected to marry the person chosen by their parents.

However, after hearing the happiness in Kavita's voice, Sheetal knew she stood a chance at happiness if she could muster the courage to defy Mama and Papa.

"There's a few things we need to talk about." Mama entered the room, sat on the bed, and patted the mattress. "Come sit, *Beti*." She used the term of affection parents lavished on their daughters. "We need to finalize the saris and *salwar* suits and..."

Mama referred to Sheetal's dowry. With the wedding four months away and numerous functions and rituals to coordinate, Mama wanted to check off as many tasks as she possibly could to stay ahead of deadlines.

"I can't believe how quickly your wedding day is approaching."

Anger rose. Sheetal couldn't believe it either.

"Your father's been in his den, working around the clock coordinating the wedding plans." Mama's milky pale complexion was a stark contrast to the evening sky.

Sheetal's room, located above Papa's ground-floor den, both in the Prasad *Bhavan*'s main tower, offered the best view of the ten-acre estate. Windows of both rooms faced the front lawn, driveway and topiary hedge, and their balconies faced the backyard. Two double-story, rectangular wings branched left and right off the tower in a V that reached toward Rosewood Street like a pair of open arms. The stone wall that encircled the estate separated the Prasads' home from Raigun City.

Six servants, two gardeners, a chef and a personal maid, Preeti, were the comforts Sheetal had grown up with. Sheetal merely asked for something and it was hers; except, six months ago, when she asked to marry Arvind.

"I'll have to call the tailor for the blouse fittings and go with your father first thing tomorrow to meet with the decorators and—"

"This marriage isn't right," Sheetal broke in.

"What?"

"It doesn't feel right. Don't make me do this. I hate Rakesh."

"You will learn to love him over time."

"'Meet Rakesh,' you said. I did. 'Go out with him a second time.' I did."

Papa had introduced Rakesh to her at a friend's party. The second time, she and Rakesh met at a restaurant for lunch. Despite being chaperoned by two of Sheetal's cousins, they dined in private, talked over lunch and got to know a little about each other. According to Mama, Rakesh was blessed with charm, wit, gracious manners and an athletic body, but sixty-six minutes with him had been more than enough.

"He's so mean. Rude. Self-centered. So...so..."—her breathing grew erratic—"full of himself!"

"You're forgetting all the virtues a woman can only dream of in a husband." Mama rose, spun on her heels and headed for the door, her green sari *pallu* whipping the air like a snake.

Sheetal followed.

"An M.B.A. from Harvard," Mama went on. "The most eligible and wealthy bachelor in Raigun. So well known, respected, and acknowledged by society. Memberships in every prestigious club..."

Sheetal hurried to keep pace, fed up with the countless blessings she was reminded she perpetually took for granted. "I could study further," she pleaded. "Work. Get a job like other girls do and—"

"They need the money to support their families. You have everything you need. It's how lucky you have been." Mama stormed down the corridor as she shook her head. "Your father spent his whole life working hard..."

There it was again, the how-hard-Papa-worked line.

"Now you want to bring the family shame like Kavita? After everything we have done for you? And prove what?" Mama took the stairs, the heels of her slippers kicking the hem of her sari.

Nothing! Sheetal gritted her teeth and followed. She had never had to prove anything to anyone. Not even to herself. She had a master's degree in arts and she wanted to continue her education, but Mama and Papa insisted she marry young and mold quickly to the ways of her prospective in-laws.

Sheetal wasn't sure what Mama and Papa wanted her to mold toward—their way of thinking or the Dhanrajs's. And whose after?

"Women from our type—our class—don't go out to work." Mama took a left at the landing and marched down the carpeted hallway. "Most people would die to have a fraction of what you do and you're ready to throw it all away?" She stopped, turned and took a deep breath. "I just don't under-stand you."

"But Mama, listen—"

Mama's glare made Sheetal cringe. "It's Arvind, isn't it?"

Sheetal's heart sank at the spiteful tone and glare.

"Ours is a centuries-old tradition. You will follow the ancestors and marry the man we have chosen. Is it so wrong if we expect that from you?"

Sheetal didn't want their outdated tradition. India had stepped into the global world. Women had torn down walls of class and culture to marry for love, to pursue their careers and live their dreams. How did it matter that she'd been loyal and chaste, qualities Mama and Papa demanded she uphold because she was a good Indian woman from a good Indian family? Being good only forced her to do even more good for the family.

Mama led her into the dining room, where floor-to-ceiling windows and a glass door flooded the room with sunlight and provided a view of the patio and the backyard beyond. Then she closed the wooden doors behind them with a thud and turned the deadbolt. "You are not like other girls. We're doing what's right. What's best for you."

Sheetal's chest tightened and she looked into Mama's eyes. "How do you know what's best for me?"

"Because I can't forget the days in Nariyal Ka Rasta. Can you?"

Disgust lodged in Sheetal's throat at the mention of Coconut Lane in Raigun's poor northern district. How could she forget the view from her second story window of murky gray water filling open, choked gutters? Roving street dogs zigzagging through the streets. Cows plopping turds on pavements while swatting swarms of flies with their tails. Human waste dripping from pipe outlets into the main drain below.

Odors rose with the day's humidity and caused bile to rise in her throat. Sheetal turned away. That was thirteen years ago. In the past. Over.

The Prasads hadn't begun life wealthy, but a lifetime of labor, perseverance, good luck and good business timing had elevated them from the lower middle class in northern Raigun to this southern posh locale. Not only did Mama and Papa want to maintain their hard-earned prestige, they wanted to secure it for life by marrying Sheetal into the elite class. But she had heard how the practice of upper-middle-class families marrying their daughters into the class of the elite, followed by many of India's iconic families, enslaved new brides.

"Look at me when I'm talking to you." Mama grabbed her shoulders and dug her fingers into Sheetal's flesh. "Do you want to spend the rest of your life cooking? Cleaning? Scrubbing? Washing up after everyone else? Queuing up for water at some communal tap? Because that's what will happen if you marry that Arvind."

"Stop calling him 'that Arvind.' He's Arvind. Just because you had to queue up doesn't mean I'll have to."

"How can you guarantee Arvind won't abandon you at this doorstep"—she pointed to the glass doors—"when he's done with you?"

"Mama!"

"What if he's using you to get at our wealth?"

"Mama." Fury flooded her veins.

"We've been through this before. There is no logic, no security in marrying someone off the street."

"He's not off the street." He just didn't have the money or the means, but he would find a way, like Mama and Papa had.

And now that Mama and Papa were well off, it was obvious they had no intention of supporting her marriage to Arvind, with or without a dowry. "Today, my life is in Papa's hands. Tomorrow, Rakesh's." Her tone crossed acceptable boundaries. "How can I do what I want when I want to marry Arvind?"

Mama marched past the ten-seater dining table to the other side of the room and pushed open the glass door. "Then go marry him."

Sheetal froze.

"You want to marry Arvind, then you leave right now with only the clothes on your back and nothing more. Like Kavita." Her voice brimmed with disgust. "She eloped with Gaurav and look what shame and embarrassment they caused. Her parents can't show their faces to anyone."

Sheetal gulped.

"And if he leaves you bloated with child at our doorstep, don't think for a second you can just walk back in. We will have nothing more to do with you."

3
COFFEE TALK

Café Coffee Day, a franchise coffee shop in the heart of southern Raigun, blared rock music and hummed with the conversations of college students who occupied its tables. The combined aromas of coffee, butter and syrup stirred Sheetal's appetite. She looked at her watch. 4 p.m. In the past, Kavita had always been the first to arrive. Today she was forty-five minutes late. Maybe she was stuck in traffic or her car had broken down or— Sheetal stopped. Kavita didn't have a car anymore.

After their elopement, Gaurav and Kavita's families had severed all familial ties and financial support. Sheetal figured Kavita used public transport and that's what took her longer than usual. Kavita had moved from the posh locale of Green Park, several blocks from Rosewood Street, to a one-bedroom apartment in the northern districts around Nariyal Ka Rasta.

During their college days, Sheetal and Kavita used to tie up the landline for hours, and Mama yelled at her to cut short conversations. Now, Kavita didn't take calls at her new residence. She and Kavita had spoken twice in the month since Kavita's first returned call. Kavita's conversations had been filled with pauses and long eclipses of silence, and Sheetal had struggled to come up with words to fill the one-way conversation.

At least today, they'd be able to enjoy each other's company over a cup of iced coffee—Kavita's favorite—like old times, and Sheetal could figure out a way to still marry Arvind. Maybe she and Arvind could talk to Mama and Papa together and reason with them. If that didn't go well, they could elope like Gaurav and Kavita.

A barista in a bright orange apron smiled at Sheetal from behind the glass display of muffins, croissants, sandwiches and pastries. She'd caught him glancing her way while serving customers, and now he turned in her direction on the pretext of arranging food items on display that were already neatly arranged. To avoid eye contact, Sheetal sipped her iced latte, then reached into her handbag, withdrew a Sidney Sheldon paperback, opened it at her bookmark and began reading.

"Hey, Sheetal?"

Sheetal looked up, jumped to her feet, dropped her book and hugged Kavita. "You made it!"

Kavita returned her hug and then pulled away, her sunglasses, two black ovals shielding her eyes. She pulled out a chair opposite Sheetal at the round table for two.

Sheetal noticed how quickly Kavita had ended their embrace. "Are you okay?"

Kavita removed a handkerchief from her handbag and wiped sweat from her face and neck. Her blue polyester blouse clung to her with perspiration, and dark patches marred the fabric under her arms. She removed her sunglasses. Dark circles shadowed her eyes and her cheeks were sunken.

"What happened to you?" Sheetal took her seat. "You look half dead."

"Wouldn't you, if you had to wake up at five every morning because the water supply cuts off at nine?"

"You don't have running water?"

"Rationed water where we live."

Some poorer districts in northern Raigun suffered water rationing. Residents collected water in buckets and large vessels during specified hours of operation.

"Plus, I have to get to work by nine thirty, so there's a mad rush every morning."

That explained why Kavita had returned so few calls. She kept busy with a job, a home to run and her husband.

Kavita withdrew a reusable plastic water bottle from her handbag and took a long drink. In the ten years they'd known each other, Kavita had never carried a water bottle. Sheetal didn't know how far Kavita had travelled to meet her, but from the day's heat and the dampness of her clothes, she must crave an iced coffee.

"Do you want to order something?" Sheetal asked.

"I'm fine. Water's good enough."

"But you love the cold coffees here."

"Not when it's two hundred rupees. That's equal to my bus fare home and a portion of the grocery bill."

Sheetal leaned back. Where was the fun-loving Kavita who couldn't get through a day without her fix of cold coffee? The carefree Kavita, full of life and laughter, the main entertainment at any party? "So, you weren't ignoring me when you didn't call back."

"How can I ignore you when I don't have the time?"

"I called for months and you didn't—"

"Gaurav and I didn't want anyone to know where we were. Then—life took over. Not a minute to breathe."

"But aren't you happy that you're finally a career woman and living the dream life with Gaurav?"

Kavita raised her eyebrows and shook her head slowly.

"I admire what you did, Kavita. It takes guts, and I've been thinking hard since we first spoke."

"What's there to think about?"

Sheetal fished in her handbag and withdrew a white envelope about the size of her palm. "Please give this to Arvind for me."

Kavita grabbed Sheetal's hand and stared at the ten-carat diamond ring on Sheetal's third finger. "Your engagement ring?"

Sheetal took a deep breath and nodded.

"Arvind got you this—"

"No. I'm not seeing him anymore."

"But you love him. I thought you two planned on—"

"It's not going to happen. I'm engaged to someone else."

"Who?"

"Some rich foreign-return guy who runs his father's business." Sheetal didn't name Rakesh Dhanraj because everyone knew his name and would say she was a fool to choose Arvind over him.

"Arvind knows?" Kavita leaned forward. "You told him, right?"

Sheetal nodded, her heart heavy as lead. "I had to."

Kavita took the envelope, slipped it into her handbag, folded her sunglasses and shoved them in. "So that's why you wanted to meet me."

Sheetal nodded. "And I wanted to know how you're doing. How you're *really* doing."

"Never mind me, at least you're doing the right thing. Look at the diamond on that sucker!" She let out a whistle.

Sheetal looked up, shocked. How could she say such a thing? Kavita knew how much she loved Arvind. It's not like she'd walked away by choice or chose the money.

"Look, *yaar*"—Kavita used the slang reserved for friends— "being in love is one thing, but real-life sucks. Ask me. I'm living it."

"I thought you were happy with Gaurav."

"We can barely afford rent. Our apartment is half the size of Mom's living room. We have to scramble for water first thing every morning and we argue every evening after work. We're both exhausted and just want to sleep. But someone has to cook, right? And guess who that someone is?"

"Doesn't Gaurav help around the house?"

"Of course, he helps." Kavita crossed her arms. "He helps create a mess, a fuss. Complains from the moment he wakes up to the moment he sleeps. The apartment is too small. The mattress is too rough. The sofa is ripped. What do you expect from second-hand stuff? Where's all the money coming from when we've both been kicked out of our homes and have to start on our own? Our life is shit."

Sheetal bit her lower lip. Should she ask for the envelope

back? Her attention flew to the hollow at Kavita's collar bone. Was she getting enough to eat?

"Look, I've got to get home before six so I can get water. Three hours of water, yeah!" She raised her hands and waved them in mockery. "But good seeing you again, and glad you're smarter than I am." She stood.

"About what?"

"Leaving Arvind. It wouldn't have worked out. Look at me."

The air thickened with the overwhelming scent of coffee. The surrounding student chatter deafened her. "I can drop you home." Sheetal stood, skirted the table and started toward the door. Kavita pushed in her chair and followed.

"I'll make my own way. Don't want your chauffeur to see me. Besides, no point sitting in your car and remembering what I gave up. It'll just hurt. Oh look, my bus!" She brushed past Sheetal and hurried toward the door as a double-decker pulled up to the curb and heaved to a stop. On the way, Kavita fished her sunglasses out, slid them on her face, waved to Sheetal and left, oblivious to a thick, rectangular paper that fell to the floor. Sheetal was about to call to Kavita that she'd dropped something, but a crowd of students gathered on the spot, and when they filed out the door, the paper was gone.

4
MIRAGE

The warmth of the night closed in upon Sheetal. She whimpered and tossed in her sleep...

Barefoot and seated cross-legged, she turned her face away from the heat of the *agni*, the religious fire, burning in a square metal *havan* on the carpeted ground three feet away. Flames blew in her direction, their tongues reaching, beckoning her closer. She had to get out of there before the fire consumed her. She reeled right and bumped a man who also sat in a lotus-like position.

"Excuse me," she blurted, "I—" The statement caught in her throat.

Embroidery and gemstones adorned the full-sleeve shirt of this gentleman's bronze *sherwani*. The hem of his shirt touched the knees of his tightly fit, tapered trousers. Despite his expensive clothing, uneasiness caused her to draw back. Curious, she leaned forward and tried to glimpse his face, but a curtain of tiny white *mogra* flowers, tied to a cord around his forehead, shielded his face.

Ninety degrees to the stranger's right, Mama and Papa— Rana and Indu Prasad—sat in the same austere fashion. They, too, wore costly clothing. Behind them, uncles, aunts and cousins sat on the rug dressed in brightly colored chiffon, silk and organza saris, heavy jewelry and dark suits with bright ties. Whose wedding was this?

Everyone's attention remained focused on the havan. Clouds of gray smoke billowed toward the twenty-by-twenty-feet canopy of yellow silk and escaped out the open sides into the star-studded sky. The silk ceiling dipped several inches on all sides under the weight of tiny pearls and small ingots of gold. Four pillars held up the canopy, and seven *matkis*—earthenware pots—of decreasing size, stacked one atop another, leaned against each pillar.

Two Hindu *pundits*, dressed in yellow and saffron-colored robes, sat cross-legged to the left of the fire. The priests poured ladles of ghee into the havan while chanting religious *shloka*s.

A fireball spiraled up from the havan. Its heat caught Sheetal in the face. Soot irritated her lungs and grated her eyes. Her stomach cramped. The canopy was bound to catch fire.

The pundits' sonorous chants blended as they fed more ghee and dry grains of rice into the havan. Sheetal leaned aside and coughed as beads of sweat oozed down her neck and back and gathered at the curve of her waist, dampening the throt-tling stitches of her outfit.

Another billow of smoke spiraled. Sheetal turned her head away and tried again to catch a glimpse of the stranger seated beside her. Her failed attempt incited murmurs of disapproval from other guests. She looked at her father for an explanation, but his attention remained fixed on the havan.

Unable to bear the heat, she rose to leave, but the stranger grabbed her right hand and forced her down. She tried to wrench free, but he tightened his ice-cold grip, causing the curtain of flowers masking his face to swing like windshield wipers. Sheetal flattened her left palm on the rug in preparation to inch away from the flames, but the crush of people seated behind her prevented escape.

Suddenly, someone yanked her left hand behind her and ran their fingers up and down the rungs of her bangles. Sheetal twisted to see who held her.

"Just lovely!" cried the girl who held her wrist. "And ooh... look at her *hathphools*! Bet they cost a fortune."

The girl examined the four rings on each of Sheetal's henna-laced fingers, each ring linked by golden chains to a bracelet. She traced a finger up the red henna designs that crawled from Sheetal's fingertips to halfway up her elbows in spirals of thorns and creepers.

Sheetal tried to free her hands, but her dupatta's sharp zardozi embroidery pricked her cheeks, and the sway of her heavy earrings tugged at her earlobes. She managed to yank both hands free.

The stranger tossed grains of puffed rice into the havan, causing the fire to leap in a scorching frenzy and devour the food. A pundit placed a few grains of puffed rice on Sheetal's right palm and ordered her to do the same. Sheetal stiffened. She didn't want to. But Papa's pointed scowl meant, *Do as you're told*. She reached to toss the rice into the fire but the grains fell near her foot. Sheetal pulled her knees to her chest and hugged her legs, not daring to meet Papa's gaze.

The other pundit ordered Sheetal and the stranger to their feet. The thick choker around Sheetal's neck tightened. She tugged at the choker. Papa smiled, like he'd been waiting for this moment. She had to run away. Not because of the fire. Because of him. This stranger. His stare drilled into her through the windshield of flowers and caused her to squirm.

This had to be a dream. Sheetal opened her mouth to say so, but smoke choked her and clouded her vision. Then she glimpsed her reflection in a brass vase that leaned against a matki. This wasn't just any wedding. She was the bride! And she was marrying this stranger. She raised her right hand to signal Mama for help, but the stranger seized her wrist and forced her to rise.

A pundit tied the sash draping her left shoulder to the stole hanging from the groom's shoulder and ordered her to lead the first six of seven sacred perambulations around the havan.

Sheetal crushed the carpet under her toes, the weight of her golden anklets weighing each step. The skirt of her richly embroidered red *ghagra,* complete with matching blouse and sash, noosed her in its cocoon. She inched forward and the ghagra dragged behind in a blood-river of red silk.

A dream. This had to be a dream.

After completing six of the seven *pheras,* Sheetal brushed past the groom and glimpsed his face through the slits of mogra flowers before taking her place behind him. Her heart pounded. Had that really been a pair of empty sockets where his eyes should have been?

A dream, she reassured herself.

One last phera would render the marriage complete. Clouds of soot billowed under the canopy and smothered the air. She should run. But where to? He glided forward and she followed. Halfway around the fire, inches away from being bound to this devil for a lifetime...

It's now or never.

Sheetal clutched the sides of her ghagra and stepped into the fire. A thousand needles stabbed her feet. Ash rose like a volcano as flames engulfed spirals of embroidery and red fabric. She gasped, but smoke filled her lungs and she coughed. Someone yanked her arm, but she resisted the pull to safety.

"Sheetal!" Mama's screams soared above the ocean of panic-stricken screams. Mama reached out to grab Sheetal's hand but recoiled from the flames.

A vortex of heat spiraled up Sheetal's gut. She screamed as flames danced on her hand, leaping to the hathphools, *mehndi* and gold bangles.

This couldn't be happening. But it was real. She was burning. She was on fire. She was fire.

"*Bachao! Bachao!*" Papa yelled as men ran back and forth and women lunged to cover the eyes of children.

No one could save what was beyond help.

5

DRIZZLING DIAMONDS

"Sheetal... Sheetal?"

Under the bed covers, Sheetal sluggishly ran her fingers down her satin nightgown. Today was her wedding day. She let her hand fall back to her side.

"When you grow up, you will marry a prince, a *Rajkumar*," Mama once proclaimed. "And that will make you happy. Very, very happy."

Other childhood images flooded her mind. How she loved to stretch out her arms and spin on her toes under the rotating ceiling fan as her white dress flared and strands of her silky, waist-length hair flew around her face like a dark cloud.

Mama would clap in time to the music playing on their imported Sony stereo cassette player as rungs of colorful glass and gold bangles jingled to long, melodious notes of the harmonium and sitar. The sari pallu around Mama's head always slipped, revealing a river of vermilion *sindoor* running down her hair's middle parting. Mama was quick to pull the pallu back over her head out of respect, inevitably hiding the mark of a married woman, should Asha, her mother-in-law, suddenly walk in. Then Mama threw back her head and laughed, her diamond nose-pin sparkling in the sunlight against her milky-white complexion. No one was more beautiful than Mama. Not even Sheetal, who didn't inherit Mama's fine-cut features, hair that curled natural, or the milky-white complexion that was every Indian woman's dream.

"Louder! Louder!" Sheetal called.

Mama fiddled with the knob on the stereo until music engulfed the room, creating a bubble-like universe no one could burst. The fan, walls and carpeted floor blurred in Sheetal's vision and the white of her dress was all she could see. She collapsed in Mama's arms and the two giggled, their laughter reverberating beneath the fan.

"You're going to make everyone in your *mahal* dizzy with all that spinning." Mama pulled Sheetal close to her chest and the thump of her heartbeat filled Sheetal's ears.

"I don't have a palace."

"You will, my darling. When you're all grown up."

"Will I be like you?" No one was more loving or more caring than Mama.

"You will be better than me."

Sheetal jumped up, stretched her arms out and spun in circles all over again. "You! I want to be just like you."

Now, thirteen years later, at the age of twenty-two, Sheetal didn't want to be like Mama. She didn't want the boredom of Mama's married life, which had been arranged thirty years ago by some middleman who knew both families and concluded that Mama would be a perfect fit for Rana Prasad. She wanted the dizzy euphoric rapture of being in love. Of meeting the man of her dreams, like so many women did in romance novels and Bollywood films. She wanted a man to woo her, to pursue her in gentle ways and say 'I love you' until she said it back. Arvind had fulfilled all those wishes. Arvind was everything she could ask for in a man. But Mama would have none of that.

"Sheetal? Come now. Wake up." Mama's voice blended with the outside coo of the *koyal* birds and the chirp of sparrows.

Usually, Sheetal wouldn't have minded waking. Today, however, she wanted to curl into a ball beneath the sheets and pretend the day didn't exist. She rolled onto her side and raised the sheet over her exposed ear.

The mattress dipped near her pillow, causing her body to tilt. Loose wisps of hair were brushed away from her face and she opened her eyes.

"It's your wedding day!" Mama sang in Hindi. "The whole house is buzzing. Can you believe this special day is finally here?"

Sheetal's head throbbed. She pulled down the covers. "I had a bad dream, Mama. This marriage isn't right."

"It is." Mama was firm. "And don't give me the nose. You're just having butterflies. There's so much happening. You're nervous. Worried. It's perfectly fine to feel—"

"I'm serious, Mama."

Mama wrapped Sheetal's fingers in the palms of her pashmina-like hands as a summer breeze from the open balcony door carried the scent of jasmines, roses and chrysanthemums into the room. "I know how you feel. Like there's too much going on at once. But trust me. Everything will go perfectly as planned."

"I hate him."

"You will learn to love him over time."

"Love isn't"—Sheetal faltered for the right word—"automatic. You can't just water it like grass and expect it to grow. You and Papa had to marry whomever your parents chose for you, but I don't. Times have changed. A woman can—"

Mama pulled Sheetal to her chest. "You must calm down, my darling. This kind of temper at your in-laws' just won't do. Even though that dimple on your cheek makes you look so beautiful. Perfect. Well...almost perfect." She teasingly pinched Sheetal's nose.

Sheetal gritted her teeth.

"You will be a wonderful wife. And soon, an equally good mother. But how will I carry on without you?" Mama rocked Sheetal in her arms, counting each year gone by with a string of kisses on her head. The fragrance of lily joss sticks meant Mama had probably come up from her morning prayers.

Nineteen...twenty...twenty-one—

Sheetal waited for one last kiss to mark her twenty-second year, but none came. Or maybe she just didn't feel it. She flexed the fingers of her right hand. The engagement ring obstructed her movement.

"Look at how special you are."

There it was again, the how-special-you-are line.

"Every inch... Brahma has truly created you."

Her head pounded. She was sick and tired of being special, of being told she was Brahma's one perfect creation. She pulled away and looked past the pink and yellow sari pallu covering

Mama's head to the wall clock behind. She had fourteen hours to end this wedding nonsense. "I'm not doing this."

"You are not like other girls. Remember, we're doing what's best for you."

Women of Mama's generation believed that a daughter's real home was the husband's home, and until she married, she was a liability for her parents. Did Mama see her that way? No. It's just that this alliance offered her parents an opportunity to maintain their hard-earned prestige and secure it for life by marrying her into the elite class.

Technically, the dowry was hers to keep even though it was directed to the in-laws. Her only way out was to go through with this marriage, convert the dowry into cash and then contact Arvind. They could use the money to buy a flat in a decent locale, furnish it with basic necessities, find jobs, and life wouldn't be as miserable as Kavita and Gaurav's. Still, the thought of marrying someone else clawed at her heart and tears stung her eyes. How could she go through with this? "You don't know what's best for me." Sheetal's chest tightened. "Just because you raised me doesn't give you or Papa the right to—"

A sharp sting blasted across her right cheek, and Mama retracted her hand. "Look what you made me do, all because of that Arvind. He's not worth any of this. Forget him."

Sheetal closed her eyes to hold back tears, her face burning.

"If anything goes wrong today," Mama warned, "it's your fault." Then she turned to leave.

Sheetal clenched her fists. "I hate Rakesh. I will always hate *that* Rakesh."

Mama headed for the door.

Didn't Mama hear?

Mama paused, one hand on the doorknob. "I'll send Preeti up shortly." Mama kept her back to Sheetal. "She'll help you get dressed and escort you downstairs. We are waiting."

For the next ten minutes, Sheetal paced her room. She could run away. And go where? What would the scandal do to Mama and Papa? What about the caterers, decorators, engineers, and technicians who had worked for a whole week? And family, friends and families of friends who had flown across India and overseas for the occasion?

A knock at the door intruded upon her thoughts. Sheetal flopped onto the bed. It was useless. There was no escape.

"Sahiba?" Preeti called.

Sheetal turned her head toward the door and took a deep breath. A summer breeze swept across the room, drumming the fabric of Sheetal's nightgown against her curves and causing the scent of lavender, from the bed sheets, to fill the air. The scent usually soothed Sheetal's nerves, but nothing could ease the present tension.

"Sahiba?"

"Come in," Sheetal answered.

Preeti entered, dressed in one of Sheetal's hand-me-down salwar suits. She beamed from ear to ear. "*Memsahib* say help you get ready. So many people waiting downstairs." The pitch of her voice rose in excitement as she crossed the room. "Man with big light. Holding big camera." She pronounced it 'kamraa' because English, for Preeti, was a foreign language, as it was for many locals.

"How many people?" Sheetal asked.

"Fifty...sixty...maybe one hundred."

Sheetal rolled onto her side, turning her back to Preeti.

"I see your mehndi?" Preeti referred to the henna lattice-work running from the tips of Sheetal's fingers to her elbows. Preeti lifted Sheetal's wrist. "Look at color. Very red. You know, Sahiba, it meaning?"

Preeti traced doodles on Sheetal's hand, which reminded Sheetal of the gentle brush of Arvind's fingers. If Papa's business hadn't succeeded, she could have been in Preeti's shoes. She pulled away from the girl's hold.

"It mean your husband love you lots. Other one...other one...show. Show!"

"Really, Preeti." Sheetal sat up, annoyed at the girl's begging. Here she was trying to figure a way out and all Preeti wanted was to decode the color of her mehndi.

"Sahiba, please open fingers. It so-o-o beautiful. So red. Think how pretty you look with all your jewelry on."

Sheetal left the bed, crossed to her cupboard, opened its door and flipped through her clothes. "Here we are." She pulled a silver hanger off the rod and swiveled the floral-printed, pink-and-cream salwar suit she had worn to the Broken Fort. It was easier to get rid of it than try to explain how the dupatta had ripped if Mama came across it later.

"Oh, Sahiba! It...it beautiful," Preeti said. "You take this?"

"No." Sheetal yanked another hanger off the rod, which held the matching trousers and dupatta, the tear hidden between its folds. "It's not new, but it's one of my favorites.

And I want you to have it. There's a little tear in the dupatta. No need to tell Mama about it."

Preeti raised her hands to her mouth in awe. "Oh, Sahiba."

"Think of it as a goodbye gift." Sheetal folded the salwar suit, pulled open a dressing table drawer, located a yellow plastic bag and stuffed the attire in. Then she dropped the bag on the floor near the dresser. "Remember to take it with you when you go home."

"Sahiba?"

"Mmm?"

"After you go, this still your room?"

Sheetal knotted her waist-length hair into a make-do bun. "Nothing will change after I go. Mama promised to keep everything as it is."

"Your board?" Preeti pointed to a corner of the room.

"My what?" Sheetal turned to look at the corner that held her oil painting equipment. An easel stood upright beside a desk. "Oh, that's going. It's the only used thing I'm taking. Everything else is supposed to be brand new." She went into the bathroom and brushed her teeth.

Seconds later came a knock on the bathroom door. White foam covering her lips, Sheetal sighed at her reflection. "What now, Preeti?"

"It's me. Your grandmother," called Asha Prasad, Papa's mother. "Hurry up. Everyone's waiting downstairs."

Like all the Prasads, she was in a hurry when it came to attending public events.

"I'm trying, *Dadi*." Sheetal used the term of respect to address Papa's mother and then pressed her ear to the door.

"Well, you'd better be ready before I die of old age. Or I'll just have to get the camera man and all those singing women up here." At sixty-six, Dadi was nowhere close to dying.

A split-second later, Dadi's voice shot an order for Preeti to spread a brand-new, yellow-gold sari on Sheetal's bed, which set in motion another auspicious ceremony to mark Sheetal's wedding.

TWO HOURS LATER, SHEETAL RETURNED FROM THE *PITHI* CEREMONY that had been held on the Garden Terrace. The ceremony took place before Lord Ganesh, the elephant-headed god, worshipped by Hindus before initiating anything of significance. Female relatives had dabbed Sheetal's cheeks with pithi, an herbal mixture of yellow, moist chick-pea flour peppered with turmeric, oil and sandalwood, to initiate the cleansing of the bride and mark her transition from one household to another. After the ceremony, Sheetal was escorted back to her room so that Mira Bai, a masseuse, could complete a massage.

After Sheetal changed into a yellow petticoat that covered her from waist to toes and wrapped an orange towel about her upper torso, Mira Bai directed her to sit on a footstool in the bathing corner of her bathroom. Sheetal's bathing area consisted of a tap, located three feet above the tile floor, and a plastic bucket with a floating plastic mug. As she bathed, excess water ran over the bathroom floor and spilled into a corner drain.

Sheetal hated the sandpaper texture of Mira Bai's calloused fingers covered in layers of sticky yellow pithi, which scratched back and forth along the length of her upper arm. And the way Mira Bai chewed *paan* like a cow, grinding the condiment-stuffed betel leaf, made Sheetal sick. She hoped the woman had the decency to spit the blood-colored juice in the sink when the time came.

The pain of having a body wax three days ago, then having her eyebrows and upper lip waxed yesterday, and now this pithi massage, were all taking a toll on Sheetal's sanity. But tradition demanded a bride be cleansed and purified in precisely this manner over a two-week period prior to the wedding day. A bride had to be absolutely perfect for the groom when the couple consummated the marriage.

Sheetal had not even visited Rakesh Dhanraj's home on Barotta Hill, and here Mira Bai was preparing her for his bedroom. Sheetal squirmed with the thought of the 'first night.' It was the only thing the women downstairs had been discussing in hushed tones during the Pithi Ceremony. She tightened the towel around her torso, careful to keep her feet away from puddles of water on the floor that still hadn't dried.

Mira Bai gathered the front pleats of her tattered, dark blue sari, yanked them up between her legs and tucked the fabric in back at the waist. Then she squatted on the floor, facing Shee-tal, causing the sari to puff in two balloons around her brown knees.

Mira Bai raised her eyebrows and her large red *bindi* glinted like a third eye. "Now pull up your petticoat so it doesn't get wet."

Sheetal squirmed. She inched her petticoat up her ankles, aware she would insult Mira Bai if she questioned her order because Mira Bai held an unprecedented reputation in Raigun for polishing up a bride like no other masseuse. "Thank God this is the last day," Sheetal murmured.

"You're going to miss all this tomorrow. No more pampering." Mira Bai tilted her head back, no doubt to prevent the paan juice from drooling out of her mouth. "You only get to be a bride once in your life. Every girl looks forward to this day. I know. I see it in their eyes." She let go of Sheetal's left foot, grabbed her right arm and dragged her fingers back and forth, spreading the pithi to the tip of Sheetal's elbow, skillfully avoiding the mehndi. "I've seen at least half of all the brides in Raigun, but the pithi only shows its true colors on you." She smiled and her nose pin gleamed in the soft, yellow light.

"You're hurting me," Sheetal squealed.

"Not as much as our new *Sahib* will tonight." Her attention flew to the ten-carat princess-cut diamond ring on Sheetal's finger. "Pretty. Always good for a woman to have beautiful jewelry and wear beautiful things. Precisely why some of us are blessed. But not all are lucky. Poor people like me can only make enough to put a decent roof over our heads and a little food in our bellies."

Sheetal hated the attention Rakesh Dhanraj's ring drew. First Kavita, now Mira Bai. When Mira Bai turned away, Sheetal rotated the ring with her thumb so the diamond faced her palm.

"Now, off with that towel."

Sheetal held on to the orange fabric.

"Relax, Sheetalji." Mira Bai raised both hands. "There's nothing I haven't seen."

Blood rushed to Sheetal's cheeks. She protested, but Mira

Bai lathered more pithi along her collarbone and neck and then suddenly reached for the towel.

"Oh no, you don't." Sheetal twisted out of reach.

"But Sheetalji, don't you want your husband to melt in your beauty? The most eligible bachelor in Raigun, I hear. He's going to see you for the first time."

Goose bumps rose along the length of Sheetal's pithi-plastered arms. *The first night? Alone? With Rakesh Dhanraj?* "No one touches me."

"As you say. Still, not a disappointed husband whose bride was in my hands. Every one of them blessed with at least three children."

Sex...children... The thought of Rakesh's naked body touching hers and the agony of his organ ripping through sent a shudder up her spine. Would he force her into sex? Would he leave her stiff and rigid like the layer of pithi drying on her skin? From what she remembered, he was supposed to be graceful. Charming. Suave. Too refined a man to force her against her will.

Mira Bai turned her face away and spat out the betel juice, staining the white marble floor in reddish-brown streaks. Then she casually dipped the plastic mug into the bucket and sloshed water across the floor. Juice glided toward the drain staining the tiles in dirty red streaks.

Cold water filled the hollows between Sheetal's toes, and she curled them in. It was twelve-thirty. Ten and a half hours left. She had to dress and find Mama. Now.

UNDER A WHITE TENT ON THE FRONT LAWN, RELATIVES AND FRIENDS clustered around a buffet table mounded with artfully displayed food. The aroma of fried onions, tangy tomato gravy and spices flavored the air as waiters, dressed in black and white suits, passed in a steady stream from the kitchen to the lawn and back, burdened with silver trays of food and drink. The guests helped themselves to the fare and spilled out across the lawn, their plates loaded with curries, saffron rice and *tandoor*-cooked breads.

A topiary hedge of peacocks, elephants and deer surrounded the garden, and guests wandered from one display to another while eating.

Sheetal spent fifteen minutes looking for Mama to convince her to stop this wedding. She couldn't just sleep with some stranger on his bed and have sex with him for the rest of her life. There was enough time for Mama to talk sense into Papa and call off the event.

Sheetal gently urged people aside so she could make her way across the lawn while congratulations flew at her from all directions.

"There you are!" someone shouted.

A fishy odor fouled the air, and Sheetal froze. Only one person could tear through a commotion in just three words. Hemlata Choudhary, Papa's younger sister, known among the family as Hemu.

Dressed in a gaudy green sari and balancing a plate of food, Aunty Hemu made her way toward Sheetal. "*Hambe!* Let's see it."

Sheetal drew her right hand behind her back. "I'm looking for Mama. Do you—"

"Come now. The ring." Aunty Hemu swallowed a spoonful of sweet almond *halwa* coated in a leaf of edible silver. "About time I see what I've been hearing for weeks." She swiped the mixture of mashed almond, ghee and sugar from the corner of her mouth with a napkin then squeezed the soiled end of the fabric between her teeth and sucked hard. "Out with it."

Sheetal held out her hand for Aunty Hemu to see.

Aunty Hemu leaned in for a closer look, her shadow falling over the ring. A trinket in Sheetal's world was a fortune in Aunty Hemu's.

Without warning, Aunty Hemu spun around and her waist-length plait lashed Sheetal. "Look, Veena, Rita, Meenu!" She waved, summoning three of Sheetal's aunts. "I was right. See! I was right."

The three plump women rushed over. One grabbed Sheetal's hand and held it up for a crowd of more than fifty to see.

"I told you it was a princess cut," Aunty Hemu declared. "Not five, but a whole ten carats!"

"Let me see!" Aunty Veena seized Sheetal's wrist.

"And me!" a stranger declared from the crowd.

"How about us?" someone else yelled. "We want a look."

"It must have cost at least—"

"Take it off," Aunty Hemu ordered. "I want to see that ring. Now."

The air thickened with tension.

Sheetal grasped the ring and started to twist if off when Mama called, "There you are, Sheetal!"

Mama made her way through the crowd, and Sheetal exhaled in relief.

"Shashiji's waiting upstairs in your room," Mama said.

"You need at least two hours, if not more, to get dressed. Now, off you go. Quickly! I'll have lunch sent up for you."

"I must say, *Bhabhiji*," Aunty Hemu addressed Mama, "all I asked Sheetal was to give me the ring. For a minute. Just one minute. But she refuses."

Liar! Sheetal ground a heel into the grass.

"*Hambe.* As if I'm going to keep it." Aunty Hemu didn't slow, oblivious to the irritation in Mama's expression. Then she pressed a palm to her head and flattened the black strands of oiled hair. "I would never even think of such a thing. How could I? After all, I'm...I'm her own blood—in a way. But young girls nowadays..." She clucked her tongue while the crowd mumbled its disapproval. "Spoiled."

Sheetal tugged Mama's hand. "We need to talk."

"Later, Sheetal." Mama raised her voice, "Now, now then, Hemuji, that's such a small thing to worry about. I have so much more of Sheetal's jewelry you must see before it leaves for her in-laws' house."

Sheetal curled her right hand into a fist. Why did Mama have a soft spot for Aunty Hemu when all Aunty Hemu did was meddle in family affairs and make life difficult?

Two years ago, when Papa bought a new car, he first called Aunty Hemu to share the details of the purchase. When Sheetal passed her master's exam, Mama and Papa first shared the good news with Aunty Hemu. The reason was always the same...Aunty Hemu was family and had once been a Prasad. Because she was not as well-off as them, Mama and Papa continually kept Aunty Hemu engaged in the loop of their lives. Because they had risen in wealth and status shortly after Aunty Hemu's marriage to a man of the lower class, they still lived with the guilt of having left her behind. Though Mama and Papa had consulted several family members about Sheetal's dowry, as was customary, Aunty Hemu was given priority over everyone else. This time, the excuse was that any family member who had not been consulted would feel left out, take offense, and possibly try to sabotage the wedding.

How was an attack possible, when weddings gave families an opportunity to come together, rejoice, renew family ties and forge new ones? In any case, this was too much! Mama had given Aunty Hemu more than her share of attention during the Pithi Ceremony this morning. And during Aunty Hemu's son's wedding, Mama had practically managed the event. Sheetal needed Mama now. "Mama, I need—"

"Sheetal." Mama was firm. "Later."

Mama placed a hand on Aunty Hemu's shoulder and steered her away from the crowd, curtailing the opportunity for more public fury. "Now, Hemuji, I need your advice for the most important..."

The cluster of women followed Mama and Aunty Hemu to the dowry room, and Sheetal, furious, broke away.

"HATTO CHOWKIDAAR," INDU PRASAD ORDERED ASIDE ONE OF THE fifty security guards manning the three thousand square foot hall and invited Hemlata and the women in. According to rumor, Rana Prasad had arranged for a fraction of Raigun's military to guard the dowry.

Thirty designer *salwar kameezes*, one hundred and one saris and a dowry fit for a princess glowed beneath twelve crystal chandeliers. Each sari had been puffed, pleated, folded, and pinned into an endless display of shapes and designs. A pink crepe silk sari, shaped to resemble a rose, lay beside a yellow sari resembling a sunflower. A boat of red organza sailed on an ocean of blue chiffon. An olive-green sari, folded to resemble a kite with gold trimmings and a tail of bright pink chiffon, was followed by a succession of colorful silks, tissues and organza.

The display of Sheetal's clothes went on and on in different hues of burgundy, cream, yellow, blue, maroon and silver until there wasn't a color in the rainbow unrepresented. In the center of it all, mounted on a pedestal, under the grandest crystal chandelier, a golden tissue peacock, pleated together from fifteen different saris, stood proud, jubilant and five feet tall. Brocaded in threads of emerald-green and ocean-blue, the bird's tail fanned over an array of twenty open-top jewelry boxes wrapped tightly in sheets of transparent cellophane with guards positioned to protect their contents.

Word spread quickly that the dowry room was open and a crowd of three hundred gathered in less than five minutes. In one of the twenty jewelry boxes, the curve of a pearl necklace separated a pair of matching earrings and a triple-string bracelet. A golden Cartier set in another box, dotted with pigeon-blood rubies and pink sapphires, was fashioned in loops and rings. Drops of white gold graced the edge of a swan neck choker, and fine latticework encrusted with diamonds sparkled in the center. The spectators drooled, uncertain where to look or which way to turn. There was so much to see and so little time.

Then Hemlata Choudhary sidled between several people

and made her way to the teardrop necklace from Belgium, matched with a pair of earrings and a double-string bracelet. Strands of one-carat diamonds, woven with slivers of white gold, converged upon a two-inch wide pendant. She put a hand to her throat, her chest heaving, as if struggling for air.

Indu led the women forward, ordered two security guards to step aside, and pulled open panels of white chiffon curtains, revealing the hidden dowry.

Wedgewood Serenity Goblets encrusted with sapphires nestled on a blue velvet bed. Two dozen Araglin glasses marched across a red tablecloth. Each tulip-fluted glass, fashioned with diamond-shaped vertical wedges, reflected light from a chandelier. A Paris Evening tea set in copper and gold hosted five-dozen teacups, enough to serve fifty guests. Matching globe sugar bowls, cream holders and teapots complemented several velvet display boxes brimming with sterling silver cutlery. Fancy soup bowls, custard troughs, decanters and punch bowls, all bearing the same zigzag pattern, trailed like a never-ending maze.

The dowry was, everyone agreed, a grand display of affection. All this was intended for Sheetal's mother-in-law, Pushpa Dhanraj, to use as she deemed appropriate.

"And those are Sheetal's personal things." Indu diverted the crowd's attention to three Louis Vuitton suitcases in one corner of the room, the only items not open for display. "And this is for Rakeshji." Indu pushed a green button on a remote control and a wooden folding wall on the left began to lift, revealing sharp streams of daylight.

Hemlata Choudhary squealed and stumbled backward, and

spectators gasped as a car, unlike any ever seen, rolled into view.

The convertible's metal and chrome chassis shimmered in the pool of sunlight. Its hood sloped with the same vicious slant of a hammerhead shark. The exterior mirrors had been sculpted to resemble the mammal's wide-set eyes.

"It's...it's..." Hemlata's jaw dropped.

"It was flown in from Italy. A Lamborghini. Onyx Diablo," Indu said. "A twelve-cylinder purchased well in advance. Three years, in fact, because only eighty have been released." Then she pulled a handkerchief from the sleeve of her blouse and unfolded the yellow fabric to reveal a car key. She pushed a button and the doors of the vehicle opened skyward, revealing a tan leather interior shaped like an airplane's cockpit.

The crowd crept closer to the vehicle. Hemlata leaned forward, a hand extended toward the mullet-shaped exterior, when Indu placed a hand on her arm and urged her back.

"We have been planning this for some time. For the lucky man who would marry Sheetal."

"Remember your time, Hemu?" Asha, Indu's mother-in-law, turned to Hemlata. "I packed everything in your dowry when you were married. From your toothbrush to the four saris, petticoats and whatever else I could." She lowered her voice to a whisper. "I tried to do the best so...so you were well supplied for at least a year. It was so simple then. So easy in our two-bedroom flat, compared to this."

Indu's attention wandered to the Lamborghini. "You know your brother when it comes to giving. He's all heart. Remember how much he spent on your son Vikram's wedding two years

ago? I—" She turned to look at Hemlata, but Hemlata had
slipped away.

A RENOWNED BEAUTICIAN HAD BEEN CALLED UPON TO DRESS SHEETAL
for the wedding. With more than twenty-five years' experience
in the bridal business, this woman maintained a flawless reputation, and was hired to assure that Sheetal outshone any other
bride. But the robust woman, in her mid-forties, merely looked
from Sheetal's cousin Tina to the golden wedding gown spread
across the bed, to Sheetal, and her eyebrows plunged into a V.
She made her way to the fishtail ghagra—designed by Anita
Dongre, India's leading fashion designer—that lay glimmering
in the sunlight. "Is *this* what I'm supposed to work with?" She
shook her head and her large earrings trembled.

Sheetal wiped the corners of her lips with a white napkin
and covered the half-finished plate of food. "Is something
wrong?"

"We need to begin right away. There's no time to lose. Just
look at your ghagra! I've never— Why, the world has never
seen anything like it. It's...it's an Anita Dongre creation! I can
tell by the look. Your make-up, your hair...they have to live up
to this masterpiece. Everything must be perfect. Absolutely
perfect." She glanced at the watch on her wrist and frowned.
"Two and a half hours. Hair, make-up, clothes—" She clapped
her hands and turned to face the team of three beauticians and
Preeti. "Right, girls. Air condition on full. A bowl of ice-cold
water. Take out the number five brush, compacts fifteen, four

and nine..." She reeled off a list of items and then stopped, slapping herself on the thigh. "How silly of me." She turned to Sheetal. "I forgot to introduce myself. I'm Shashi Behn."

Sheetal knew who she was.

"Now, let's mo-o-o-o-ve it!"

Within minutes, sponges, brushes, lipsticks, powders and hair clips cluttered Sheetal's room. Excitement buzzed in the air, and Shashi Behn orchestrated her staff with the precision of a symphony conductor.

An hour later, Tina left Sheetal alone with the women and returned shortly with a thick, white towel pressed to her chest. "I don't know what's going on," she panted, closing the door behind, "but I heard something about a commotion in the dowry room."

Sheetal tried to catch a glimpse of Tina from the corner of her eye, but Shashi Behn, who ran a comb through her hair, tightened her hold on the strands and nudged her head back into position. "What commotion?"

"Something missing." Tina lay the towel on the bed, opened its overlapping folds and was about to lift the lid of a jewelry box when the creaking of the bedroom door and the thick odor of fish caused her to snap it shut. She rewrapped the jewelry box, placed the towel and its burden on a chair and sat on top of it, fanning the folds of her A-line *kurti* around the chair's edge.

Aunty Hemu entered and made her way across to the golden ghagra. "Very lavish." She reached for the gown with long brown fingers, a look of regret in her expression as her chipped nails caressed the pool of molten gold fabric encrusted with diamonds.

"It's designed by Anita Dongre. Designerwear." Tina apparently added the explanation for Aunty Hemu's benefit. "It's the latest in bridal outfits."

"*Hambe.*" Aunty Hemu waved a hand in the air. "That's the trend I hear, nowadays," she sneered, oblivious to six women frowning at her obtrusive manner. "In our days, we wore our wedding sari several times. Got our parents' money's worth. It's precisely why our mothers had things so sensibly made for us. Nothing too heavy, too expensive, or overly done. So we could wear them again and again."

"That's odd," Tina said. "Didn't you just say this morning at breakfast that weddings are a once-in-a-lifetime opportunity, and that every bride should have the best?"

"The best doesn't have to mean the most expensive," Aunty Hemu retorted and approached Sheetal. "Some parents can't afford what they want for their children. And we never forced our mothers to buy us the best. We understood. We compromised. We—"

Sheetal tightened her jaw at Aunty Hemu's audacity.

"Didn't you say you didn't have much in your time?" Tina interrupted. "So even if you wanted, you couldn't really do much about it."

"Relax now." Shashi Behn tapped Sheetal gently on the chin and Sheetal relaxed her jaw. "Loosen up or the style and setting will go wrong." Shashi Behn then ran her fingers through Sheetal's hair, sprayed it with water and chemicals from several bottles, and then started blow-drying the strands.

"*Hambe.* I see you still have a long way to go." Aunty Hemu raised her left eyebrow. "Strange—no? Beauty. Supposed to be natural, but you girls nowadays go to such extremes to achieve perfection. Adequately blessed, but still want to be better. Tch... tch...tch... Will there ever be an end to all this madness?"

Shashi Behn took a deep breath and twirled a fistful of Sheetal's hair into a knot. "What you call madness will end on the day love dies, or when women stop caring for their men— and what their men think of them. Love works both ways. Anyway"—she whirred the hairdryer back and forth, blowing strands of hair into Sheetal's face—"I heard your son was married only recently. Two years ago—yes?"

"Oh, yes. A beautiful wedding in Vilaspur. The talk of the town!" Aunty Hemu smiled. "For weeks and weeks that's all everyone went on about."

Aunty Hemu had been going on and on about it until the announcement of Sheetal's engagement to Rakesh Dhanraj.

Shashi Behn turned off the hairdryer and silence filled the room. "In that case, I'm sure you know all the wedding preparations are happening outside. Not here. Now, if you don't mind."

Aunty Hemu raised a hand to her chest, took a deep breath, then turned and stormed out the door.

"Negative energy," Shashi Behn murmured. "Doesn't do any good. Ever."

"Thank you." Sheetal took a deep breath and exhaled, grateful for Shashi Behn's intervention. Any trouble today would give Aunty Hemu reason to glorify the Prasads' faults, to gossip, and to mar the family's reputation.

"Don't thank me," Shashi Behn replied. "I'm used to dealing with obstacles in life. And you will learn, too. It all comes with experience."

An hour later, one of the servants asked Preeti and the team to come downstairs in order to give Sheetal some privacy. Tina and Shashi Behn stayed back, helped Sheetal into her wedding gown and added the final touches to her make-up.

Shashi Behn contoured the edge of Sheetal's lips, dusted her bun in glitter and darkened her eyebrows. She took the golden chiffon dupatta between her fingers, fanned it behind Sheetal and pinned it to Sheetal's chignon. The paper-thin leaf of fabric, embroidered and dusted with diamonds, fell to rest along Sheetal's voluptuous curves. Gold tassels, edging the dupatta, tinkled and chimed on brushing the lower half of the fishtail paneled skirt.

"Come now, quickly." Shashi Behn flipped open the jewelry box and pointed to the earrings. "Hand me those first."

Tina did as she was told, and Shashi Behn clipped the earrings on Sheetal. Then she fastened the choker, adjusting it to the left and right until the pendant hung just above Sheetal's cleavage. She hooked a thin strand of gold to Sheetal's chignon and ran the six-inch-long *maang tikka* down the middle of her head like a river. A diamond teardrop at the end rested on Sheetal's forehead. Then she slid thin, gold-colored glass and diamond bangles along her wrists. "Perfect."

Sheetal wriggled. Nothing was perfect. The gold-colored blouse with diamond strands woven between swirls of leaves and flowers that exploded at the cups of the bodice in a firework, stuck to her like a second skin. She preferred loose, airy clothing, not body-hugging outfits that padlocked her behind its stitches. Sheetal tugged the choker away from her throat and took a deep breath, but the air wouldn't come.

"Uh-uh-uh." Shashi Behn shook her head. "No fidgeting. Just stay away from the sun. These impossible summers, you know! And if those camera lights at the reception get too much, I'll be there to freshen you up. Well, I must be off. Two other brides to dress, but I'll see you later this evening—and, oh yes!" She leaned toward Sheetal and whispered in a hurry, "If you need...you know...to do your business, have at least two people hold up your ghagra. Or better, slide out of the skirt, do your thing, and then slip it back on." Then she kissed Sheetal's head and turned to leave as Tina giggled.

"What's so funny?" Sheetal whispered, catching the loose ends of the dupatta. She crossed to her bed, her feet snug in open-toe, golden Manolo Blahnik sandals, and fanned the paper-thin sheet apart before lowering herself onto the mattress's edge, careful not to sit on embroidery that would crush under her bottom. Then she let go and the golden leaf of chiffon drifted from her French-manicured nails to the crimson duvet.

Shashi Behn reached for the doorknob just as the main door swung open and Mama entered. She surveyed Sheetal and turned to Shashi Behn. "You have truly outdone yourself."

"Nothing more than was already created by God," Shashi Behn replied modestly.

"This is a work of art. You...you absolutely must have lunch with us before you leave," Mama said.

Shashi Behn glanced at her watch. "I'm running late. Two brides are waiting for me and—"

"I will not take no for an answer," Mama insisted. "Please join us."

"All right, then." Shashi Behn smiled and left, closing the door behind her.

Mama approached Sheetal. "You look absolutely beautiful."

Beautiful. Isn't that what Arvind used to say?

"Gorgeous," Tina agreed. "Isn't Shashi Behn amazing? *Taiji*," she addressed Mama with the respect due to her father's older brother's wife, "what was all that commotion downstairs a while back?"

"Oh...nothing." Mama frowned.

"I heard something about a theft."

"It's...it's...really nothing."

"What happened?" Sheetal asked. "Tina said something was missing from the dowry room."

"One of the necklaces. No one understands how...what... I don't know exactly when it happened, but Hemuji came running to us outside. She was the first to see the cellophane on one of the boxes slit through and the necklace gone."

How did this happen under such tight security? What would this do to Papa? The wedding? "Which one?" Sheetal asked.

"The diamond-drop from Belgium."

Ten million rupees!

Papa was probably tearing up and down the dowry hall this very minute, sealing off the premises, hyping up security and shooting a hundred orders at once.

Maybe he'll call off the wedding and order an immediate search.

That would be bad.

No, not bad. Awful for the family's reputation. An omen.

No. A secret intervention from God to stop the wedding.

Sheetal turned to look past Mama at the clock. Five o'clock. Three hours to inform Rakesh's family that the wedding wouldn't take place. "Did the guards see—?"

Mama shook her head. "Four hundred guests in the house. Three hundred of them, family. Your father and I can't even imagine the humiliation that would cause. Even if we ordered a search, even if one of the servants took it, it's probably gone by now."

"So, what happens?" Her heart raced with hope.

"I…I don't know," Mama said. "I'm going downstairs with Tina. She needs to get dressed. Keep the door locked. You're wearing five million rupees worth of jewelry, and I simply can't risk anything more going wrong. As soon as one of us is dressed, we'll escort you downstairs."

"So, everything is going as planned?"

"Of course. What did you think?"

Sheetal's heart sank.

"I don't want you outside until I call for you," Mama cautioned. "And Tina," she turned to look at her, "I want you to change and be back before the hour. You will stay with Sheetal until we leave. If I'm back first, I'll wait for you to return."

"Yes, Taiji." Tina left and closed the door behind.

Sheetal straightened her posture. "What if we don't find it?"

"I don't know." Mama sighed.

"I need your help, Mama. Listen to—"

"I can't deal with any more right now, Sheetal. I know how distressed you are with the awful news. But I'll deal with the theft after the wedding is over." Then she made for the door, punched the lock in place and closed it behind her.

Sheetal's heart grated the pit of her stomach. She rose, walked over to the dressing room mirror and stared at her reflection, searching for the woman she knew. But a mermaid with hips cast in golden scales and thousands of beads and diamonds stared back. Who was this golden Venus?

Sheetal opened the balcony doors in search of fresh air. She needed light. She needed to breathe. Sunlight streamed in and spilled across the carpet. She remembered Shashi Behn's warning, turned and headed back in, away from the balcony, so that her makeup wouldn't melt. She closed her eyes and took a deep breath to calm herself.

A hand clamped over her nose and mouth.

6

RUNAWAY

Sheetal struggled against the stranger's grip but couldn't draw enough breath to scream.

His grip loosened, two fingers pressed her lips and the familiar scent of musk filled her lungs.

"Stop, Sheetal. It's me." Arvind released her.

Sheetal spun to face him, her heart racing. "What are you doing here? What if someone sees you?"

Drops of sweat beaded his stubble and dampened the collar of his black-and-white server's uniform. His gaze travelled down her body. Sheetal's heart grated in guilt at the risk and effort he had taken to be with her.

He placed the knuckle of his index finger under her chin and tilted her head until she looked him in the eye. "You are beautiful." He knelt on one knee and gently coaxed her fingers open, his thumb pressing the ring. "For the last time, marry me. Please."

The white panel of curtains billowed in the breeze, and her heart fisted in her throat. He had risked his life for her, but that would mean nothing to Mama and Papa. There was no telling what they'd do if they found him here.

Arvind gestured to the balcony. "We can run away. No one will see us."

Sheetal tried to pull away, but he held tight. "I can't."

"Sheetal."

The image of open gutters lined with gray filth, dirt-infested streets and flies swarming clumps of turd whirled in her memory. She took a step back and wobbled on the three-inch high sandals as the tips of his fingers began slipping from her hand.

He tightened his grip, rose and gently pulled her by the hand toward the balcony. "I know you love me."

She tried to swallow, but her throat was choked. She couldn't leave. What would happen to the dowry? To the ambassadors, politicians and Bollywood magnates who had flown in from all over the country for the occasion? What would they say upon learning that a necklace had gone missing and the bride had run away? What would an elopement do to Mama and Papa? "My family. I—"

"For God's sake, Sheetal. It's about you. Your life. Not theirs."

She dug her heels into the carpet. "They sacrificed so much so I could marry the right person."

"The right person," Arvind scoffed, "is ten years older than you."

"Eight."

"Eight. Ten. Same thing."

"I can't just walk away."

"It's not about you. Don't you see? It's never been about you. It's a business transaction. And you're the deal."

Anger revved through her veins. Papa would never barter her for anything! They wanted her well taken care of.

"And your mother," he went on. "Of course, she'll agree with everything your father says. Not as if she or anyone can stand before the great Rana Prasad—"

Sheetal pushed him, sending him staggering back.

"Coward!" he shot at her.

"I'm not a coward."

"Too damn scared to stand up for yourself."

"I owe Papa—"

"You don't owe your father or anyone, anything. It's just a load of bull stuffed in your head so—"

"How dare you!"

"You love me. But you're too damn scared to admit it."

"It doesn't matter. I told you—"

He grabbed her wrist and dragged her toward the balcony. "Just leave this madness behind."

He was the madness. What if Mama was right? What if he used her to get at their wealth? And if he abandoned her at their doorstep with child, where would she go? What would she do? Papa would never allow her back. And she'd be a fool—a bigger fool—to have run away with him for nothing. She yanked free.

A knock sounded at the door. "Sheetal?"

Mama! "Arvind, you have to go."

He narrowed his eyes and shook his head.

"Sheetal!" The knocking continued.

"Listen to me. A friend and I. We're talking about starting our own business."

Her heart pounded. "This isn't the time." He had to leave. Now.

"It's a guaranteed plan. I can give you a good life. Trust me."

Mama was right. He was desperate. Afraid to lose a chance at her fortune. She shoved him past the panel of curtains as more people called out. The balcony railing stood two feet away. A fifty feet drop to the ground. If he had climbed up, he could easily get down.

"Marry me. I love you. I promise—"

"Arvind, I already told you, I—"

"Forget them. Think of what you want. What you—"

"Sheetal Beti!" Mama called again.

The door. They were going to break it down.

"Sheetal!" Mama yelled.

The expanse of grass separating the house from the stone fence was an easy five-minute sprint. "Get out while you can," she snapped.

"Just look at you. I never expected you, of all people, to be two-faced. I thought you were different. But you're the same. All of you."

The pounding on the door stopped and the corridor grew silent.

"I have to let them in." She turned her back to him and headed for the door.

"Sheetal!"

Papa never used that tone of voice. A shiver ran up her spine. Sheetal reached for the doorknob and looked back. The balcony door shifted in the breeze as the curtains billowed in the emptiness.

WITHIN SECONDS, MAMA AND PREETI REACHED SHEETAL'S SIDE AND A cluster of brightly dressed women followed.

The thick fragrance of Givenchy perfume flooded the room. Papa entered, his gray and white moustache quivering as he pushed thick, black-rimmed glasses up the bridge of his nose. "What on earth is all this?"

Sheetal lowered her gaze to the floor to avoid the stares. Papa's cream-colored silken pajamas and the pointed toes of his embroidered silk shoes filled her view. "I... I was in the bathroom. I didn't hear you call. I was—"

"What nonsense!" Papa yelled, his *juttis* thudding the carpet. "She's wearing five million rupees worth of jewels and you leave her alone, Indu? What's wrong with..."

A business transaction... Her heart sank.

Mama escorted Sheetal to the bed and sat her down as the women speculated in hushed whispers. Mama ordered Preeti to get Sheetal a glass of water and sat beside her. "I was here the whole time until Tina and I had to go and change. So, we left her alone for a few minutes. But she's fine. There's nothing to worry about. We should try and find the missing necklace. Did—"

"What's gone is gone," Papa said. "We can't go looking for

it now or we'll ruin everything. Get Sheetal out there or we'll be the laughingstock of Raigun if the Dhanrajs reach the reception ground before we do. Now come on, everyone. We have a wedding to show the world." He marched off, the smack of his juttis on the corridor floor fading rapidly in the distance.

The women surrounding Sheetal exchanged hushed remarks about how Sheetal shouldn't have been left alone, how guards should have been placed outside her bedroom door and extra guards stationed near the jewelry sets in the dowry room. Their whispers buzzed like a thousand angry bees. Sheetal pressed a palm atop Mama's hand for support and curled her fingers around the edge.

"Perhaps you should all head down now," Mama interrupted. "We can't be late, and I need some time alone with Sheetal."

The women filed out the door.

Mama looked at the broken glass bangles near the balcony door and then narrowed her attention on Sheetal. "He came for you, didn't he? Arvind."

Sheetal turned away from the press of Mama's stare.

"And you didn't go."

"I couldn't. You and Papa. I thought of—"

"Forget him. You did the right thing. Now, let's go."

Sheetal rose to her feet and looked about her room one last time. The walls had sheltered her childhood. The bed had lulled her into a million dreams. The minutiae of her life, from dupattas, hair clips and cosmetics, to hangers and pairs of sandals, lay scattered around the room after the hustle and bustle of the afternoon. She imagined Preeti clearing up this room after all the guests left, the skinny brown figure picking up twenty-two years of her life and putting them away.

"Let's go."

Sheetal took one step forward and let go.

7
ROYAL RENAISSANCE

At precisely six o'clock that evening, Rakesh Dhanraj mounted a white mare and rode toward the Royal Renaissance Hotel's Waterfront Garden entrance while the wedding procession accompanied him on foot. A shiny brass band, bolting out renditions of famous Bollywood tunes, preceded three hundred and fifty family members and close friends dressed in heavily embroidered saris, suits and *kurta* pajamas, while fifty senior members of his family rode to the hotel in white limousines.

A piercing honk from a trumpet caused the mare to reel back and stomp her hooves, which made her brocade caparison tremble. The horse's owner, who walked alongside Rakesh with a firm grip on the reins, tugged to control the unnerved beast.

Rakesh swayed and shot a hand up to secure his white turban and the fifteen-carat diamond that glittered at the center of the *saafa*.

The entourage paused when some of the wedding procession formed a dance circle behind the band. Rakesh nodded
approval, pleased with the laughter and good cheer, and
straightened a string of pearls around his neck. He adjusted the
low-cut Mandarin collar of his two-piece, pure white crepe
wool sherwani. Kashmiri embroidery in a shade of stone blossomed along the length of the shirt and unfurled down to his
knees. He tightened his legs against the horse's belly to secure
his position should the mare grow nervous again, and the
matching, skin-tight *churidar* clung to the taut muscles of his
calves.

Passers-by and oncoming foot traffic stopped to gawk at
the procession, and Rakesh's heart swelled. How could people
not stare at his attire, custom-designed by India's premier
fashion guru, Arjun Khanna? And it wasn't just any collection
but came from the House of Khanna Classic Couture.

The ring of dancers broke apart and the procession
advanced toward a pair of elephants that stood guard at the
hotel's entrance, their bodies draped in glittering, embroidered
caparisons and their heads covered in golden, jeweled *nettipat-
tams*. The entourage stopped as the elephants raised their
trunks and trumpeted the joy of the groom's arrival. Rakesh
accepted a silver stick and touched it to a religious placard
mounted overhead. The crowd cheered at this formal signal of
his arrival.

A throng of pundits, women and children wearing brightly
colored, sequined clothing, followed Indu Prasad toward the
groom. Indu carried a *thali*, a sterling silver plate, in her left
hand, which contained separate mounds of dry rice; yellow,
vermilion and white powders; and a small, sterling silver vessel

of water. Indu stopped at the main entrance as Rakesh dismounted and stepped onto a decorated footstool before her.

Indu dampened her right thumb and third finger, then dipped both fingers into the vermilion powder. She dotted the gap between Rakesh's eyebrows, then used her thumb to extend this dot upward in a vertical line. Then she dipped a finger into the dry rice and dotted a few grains onto the base of the vermilion trail as pundits chanted shlokas. She held the thali and circled it clockwise before Rakesh to officially welcome him to the family. Only then did Rakesh step off the stool.

Members of the bride's family cleared a path for the groom's entrance. Six female ushers dressed in sequined ghagras of white silk with black sashes broke away from the crowd in pairs and preceded Rakesh down a hall, scattering rose petals on the red carpet. Golden trellises woven with vines and flowers lined the hall, the scent of tea roses perfuming the air.

The trellises gave way to a bridge that arched gently over the sunken wedding ground almost twenty feet below. Rakesh gestured for the entourage to slow and kept his gait relaxed so it didn't appear that he hurried to marry Sheetal. He certainly didn't, and the guests needed to know that.

He looked across the right railing. Buffet tables, laden with golden serving dishes that offered cuisines from around the world, awaited the grand feast. The floral arrangements had been flown in from Holland, while bottles of wine and champagne were imported from France, Portugal and Italy. His heart soared at the ostentation. It was going to be a fabulous wedding, indeed. A wedding to remember.

A breeze swayed strands of miniature lights woven through the branches of trees. While those around him oohed and aahed, Rakesh kept his expression blank, like he had expected the Prasads to spare no expense. After all, their daughter was to marry the most sought-after bachelor in Raigun.

A fifteen-feet-tall yacht, with *Destiny* in golden letters across the bow and surrounded by a moat, was the stage upon which he and Sheetal would be presented to the world. The yacht's gold sails flapped in the breeze. Behind the yacht, a collage of roses, blue bells, marigolds and sunflowers depicted a sunrise. Two staircases, one on either side of the ship, provided access to the deck.

The moat branched into channels that circled the inner perimeter of the wedding ground. Rock pools, flora, lotuses and multi-colored lights peppered the trickling waters. Crystal fountains sprouted silver webs of water that locked and wove apart with the breeze.

Rakesh signaled the entourage to continue and followed the litter of rose petals to a ramp that angled toward *Destiny*. He straightened his posture as the waiting crowd beamed at him.

He was ready to take on the bride and her world.

8
DESTINY

Ten women escorted Sheetal up *Destiny's* left staircase as she struggled under the weight of her jewelry. Halfway up, she gripped the banister decorated with alternating yellow and purple tulips to steady herself. A dark abyss gazed back at her. Was that an eight feet drop, or more? She couldn't tell. When she neared the top, a spotlight fixed on her. *Breathe.* The air seemed too thin, and she struggled to inhale against the throttling pressure of her choker.

Finally, she reached the deck, stepped aboard, was led to the vessel's bow, and halted before two majestic thrones plumped with satin cushions.

Surrounded by an entourage of men, Rakesh approached from the opposite staircase and stopped two feet away.

Sheetal's knees weakened, but female relatives coaxed her to close the gap between her and Rakesh. On her right, a thousand guests watched. She held her breath. What if Arvind suddenly climbed over the railing and whisked her away?

A photographer called out to her. Sheetal glanced up as a flash of hot white light blinded her. Another breeze swept past, and the satin sails flapped, their thumping synchronized with the beating of her heart. The audience raised their fluted glasses to toast and waited for Sheetal to make the first move.

A five-inch thick, ten-pound string of flowers was thrust into her hands. Rakesh grabbed a similar garland from a sterling silver thali carried by one of his friends for the Garlanding of Flowers, Varmala Ceremony. They were to drape the garlands around each other's neck to signify acceptance of the other as husband and wife. But how could she accept this man when she wanted nothing to do with him? Her heart pounded. She crushed the flower petals and sap trickled down her wrists. She turned to Rakesh. The stone hardness of his perfectly chiseled features sent a shiver down her spine.

He towered a foot above her. Too high. Out of reach.

Sheetal raised the garland until it hung like a halo of flowers before Rakesh's face. She tiptoed and rocked forward, paralyzed by the knowledge of what she was about to do. She hated everything about Rakesh and here she was accepting him as her husband. She released the garland and almost lost balance. The garland slipped from her fingers and draped the Mandarin-cut collar of Rakesh's sherwani.

Waves of applause filled the air. Fluted glasses clinked against one another, accompanying the drumming of the *tabla*. Sheetal was about to rock back and regain her balance when Rakesh tossed his garland around her neck. The string of flowers lunged at her like a noose, causing her to stagger back into the arms of the women behind her, who laughed and pushed her back on her feet as the crowd cheered louder than before.

A minute later, Sheetal sat down on a throne beside Rakesh, bearing the full weight of his authority, on display for all their guests.

AT EXACTLY ELEVEN O'CLOCK, AS STARS TWINKLED ABOVE THE *MANDAP*, Sheetal and Rakesh sat cross-legged and barefoot on the floor before a fiery havan, her right hand locked in Rakesh's ice-cold grip.

Two pundits dressed in saffron-colored robes chanted Vedic shlokas and poured ladles of ghee into the havan, causing thick gray smoke to fan across the guests. Sheetal turned away from the flames, her skin scorching in the heat. A pundit ordered them to rise from their lotus-like positions, then tied her golden dupatta to a stole, draping Rakesh's left shoulder. Sheetal scrunched the carpet under her toes and inched forward carefully, leading the first of seven perambulations. The first signified the family's prestige. The second, their honor, and the third, their integrity... Family, she reminded herself. She was doing this for her family.

Then Rakesh took his position in front of her, and she followed him for the final phera.

It was now or never.

She was halfway around the fire, inches away from losing her freedom. Sheetal gathered the sides of her golden ghagra and just before the final step, a flash of hot white light blinded her, causing her to lose her footing and stagger. She bumped Rakesh's back and the wall of his white sherwani suit filled her view. As fire raged in the havan, the crowd joked about the bride's hurry to marry Rakesh and have him.

The photographer wildly gestured for her and Rakesh to stand closer together and face him. "Smile!"

Sheetal stared into the camera lens as another flash of light blinded her.

It was over.

9
SOLITAIRE

Rakesh Dhanraj watched as family and friends prepared for a prayer to seek the Lord's blessing before he slept with his bride for the first time.

The pundit asked Rakesh to fold his hands in prayer and Rakesh gritted his teeth. *Why pray when a glass of scotch cured all ills?* Stares from family members and relatives caused him to align the palms of his hands. His head pounded. His throat was parched. He hadn't had a drink in more than twenty-four hours. Or a cigarette, for that matter.

Alcohol wasn't supposed to be consumed on auspicious days. Not only did drinking violate tradition, it insulted the gods. Rakesh didn't plan on making tradition a habit.

A priest dotted Lord Ganesh's forehead with vermillion powder and dry grains of rice, then instructed Rakesh and Sheetal to do the same.

Sheetal obeyed, but Rakesh turned away, sick to his stomach. Hadn't he followed enough orders by now? The surrounding crowd frowned. Rakesh turned back, dipped the third finger of his right hand in a tiny trough of water, then into red powder, dotted Ganesh's head and wiped his hand on a tissue. His fingers trembled. He gulped.

He slid his right hand along his thigh toward a hip flask fastened to his belt. After the Varmala Ceremony, he had changed into a suit and tie and equipped himself with enough scotch to make it through the night. He curved his fingers around the cold metal as loud Vedic hymns pealed the air. *Not now.* He patted the bottle. *Later. When alone.* Then he slid his hand into the right pocket of his suit and ran his thumb over the fine latticework of the Belgium diamond-drop necklace. *Later. When alone.*

10

BLACK KNIGHT

Sheetal took four steps into the bedroom before she turned back toward the corridor, but the door clicked softly shut. She stood alone in Rakesh's bedroom. The nuptial bed stood hidden behind a curtain of red and yellow tulips threaded in neat vertical rows. The fragrance of flowers and mint made her dizzy.

According to romantic Bollywood films, she was supposed to take her position in the center of the bed and coyly wait for Rakesh to enter. Instead, she stumbled to a sofa, grabbed an armrest, and sank onto a blue cushion, nearly toppling a swan-shaped silver jug and matching sterling glasses on a nearby table. She blinked, her eyes heavy with exhaustion. The room blurred into two of everything. Goosebumps puckered her arms and legs. She wrapped the chiffon dupatta around her shoulders. It provided little warmth. Her legs ached from sitting cross-legged for hours and then standing all evening. She raised her feet onto a coffee table, closed her eyes and slumped against the corner of the couch.

All she had to do was keep Rakesh's hands off. Stay pure. Untouched. Manage for a few weeks, then go home and prove to Mama how wrong she and Papa had been. They'd see their fault, give in and then let her marry Arvind.

So what if Papa had forced her to marry Rakesh? There was no way that he or anyone else could force her into Rakesh Dhanraj's bed.

FIVE HOURS LATER, WHEN SHEETAL WOKE, THAT'S PRECISELY WHERE she was.

She reeled back, disturbing the strings of tulips surrounding the bed.

"Easy, easy." Rakesh raised a hand. His steely complexion filled her view. He lay along her left side, an elbow propped on a pillow and his palm cupping the side of his face. From his easy manner, it was obvious he'd been waiting for her to wake.

A deep impression on the pillow, where her head had lain, indicated she'd been here for some time. "How did I get here?"

He reached out and traced his index finger down her nose, lips and across the right cheek. "I carried you." He continued gliding his finger down to her chest, past folds of wedding gown, and stopped at her cleavage.

Sheetal pushed his hand away. "Get off me!"

"I'm not on you."

"Move back or I'll—"

"Scream?" He smiled. "They're expecting that." He gestured to the bedroom door. "Now, allow me." He leaned over, inched his finger down her cleavage, and pulled her closer, his eyes glinting in the bedroom's soft, yellow light.

Sheetal flinched, but Rakesh was quicker. He grabbed her wrists, pinned her arms against the pillow, and kissed her on the lips. His tobacco breath burned her throat, the stubble on his cheeks grated her skin and she cried out when his teeth cut her lip.

She kicked, managed to free her hands and shoved his bare chest, but Rakesh ripped off her dupatta and began unfastening her blouse. She grabbed his wrists but he kissed her again, filling her lungs with the odor of burnt copper. The stench of alcohol caused bile to well up her throat. She thrashed her head. His saliva smeared her lips and cheeks.

He ripped apart the final blouse hooks.

She cried out and swung an arm to cover her nudity but struck Rakesh's head as the tips of his canines grated her breast. Rape... Was this rape?

She opened her mouth to scream, but Rakesh clamped a hand over her lips and drove his teeth into the flesh above her left collarbone. A scream gurgled up Sheetal's throat and erupted as the wail of an animal.

Rakesh tossed aside the duvet, and cold air blanketed Sheetal's body. She lay unmoving, numb.

Rakesh walked to the other side of the bed, slid beneath the blue quilt, turned off the bedside lamp and immersed Sheetal in darkness.

THE NEXT MORNING, PUSHPA DHANRAJ, SHEETAL'S MOTHER-IN-LAW, who she was to address as Mummyji, threw open the bedroom door and marched in.

Sheetal yanked the bedsheet to her chest and jerked upright. Rakesh—

He was gone.

She ran a hand over her crushed gown, then the mattress and encountered a soft tissue-like fabric. She pulled out the dupatta. A safety pin had gashed the fabric. She looked toward Mummyji, opened her mouth and stopped. Who would believe her? They'd say Rakesh only did what he was expected to do.

Mummyji crossed the room, stopped between the bed's footboard and the entertainment unit and thumped the right wall with a palm. A portion of the wall glided right. Yellow light bathed her brown complexion dotted with black freckles. She entered the previously hidden space, her white sari billowing around her bulbous frame.

The tail of Mummyji's sari pallu disappeared behind the closet door and soon after, metal clanged against metal.

"Mummyji?" Sheetal said. When the woman didn't answer, Sheetal called louder, "Mummyji?"

No response.

Sheetal leaned forward for a better view of the hidden room but couldn't make out much with Mummyji's bottom obstructing the doorway. She pulled together the edges of her blouse but the bent hooks wouldn't latch. She dragged the sheet as she slid out of bed and wrapped it around her body. She approached the enormous walk-in closet. Double rows of horizontal rods on each side of the room formed upper and lower berths for hanging clothes. Empty, golden hangers swung gently between rows of mostly empty shelves.

Mummyji bent to reach something she had apparently dropped. As she wriggled left and right, her movements caused the hangers on the lower rods to tinkle. A ten-inch-thick fold of flab spilled through the gap between the hem of her blouse, which ended just above the waist, and the sari fastened about her hips. She straightened, turned toward Sheetal, raised her thick, perfectly shaped eyebrows and sighed. Then she handed Sheetal a red and gold silk sari adorned with a latticework of diamonds and sequins. She added a matching petticoat and blouse from a shelf, grabbed a blue velvet box and flipped it open to reveal a gold and ruby jewelry set. Then she marched to the bed, shoved the strings of tulips aside and placed the jewelry box on the duvet. "The clothes and jewelry you are to wear today. Be dressed, I tell you, in the hour. Vikram will come to pick you up."

Tradition dictated that the bride's brother escort the bride to her mother's home the day after the wedding, but because Sheetal didn't have a brother, Vikram, Aunty Hemu's son, would fulfill the duty.

"Mummyji, last night Rakesh—"

"Yes, he left late last night, very late, I tell you, to attend to business matters. No need to feel alone. I am here. I am always here, and now I have the extra duty to manage you, *Hai Ishwar!*"

Three female servants entered, each carrying a Louis Vuitton suitcase. Sheetal clutched the sheet tighter and cringed. Didn't anyone have manners? She was dressed in a bedsheet, for God's sake. Couldn't Mummyji have told the servants to wait outside?

Mummyji ordered them to leave the luggage near the closet door beside Sheetal.

The first servant bent, placed a suitcase against the wall, glanced sideways at Sheetal and raised her eyebrows. Sheetal's cheeks flamed.

Then the servant straightened and left. The other two placed their suitcases then followed the first from the room.

Mummyji unclipped a ring of keys from her sari and jingled the bunch in her hand. "All these, I tell you, are keys to the boxes of dowry your mother sent." She removed three keys from the ring and handed them to Sheetal. "But those are all you will need." Then she fiddled with the white pleats of her sari before staring at Sheetal's neck. "Anything else?"

"May I have the other keys to my dowry?"

"*Hai Ishwar!*" Mummyji gasped. "Your dowry? Haven't your parents taught you anything? Now that you are a Dhanraj, what's yours is ours and what's ours is yours. All one and the same, I tell you. Obviously, you've not been brought up well. Clearly not only are you selfish, self-centered, full of yourself and demanding, but you have no respect for elders. This won't do."

Warmth crept up Sheetal's shoulders. "The bathroom? I...I..."

"Why there, of course." Mummyji pointed to a wall on the far right. "Just tap the wall and another door will slide open. Didn't Rakesh tell you?"

Sheetal shook her head.

Mummyji patted her black chignon. "Plenty of towels

inside, I tell you, and lots of other things you might need. Make sure you go to the Prasads' looking like a Dhanraj."

A Dhanraj. What was that supposed to mean?

"Last night, Rakesh hurt me," Sheetal blurted.

"Well now, I tell you." Mummyji straightened her shoulders. "If you misbehaved with him last night, I'm not surprised. What were you expecting? And don't tell anyone you didn't sleep well last night." Mummyji pointed to Sheetal's neck. "Make sure to hide it."

11

HOMESICK

The Prasads' blue Maruti turned into Prasad Bhavan's driveway, rolled past the topiary hedge and braked fifty feet behind a luxury coach parked in the porte-cochere.

As guests exited the house and crossed to the waiting vehicle, Vikram, seated in the Maruti's front passenger seat, gestured to an available parking spot to the left of the bus. "Well, Dinesh. Go on farther."

"Cannot, Sir." The chauffeur switched off the ignition and unclipped his seat belt. "Sahib say no park, and to leave empty so people can board bus."

Sheetal glimpsed Vikram's glare when he turned his head toward the driver. "Well, I'm ordering you to pull up there."

Mama and Papa emerged from the glass entrance and hurried toward the Maruti. Aunty Hemu followed close on their heels. Mama's orange sari glowed like the rising sun. Their expressions lit with smiles.

"Sahib say park here," Dinesh said. "You can check with him if you want, Sir."

"It wouldn't kill you to drive up a few more feet. They wouldn't have to walk all the way down," Vikram said.

"Sorry, Sir." Dinesh fidgeted with the collar of his starched white shirt, left the vehicle, and walked around the car to Sheetal's door.

"Sorry, Sir, my foot." Vikram unclipped the seat belt and swung open the door. He turned toward Sheetal. "You know your problem? Just because you guys are loaded, you think you can trample over everyone."

Bitterness crept up Sheetal's heart. "Dinesh works for Papa. Of course, he'll take his orders from him."

"Well, every dog has his day. Enjoy your visit, because before you know it, your time will be over." He extended one long leg out the vehicle, rose and slammed the door shut.

Dinesh opened Sheetal's door and she stepped out. "Don't mind him," she whispered. "Vikram—he just takes offense at the smallest things."

The sari that belonged to the Dhanrajs weighed on her like a burden stitched to the fabric of her skin. Or did the safety pin on her pallu, digging into her shoulder, cause the discomfort? The driveway she'd walked countless times before felt smaller, perhaps due to the enormous bus and the crowd of people that took up so much space. She trudged partway up the driveway before Mama and Papa joined her.

"Ah, Sheetal Beti!" Mama and Papa reached and hugged her, and the familiar scent of sandalwood aftershave and lily joss sticks soothed her nerves.

"Splendid. Looking absolutely splendid." Papa's eyes

sparkled. "I can't believe my little girl's all grown up, married and with her new family. And how is our new son-in-law?"

"Now what kind of a question is that?" Mama ran a hand soothingly down Sheetal's arm. "Both must be so exhausted after the wedding."

"*Hambe.*" Aunty Hemu squeezed through the ten-inch gap between Mama and Papa and ran her fingers over the embroidery on Sheetal's pallu. "Such heavy work! So pretty. Must be so expensive and—"

"There you are, Bhabhiji!" Aunty Veena called Mama as she hastily approached, her silver blouse reflecting the sun's rays. "The chef is going mad, just mad, looking for you. He's got one hour before lunch preparations and— Sheetal!" She embraced Sheetal as if they were meeting after a years-long separation.

"Look how delighted everyone is to see you!" Papa patted Sheetal's shoulder. "Now come on, everyone. Back inside before the heat picks up. Got to get our tourists on their way."

They made their way up the porch and entered the house just as Uncle Ashwin, Papa's younger brother, entered the foyer. Except for narrower shoulders, a thinner frame and a softer voice, Uncle Ashwin was almost a spitting image of Papa.

"Ah, Sheetal Beti! How is our new bride?" His bushy eyebrows lifted and his thin lips parted in a smile.

"Fine, Uncle."

"Good, good. I'll join you a little later. Have to make sure we get the tourists off on time." He turned his back to Sheetal, cupped both hands around his mouth, and hollered, "Leaving in ten minutes. *Jaldi, jaldi!* Hurry up, everyone!"

A cluster of second, third and fourth cousins who wore capris, jeans, T-shirts and visors rushed past Mama and Papa toward the waiting bus. The rev of an engine caused Sheetal to turn. Another coach pulled into the drive.

"Oh, look!" One of Papa's business acquaintances from Canada exclaimed, "Sheetal's here." The woman approached and several men and women surged forward. Papa's business acquaintance reached her first, flipped up her sunglasses and perched them on her head. "Why, you look gorgeous. So gorgeous."

"Thank you, Aunty," Sheetal addressed her respectfully.

"So, how is the new Mrs. Dhanraj feeling?" asked an uncle with a wart on his left cheek.

"Arrey." Another uncle joined in. "Like a million dollars?"

The growing crowd erupted into laughter.

The groan of an engine followed by a honk cut short the jovial atmosphere and wart-uncle raised a hand. *"Challo, challo. Bus choot jayegi."* He gestured for others to follow him and pushed through the door.

"Got to go, honey." Canada-aunty cupped Sheetal's cheek, leaned forward and kissed the air over her left cheek. "Good luck to your future and keep us posted. I'll make sure to read up on you in the news." Then she left and choruses of "Good luck," "Wish you well," and "Many many years of togetherness" followed.

"Jaldi karo!" Wart-uncle joined Uncle Ashwin in the driveway and waved for people to hurry.

Something tugged Sheetal's right earring. She swept her hand to free what felt like a loose thread snagging the jewelry and, from the corner of her eye, caught Aunty Veena quickly withdraw her hand.

"Just brushing away a fly on your earlobe." She chuckled as Mama turned back.

"I could go too, you know," Aunty Hemu said as a line of children passed them and rushed toward the coach, "but I think to myself, 'How will Bhabhiji and Rana *Bhaiya* manage without my help?' So, I sacrifice a day of enjoyment to help them."

Mama turned to Aunty Hemu. "And we will never forget all that you have done for us. You did so much more than a real mother could have done, which is why I'm going to ask you to escort Sheetal to the Great Hall and stay with her until I'm free. We can't leave her alone, and you're the one I trust most to sit with her."

Aunty Hemu? Trustworthy? Sheetal tapped Mama on the arm, leaned close and whispered, "I can wait in my room. Surely Tina can spend time with me until you're free."

"She's out shopping," Mama said. "I don't expect her to return until this evening, and Preeti hasn't cleaned your room yet. You'd better wait here. Besides, everyone will want to see you and should know you're here."

"They can see me upstairs, if they want," Sheetal said.

"No arguments. I'll see you later." Mama headed toward the backyard.

Sheetal sighed and followed Aunty Hemu. The floor-to-ceiling wall of glass, which offered a view of the topiary hedge and driveway, reminded her of a glass tank. The clippety-clip of the gardeners' clippers snipping away at bushes or sculpted animals and the hiss of water spraying the grass had been among the first sounds of every morning. Today, cries of "*Jaldi karo*" and the commotion of people rushing from the backyard and across the main hall to the waiting buses replaced those familiar sounds.

"You sit here." Aunty Hemu gestured to the U-shaped sofa that faced the window.

Aunties Veena and Meenu followed on Sheetal's heels. Sheetal pursed her lips. A few hours of being a Dhanraj and not only had she been escorted from the car and up the driveway by family, she was now being herded by a troop of aunties and seated center-stage for visitors who wanted to meet or greet her. What had she turned into? An exhibit?

Sheetal lifted aside a cushion and sat down beside the arm rest. She wanted to talk to Mama. In the privacy of her room, she wanted to slip into her old clothes and clear her head to think. How would she tell Mama about last night? Should she tell her everything? Once Mama heard the truth, she'd admit the marriage was a mistake and take her back. There'd be no returning to the Dhanrajs's, for sure. Perhaps Mama would agree to Arvind and apologize for what she'd said about him.

The luxury coach reversed out the entrance gate, made a wide turn and left.

Sheetal's attention drifted to the topiary hedge. No one deserved to be with a man like Rakesh.

"You worried about something?" Aunty Meenu took a seat beside Aunty Hemu.

Sheetal suddenly realized that her right thumb was tapping her left wrist. "Umm, no." She stopped.

Aunty Meenu crossed her legs. "I've heard there are twenty-five bedrooms in the Dhanraj mansion. Does that include attached or shared bathrooms?"

"*Hai*, I'm hearing the taps are made of gold. Pure gold." Aunty Veena gripped her elbows and leaned forward. "Are you seeing the swimming pool? I'm hearing it's endless. Or appears endless."

"Infite pool," Aunty Meenu said. "They call infite pool in English."

Sheetal had heard about the grandeur of the mansion but didn't know the premises accommodated a swimming pool, let alone an infinity pool.

Shortly after her engagement, the Prasads had been invited to tour the Dhanraj mansion, but half an hour prior to leaving, Sheetal had feigned a headache.

"Well, take a Saridon or something," Mama had said. "We can't go without you. What will they say?"

"Nothing, if you tell them my head's going to split."

Now feeling like her head would truly split, Sheetal pressed her forehead.

"Maybe Sheetal is not seeing much." Aunty Meenu cupped her chin and leaned forward. "You know, first night—how say in English? All nighter?" She covered her burgundy lips and chortled.

"What could I see in seven hours after all the wedding rituals?"

"Well, of course, you'd see the bedroom," Aunty Veena said. "Where else would you be on the first night?"

Another round of giggles.

What was taking Mama so long? Sheetal craned her neck to look toward the door. Her heart sank. A cluster of aunties wearing too much makeup headed toward her from the east wing.

"Hambe." Aunty Hemu leaned toward her. "Did they treat you well?"

Sheetal swallowed. Why would she tell Aunty Hemu, of all people, the truth? The woman already knew so much about her personal life.

Aunty Hemu pulled back as if realizing she'd said something she shouldn't have. "I mean—he—Rakeshji—he behaving nice? Decent?"

"Yes, very decent." Sheetal could just imagine their reactions if she told the truth. "We still have to get to know each other."

"All the more reason to tread softly." Aunty Meenu nudged Aunty Hemu with an elbow.

Sheetal felt a tug on her earring and from the corner of her eye, saw Aunty Veena trace her chandelier earring. The woman's face drew close, so close that her lips hovered inches from Sheetal's nose. The smell of grease, onions and spices peppered the air. Sweat dotted Aunty Veena's upper lip. She cradled the earring in her palm. *"Hai,* so dark. So red! This alone must be worth twenty-five *lakhs."* She meant twenty-five hundred thousand rupees.

"Bloody pigeon, the name." Aunty Meenu clicked her tongue and raised her eyebrows. "So? Twenty-five or more, you think?"

Where on earth was Mama?

"Pigeon-blood ruby," Aunty Hemu said.

"Well, look who's back." An aunty from the new pack took a seat beside Aunty Meenu. Other members of the group filled the remaining empty seats and three ottomans.

"Ouch, Aunty. Please let go." Sheetal brushed Aunty Veena's

hand aside and straightened her posture. "This thing is heavy enough without—"

"*Hai! Dekho, dekho!* Look, look!" Aunty Veena released her grip and the earring swung like a pendulum. "Now she's showing off like a Dhanraj."

Sheetal pressed her earlobe gently to curb the swinging motion of the earring and soothe the pain searing her lobe.

"What a little snob you are." Aunty Veena inched away. "Married a few hours and already acting snooty."

"Of course, it's heavy. We can all see that, can't we?"

Silence engulfed the room. Sweat beaded the sides of Sheetal's neck and armpits and she fidgeted with the pleats of the sari pinned at her left shoulder, hoping the bruise remained hidden.

"And the necklace. My, my!" Aunty Meenu added. "So gaudy and—"

"So what if its gaudy?" Aunty Hemu cut her off. "*Hambe.* So much money the Dhanrajs have. Too much for ordinary people like us. What do we know of—"

"So, tell us," a newcomer aunty in a bright purple sari asked. "Are they really as glamorous as they appear? Do they eat off eighteen-karat gold plates? Are you protected by an army of servants and security guards?"

"Yes, tell us."

Aunty Meenu raised a hand. "More important, do they only wear silks and chiffons? I heard..."

Sheetal's head throbbed harder. She had to speak to Mama. There was no way she was going back.

"*Hambe,* how matter what they wear or eat? More important, how quickly Sheetal fits in their lifestyle."

"All depends on Induji," Aunty Meena said. "If Indu taught her well to listen, not talk back like so many girls do nowadays, and learn the family's ways, she'll hold up the Prasad's *naak*."

Holding up the family's nose was a measure of reputation, but Sheetal didn't care about upholding anything. Why were they talking about her, in front of her, as if she wasn't there?

Aunty Hemu ran her fingers over her greasy hair. "All in Sheetal's hands now. What she is doing. How she is behaving to hold up the Prasad naak."

"Oh yes, of course," Aunty Purple-sari added. "Didn't we all, in our time? Had I failed to please my husband and in-laws, why, that would be the end of me. Where to go?"

Aunty Hemu halfway curled the fingers of her right hand and waved that hand side to side. *"Log kya kahenge?"*

"Not just a question of what people will say." Aunty Meenu brushed the air with a hand. "What after? Mess up with your new family. No turning back. Not even to your parents' home. Just drown in shame."

Mama and Papa wouldn't force her to return. Not after she'd done everything they'd wanted.

"And take your parents down with you," Aunty Veena added. "And everyone else you're tied to."

"And then," Aunty Meenu added, "what man will want you after all that?"

Sheetal pursed her lips. Arvind would always want her. If, for some reason, he didn't, she would find a way to make a new life for herself. She owed herself that much.

"Does anyone know where Mama is?" she broke into the cacophony of simultaneous conversations. "I saw her briefly and then she had to leave to attend—"

"We're all busy," Aunty Veena answered. "Can't you see? An extremely busy time for a bride's mother. So many responsibilities and so much to do after the event. And she has to attend to us, as well, considering how far we travelled for you."

"Just for you," Aunty Meenu added.

Mama and Papa had paid for their relatives' tickets. All they had to do was pack and come. Clearly, no aunty intended to help, so Sheetal rose. Aunty Veena grabbed her wrist. "No need to get upset. I'm sure Induji will be here soon."

Soon? Sheetal's chest tightened. She had to speak to Mama now.

"Why so agitated?" Aunty Purple-sari asked.

"Is something wrong with their family?" An aunty in a turquoise salwar suit scooted closer to Aunty Purple-sari.

"Come now," Aunty Veena whispered. "You can tell us."

Aunty Hemu tapped Sheetal's wrist and leaned close. The odor of warm coconut oil and fish caused Sheetal to hold her breath. "He real gentleman? *Hambe*, Beti, tell me. I read in newspaper, he has high education, very good manners, talk like Amrikan. He treat you gentle, like precious flower?"

Sheetal slumped against the couch, the pallu's weight dragging her down. What was she supposed to say?

A group of older men walked by and Aunty Veena pressed her index finger to her lips.

A clean-shaven uncle wearing suspenders veered toward them. "Oh, ho! The new bride will be benefiting from all your experience and womanly advice. Good, good."

Aunty Veena raised her finger in the air. "Precisely why we're attending to her."

He clapped his hands and squeezed them together. "Well,

then we'll just leave you women folk to your business and be on our way to lunch." He led the troop of men into the main hall, headed toward the backyard.

Aunty Veena tucked a loose wisp of hair into her bun and crossed her arms. *"Hai,* you look somewhat troubled. Didn't the first night go as planned?"

"There was a plan?" Sheetal swallowed the bile rising in her throat. She was going to be sick.

"Unless, of course, he dozed off," Aunty Veena said.

Aunty Meena hid a smile behind her hand.

"Or," Aunty Veena continued, "Rakeshji's nowhere close to the dynamic and charming man he portrays to the world and *you* fell asleep."

The women broke into fits of laughter.

Sheetal's throat tightened.

"Hambe." Aunty Hemu cleared her throat. "In my time, wedding was a two-day event and done. Now, four, five, six days and so many functions. Keeping up with this, that—after second day, I am falling asleep."

"You're comparing today to your time twenty years ago?" Aunty Turquoise-salwar suit called. "You are her mother's age."

"Now, hush everyone. Not a word more of the first night." Aunty Meenu chortled and gestured to Sheetal's neck. "We can clearly see."

Sheetal reached for the pallu on her left shoulder and tugged the fabric to hide the bruise. A cold palm covered her free left hand. She looked down. Aunty Hemu's hand rested there.

"Is hurting?" Aunty Hemu whispered, her eyes welling. "So deep?"

Sheetal fumbled for an explanation. "I...I guess I'm not used to wearing such heavy clothes. The safety pin must have dug into my skin all night long."

"What rubbish," Aunty Meenu snapped. "It should hurt. In English, how they say? No pain, no gain?"

"Infinite gain for this one here," Aunty Veena added icily. "She'll rule her palace like a queen."

Sheetal's heart grated the pit of her stomach. She swallowed back tears. If only they knew.

"How you all behave!" Aunty Hemu snapped. "Someone get her Boroplus." She referred to an antiseptic cream that claimed to cure most skin ailments.

"It's not infected," Aunty Turquoise-salwar suit replied. "An icepack three times a day should cure. Three to four days, at least. Not like a headache, one pill and gone. Pure common sense."

"Arrey, what makes sense is perhaps the Dhanrajs aren't as polished and refined as Induji and Ranaji make them out to be." Meenu Aunty raised her eyebrows. "Just because you have money, doesn't mean you have everything. You know how some people exaggerate the truth to make another look grander, especially when it's about the family they've married their children into."

Sheetal straightened her posture. "My parents don't lie."

"*Hai!*" Aunty Veena cupped a hand to her mouth. "*Dekho, dekho!* Now she insists we are accusing her parents of lying."

"I didn't say that." Sheetal looked from Aunty Veena to Meenu and back. "I only meant—"

"Tell us what you mean," Aunty Purple-sari said. "I've been hearing about how perfect the Dhanrajs are for years. Not a blemish. Not a scandal to their name. How to believe for a second the Prasads could have scored an ace alliance in the first go without something up their sleeve? Every family has weaknesses."

"Loopholes," someone threw in.

"Induji and Ranaji are hiding something," Aunty Veena said. "I can smell it. Or why would a family the likes of the Dhanrajs"—she raised a hand in the air—"take a girl from the Prasads?" She lowered her hand halfway and her bangles clinked. "I sent my Nandini's photo and biodata to them, but no word back." Nandini was Aunty Veena's oldest daughter and because her proposal to Rakesh hadn't been accepted, Nandini had refused to attend the wedding. "My Nandini is twenty-six. Perfect match, four years younger than Rakeshji. Not a child of twenty-two."

"Loophole. De-fi-nitely b-i-g loophole," someone joined in.

"*Hambe.* Give her a chance to say something," Aunty Hemu raised her voice.

"We're all ears," Aunty Veena said. "How did your parents hook you two up? Speak."

Sheetal calmed her breathing. "Mama and Papa did absolutely nothing wrong. Rakesh is the perfect gentleman. Mummyji was there for me first thing this morning, and I don't have to lift a finger in my new home."

"Sheetal? That you?"

Sheetal craned to see past the heads of Aunties Hemu and Meenu. A slender woman in black trousers and an orange blouse stood at the main door. The young woman hurried across the room.

"Kavita!" Sheetal jumped to her feet, wove through the

barricade of women's legs and hugged her best friend. "Where have you been? There were so many people, I didn't see you at the wedding."

"Tied up." Kavita tried to pull away, but Sheetal held tight. "Don't want to spoil your clothes, if you know what I mean."

"They're just clothes." Sheetal allowed her to pull away but held onto Kavita's shoulders.

Kavita skimmed Sheetal from head to toe. "Don't want to mess up the look."

Sheetal's heart ached. Had money now distanced their friendship? First Arvind, now Kavita. Who else would she lose because of this marriage? She led Kavita toward the east wing and stopped well away from the aunties and their side-eyed stares.

"Something wrong?" Kavita asked.

"Last night... I— He hurt me."

"What do you mean, *hurt*?"

"I didn't want to—you know. Rakesh forced me and there was nothing I could do to stop him."

"He raped you?"

Shame welled up Sheetal's throat. "I..."

Kavita's jaw dropped. A deafening silence hung between them. "Have you told anyone?"

"Just you."

"Tell your mom. This is unacceptable. He doesn't have a right to— No one has a right to and get away— Does anyone— Your in-laws know?"

"Just my mother-in-law, who barged into my bedroom this morning and started commanding me around."

Kavita raised a hand to her temple and stared at Sheetal. "You have to tell your mom."

Sheetal took a deep breath to maintain her composure but a tear spilled. She turned her back on the women. "I don't want to go back. He'll hurt me again."

"I can't imagine what you're going through. Look, your mom's headed this way. Tell her now."

Sheetal looked over her shoulder. Mama strode toward them from the main entrance. The cluster of aunties called out to her. Mama's attention shifted from Sheetal to the congregation.

"Go tell her now before those cows hog her attention." Kavita pulled Sheetal by the arm toward Mama.

"Kavita." Mama halted near the cluster of aunties. "What are you doing here?"

"Hello, Aunty." Kavita released Sheetal and pressed her palms together. *"Namaste."*

"Don't *namaste* me. I don't remember inviting you."

The aunties murmured and scooted closer. Mama led Kavita and Sheetal toward the glass wall. "She doesn't need any more of your bad influence. First you elope and shame your family, then to prove you're right, you're here to turn Sheetal against her husband and family?"

The air thickened. Is that why she didn't see Kavita and Gaurav at the wedding? Why didn't Kavita tell her? And what about the letter? Did Kavita give it to Arvind?

"Oh my!" Aunty Meenu squeaked. "She's the girl who eloped and—"

Shocked murmurs erupted in the cavernous hall. "Shhh," someone hissed.

"Some things never change," Kavita murmured and glanced sideways.

"Why is she even here?" someone asked.

"What did I say about selfish girls?" Aunty Veena demanded. "First, they elope against their parents' wishes, then expect a welcome. What's wrong with this generation? What are they thinking?"

"Arrey, they are not thinking," Aunty Meenu said. "That's why they end up the way they do."

"Aunty," Kavita kept her voice low, "Sheetal has something important to tell you."

"And what could be so important that you must intervene?"

"We need to talk, Mama. In private."

Mama crossed her arms and faced Kavita. "What have you done now?"

"Nothing," Kavita said.

"This has nothing to do with her," Sheetal said. "It's Rakesh."

"I see." Mama raised her eyebrows at Kavita. "So, you have already turned her against Rakesh."

"Mama!" Sheetal grabbed Kavita's wrist. "She's not turning me against anyone—"

"Enough." Mama looked at her watch, then at Kavita. "It's not enough that you shamed your family. Stay away from her. I have ten minutes to spare, then I have to see to lunch preparations."

"Ten minutes?" Sheetal felt lightheaded. "This is about my life."

"Not here." Mama glanced sideways at the aunts who had lowered their voices even more, no doubt to eavesdrop. She looked at Kavita. "You're more than welcome to leave." She turned to Sheetal. "Follow me." She headed toward the hall.

Sheetal followed, entered Papa's den behind Mama and closed the door. She turned.

Mama pulled a chair for herself, swiveled it ninety degrees and sat at Papa's table. She propped her right elbow on the table's edge, cupped her head in her palm and glanced at her watch again. "That girl's nothing but trouble. Stay away from her."

Sheetal leaned against the door. "I'm not going back."

"That's your home now. Your duty lies first and foremost with them."

"That's not my home."

"Look, Sheetal, I just sent off about sixty people for a sight-seeing tour. I've got to supervise preparations for lunch because there's easily another hundred people or so in the house and I'm expecting another forty or fifty who didn't go on the tour and—"

"Mama. Did you hear me? I'm not going back."

"What is it with you and your never-ending drama?"

Sheetal swallowed through a dry throat. Is that all her problems were to Mama? Drama?

"If this is about Arvind—"

"He hurt me."

"I told you all along he'd hurt you. On the day of your wedding, he came to harass you. Wasn't I right?"

"I'm talking about Rakesh. He hurt me last night."

Mama's neck and cheeks turned a light shade of pink. Her elbow slid off the table's edge and she looked away. "Well, you know these things are—" She fidgeted with the bangles on her wrist. "Every woman must deal with it in her own way and..."

Sheetal tried to make eye contact, but Mama looked down at her orange sari pleats. "He used force on me."

Mama took a deep breath and shook her head. "Look, Sheetal. It's in your nature to fight. To go against anything you disagree with instead of reasoning things out. That's how you are, and that Kavita has put ideas in your head. But just because Papa and I tolerated your rebellious behavior all these years doesn't mean others will. Learn to think of others first."

Sheetal lowered the pallu on her left shoulder and her heart welled in her throat. "You mean like this?"

Silence filled the room and Mama cupped a hand over her mouth. "He did this?"

Sheetal nodded.

Mama's attention fell to the floor. "I...I know it's hard, but... but try to be a good wife. An understanding wife, so this doesn't happen again. Agree to and adjust to their ways. Don't make it harder on yourself."

Sheetal swallowed. "I tried, Mama. I told you he's—"

"Try harder. You've only been married a few hours. Your whole life is ahead of you, but if you do anything or say anything stupid, you're giving all those women out there a chance to spread gossip."

Anger fueled a fire in the pit of her heart. Didn't Mama want to know what happened? Didn't she care? "Why do you assume Kavita's behind this? Or—"

"You didn't say— Tell those women what Rakesh did, did you?"

"I lied. I made up something about the safety pin digging into my skin."

"Did Kavita say a word?"

"No."

"At least that girl did one thing right." She rose. "Speak good of the Dhanrajs because their reputation is now in your hands. And don't think for a second you can just walk back in when you feel like, because now you are like a guest in this house. You need your in-law's permission to come here. And that's exactly what Veenaji, Meenuji and the others are waiting for. One chance to prove they are right."

12

MIRROR MIRROR

By the second night, the curtain of flowers around the nuptial bed had been removed. Sheetal slipped under the quilt, on the side of the bed closest to the bathroom, so she could run and take cover should the need arise. She turned to face the wall, her back to the empty half of the bed, and closed her eyes, willing sleep to come quickly.

A soft swish filled the silence. The scent of mint preceded a slight jostle as the mattress springs lifted gently and then settled back. *Rakesh!*

"So, darling, how far do we take it tonight?" Rakesh cupped the right side of her face and forced her to look at him. He slid his other hand under the pink satin nighty and snapped open the clasp of her bra.

Sheetal stopped breathing and stared into the two moons of his eyes. *Do not give into fear.*

"A challenge?" He inched away. "Interesting. Perhaps I should leave you alone and just continue my good ol' bachelor ways. Assume I never married you. Nothing between us." He grabbed a pack of cigarettes and a lighter from the bedside table.

"There *is* nothing between us."

"Oh, so you talk! Not just a pretty face in pretty clothes." He tapped out a cigarette, lit it, and puffed white clouds of smoke. "I realized from the get-go you were different from the other thirty ladies dying to be Mrs. Dhanraj. There was something about you..." He waved the cigarette in the air. "Secrets."

Did he know about Arvind?

"The whole thing has obviously been embarrassing for all of you. And the embarrassment will continue if you don't listen. Stick to the rules and you'll be safe." Rakesh swung the cigarette until it hovered above the carpet and tapped the end. "Number one. You go nowhere without my permission. Rule number two. As my wife, I expect appropriate behavior at all times. My public image is top priority. Understand?"

Sheetal stiffened.

"Do I make myself clear?" he bellowed.

Sheetal nodded.

"Ditto." He curled his lips into a smile. "Oh, yes. Rule number three. Try filing for divorce and I'll spread rumors that you failed to please me as a wife. I'll make life so miserable, your family will never show their faces anywhere again." He took another drag and the end of the cigarette burned neon red before Rakesh extinguished it in the crystal ashtray. "Do we understand each other?" his voice tightened. "Well? Do we?"

Sheetal nodded.

"Good." He swung his legs across the bed, rose to his full stature, and the mattress sighed in relief. He lengthened his stride, causing the cream-colored kurta to unfurl to his knees and swish against silk pajamas as he headed for the mirrored wall.

He's going to crash into the glass!

Rakesh raised a hand to the mirror and a portion of the wall swung open, swallowing him in darkness before it closed.

13
SISTERS 'N SPICE

Two days later, Rakesh's sisters, Megha, seventeen, and Naina, twenty, knocked on Sheetal's bedroom door and asked if they could help arrange Sheetal's closet. In addition to her dowry wardrobe, ten of Sheetal's paintings had been brought up to her room and stacked in two groups of five, placed at an angle against a wall. Thrilled with the offer, Sheetal welcomed the opportunity to get to know her sisters-in-law.

Shortly after Sheetal's engagement to Rakesh, the Dhanrajs announced Naina's engagement to Ajay Malhotra of Calkot. The marriage was scheduled for a year after Sheetal's, thereby giving Mummyji time to prepare for a second wedding. Acres of land on the shore of Lake Pyasi, which lay to the east of Raigun, was being cleared for a mammoth construction.

Naina, wearing a green salwar suit, approached the paintings, paused, then began flipping through them, resting them against her knee. She stopped and stared at one. "What's this?"

Sheetal walked over and looked down at the canvas. "Oak trees."

Naina flipped to the next canvas. "And this?"

"Conifers."

"They look the same."

"Oaks have branches that spread out like a cauliflower, whereas conifers—"

"A tree is a tree, no matter what." Naina gave the paintings a hard thwack. The canvases knocked each other and fell like dominos.

Sheetal rushed to stop the fall, but they clattered and banged against the floor as Naina walked away. *How dare she?*

"Now, what's all this noise here, I tell you?" Mummyji rushed in.

"N-Naina was b-being rude," Megha answered. Dressed in a T-shirt two sizes too large and wearing a pair of round eyeglasses that wobbled on her nose, Megha dropped a pile of Sheetal's blouses on the bed and rushed over to help Sheetal restack the paintings. "B-Bhabhi is right." Megha used the term of respect reserved for an older brother's wife. "This is a p-painting of c-c-conifers and those are oaks. But N-Naina was arguing that they're the s-same. Anyway, you c-can't expect N-Naina to know an-n-n-y of this."

"Now, now." Mummyji turned to look at Naina. "Here I was thinking you three would work together so Sheetal could have her things quickly arranged, I tell you. But instead of—"

"I just think—" Naina interrupted.

"Never mind what you or anyone else around here thinks, I tell you. Sheetal is new and needs time. The quicker she plants her roots, the sooner she'll fit in. And I will teach her all there is to know, now that I have the extra duty to manage her. *Hai Ishwar!*" She spun on her heel and left.

Rumor claimed that Rakesh's father, the late Ashok Dhanraj, had married Mummyji shortly after the death of his first wife, Rashmi. Mummyji, only eight years older than Rakesh, had been almost half Ashok's age. Ashok's death three years ago meant the death of her normal life. A widow wore only white and was expected to avoid festivals and celebrations so that her inauspicious shadow didn't fall on another. Her somber life was to be devoted to raising her children—which now, apparently, included Sheetal.

Megha and Naina had moved to the mirror-wall. "N-Naina, you're n-not l-listening," Megha said. "C-conifers have s-spiky n-needle-like l-leaves. They're—"

A scream suddenly pierced the air. Naina tossed her hair away from her face, stamped her foot, pivoted, stomped off and slammed the bedroom door behind her.

"What was that?" Sheetal asked.

"That m-m-my d-d-dear B-B-Bhabhi, is N-Naina D-Dhanraj." Megha pushed the silver frames up the bridge of her nose. "Welcome to the f-f-family."

ON THE FOURTH MORNING, AS SHEETAL READ THE JUNE ISSUE OF *NEW Woman* magazine in the privacy of her room, Mummyji barged in and handed her a sheet of paper.

"What's this?"

"Read. Rote. Revise." Mummyji smiled. "I drew it all up on

my own. Your routine beginning tomorrow, I tell you." She turned around and left Sheetal with a timetable dictating what time she was to wake, dress, and attend morning prayers. Breakfast, according to the schedule, took place at eight-thirty, followed immediately by Sheetal's educational time, which meant reading the newspaper, learning the family history, and the family business. Lunch was served at twelve-thirty, after which she was to help Rakesh with his work in the office until six in the evening. Only after this was Sheetal officially free.

Free? Sheetal took a deep breath. She had always done things at the time and in the manner she wanted. How dare Mummyji dictate her schedule? She was about to scrunch up the paper when a footnote scrawled at the bottom caught her attention. Sheetal was to rote-learn the family's achievements and web of relatives for a pop quiz at the end of the month.

With eleven days to go before the end of the month, Sheetal was determined not to learn anything at all.

That afternoon, Janvi, one of the fifteen servants, knocked on Sheetal's bedroom door. "Choti Sahiba?"

"Yes?" Sheetal set aside her Danielle Steele novel.

"Memsahib is calling you downstairs for lunch."

"I'll be there in a minute." It took longer than a minute to reach the Marquette Dining Room. Getting from one floor to another meant a walk along one of the mansion's wings, going down the main stairs, across the hall and through a short corridor. The Dhanraj mansion sprawled on acres of land and accommodated seventy-thousand square feet of living space: forty thousand on the ground floor and thirty thousand on the second floor.

A private Japanese garden, the only one of its kind in Raigun, occupied the space behind the mansion. Four garages and servants' quarters situated outside the west wing were equally matched on the east by an infinity pool that overlooked the Dhanraj's private lake and a view of the mountains.

The U-shaped driveway passed through a lush green lawn and was bordered with flowers, colored pebbles and a sculpted hedge. A pair of black, wrought iron gates closed the driveway's entrance on the left and exit on the right, each monitored by a manned security post. A porte-cochere, supported by six Venetian pillars, shaded fifteen marble steps covered in red carpet that ascended to a pair of huge mahogany doors.

Sheetal emerged from her bedroom on the north wing and silently passed Megha's room, situated directly above the Marquette Dining Room. She peered over the marble railing of the balcony that ran the length of the mansion's inner perimeter. No one stirred downstairs.

A flight of stairs bisected the north wing's corridor and flared in an A at the ground floor. A tessellation of alternating black and white tiles covered the ground floor, and a pair of crystal chandeliers, hanging from the sixty feet high ceiling, framed the stairs.

The left chandelier illuminated an informal sitting area that contained a nine-seater Bradford Brown settee pampered with soft, brown cushions, and a Russet Legacy coffee table. The right chandelier hung above a mammoth, sixteen-seater, U-shaped Fulton White seating arrangement complete with five ottomans, each piece padded with sturdy appliqued white cushions. This seating arrangement was fronted by two gray marble elephants that faced each other, each elephant adorned with gold collars and silver-and-pewter anklets. Their heads and S-shaped trunks supported a six-feet long sheet of beveled glass. The table was rumored to be worth a fortune.

However, this good fortune meant little to Sheetal who preferred to watch streaks of yellow sunlight angle across the squares of black and white marble and soak in a little sun that streamed through the French windows behind the Bradford Browns at dawn and across the Fulton Whites at dusk. She craved warmth in this mansion of hard, cold marble where all the bedrooms, except for Mummyji's on the east wing, ran along the north wing.

Sheetal made her way down the stairs and paused behind the Bradford Brown sofas in a spot of sunlight, hoping to warm herself. Janvi called out again.

Sheetal hurried to the dining room. Mummyji was likely to fuss about how improper and unacceptable it was for a daughter-in-law to loiter around the house when so much work needed to be done.

Mummyji sat tapping her French manicured nails against a plate, diamond bangles glittering on her wrists. Sheetal understood why as she entered the dining room. Three serving bowls, full of curries, graced the center of the dining table set for two.

Sheetal had heard that Mummyji had wasted no time after Ashok died in exchanging her ruby, sapphire and emerald bangles for diamonds and pearls. Sheetal took her place opposite Mummyji, pulled in her chair and spread a serviette across her lap.

"Well, what do you think?" Mummyji asked.

"Think of what?"

"Your schedule?"

Sheetal took a deep breath. "It's like being back in school."

"Exactly what the first few years are all about for any bride, I tell you!" Mummyji clapped in delight. "Marriage means school. An education. Learning to do everything in a new way. *Our* way."

"But—"

"No buts, I tell you. Forget what you were. Look at who you are. A Dhanraj." Her cheeks swelled with pride. Then she leaned forward and helped herself to servings of spicy *mutter korma, chana masala* and yoghurt *raita*. The freckles on her face darkened as she accidentally dribbled gravy from the spoon onto the cream-colored tablecloth. "Now, if you need me during the afternoons, I'll be at the club. I'm the best card player, I tell you. I always win."

Sheetal didn't care if Mummyji lost. She had to do something about that ridiculous timetable. "Where's Nainaji?" She added the 'ji' as a form of respect when addressing any in-law.

"Naina won't eat." Mummyji tore a piece of *chapati,* rolled it into a cone, filled it with curry from her plate and popped it into her mouth. She said while chewing, "I understand Naina hasn't been on her best behavior lately. This just cannot continue, I tell you. The two of you arguing over trees and now one on a hunger strike. Aren't you going to eat?" She gestured to Sheetal's empty plate.

"I tried to reason with her," Sheetal said, "but she wouldn't listen." The argument over conifer and oak trees had cropped up again last night when all four women were watching TV in the lounge and Naina continued to pass sarcastic remarks about Sheetal's paintings. Furious that no one stood up in her defense, Sheetal had excused herself and gone upstairs to her room.

"There's only one way to sort this." Mummyji raised a greasy index finger. "An apology."

Finally! They agreed on something.

"You should go to Naina's room right now."

"Why?"

"To apologize, of course." Mummyji glared at her. "Not everyone cares about trees or trivial things the way you do."

"Me?" The blood rushed to Sheetal's head. "Apologize?"

"Of course, what did you think?"

Was she even supposed to think, or was Mummyji supposed to do all the thinking around here? She reiterated how the argument had begun, but Mummyji would have none of it. According to Mummyji, it was Sheetal's fault and an apology to Naina was pure common sense.

Nothing made sense. Her first week as a Dhanraj—bridal mehndi still laced her palms–and she was supposed to apologize for something she hadn't done?

Sheetal finished her lunch in silence. Then she marched upstairs and apologized through Naina's locked bedroom door.

Over the next two weeks, Sheetal saw Rakesh a total of four times and ate fourteen dinners without him. She had never seen him eat, drink, sleep or interact with any family member or staff. Sometimes, he worked out late at the gym, or he saw clients all evening, and she learned of his whereabouts from eavesdropping on Mummyji's conversations with the servants. But to ask any of the Dhanrajs directly about him was unthinkable. What would they think of her and her supposed intimate relationship with Rakesh? The blame for any fault in the marriage would fall on her.

If she returned to Mama and Papa and said things weren't working out between her and Rakesh, she'd be forced right back with instructions to give this marriage time and patience. To 'get to know' Rakesh before making hasty decisions. Which is why it was crucial to spend time with her husband, to get to know him, and find reasons why it was impossible to live with him and his family. She needed proof that this marriage was over and there was no chance of a return.

Each night, Sheetal tried hard to stay awake, but fell asleep before Rakesh arrived home. By the time she woke in the morning, he was gone. The only clues of Rakesh having slept with her were the distinct odor of nicotine seeping from his side of the bed and a slight indentation in the mattress. Clues like this left her feeling bad. But nights when the other half of the mattress lay cold, empty and flat, without a wrinkle or impression, left her feeling worse.

Finally, Sheetal entered the dining room one evening and turned left into the kitchen. There were no voices, only the rattling and clanking of pots and pans. Which meant Laal Bahadur, the chef, worked alone. She paused at the open doorway as Laal Bahadur tossed some cumin seeds into a wok of hot oil. A crackle and splutter filled the air as wisps of smoke rose from the pan. "Smells good."

"Oh! Choti Sahiba!" Dressed in a chef's white hat and starched, white uniform, Laal Bahadur mopped his cherry-round face with a tea towel before turning to face her. "Welcome, welcome!" He clanked a flat griddle on one of the four burners and then tossed some diced green chilies and ginger atop the cumin seeds.

Sheetal rarely had an opportunity to speak to a member of the staff. The first time was the day after her wedding. Fifteen Dhanraj servants had lined up and Mummyji had introduced her as the Choti Sahiba, after which the servants introduced themselves to her one at a time.

"What's cooking, Laal Bahadur?" she asked.

"Oh! *Paneer korma, dal palak,* and"—he indicated the wok —"a *phool gobi* mix." He tossed in florets of cauliflower and began to stir-fry the contents. "Just ten more minutes and I'll be done. You are hungry, no?"

No. She wasn't hungry, and she didn't have ten minutes. Mummyji would be down any second. "I was just wondering... do you warm dinner for Rakesh when he returns at night?"

"Oh! He not eating here." Laal Bahadur paused to look at her. "I don't know much. I am given instructions never to ask anything. But, oh, I know he is usually returning by one or two at night. I am leaving his dinner on the table, as I am told to. And that's exactly how I am finding it every morning."

"He must eat out then. With friends? Business clients?"

"Maybe." Laal Bahadur shrugged. "How else can a man like

him manage Dhanraj & Son alone and work nonstop? Fifteen hours a day, sometimes."

Sheetal didn't know how. But she was determined to find out.

THE NEXT MORNING, MUMMYJI BARGED INTO SHEETAL'S BEDROOM AND thrust another sheet of paper in her face. "This is the menu for the rest of the week, I tell you." She panted– no doubt, from the speed at which she must have raced to give this to Sheetal. "And from now on, I will give you one every Monday so you don't go around asking the cook what's for lunch! Before I know it, you'll be asking the servants where they live and what they do."

Sheetal opened her mouth to reply, but Mummyji didn't give her a chance to speak.

"Rule number one, I tell you. You do not make casual conversation with the staff in this house." She locked her Kit Kat thick fingers behind her back and started pacing the room. "Rule number two. You do not frolic about the house. Ever. Or just loiter around. A Dhanraj walks with poise, pride and elegance." She straightened her posture, raised her head high, looked at the ceiling, and almost banged into the entertainment unit. "You should command sophistication, respect and dignity so everyone will respect you."

Was this a mental institution or a military school?

"You carry on the way you did yesterday and you'll find little difference between yourself and the servants. I don't know how you went about doing things in your mother's house, and I don't want to know. But from now on, I tell you, you do everything our way. You have married into the Dhanraj household and you will behave like one of us, I tell you, or you will never become one of us. Furthermore…" Mummyji spat out another twelve don'ts, and when she finished, she paused to stare at Sheetal. "We're in the first week of July. You have learned the list of family members and relatives—no? For a surprise quiz?"

How could it be a surprise if she knew about it? "No." Sheetal crossed her arms. "And I don't plan to, either."

"Well"—Mummyji raised a palm in the air, causing diamond bangles to jingle—"we'll see about that. As for mealtimes—"

"I don't think I'll be hungry again." Sheetal tossed the paper aside, full to the brim with commands, lectures and resentment.

"The hunger strike thing, no? We'll see how long that lasts, I tell you." Mummyji adjusted the sari pleats that fanned across her chest, then marched out the door.

A hunger strike. Sheetal sighed. Like anyone would care.

Sheetal phoned Mama twice or thrice a week, and every time she begged to come home, the conversation took the same turn. "You know coming here is not the answer, and it will only unsettle you," Mama said this afternoon. "Your in-laws' place is your home and you must give yourself time to understand the ways of their family."

"But I need some time away from them. To think. To be myself," Sheetal said.

"I will have to talk to Pushpaji about a good time for you to come and spend a month with us."

Sheetal's grip on the handset loosened and the instrument begin to slip. "But Mama, I can't wait that long. It could take forever. And they're so difficult. So obnoxious. So rude. Self-centered. And Mummyji keeps a close watch on me all the time. She even dared to—"

"Sheetal—"

"And Rakesh doesn't care. He—"

"He's your husband and the only earning member in the family." Mama was firm. "Are you expecting that he wait on you hand and foot?"

Sheetal paced the length of the phone cord. "I'm not expecting anything. Just that—"

"It was the same when I married your father. I only saw him in the mornings before he left for work and late in the evenings when he returned. I spent all my time with his mother. But a woman like Pushpaji," she raised her voice as if in awe, "to preserve the Dhanraj name, she must keep a close watch on everyone and make sure no one strays. So much pressure and effort to keep balance and unity in the family."

Sheetal shook her head in disbelief. The marriage celebrations were over, the guests had gone home, but Mama was still fixated on the Dhanraj label.

"You are a grown woman now. Not a child. You will always be the apple of our eyes, but you shouldn't expect—"

"You don't understand, Mama. They keep shoving lists of rules and regulations down my throat. And act as if—"

"You're not on holiday. Or a guest. And you're not an only child now. You have two sisters-in-law and a responsibility toward them."

Even though Naina was twenty and Megha seventeen, custom demanded that Sheetal be mature, understanding and assume a mother-like role toward her husband's younger siblings.

"You must try and settle in," Mama continued. "Respect your husband and mother-in-law. And remember—"

Sheetal tightened her grip on the handset. "I'm not comfortable here. Always on edge. Always—"

"Comfortable?" Mama cut her short. "We didn't have a fraction of your comforts when I married your father. And until you were nine, we lived in Nariyal Ka Rasta. Have you forgotten? Sometimes, we scraped by with two meals a day. Remember that time? On the way back from school, you insisted on buying the ten-rupee coloring book. You must have been eight then."

Sheetal thought hard but she couldn't remember ever missing a meal. Mama would drop her off and pick her up from school every day on foot and Sheetal, like any other child, wanted to buy some trinket from the roadside stalls. However, one day she insisted on buying a coloring book from a magazine stand. Mama explained that it was expensive and they should let it go. Eight and stubborn, Sheetal insisted on buying it and Mama gave in.

"I know, Mama. You've told me before."

"I was meant to use that money to buy vegetables for the

evening's dinner. And spent it on the coloring book you wanted."

Sheetal's heart sank. Mama had never told her they'd gone hungry because of the incident. "So, what did you eat?"

"We managed."

Her heart fisted in her throat. *They managed to stay hungry because of me?* Sheetal bit her lip and her attention fell on the princess-cut diamond ring. The ring would have fed her family for years back then. It could have bought them proper windows instead of chipped wooden shutters to keep out the stench from the streets. It could have repaired the flush so that they didn't have to pour buckets of water down the sit-and-squat-on toilets. It could have—

"And you must learn to manage now." Mama's calm voice filled the speaker. "You have everything any woman could want. Learn to fit in. Find your place in your new home."

WITH NO BETTER ALTERNATIVE, SHEETAL DECIDED TO LEARN ABOUT the Dhanrajs and their history. She read past newspaper clippings and magazine articles carefully filed over the years in transparent sheet covers, which filled several binders.

She returned the pop quiz unanswered, much to Mummyji's dismay, and spent evenings reading in the peaceful quiet of the Japanese garden behind the mansion.

The Japanese garden, shaded by clusters of trees rich with lush foliage, offered Sheetal respite from the mansion's cold temperature and the outdoor heat. Landscaped with bridges, ponds, miniature waterfalls, rockpools and bonsai trees, this extension meandered to a clearing at the far back where the gardener burned dead trees, hedge trimmings and dried leaves.

Sheetal took her favorite spot on a bench on the far right, near the pond of Japanese koi, and began reading an article from three years ago, written after the late Ashok Dhanraj's death. It described how Ashok had died of a heart attack, and how Rakesh took over Dhanraj & Son immediately after and guided it into a multi-million-rupee empire.

Rakesh was described as the Harvard graduate-returnee who made it big by proving industry pundits wrong. Industry leaders claimed that new business strategies and innovative marketing techniques learned in the U.S. would not work in India. They believed the only way to keep the Indian economy strong and self-reliant was by barring international goods. However, Rakesh pointed out that the international playing field was levelling and the country couldn't function in isolation anymore. Collaboration with international brands, allowing them access to the Indian market and, in return, gaining access to markets abroad, was the only way to prosper and fuel economic growth. The jump in Dhanraj & Son's stock price months later proved the point.

Sheetal was about to turn the page when the tink-tink of porcelain rattling on a trolley caused her to look up.

Mummyji was making her way toward Sheetal. A servant followed, wheeling a tea trolley. "My meeting at the club was called off, I tell you." Mummyji reached and settled upon the stone bench. Her body blocked the sunlight. "So, I decided to spend my evening with you."

How thoughtful. Sheetal smiled as the gray-uniformed servant poured hot *masala chai* into two teacups.

Mummyji grabbed a cup and saucer and began sipping the tea in loud, irritating slurps. The servant handed Sheetal the second cup. She took it reluctantly.

"Perhaps it's good my meeting got cancelled, I tell you. With Naina so miserable and upset, I shouldn't leave her alone until she gets better."

"Is Nainaji all right?" Sheetal asked. "I haven't seen her in two weeks." After the incident over the trees, Sheetal had steered clear of Naina, making sure to avoid crossing paths or being in the same room with her. This was relatively easy, considering the mansion had endless corridors and rooms. However, lately she hadn't seen Naina, at all. Clearly, something was wrong.

"I know." Mummyji sighed. "It's something you must get used to."

Sheetal stared at the tea in her cup and winced. "I don't drink tea. I prefer coffee."

"Well, you'll get used to the taste over time, no, I tell you."

Sheetal was about to emphasize that she didn't like the spicy, milky flavor, but Mummyji didn't give her a chance.

"In her room for ages now. My Naina refuses to eat or do anything, I tell you. *Hai Ishwar!*" She fluttered her thick brown eyelids and coughed. "She goes through...these...these phases where she needs to be alone. After a while, once she's her usual self again, she's normal. Nobody understands. Poor child." Mummyji's voice cracked, and a tear glistened in the corner of her eye. "It all started with Ashok's death. Of the three children, I tell you, only Naina loved him the way a real daughter should.

She's the only one who really cared for him. She was so hurt after his...his..." She sobbed.

Sheetal's throat tightened. She hadn't meant to upset Mummyji.

"Anyway." Mummyji wiped the tears with her fingers and instantly stopped crying. "Let's talk about you now."

So, Mummyji wasn't here to talk about Naina. She was here to exchange information about Naina in return for some of hers. Sheetal gritted her teeth.

"Are you more comfortable here?" Mummyji fidgeted with her necklace's diamonds. "It's been three months."

Sheetal didn't want to appear difficult. "Everything's a little different. It's still taking a while to get used to. New home. New place. New faces."

"Oh!" Mummyji's cheeks ballooned into a smile. "I'm sure you must find everything here, the quality of being a Dhanraj, so much better, grander, richer. No?"

No! Was being a Dhanraj all Mummyji or anyone else cared about?

"Anyway"—Mummyji waved a hand in the air— "I often worry about you and Rakesh. Are things all right between you two? I know Rakesh doesn't give half the attention you deserve. Perhaps he's a little uncomfortable with you, no?"

Me? Wasn't it obvious she was the one uncomfortable with him? She was uncomfortable with Mummyji, too. Had Mama talked to Mummyji behind her back?

"I wonder sometimes whether you two are as intimate as you should be. What with your honeymoon to Europe cancelled, I tell you."

Something urgent had came up at the office and the

planned two-week trip to Europe had been cancelled, much to Sheetal's relief. Two nights with Rakesh was enough discomfort to last a lifetime.

"With Rakesh so busy, I think you should join him in the office," Mummyji continued. "That way you'll be more helpful and can spend time together. I have no clue, I tell you, what's happening in the company since Ashok died. Rakesh doesn't tell me a thing. And because he doesn't spend time with you, I" —she pressed a hand against her chest— "am doing my personal best to help you fit in. All the socializing, I tell you, we've been doing together...it's only brought us closer—no?"

Sheetal had accompanied Mummyji to several dinners, charity events and exhibitions, but she hardly knew anyone in the Dhanrajs's circle of friends and business acquaintances and felt more like a model used to showcase the latest designer sari and jewelry than a family member.

"You don't know how worried I—"

Sheetal broke in, "We're fine, Mummyji. We're old enough to manage our relationship. You do understand," she softened her tone, "bedroom doors were made for a reason. So that people knock before entering. Perhaps the reason we don't have the intimate relationship we should is because you barge in whenever you want." With that, she snapped the hefty black binder shut and walked off.

14

PICTURE PERFECT

Rakesh grabbed a black DuPont pen from his six-feet-long cherry wood office table and leafed through a stack of papers. Tiny red arrow tabs marked several black lines, indicating where he should sign. He twirled the pen between his fingers and sighed. This would easily take thirty minutes. He skimmed the fine print. On second thought, fifty-five.

Rakesh read every document in detail before he signed, especially the fine print, because that's where the loopholes were placed. And he was not one to fall for them.

Yet, he'd managed to get stuck in the biggest loophole of his life. The guests had come and gone, Pushpa had enjoyed her week of glory as the groom's mother and everyone else had witnessed the matrimony of a lifetime. But he was now stuck with a wife.

The pen accidentally left his fingers and landed near a wedding photo of him and Sheetal taken after the Varmala

Ceremony and now sealed inside a black and silver frame. They were frozen in time, like gold and silver mannequins, and from Sheetal's expression, she'd just woken from a nightmare.

The feeling was mutual. No contract to dictate the parameters of the deal. No fine print to hunt for hidden clauses. Just a marriage certificate they signed after the wedding, binding them as husband and wife. He shook his head and swiveled his chair to face the swarm of skyscrapers beyond the floor-to-ceiling window.

At least, he'd established authority in their first week and established the marriage rules—which was good. So far, Sheetal hadn't interfered with his work or caused any trouble. Still, the thought of her presence in his home, room and bed was enough to make him wince.

Rakesh propped his right elbow on the armrest, stretched his legs and swiveled away from the crowded view. He had explained to Pushpa that he wasn't cut out for marriage or settling down and that he was content as a bachelor. All he wanted was breathing room. However, Pushpa argued that most good Indian men married in their late twenties—thirty, at the most—and if he didn't, all the 'good girls' from 'good families' would be snapped up.

"Leftovers. That isn't what you want, I tell you," Pushpa's words from that night swirled in his head...

He remembered as if it had happened yesterday. He returned home from work and she'd started again. "For how long will you live like this? Reckless. *Awara*."

Rakesh tensed. He wasn't a nomad.

"Clubbing every day, I tell you. Drinking. Spending time with clients. How many dinners? How many—"

"It's for work." He dumped his Saatchi briefcase on a Fulton White ottoman and sat on a single seater.

Pushpa had arranged thirty photographs of eligible bachelorettes on the glass table. Some women wore saris, others wore salwar suits, but they all shared one thing in common. They came from wealthy families.

Rakesh was about to protest, then stopped. What was the point? Pushpa would have her way in the end, like she had seventeen years ago, shortly after his real mother, Rashmi, gave birth to Megha and then died of post-natal complications. Pushpa and three-year-old Naina marched into their lives a week after Mumma's funeral, and Ashok introduced the two as the new mother and sister—a hasty court marriage after which Pushpa had been quick to take control of their lives.

Rakesh was ordered to consider Naina as much a sister as Megha and refer to Pushpa as Mumma. No one was to speak of the past. However, Rakesh refused to call Pushpa Mumma because that would mean Mumma no longer existed.

Pushpa grabbed a photograph, flipped it so that the candidate's information, scrawled in black marker, faced him, and turned to Rakesh. "Sasha. Five feet nine..."

The backs of each photo listed all the pertinent information, from the candidate's height, body measurements, complexion, education and hobbies to the family's net worth. But Pushpa had obviously spent so much time preparing for this moment that she had memorized their details. Though an Indian man was expected to study hard, marry in accordance with the parents' wishes, have children and provide for the family, Rakesh was sickened by her behavior.

"You have to marry," Pushpa insisted. "Don't turn away, I tell you. How else will I find a suitable boy for the girls?"

'The girls' meant Naina.

"They will think something is wrong with you. Us. And then what future is there for the girls, I tell you?"

Because Rakesh was ten years older than Naina, he had to marry first so they could move forward with Naina's matrimony. It was the only way to get rid of her.

"You must think of your sisters and their futures. If not for that heart attack three years ago, your father would still be here and handling all this. But he isn't. And you owe us this much, at least."

His attention fell on the photographs. Saliva lodged in his throat and he gulped.

Pushpa reached for a photograph of a woman in a blue and magenta salwar suit. The woman had a pleasant expression and leaned against a waist-high pillar. "Nupur. Twenty-four. Five feet ten. Bachelor's degree in arts. Working in her father's jewelry business, I tell you. Likes to dance, watch movies, play the piano..."

Rakesh leaned over for a closer look. She was pretty but overconfident. Given her business experience, she'd probably try to meddle with his affairs at Dhanraj & Son.

"No? Another good prospect here." Pushpa grabbed the photograph of a woman wearing a blue-and-gold-bordered sari. "Very talented, I tell you, this one. Rakhi Sengupta. Twenty-six. Five feet eight. Studying to be a doctor in Amrikaa. Parents are both doctors in Amrikaa and they recently inherited a huge estate on the outskirts of Raigun."

"America," Rakesh corrected her and perched both elbows

on his knees. He linked his fingers into a fist below his chin. *A doctor in the house?* She'd be more focused on starting her own practice—if she wasn't already running one—and not have time to be a mother-figure to Megha. Any conflict in schedules meant she could back out of social obligations on a whim and leave him high and dry. Besides, her complexion was too dark. She wouldn't complement his height, sharp features or good looks. He needed someone he could take out to dinners, parties and clubs. "No can do."

Pushpa replaced the photograph in its slot and picked up another of a woman dressed in a lime green salwar suit. She began rattling off a list of the woman's attributes, but Rakesh's attention snagged on a woman wearing an orange sari, her photograph tucked on the far-right corner of Pushpa's display.

"Oh, now you are interested, I tell you?" Pushpa grabbed the photograph and raised it to eye level. "Not on top of my list. But well-established family in Raigun. Only twenty-two. Very young. Too young for you, perhaps, no?"

Not too young. Not too dark. Her skin was a light latte color and her eyes brown and soft. Not overconfident, as revealed by the hint of a forced smile.

"Master's degree in arts or something. Let me see." Pushpa flipped the photograph and read the details. She'd obviously not given this one much attention. "An oil painter. Good, maybe, no? For family reputation, and my Naina to have some creativity, some inspiration around here."

Rakesh leaned closer. Didn't he meet her at a dinner party two weeks ago? The father had introduced his daughter.

"Sheetal Prasad. Family owns a telecommunications business. Rana Prasad runs operations in India, and his brother in

New Jersey, U.S." Then she flipped the photograph right side up. "Induslink Corporation."

"Is she established yet?"

"Of course! I just told you, I tell you. Her father's company—"

"I mean, career-wise. As a painter. Artist. Whatever. Does she have her own business or art studio?"

"No. Just painting at home for leisure. But she is good, I hear."

Pushpa lived within hearing range of gossip, and whatever didn't come through friends and family, passed through the club's grapevine. "Good family. Decent family. But we can do better with that other girl, Rakhi. Such a powerful, strong family. Like us. Even that Nupur—"

"I'll meet this one first." He pointed at Sheetal's photograph. "Then we'll see."

"Good!" Pushpa clapped her hands. "What a good day, I tell you. At least you agree to meet someone. And if you don't like her, we can move up the ladder. Plenty of room for more opportunity, considering there are at least five families way above the Prasads."

RAKESH RESERVED TWO TABLES AT THE MEDIT, AN INTERCONTINENTAL restaurant notorious for its over-priced menu, chic décor, imported ingredients and chefs with experience from the finest restaurants in Europe. Rakesh and Sheetal dined at one table and Sheetal's female cousins dined at another.

Before dinner, Rakesh asked Sheetal if she would like a glass of wine, but Sheetal said she didn't drink alcohol and ordered a glass of juice. Over dinner, Rakesh asked about her interests and Sheetal answered, "Painting, reading, music."

He waited for her to ask a question or two, but Sheetal kept looking at her watch, flipping the latch on her purse or shifting her attention to other diners. Since it was obvious she didn't have any interest in talking about herself, Rakesh explained his lifestyle, routine and the travel involved in his work as CEO of Dhanraj & Son. Before he could order dessert, Sheetal thanked him for the dinner and left with the chaperones, leaving Rakesh, as expected, to foot the bill.

She was perfect.

15

GARDEN OF RUBIES

After three and a half months of loneliness, Sheetal forced herself to stay awake one night to see if Rakesh came home.

She closed the bedroom door and settled on the sofa with a romance novel. The heroine met the veterinarian hero when she brought her Corgi to the clinic for a check-up. As the hero ran his hands over the dog's back and checked its eyes, ears and tail, the heroine watched his slim fingers, gentle strokes and noticed the absence of a wedding ring. The dog squirmed and whined, clearly uncomfortable with the stranger's touch, but the heroine appreciated the doctor's patient and calm manner.

He was gentle...so gentle. Like Arvind.

The words blurred. The meeting at the Broken Fort—his warm skin under her hand, the comfort of his arms around her —and her eyelids grew heavy.

A noise startled her awake. She looked at the bedroom

door, but it remained closed. The digital clock on her bedside table displayed one-thirty in the morning. She rose, checked the bathroom and Rakesh's walk-in closet. No one. She resumed her position on the sofa and returned to the book-marked page.

The dog howled, and crinkles formed at the corners of the doctor's lips and eyes. Even as the heroine assured the Corgi that it was in good hands, she was drawn to the doctor's kind expression and couldn't take her eyes off him.

Arvind.

She lowered the book to her lap.

He could see right through her. Whenever she looked into his eyes, he held her gaze. He *saw* her. Read each unspoken thought.

Sheetal rose and pressed the mirror-wall, hoping to find clues about where Rakesh went and what he did in his free time. She had tried the door numerous times, and on each occasion, found it locked. She paced the room, aching to lie on her side of the mattress.

No.

She left the bed's footboard. She had to stay awake so she could find out what was going on.

She returned to the sofa, opened the novel, leaned against the armrest and blinked in an attempt to clear her sight enough to read.

Rakesh walked in dressed in a navy-blue Armani suit. Sheetal looked at the time on her watch. It was two o'clock, and she waited for him to say something, to offer an explanation for his late arrival, or ask why she was up so late, but he simply loosened the knot of his red-and-blue tie and headed for the bathroom. He didn't even bother to acknowledge her.

Running water drummed the glass shower box. Sheetal tried to concentrate on the words of the novel. She would return to Arvind soon. Just a few more weeks and all this nonsense would be over.

Her attention wandered to the mirror-wall on the left and the reflection of the bathroom door. She imagined drops of water beating against Rakesh's chest, trickling down his smooth skin, white fog from the hot spray shrouding every inch of muscle while he ran his fingers through his gelled black hair. Blood charged through her veins, and she bit her lower lip in guilt. Did such thoughts betray Arvind?

Then the splash of water halted and seconds later, the bathroom door glided open. Rakesh emerged, a green towel wrapped around his taut waist while he dried his hair with a smaller towel. Droplets of water glided down the bulge of his muscles.

She forced her gaze back to the book but stole glimpses of his reflection. Then Rakesh tapped the wall of his walk-in closet adjacent to Sheetal's. The door glided open, and he bent to one of the shelves.

A hot, moist sensation welled, rising and sinking, as her groin throbbed. The heroine of her story must have felt the same way with the veterinarian. Perhaps, the author had chosen not to write the details. She looked away. She wasn't supposed to look at him. Not like this, even though they were married.

She moved to another seat, her back to him and his reflection clearly visible. Then Rakesh rose to his full stature and turned toward her. The towel around his waist fell to the floor. Sheetal tried to look away, but her eyes were glued to his reflection, and she snatched a glimpse of the naked manhood that throbbed between his legs. Their eyes locked and for a split second and she felt her soul being sucked away. Then he grinned, turned his back, and she could breathe again.

Sheetal tried to focus on the warmth of Arvind's touch, the rugged strength of his arms, but his features faded like a wall of fog misting between them.

SHEETAL PACED HER ROOM, NERVOUS OVER THE PROSPECT OF HER FIRST public appearance with Rakesh. Three hundred guests were expected to attend the anniversary party at the Hyatt Hotel's Ruby Garden, including some guests from the U.S. and U.K. How was she supposed to behave as Rakesh Dhanraj's wife in public when she still hadn't figured out how to do so in private?

At precisely eight o'clock, Sheetal and Rakesh entered the Ruby Garden hand in hand, passing beneath a canopy of trees threaded with miniature lights. The hosts, Aradhna and Akshay Damani, welcomed and led them to the reception, where fountains sprouting golden cobwebs of champagne danced in the breeze. A quintet of musicians, including a saxophonist, seated on a miniature dais played a soothing melody as Rakesh and Sheetal mingled with the guests. Rakesh placed Sheetal's hand on his arm and led her from one group of friends to another. He addressed individuals by their first names and slipped into conversations with such ease, it was as if he'd grown up with these people all his life.

Other Indian men, all crème de la crème of Raigun's posh society, wore expensive clothing and spoke the Queen's English that Sheetal had learned, but their words were coated in a thick Indian accent and they didn't carry themselves with half the suave sophistication of Rakesh.

Blessed with an unusually fair complexion and fine features, Rakesh, at six feet two, stood several inches taller than most Indian men. When he walked, he exuded a confidence that few of his contemporaries matched. When Rakesh spoke, his audience held their breaths. No one sipped wine or champagne, perhaps afraid of missing something significant. And when they wanted Rakesh's attention, they made eye contact, awaited his nod of approval and then spoke. Some broke away from another group to shake Rakesh's hand or called the photographer to have a picture taken with him, adding a quick reminder that the photographer send them the link to the online album. Because Rakesh had graduated from Harvard and taken over a business empire at an age when others were still apprentices, he could speak his thoughts with ease while others thought through their responses. He infused every sentence of the English language with American slang while others struggled to keep their British English intact. He drove an Italian Ferrari while others drove Marutis, Hondas and BMWs.

"Look here!" a photographer called out. "This way, sir. Madame?"

Sheetal raised a hand in silent protest and turned away from the camera's flash. She withdrew her hand from Rakesh's elbow, but he slid his left arm around her waist and pulled her back, digging his fingers into her midriff. The air thickened.

Then a woman rushed toward Rakesh, gripped his right shoulder, aligned her body to his contours and pecked him lightly on the cheek.

Sheetal tensed.

Someone remarked upon Rakesh's close proximity to the woman, but Rakesh laughed and ran a free hand along the back of his gelled hair. He pulled Sheetal closer, draped an arm casually around the other woman's shoulders and whispered something in her ear that caused her to cock her head back and laugh.

The woman stepped away.

Rakesh erased the lipstick mark with his pristine, white handkerchief. "Jealous?"

Sheetal struggled not to explode.

"Calm down. She's an old friend."

So, just because Rakesh knew her, that gave this tramp an excuse to pounce on him? Sheetal turned away and the crowd blurred in her vision, their high-pitched voices and laughter, coupled with the music, making it hard to think.

"Sheetal? Sheetal?" someone called.

Sheetal turned toward the speaker. A camera flashed.

"Where did you and Rakesh go?" asked a woman in a red halter-neck evening gown and matching lipstick.

Sheetal closed her eyes and took a deep breath. *This woman? The hostess. Her name? What was her name?* Her head spun. She opened her eyes. How could she forget when she'd just met her an hour ago?

Sheetal had spent all evening trying to remember the names and faces of people she'd met, but she kept getting confused. She had tried to associate a person's name with some element of their clothing, but when two people shared the same name, that method failed. "Go—where again?"

"Your honeymoon, for God's sake. Weren't you listening?" The woman swayed to the beat of the music, causing the sash of her gown to brush the grass in long strokes.

Aradhna! That's it. Sheetal bit her lower lip, embarrassed. She was about to explain why the honeymoon had been cancelled when Rakesh leaned over and whispered in Aradhna's ear.

"You're hilarious!" Aradhna giggled, playfully slapped Rakesh's shoulder, then wrapped her long arms around him and hugged him close. When she released him, she grabbed her husband by the arm and dragged him toward the dance floor.

Rakesh raised another glass of champagne to his lips and drained it. He turned to Sheetal and wrinkles tightened the corners of his eyes and lips. "Look what you did." He reached for Sheetal's waist and tightened his grip until she winced. "Embarrassed me. At this rate, we'll be the laughingstock of Raigun."

Laughingstock. First Papa. Now her husband. Was that all she was?

"Let's dance."

Sheetal broke free of his grip. "I don't feel like it."

"What the fuck does that mean?" He thumped his empty glass on a high-boy table and dragged her to the dance floor while Sheetal struggled to keep pace. "Dance when I say dance.

Understand?" He spun her around until she faced him. Swirls of sharp, silver zardozi embroidery pricked her skin. Her neck-lace's double-string of mauve-colored diamonds pressed against her collarbone.

The crowd parted, Rakesh strode to the center of the dance floor and people closed around them as the beat of bass thick-ened. Gripping Sheetal's left hand, Rakesh flung her out of his embrace and then rolled her back again into the cave of his chest. She spun in and out of his arms, twirling and whirling as the pallu of her lavender sari swirled to the tempo of Rakesh's force. He pushed her back, pulled her forward, and her body gave in to his demands.

The crowd cheered in frenzy. The dance went on and on until the moon, stars, trees and miniature lights became one dizzy blur.

Then the music revved to a climax, and Rakesh spun Sheetal halfway out of his embrace.

She reeled back, tipped on the heel of her left stiletto and began to free fall. The moon and stars blanketed her vision just as her back slammed into the rail of Rakesh's arm. She tried to stand, but the barrier of Rakesh's body kept her down.

She needed light. Air. Breath.

Rakesh's head eclipsed the moon, casting Sheetal into shadow. His lips, a hair's breadth above hers, parted and the odor of alcohol washed over her. He pressed his lips against hers and drove his tongue between her lips. The thick, heavy taste of cigarettes burned Sheetal's throat. The crowd roared, and Sheetal gasped for air.

"Now, that's what I call dancing," the DJ bellowed over the microphone.

Rakesh abruptly straightened, and Sheetal struggled to remain upright as he forced her off the dance floor and made for the entrance. Strings of catcalls followed their exit as servers uncorked bottles of champagne.

A breeze swept across the sidewalk, but only now did Sheetal feel the chill. She tightened the sari pallu around her right shoulder as Rakesh ordered a valet to bring their vehicle.

"Yes, sir." The man darted around a corner of the building, no doubt, frightened by Rakesh's tone.

Rakesh lit a cigarette—the third this evening—took a drag, blew hard and lowered his fist to his side. The cigarette smoked in his grip. He tightened his fist until the knuckles turned white.

The valet pulled in two minutes later with the Ferrari and handed the keys to Rakesh.

Sheetal slid into the passenger seat, and the valet shut the door. She clipped her seatbelt, then leaned forward to straighten her sari pleats.

The tires screeched and she was thrown against the backrest as Rakesh sped off into the night.

Sixteen minutes and thirty-five seconds later, Rakesh dragged Sheetal upstairs to their bedroom, slammed the door behind them and hurled her across the bed.

Sheetal struck the duvet face down, heart pounding. Her panting blocked out any other sound, and she tensed in anticipation of a strike. A second rape. She closed her eyes and prayed he'd leave.

The roar of the Ferrari engine through the closed window caused her to snap her head up and around. The bedroom door stood open. The room was empty.

Seconds later came the screech of tires and shattering of glass.

16

TYPHOON TYCOON

The next morning, the Dhanrajs gathered in the Marquette Dining Room for breakfast, where a basket of croissants, platters of vegetable cutlets, *upma*, steamed vegetable semolina cakes and platters of fruit embellished the table.

Naina slurped tea while Megha helped herself to a semolina cake. Seated at the head of the table, a Band-Aid and gauze taped across his forehead, Rakesh reached for a croissant.

Mummyji stormed in and slapped *The Raigun Herald* atop the cutlets.

The headline on the "Life and Leisure" section read, "Typhoon Tycoon's Kiss of Life." A four-by-six colored photograph of Rakesh kissing Sheetal at last night's party accompanied an article about the Damanis who had celebrated their first anniversary with such flare. However, the focus was on how Rakesh and Sheetal had lit the evening with their "fiery performance."

Mummyji's cheeks ballooned and she raised her eyebrows.

Sheetal sighed. Who would she have to apologize to this time?

Rakesh continued to butter his croissant as Mummyji walked over to Naina, stood behind her chair, pumped both hands on her hips and turned to Sheetal. "I hope there's an explanation for this, I tell you. I expected you, of all people, to know better."

"Leave her out." Rakesh didn't look up. "I'm responsible.

"*Hai Ishwar!* Sheetal's also to blame."

"I forced her."

"And what were you thinking?" Mummyji gripped the finials of Naina's chairback. "Your father was photographed for meeting prime ministers and presidents at conferences and conventions. Not once, I tell you, did he tarnish our family name. And just look at what you've done. Nothing but night clubs, bars and showing off your playboy lifestyle to the media. For heaven's sake, I tell you, grow up. At least live up to you father's reputation, if nothing else."

"I am not my father." Rakesh clanked his knife onto the plate. "What I do is my business."

"Last night you bang your car into a lamp post. Your business. You refuse to discuss it. Your business. It's supposed to be all right, no, I tell you? Because it's your business." The freckles on Mummyji's face darkened. "I—" She raised both arms in the air and was about to say something when she lowered them. "What if something happened to you last night?" She softened her tone. "What if—"

"So, I'd be dead."

"How does Sheetal feel listening to you talk like this?"

"Thrilled."

"What you do affects us all. The family. Friends. The business—"

"You focus on family and friends," Rakesh cut her off. "Focus on your share of the will. I'll focus on the business. Why should my social life affect you now when it's never affected you before?"

"Because everyone will see this." She pointed to the headline damp with grease. "The phone's bound to ring all day, I tell you. What will I say?"

Rakesh shrugged. "Just tell them that Rakesh was doing what every man should with his wife. Having fun."

"*Hai Ishwar!* If your father were alive today—"

"If. He isn't. I've never shaken hands with the PM. Yes, I love hanging out at bars and clubs. That's who I am. Look at our finances. Our profits are over the roof and my business is better than ever."

"Your business?"

"Yes, my business. Like my wife." He pointed to Sheetal as if she were a commodity. "With whom I can do whatever I want. Screw whenever—"

"Such foul language, I tell you. What impression will it have on the girls? Naina. Megha." Mummyji pointed to the dining room door. "Out now."

Both girls rose from their seats and left the room.

"How dare you speak like that? You didn't earn any of it. Your father built Dhanraj & Son with his own hands. He created a whole empire. You just walked in, took charge, and now look what you're doing to the reputation. So selfish you are, I tell you. No interest in keeping relations with Naina's prospective in-laws. What will the Malhotras think?"

"Fuck up!"

"Ae-ee!" Mummyji cupped her mouth.

"Now, you listen to me. I did everything you wanted. No one to run the business. I took charge. Get Naina married. I networked and found someone for her. That too, just before my own wedding. Get married. I did, for your peace of mind. You got everything you wanted. Everything. Now leave me alone. All of you."

"I told you so many times." Mummyji leaned forward. "But you didn't listen. That other girl, Rakhi. Or Nupur, I tell you. They were better choices. From better families. Almost as financially strong as we are, but *she* was your choice."

Sheetal's gut knotted. So, she was here out of convenience? A settlement? Is that why Rakesh chose her over the others? Arvind was right all along. She was a business deal.

"Sheetal could be so useful in the office, I tell you. I mean, she has nothing to do here all day and—"

"Her place is in the home. Not my office. If she steps foot in my office, I will not step foot in this house." Rakesh rose and spun on his heel.

"You can't just walk out—"

Rakesh left the room.

Mummyji collapsed in an empty chair and stretched her thumb and index finger across her forehead as if to ease a headache.

Sheetal's heart was ready to explode. She rose to leave.

Mummyji jumped to her feet. "I'm so sorry, Sheetal. I...I forgot you were here. And...and... *Hai Ishwar!* Now you heard everything you shouldn't have. But it's not what you think. Give me a chance. I can explain."

Sheetal didn't want to hear any explanations. She left. Wasn't it enough that their photo was splashed in *The Raigun Herald?* But to now have her marriage spread out in the open like this? Bile rose in her throat and she swallowed. Her throat burned. She was fed up being treated like a ball of dough that anyone could roll, flatten and toss at will.

"Sheetal! Sheetal!" Mummyji followed her. "It's not what you think, I tell you."

Sheetal took a left at the upper landing and marched along the north wing. She turned into her bedroom, slammed the door, twisted the lock in place, and pressed her back against the door. Then she sank onto the floor as anger rippled up her chest in waves. She pulled her knees to her chest and scrunched herself into a ball.

"Listen," Mummyji pleaded through the door. "Just listen to me."

Sheetal took a deep breath and exhaled. She was done listening.

17
REV

Rakesh stormed out of the mansion, and a guard in a gray uniform saluted him. Rakesh didn't bother to nod. He took a sharp left and made for the garage.

He hadn't meant to lose his temper at last night's party, but he couldn't stand all the hype around Sheetal. How she carried herself so well with such poise, grace and charm. How he was so lucky to have found someone like her...someone so beautiful, so young and so well mannered.

Rakesh stopped at the garage entrance and pushed a red button mounted on a wall, causing the door to roll up vertically and reveal a fleecy black sheet that draped a vehicle. How dare the photographer ask him to smile and then gesture to Sheetal! *Fuck!* Well, he showed them who was boss on the dance floor.

Rakesh grabbed the car cover, balled the sheet and tossed it aside. A gift from the in-laws. He slipped behind the Diablo's steering wheel, switched on the ignition and eased the vehicle out of the garage.

Two pairs of black wrought iron gates and two security posts, five hundred meters apart, marked the entrance and exit to the Dhanraj mansion. But when Rakesh test drove a vehicle, they served as test points. Three years ago, the Ferrari, a graduation gift from Papa, had made it through in three seconds flat.

Rakesh revved the accelerator and the V12 engine roared, but he restrained the vehicle.

A security guard in the left guard post glanced at him and pounded a button. The gates quivered and slowly swung apart. The guard's job depended on Rakesh passing through the gates without a scratch on the car's chassis.

Adrenaline tingled through Rakesh's veins. He wriggled his toes in the leather Bally shoes and pressed the accelerator. The arrow on the tachometer inched right...nine thousand...nine thousand five hundred...six hundred. He shifted gear and shot like an arrow. Wind rushed through his hair as he zoomed around the semi-circular driveway. He was flying. Free! The gate's black bars loomed closer, widening in slow motion: Five feet to go. Four feet. Three feet. The gate whizzed past on the right, missing the chassis by a hair's breadth. His manhood hardened. A glance in the rearview mirror showed the guard flop down in relief. Rakesh cocked his head back and laughed. *Sweet!*

He sped down Barotta Hill as sunlight dappled through the overhanging canopy. At the four-way intersection, a policeman dressed in an olive-green uniform with a belly the size of a watermelon stood on a podium two feet high. He blew a whistle for Rakesh to stop as pedestrians started across the road.

Fuck! Rakesh braked and gritted his teeth. Didn't that

officer know who he was? That he was supposed to hold back the pedestrians and let him through? Rakesh reached over to the glove compartment, flicked it open and groped inside for a packet of Marlboros he had tossed in yesterday morning. Something sharp pricked his thumb. He slid his hand right and pulled out Sheetal's proposal photograph. A reminder from the in-laws that Sheetal was the reason he owned a Diablo?

The long, smooth curves of Sheetal's figure-eight body shimmered behind the orange translucent pleats. Her belly button winked like a hidden eye, and there was no denying the smooth, sharp curves of her lips or the almond-shaped eyes. He let go, and the photograph fell onto his lap. She was nothing more than a fixture with limited time warranty. Once she realized it was impossible to live with him, she'd leave him alone. Though he'd warned her not to file for a divorce, she might still go ahead. However, because she would initiate the separation, he'd owe her nothing.

He needed her to keep the charade going until Naina's wedding; otherwise, the Malhotras would think there was something wrong with the Dhanrajs and with Naina and break-off the engagement. Then he'd be stuck with Naina for God knew how long.

Rakesh groped in the glove compartment for the Marlboros. He pulled out the familiar red and white packet, a golden lighter and tapped out a cigarette. He was about to light the cigarette's tip when his attention fell on Sheetal's photograph again. Her orange sari glowed like a fucking sunset. Surely he could put the photograph to good use.

The policeman whistled a signal for Rakesh to advance.

With a foot on the brake, Rakesh revved the engine and basked in the roar. He was not one to take orders from anyone.

"Eh! Hurry! You're holding everyone up."

He flicked the lighter and held the photo's bottom right corner to the flame. The flame danced along the Kodak's edge, and Rakesh released the brake, rolled ahead and stopped at the podium.

"Watch it!" The policeman almost toppled off the podium but regained his balance. "Don't meddle with the law or you and your shiny black—"

Rakesh thrust the burning photograph into the policeman's hand and sped off, glancing in the rearview mirror.

The policeman blew furiously on his fingers as the burning photograph drifted to the ground. He stamped out the fire, yanked a notebook from his pocket and looked ahead, no doubt, to note the Lamborghini's license plate.

Rakesh cocked his head back and laughed, imagining the man's reaction when he saw A-5-5-H-O-L-E.

18
NORTH AND SOUTH

Sheetal headed downstairs the next morning, noticed something sparkle on the Bradford Browns and quickened her gait. At a ten-feet distance, she just made out Naina's figure on the sofa, almost as if Naina were an extra pillow.

Naina's pasty brown complexion matched the sofa's fabric, and her raisin-eyes pressed into her face like buttons dotting the center-point of each Bradford cushion. Not only was she the black sheep in the family, her complexion was darker than Rakesh and Megha's. Naina held a hand up to the chandelier, and her engagement ring sparkled in the light. "Eh na, where you going?" She wiggled her fingers as Sheetal stepped onto the landing.

"Nearby."

"Can I come?" Naina stood.

Sheetal lengthened her stride. The last thing she needed

was Naina meddling in her business instead of minding her own. "Next time, perhaps." She hurried out the door.

THREE HOURS LATER, SHEETAL SLID INTO THE REAR SEAT OF A WHITE Mercedes as the chauffeur loaded bags containing tubes of oil paints, knives, turpentine and other art supplies into the vehicle's boot.

He drove through northern Raigun, a poor section of the city Sheetal hardly ever visited. His route would cross Nariyal Ka Rasta, where Sheetal grew up, which fell halfway between north and south Raigun.

"The highway is always jammed at this hour, Choti Sahiba," the chauffeur said. "It may take us forever."

Sheetal didn't mind. No one waited for her at home. "That's fine."

The Mercedes wove in and out of traffic, jerking every time an auto rickshaw squeezed between it and the vehicle ahead or a policeman signaled to stop even though the traffic light was green. Pedestrians sidled between bumpers to cross the road while vehicles honked furiously for them to get out of the way.

The left pavement swarmed with shoppers, beggars and vendors. Hawkers yelled out their wares as the November sun beat down on their mobile carts stacked with pots, pans, Tupperware, stainless steel cookware, mops, brooms and household bric-a-brac. Smoke from open-air food stalls coated everything in a film of oil. Smog puffed from vehicles' tail pipes, and grayish liquid spilled from open gutters onto the streets. Amid the dirt and chaos, a coconut seller plucked a coconut from a garland of many, tethered to a rusted pole by a frayed brown rope. He hacked away at the coconut, poked a hole in the top, popped in a straw and handed it to a man in queue.

The Mercedes inched forward and the carts eventually gave way to colorful tarpaulin sheets spread across the concrete. Sheetal lowered her window for some fresh air but the odor of sweat and stale grease drifted in.

"Two for five!" a hawker yelled the price of fruits for sale.

"Diwali bargains! Three for five," another hawker competed in a shouting frenzy as the Festival of Lights, Diwali, approached. He rearranged slices of papayas, pineapples and watermelons while fanning away swarms of flies attracted by the nearby carcasses of fish, eels and other sea creatures that glistened on blocks of ice, their blood melting with the ice to form a reddish liquid that dripped into open gutters.

Nausea welled up Sheeetal's throat and she turned away. She was going to be sick.

The traffic light changed from red to green and the driver eased forward as a woman in her late twenties hurried to cross the road. She was dressed in a dark blue kurta and white leggings, her hands loaded with bags. A few groceries fell, and she raised a hand signaling for them to stop. The chauffeur slammed the brakes, and Sheetal rocked forward.

The woman grabbed bunches of carrots and radishes from the pavement, stuffed them back in, then hurried across the street.

"Sorry, Choti Sahiba," the chauffeur apologized. "These

people think they own the roads. Don't obey traffic lights, rules or anything."

"It's okay." Sheetal watched the woman hop onto the right pavement and stagger as she maneuvered on the broken heel of her sandal. She looked back at Sheetal and her sunburnt skin cracked as she frowned.

Is that what she could have become had she married Arvind?

A chill shuddered up Sheetal's spine and she looked away.

Just then, tiny fingers caked in grime and dust crept up the window. Children in tattered and ripped clothing with over-grown, matted hair, swarmed outside her vehicle. Gray saliva dribbled from their mouths, yellow mucus trickled from their noses, and blood-crusted, open wounds on their arms and faces oozed a mustard-colored serum.

"Bhook lagi hai. Kooch de na." Children as young as two begged for food while stray dogs barked and snarled at the pavement's edge.

Sheetal's skin crawled and she inched away from the window.

The chauffeur turned and smacked the children's hands with a folded newspaper, forcing them to retreat like snakes into their holes as the window rolled up. "Scoundrels! All of you. Only know how to beg. Precisely why you're on the streets."

The children, undeterred, banged on the windows with their tiny fists, demanding food and money.

The Mercedes shot forward and the children flaked off like mites shaken off a pashmina shawl. Sheetal snuggled both hands beneath her thighs and sank back against the plush fabric.

Shop windows displaying mannequins in expensive saris, salwar kameezes and western wear now lined both sides of the road. Bakeries, cafes and fast-food chains dotted street corners, their red, pink and green awnings offering shoppers respite from the Raigun sun. Overweight Memsahibs walked pampered pooches on designer leashes. A woman in her mid-twenties busily instructed a chauffeur to load shopping bags into a car's boot as people, armed with their own purchases, hurried in and out of stores almost knocking the woman over. Sheetal sat up, content to be on familiar turf and relieved to be close to home. This was her Raigun, where filth and poverty didn't exist.

THE FOLLOWING NOON, SHEETAL TOOK HER PLACE OPPOSITE MUMMYJI at the dining table and spread a napkin on her lap, reminding herself the law around here was this mother-in-law and asking for a favor could lead to unfavorable results. "I'd like to begin painting. Can I please have an empty room? Somewhere on the south wing, perhaps?" No bedrooms were occupied on the south and west wings. However, the west wing was only exposed to direct sunlight in the afternoons. The south wing, on the other hand, overlooked the front lawn and received sunlight throughout the day. Janvi placed a serving dish on the table as Sheetal continued, "Rakesh likes the curtains drawn, so there's not enough light in my bedroom for me to paint."

"Oh...well...I don't know what to say. I mean, this is such a surprise, I tell you." She fanned the air. "Before I forget, I talked to your mother yesterday, I tell you. And you can go to your parents' place on the first of December for two weeks. It's all sorted out."

Two weeks? Sheetal leaned forward. "Mama said I could go for a month."

"A month? What, and leave all your responsibilities behind? Too long, I tell you. Far too long for a bride. Two weeks is all you will get."

Sheetal was about to argue but realized that gave her just three more weeks here and then no coming back. Her heart was ready to burst in relief, but she suppressed the excitement. "I'll start tidying a room on the south wing. Perhaps even find some old furniture I can use while the servants are cleaning up for Diwali and—"

"No need to, I tell you." Mummyji shook her head. "We can always buy new furniture and—"

Sheetal helped herself to a curry. "I'll manage with what we have."

That afternoon, Sheetal swiveled a key in a resistant lock on a south wing door as Janvi waited patiently. Finally, the lock clicked and she opened the door. The odor of stale air and mothballs greeted her. The windows on the opposite wall were cloudy with dust.

Sheetal flipped a light switch but no light came on. Janvi

offered her a torch, but Sheetal gestured for her to put it away. Sheetal navigated through ghost-like furniture draped with bedsheets, Janvi close behind. "What's in here?"

"Don't know. No one open this room before. At least, not while I here."

Dust carpeted the marble floor, and cobwebs draped light fixtures and ceiling fans.

For two days, Janvi and Sheetal yanked sheets off furniture and dusted old lamps, vases, huge glass bowls and crystal chandeliers. On the third day, they pushed aside furniture and found a closet that contained sealed cardboard boxes. Sheetal peeled off the brown tape, opened the flaps and pulled out a layer of crumpled newspaper.

Janvi removed a child's cricket bat, helmet, knee padding, a box of cricket balls and examined a loose ball that lay in a corner of the box. The ball's cover was cracked and flaked. "So old, Choti Sahiba." She dropped the ball into the box. "Why Memsahib not throw away?"

Had this box belonged to Rakesh? She tried to imagine Rakesh playing a team sport and failed. He shot orders and instilled fear to get a job done. She grabbed a pair of scissors, slit the tape on another box, pulled apart the flaps and lifted out a photo frame. The box held more. She used the end of her dupatta to wipe the glass. A whirl of dust caused her to sneeze. Janvi offered her a rag.

Sheetal took the cloth and angled the photograph away from Janvi's view. "Why don't you wipe down the furniture?" She gestured to several chairs on the far side of the room.

Janvi did as she was told, and Sheetal studied the framed photograph in her hands. A woman in her mid-thirties, dressed in a pastel pink sari, smiled at the camera. Her black hair was parted down the middle and filled with red sindoor, the fashion of previous generations. Fair of complexion, the woman had a heart-shaped face, like Megha, a gentle smile, and warmth exuded from her eyes.

Sheetal wiped off more dust and Ashok's familiar face appeared to the left with jet-black hair, a sharp nose and a jawline that angled sharply to a heavy-set chin. His tightly pressed lips suggested a man of no nonsense, and his focus on the camera showed his determination that the shot come out perfect. If not for the thick, black glasses, Sheetal could have sworn she looked at an older version of Rakesh. She wiped the bottom half of the frame and a boy, about ten, with ruffled black hair, smiled from ear to ear. Baby fat clung to his cheeks and chin as his dark brown eyes sparkled with mischief.

"What that?" Janvi asked from behind.

Sheetal turned as Janvi peered over her shoulder. Didn't she order her to the other end of the room? "Nothing. Just some old stuff. Why don't you see if Memsahib needs help? I'll call if I need you."

Sheetal waited for Janvi to leave, then wiped other photo frames. She found one of the same boy and woman seated side by side on a lush lawn. The boy had his arms wrapped around the woman, and she held him close. Another photo portrayed a man and woman seated cross-legged on the floor in a carpeted room, their expressions somber. They were flanked by others as if they were the focus of attention at a religious function. Another photograph showed the boy and Ashok standing before the Dhanraj mansion, their arms straight by their sides.

The boy's lips were pursed and he looked straight at the camera as if he had been made to follow instructions.

Why were all these family photographs packed away and hidden?

"Sheetal?" Mummyji called out. "Where are you, I tell you?"

Sheetal hastily returned the frames to the box and shoved both boxes into the closet.

19
SHARK BITE

Rakesh crossed his arms, tired of waiting in the Japanese garden for Pushpa. At twenty past midnight, still no sign of her.

"Rakesh?" Pushpa's hushed call came from the open dining room door.

He approached her. "What's so urgent that you had to meet me like this?"

"Wait." She paused. "All right, we can talk now. No one here. Come inside."

Rakesh entered and closed the glass patio door.

"It's about Sheetal."

"I married her. My job is done."

"Shhh!" Pushpa grabbed his sleeve-covered arm and dug in her nails. "Quiet, I tell you. Someone will hear."

"This is stupid." He took a deep breath and shook his head. "Like a thief in my own home."

"The only stupid one here is you. Your wife is moving to another room and you don't even know, I tell you."

"So?"

"You fool!" Pushpa hissed. "Very soon she'll move out of our home. If she leaves, what will happen to the girls? Why, if the Malhotras find out, I tell you, they'll think something is wrong with us. With Naina. And break off—"

"Nothing will happen." He firmed his voice so Pushpa would stop overreacting. All it took was one trigger to set her off like a firecracker.

"How can you guarantee?"

"Because it's my fucking marriage. Not yours."

"Such language! But it's not just my Naina who's at risk. If Sheetal goes, you'll have no chance."

He pried her fingers off his arm, fed up with her constant schemes. She was like this huge barrel of interference that just lolled around the mansion day and night. "What chance are you talking about now?"

"The Prasad fortune."

"We don't need their fortune. We're way better off than they are."

"You have everything now, I tell you. But a shark can only survive on smaller fish. And I kept telling you those other girls, Nupur or Rakhi—"

"What's the point?"

"Sheetal is an only child. Once Rana and Indu are dead, the Prasad fortune is hers. And what belongs to Sheetal becomes yours. But only if you are still her husband."

20

THE LION'S LAIR

Over the next two weeks, servants scurried through the mansion in a frenzy of Diwali cleaning in the belief that Lakshmiji, the Goddess of Wealth, roamed the Earth on that night and showered money on those families who had cleaned their homes from top to bottom.

Even though the Dhanrajs held assets in stock, real estate and cash to last them ten lifetimes, it obviously wasn't enough for Mummyji. She had every blade of grass and flower petal on the front and back lawns hosed down. She demanded that every crystal on the twenty-one chandeliers gracing the mansion, sparkled until she could see her reflection in each.

Having never seen a cleaning frenzy of this magnitude, Sheetal watched in amusement, relieved this would be her only Diwali here.

On day seventeen of the cleaning frenzy, Mummyji marched in Sheetal's bedroom and opened her closet.

Sheetal placed her newspaper on the sofa, rose and followed Mummyji, furious. "You promised to knock before entering."

"No time, I tell you, for such formalities. So much cleaning to do."

"In this room?"

Mummyji browsed through Sheetal's sari collection. "We should take a look at your clothes first, I tell you. Must make sure everything is in order."

"How could anything get dirty or worn when I just moved in five months ago?" *Even a dust mite would think twice before invading this place!*

"No need to get all fussy, I tell you. We're just getting rid of rubbish for Diwali." She clucked her tongue, then began pulling saris off hangers. "These must go, I tell you."

"Where?"

"Donate them."

"Why?"

"Because...well, because—isn't it obvious?"

Nothing around here was obvious.

"They're not good enough."

"They're custom-designed. Mama and I spent hours selecting them."

"Well, you'll never look like a Dhanraj in any of them, I tell you."

"And what is a Dhanraj supposed to look like?"

"*Hai Ishwar!* Didn't I demonstrate recently? But you young girls nowadays just don't pay attention. Gave you plenty of time, I tell you, to prepare for the pop quiz. To follow my perfect schedule. But you—"

"I don't need instructions on how to live my life."

Mummyji dropped the saris on the rug, whipped around and pumped both hands on her hips. "Oh, but you will when no one gives you any respect. No one listens or cares what you have to say. And no one believes you. That's when you will see. In any case, I'll just remove every inappropriate sari and replace them. In fact, how does a new wardrobe sound? Good, no?"

"No." Sheetal positioned herself between Mummyji and the remaining saris. Any sari this woman replaced would be paid for by the Dhanrajs and considered their property, not hers. She wouldn't be able to use any of them when she started her new life with Arvind.

"Ai-ee!" Mummyji squealed. "I am trying to put things in order, but you just don't understand. Out of this room at once!"

"You can't kick me out. This is my room."

Mummyji shoved Sheetal out the room, slammed the door in her face and locked it from the inside.

Sheetal tightened her fingers into fists and stared at the door in shock. How dare this woman throw her out of her room? Where was she supposed to go? To the Marquette Dining Room? That was used only for meals. The Fulton Whites? That was the formal seating for guests only. The Bradford Brown sofas? That was Naina's turf, and she was bound to throw a fit and stake her claim if she found Sheetal there. The room on the south wing was still a mess.

Sheetal paced the north wing. The railings blurred in her vision. What kind of a nuthouse was this? Seventy-five thousand square feet of living space and not an inch of breathing room! Sheetal was about to leave for the Japanese garden when her bedroom door swung open.

Mummyji left the room, marched past and headed for the stairs.

Sheetal hurried in and gasped at the sight. Fifty of her saris were strewn over the floor. Five months ago, these very saris had been pleated, folded and carefully shaped into kites, peacocks, boats, the ocean, and put on display. Now, they were rubbish, according to this woman.

Sheetal squatted to gather her belongings. Two and a half more weeks, she calmed herself with that thought. And then, no turning back.

ON THE EVENING OF DIWALI, SHEETAL CHECKED HERSELF IN THE mirror one last time, determined to prove what a real Dhanraj should look like. Through the window, blue, red, green, gold and silver fireworks showered the night sky.

Fireworks signified the triumph of good over evil and Lord Ram's homecoming to Ayodhya after a fourteen-year exile, during which he defeated the demon king Ravana.

Sheetal adjusted the antique *kundan* diamond-cut ruby necklace along the curve of her collar bone and used a tissue to wipe a smudge of maroon lipstick on the lower left corner of her lip. She peeled a sticky maroon-and-gold, S-shaped bindi from a packet, pressed it between her eyebrows, ensured the sindoor running down her middle parting hadn't smudged, and aligned the heavily embroidered crimson sari pleats across her chest one final time. Finally, she was ready.

At the first-floor landing, Sheetal took a sharp right and

entered a corridor that cut diagonally beneath the stairs to the temple.

Most Indian families maintained a temple in a prominent location in the house, but the Dhanrajs's temple sat tucked away from view because Mummyji didn't want the gods to distribute her wealth and good fortune to visitors.

A marble statue of Lord Krishna holding a flute to his lips stood on a pedestal in the temple's center. A one-by-two-feet photograph of an idol of Lakshmiji, bordered in gold-leaf and glittering with crystal ornamentation, occupied a low marble platform on Lord Krishna's right. Red velvet rugs spread on the floor offered a place for worshippers to sit and pray, but Megha and Naina stood in a corner of the room while Mummyji paced. Megha had three weeks off from college while bank and office employees only had the day off.

Megha rushed to greet her. "Ooh, you l-look g-gorgeous, B-Bhabhi."

"So do you," Sheetal lied.

Megha fidgeted with the dupatta of her pastel pink chikan-embroidered salwar suit. Her kurta, a size too large for her petite frame, drooped off her shoulders and the full sleeves ran past the tips of her fingers. The hems of her straight-cut pajamas pooled in folds between her heel and the floor, hampering her gait. "I b-bought this outfit j-just l-last week." She slid her glasses up the bridge of her sharp nose and smiled, but her chapped lips quivered.

"If a prince sees you tonight, he may steal you. Then we'll have two summer weddings to prepare for instead of one." Sheetal winked.

"I wouldn't be surprised, na." Overdressed in a bright

purple sari with a string of large amethysts garlanding her neck, Naina's eyelids were clogged with purple eye shadow and her lips with burgundy lipstick. "Megha has this habit of trying to steal my moment."

Sheetal turned to Mummyji. "Is this what you meant by dressing up as a Dhanraj?"

Mummyji looked from Sheetal to Naina and back. "Are you hinting that my Naina—"

"Did you hear that, Mummy?" Naina whined.

"S-stop c-complaining." Megha crossed her arms. "It's n-not your fault if a m-mirror c-cracks every t-time you l-look in one."

"Quiet everyone, I tell you." Mummyji adjusted her eyeglasses, checked the contents of the silver *puja* thali near Lakshmiji's photograph that contained mounds of religious grains, rice and vermilion powder, then flipped through the pages of a book. "Now, where is that Lakshmiji *aarti?*" She referred to a hymn sung in honor of the goddess.

In the framed picture, Lakshmiji was depicted wearing a pink-and-gold sari, standing on a fully blossomed pink lotus. Two of her four hands held miniature pink lotuses, a third showered gold coins, and the fourth, with forward-facing palm upraised, showered blessings on worshippers.

Offerings of flowers, fruits, joss sticks and sweet *mithais* made by Laal Bahadur were arranged before the photograph.

"Let's begin now, I tell you," Mummyji announced.

"B-but B-Bhaiya isn't here yet," Megha protested.

"Prayers have to be performed according to prayer times, not Rakesh's schedule."

"Did I hear my name?" The scent of thick, heavy Zara

cologne permeated the air as Rakesh sauntered in, his black, silk kurta pajamas with gold trimmings swishing with every step.

"You're late," Mummyji said.

"I was on a business call."

"It's a holiday, *Hai Ishwar!* Who works on Diwali?"

"The Belgians," Rakesh answered. "And if you haven't noticed, I've been working from home all day."

"Honestly!" Mummyji huffed. "What do others care about our festivals or—"

"I agree." Megha turned to Rakesh. "F-from n-now on, you should t-tell your b-business c-clients t-to c-coordinate their holidays with our Hindu c-calendar."

"Enough!" Mummyji cut in and turned to Rakesh. "Don't you have a more sensible color to wear? Lakshmiji only comes when she sees beauty, cleanliness and festivities, I tell you."

"Way too much festivity going on here." Rakesh raised his eyebrows at Naina. "I thought I'd balance it out."

"Mummy!" Naina pouted.

Mummyji shook her head. "I meant something a little more appropriate, I tell you, like—"

"Sheetal's sari? I'll keep that in mind." Rakesh grinned. "Megha? Remind me to have a word with Khanna Sahib"—his personal designer, Arjun Khanna—"to match my wife's bloody maroon for next Diwali."

Heat spread across Sheetal's shoulders and she turned away.

Mummyji clucked her tongue. "Such language before puja time, I tell you. Now, sit down, everyone."

The Dhanrajs sat on the rugs, crossed their legs, and

Mummyji had Sheetal inaugurate the prayers by lighting eleven shallow, earthenware *diyas* filled with oil and cotton wicks. After the final *diya* wick flared, Sheetal dotted the edge of the *diyas* with vermilion powder and sprinkled dry grains of rice. Fifty more diyas awaited Sheetal's attention, but she would light and decorate the mansion with those after the prayers concluded. The ritual of worshipping and decorating the home with *diyas* commemorated Lord Ram's homecoming after fourteen years of exile.

Diwali, an auspicious time for inaugurations and new beginnings, gave Sheetal hope for a better year ahead away from these people.

Sheetal dotted Lakshmiji's forehead with a bit of vermilion powder and dry rice, pressed her palms together, closed her eyes and prayed for the next two and a half weeks to fly by and never return. Then she scooted behind Naina and Megha, took her place on Rakesh's left and waited for the others to offer their prayers.

Something cold tingled along her midriff. Sheetal wiggled to brush it off. Seconds later, something sharp pricked her waist and Sheetal swiped a hand to brush it away. When something slithered down the curve of her back, she gritted her teeth and turned to Rakesh.

Rakesh's eyes sparkled. He slid a hand behind the sari pleats, across her chest and traced the lower curve of her right breast.

An electric charge surged through her veins and Sheetal tensed. *How dare he, in front of everyone?* Then Rakesh snuggled his left thigh under hers. What game did he play this time?

Why was he touching her when he wanted nothing to do with her?

She inched away, but he pressed a hand on her thigh, a command to stay.

Blood rushed to her head and she exhaled to calm herself.

The snap and crackle of distant fireworks and Rakesh's constant fidgeting made her turn to Lord Krishna for help. She focused on his flute.

Stay focused. Just a few more days.

They stood to sing Lakshmiji's aarti.

"Now, Sheetal. Megha," Mummyji announced after the song ended. "You two will decorate all the rooms with *diyas*. And from now on, Sheetal will light the first firework and decorate the house with the first *diya* every Diwali."

"That's not fair!" Naina protested. "Why should Bhabhi get all the honors? What about me?"

"As the *fu-ture* lady of the house, I tell you," Pushpa clarified.

"Sheetal, Shee-tal, SHE-ETAL!" Naina screamed. "You act as if she owns the place."

"You will be married by this time next year, I tell you. And Mrs. Malhotra will do the same for you. Besides, how can Sheetal own the house or anything when the estate and mansion are all in my name, and I am alive and breathing?"

Sheetal took rapid, shallow breaths. Precisely what were Mummyji's intentions? To celebrate or insult her as a member of this family?

"I bet when she's—"

"Stop it, Naina. Enough from you, I tell you."

Naina tossed her hair away from her face, turned on her heels and rushed out in a flood of tears.

"Don't mind her," Rakesh whispered. "She's always been spoiled, but marriage should put some sense in her head."

Another eight months to go until Naina's marriage, and the last thing Sheetal wanted was to waste more time with these people. She turned to tell Rakesh she didn't care, but he was gone, leaving behind the scent of Zara.

THE DIWALI CELEBRATIONS FINALLY ENDED AT TWO IN THE MORNING, after numerous telephone calls to family, friends and relatives wishing them all a happy Diwali. Sheetal trudged upstairs, barely able to stand. Everything in her vision blurred. She eventually made it to her bedroom, closed the door and trudged toward the bed.

Her feet ached and she yearned to lie down and sink into the mattress, but she had to get out of these clothes. She unfastened the safety pins, unraveled the soft maroon sari and tossed it across the footboard. Then she unfastened a series of blouse hooks running down her cleavage, peeled the spaghetti straps off her shoulders and draped the garment next to the sari. She groped behind with one hand and released her bra clasp while pulling hair pins from her chignon with the other.

The door of the mirror-wall swung open.

Rakesh! She squeezed her shoulder blades to prevent the bra straps from slipping, grabbed the sari, wrapped herself and rushed to her closet. She tapped the wall and glanced back. He headed toward her.

She entered and the sari tightened against her chest. She clutched the fabric, turned and bit her lower lip.

Rakesh held the end of the sari and tugged gently.

She looked past his shoulder to the door. She would have to pass him to escape. "I didn't realize you were here. I assumed—"

Rakesh advanced and the sari sagged.

"I shouldn't have changed in the open, but I was tired."

"Promise, I won't bite," Rakesh said as if reading her mind. Then he wrapped the sari around her, ever so carefully, leaving a short trail on the carpet. "I should leave." Rakesh slipped an arm around her waist. His thigh pressed hers and she leaned away from him. He pulled her toward the bed and she stiffened. Then he let go. "You're not ready." He headed for the mirror-wall. "Give it time. Come, let me show you something." He pushed open the mirror-door and waited.

The sight of her reflection in the mirror-wall caused warmth to spread along her shoulders. She turned away, embarrassed at her semi-nakedness, but Rakesh returned and pivoted her so that she faced her reflection. He pressed against her hip, and the bulge of his manhood swelled and pulsed against her in a rhythmic cadence. She cringed, pulling her left shoulder away from his touch. She bit her lip and tasted her own blood. This time, Rakesh had nothing to do with that blood.

Then Rakesh led her to the mirror door, directed her into the darkness and the heavy scent of leather, tobacco and scotch snaked down her lungs. Fear gripped her. What was this room? Rakesh relaxed his grip, ran his hands down her shoulders and flicked a switch on the left, bathing the room in soft yellow light.

An enormous desk and plush swivel chair, its back to the right wall, was off set by brown sofas and a fur rug in the room's center. Sheetal entered and ran a hand along the sofa's headrest, the leather taut and cool. Shelves lined with leather-bound books dominated the back wall. She made her way across and ran her hand along the spines of volumes on business management, international trade, technology and economics.

The gentle lilt of a saxophone pierced the air, and Rakesh led her to an opaque sheet of glass, mounted against the wall, opposite the desk. Trophies, awards and plaques filled two shelves above the glass. Sheetal leaned forward to read the inscription on a trophy when he cupped her hand, pried out her index finger and made her push a button on the wall. A crackle and harrumph filled the pause in the saxophone's melody and flames leapt against the glass.

Sheetal jumped back, startled, but Rakesh caught her fall and laid her down on the fur rug. Thick strands of soft fur melted under her skin as the saxophone's long, drawn notes welled, awakening a pulse in her groin. Rakesh sat beside her, and Sheetal ran her fingers through his hair, the silken strands easing some of her trembling. He bent and kissed the upper curve of her breasts. She shuddered, and he teased the sari away from her cleavage and shifted the bra straps aside. Then he flicked her nipple with his tongue and a fire lit in the core of her being.

He raised her to a seated position, inched his fingers behind her neck, unclasped the ruby necklace, and the warm metal slid between her breasts, across her navel and stopped at her petticoat. Then he unscrewed the chandelier earrings, slid the bangles off her wrists and Sheetal was weightless. Free.

Rakesh laid her back against the rug, removed her petticoat and panties in the same smooth motion, then rose to his knees, peeled off his kurta and discarded the black silk.

He bent and ran his tongue over the slope and peaks of her curves, his bare chest glistening in the light. His strokes awakened sensitivities she'd never known existed. Moisture oozed between her legs.

The saxophone moaned with longing and desire.

She ached to be held, to be loved. And then he entered her, and the black of the moment filled with colorful sparks like a shower of meteorites.

A heaven on earth.

Sheetal woke and ran a hand across Rakesh's half of the mattress. No impression of Rakesh's body or pillow indentation. It was like he'd never been there.

That couldn't be!

Sheetal switched on the bedside lamp. Her sari and blouse lay draped over the bed's footboard. She looked at her arms. The bangles were there. All of them. She touched her ears and neck. The earrings and necklace were there. *How was that possible?* He had taken them off.

She slid out of bed, crossed to the mirror wall and positioned herself at the midpoint, where she estimated the door to be. She pushed, but the wall stood firm.

A dream? No. It couldn't be.

21
SHADOWS

Relieved to finally have her studio in order, Sheetal propped a black canvas on an easel, adjusted the easel's angle, then stepped back to approve the room.

The door swung open, and Megha clumped in wearing thick, brown Woodland shoes, jeans and a T-shirt twice her size.

"There you are! I've b-been l-looking all over f-for you."

Sheetal smiled and adjusted the canvas. During their afternoons together, Megha shared the pranks students pulled during college lectures and cafeteria gossip. While learning about Megha, Sheetal relived her college days and her stolen moments with Arvind.

Megha surveyed the studio. "Wow. You f-fixed this g-ghost r-room up real g-good. B-but it n-needs m-more work."

"We only did a quick dusting." A full clean-up had to wait because Mummyji had scheduled the servants for a three-day, post-Diwali, cleanup. But more than cleaning, the room needed renovation. Red streaks the color of faded paan juice stained the marble floor. Moss-green paint peeled off the walls in huge patches, and a faint odor of rotting wood and mold clung about the windows. With only two more weeks to go, though, the cleaning issues didn't bother Sheetal.

She arranged a palette, a jar of turpentine and a flat-blade knife on a rickety wooden table then squeezed green, blue, umber, red, yellow, gray and brown paints onto the palette. "So, how was your day?"

"G-good, yaar." Megha used the term of affection reserved for close friends. "We had a d-dissection t-today. Our b-bio p-prof was g-going to d-dissect this f-frog when he j-jumped."

"The professor jumped?"

"N-not him. The f-frog."

"So, it was alive?"

"The l-lab t-tech s-said it was s-supposed to be d-dead b-but g-good old p-prof f-found a l-leak in the g-gas chamber and f-froggy d-didn't q-quite g-get it g-good, c-catch m-my drift?"

Sheetal tried hard to follow Megha's speech, but Megha strung words without pause or inflection, and when her breathing grew erratic, she so tripped over consonants that meaning was lost behind a waterfall of sounds as large as her over-sized clothing.

"L-let's j-just s-say he was on the b-borderline of the after-life. S-speaking of which, they should t-try s-some on N-Naina it m-might d-do wonders, b-ut use l-laughing g-gas instead."

"Everyone's a little different."

"She's s-so d-different I d-don't understand her. I d-don't

think anyone d-does." She pushed her eyeglasses up the bridge of her nose.

"She's your sister."

"N-normal for a while, l-l-ike us, and then P-Papa d-died and everything changed. G-gets really weird weeks without t-talking t-to anyone, always l-locked in her room and p-pampered." She looked past Sheetal. "I m-mean, M-Mummy has all N-Naina's m-meals wheeled up and everything then—p-poof, b-bang!—one fine d-day you find N-Naina bright and chirpy as if n-nothing happened."

Her head ached at the merry-go-round of words. Did anyone else have trouble understanding Megha? And why didn't anyone try to help the girl?

"B-but it's actually m-more irritating to have her that way c-coz then she l-loses her t-temper, g-gets into all these m-mood s-swings and we all j-just have t-to d-deal with it l-like that p-painting episode when she k-kept insisting the t-trees were identical and you t-tried to t-tell her they weren't."

"Maybe Naina just thought she was right." Sheetal tried to make light of the episode even though she was still furious at having been told to apologize. The last thing she wanted was to dig up those memories.

"Even when she's wrong she g-gets away with everything."

"Why?"

Megha shrugged. "It's b-been l-like this f-forever, n-no chance except f-for the m-mother I l-lost and this one." She referred to Mummyji. "I wish I'd known m-my real m-mother."

"Do you remember anything about her?"

"Just her name. Rashmi." She calmed. "B-Bhaiya s-says she

had the house s-stripped d-down and every t-trace of m-my real m-mother removed."

"I bet you miss her."

"Wouldn't you?"

Sheetal bit her lower lip. She'd never imagined a life without Mama and realized her importance now that she didn't have Mama's ready counsel and support.

"I should g-go. L-lots of s-studying to do."

"Wait." She didn't want Megha leaving upset. "Would you like to help me?"

"With what?"

"A painting." Sheetal pointed to the canvas.

"I d-don't know m-much about art."

"There's always a first time for anyone. I need to get the lighting and distance just right and can't be in two places at once. Can you get me that lamp?"

Megha grabbed a six feet tall floor lamp, placed it beside a flower arrangement on a nearby table, and, under Sheetal's direction, adjusted the lamp's swivel head left, then right, and right again until the light hit the flowers at a forty-five-degree angle. Then Megha grabbed a folding stool that leaned against a wall, flipped it open and sat on Sheetal's left.

Sheetal added drops of linseed oil to a mixture of blue and green paint, repeatedly dragged a two-inch brush through the paint until the bristles were well coated, then used crisscross strokes to create a rough circle of color in the center of the canvas. If only she could replace the darkness of the Dhanraj world with bright hues and colors that made the heart sing.

What if she ended up returning after her 'visit' home?

She paused. Was there a chance that anything here could

change for the better?

She dismissed the thought, took a deep breath to regain focus, angled the brush, and feathered the edges of the circle in short, sporadic sweeps. Glass bangles chimed up and down her wrist.

She switched to a one-inch brush and created a coppery brown pot at the base of her dim blue-green sunburst. "See anything yet?"

Megha inched aside for a better view. "B-black. L-lots of it."

"Now for some magic." Sheetal scraped her pallet knife through green paint, deposited the mound next to the palette's umber and dragged a brush through the side-by-side colors until half of her brush held green and the other half held umber. She studied the flower arrangement for a moment, then turned back to her painting and positioned the brush tip against the canvas. With each quick, short stroke, she rotated the brush handle, widening and then narrowing the lines she created.

Sheetal paused and tightened her grip on the brush, but her fingers felt stiff, like someone gripped them. She yanked off the engagement ring, rammed it on the third finger of her left hand, flexed her fingers, and continued. *Much better.*

As she worked, the day's tension slipped away.

"I c-can s-see it!" Megha said. "I-It's—"

"Shh."

"What are you g-going t-to d-do n-now?" Megha asked.

Sheetal filled the canvas with hues of red, copper-yellow and gray. "A little mauve, blue and black is all we need." She added those colors to her palette.

Finally, she exchanged the brush for a finer one, coated the long, thin bristles evenly in red and pulled stamens out of the fantasy flowers hidden in the darkness.

"Wow! You are g-good, yaar!"

"I'm a little rusty. It's been nine months since I last painted."

"How c-can you c-call yourself rusty when you b-brought a n-nonexistent p-pot to l-life?"

"I painted what I saw. But I could have done better."

Megha brushed hair from her face. "If this is p-practice, imagine what I'd n-need."

"A canvas and paint. If I can do it, anyone can." Sheetal washed her brush in turpentine and tapped the edge against the jar's rim.

"I'm s-so happy you're here," Megha said. "You're s-so d-different f-from anyone I know."

Sheetal's heart skipped a beat. No one had said anything pleasant since her arrival. "Different in what way?"

"You're p-patient. You understand and you're honest."

Sheetal was touched. She didn't want to risk losing the only friend she'd made so far, but what if she could help Megha? "Can I ask you something?"

"What?"

"Why do you wear baggy clothes and those heavy boots? They're more for hiking."

Megha frowned. "What do you mean?"

"You're a smart, beautiful, intelligent, young woman. There's no need to hide from anyone. You should be proud of who you are."

"You're s-saying I d-don't know how t-to d-dress?"

"Not at all. I just...I can help you become better."

"I was right all along. You are s-special." Megha grabbed a brush and playfully buttered Sheetal's cheek with paint.

Sheetal numbed in shock. Only friends, sisters and brothers took such liberties.

"I'm... I—"

Sheetal grabbed a brush, dipped it in paint and turned, but Megha jumped back, giggled and ran across the studio.

Sheetal chased her around the room. She ran wild and free, bubbling with laughter as the room spun, but Megha was too fast and she couldn't keep up. Was this what little sisters did? Splatter you with paint and follow you around like a shadow? Sheetal tripped on the pleats of her lilac sari, recovered her balance and ran. When she tripped a third time, she grabbed a large section of pleats and tucked them in deeper at the waist so the hem rose six inches off the floor. "Now I'll get you." She lengthened her stride, but the spinning room tilted toward the door as if she were being pulled by a magnetic force. Inches away from Megha, Sheetal raised her brush to strike. Megha dodged left, revealing Rakesh, his hands at his sides. Sheetal tripped. She fanned her arms to recover balance and struck him with the brush.

"What the hell is going on?" Rakesh demanded.

"We're p-painting." Megha giggled, taking cover behind Rakesh.

Pleats pooled around Sheetal like a broken waterfall. She hastily tucked them in.

Rakesh pinched his T-shirt. "You call this painting?"

"It was an accident," Sheetal panted.

Rakesh crossed to the easel and Megha followed. "Isn't it g-great? B-Bhabhi d-did that j-just n-now."

"Not bad for a beginner." He crossed his arms. "Could have been better."

Beginner? Sheetal marched over to the easel and tossed her brush onto the palette. She grabbed the canvas, set it to dry in a corner of the room and headed for the door. "I need to wash up." She left.

If not for Rakesh, she wouldn't have stumbled. Or made a fool of herself. Or ruined his T-shirt. Why did she always have to be at the wrong place at the wrong time?

Sheetal lathered her face, splashed cold water, and checked her reflection in the bathroom mirror. Her face remained a collage of blue and brown paint. She grabbed a bottle of olive oil from the mirrored cupboard above the sink, poured some in the palm of her hand, pumped more soap from the dispenser and lathered the mixture over her face. She used her fingernails on the paint, but patches refused to wash off. Fifteen minutes later, cold water streaming down her cheeks and into the crevice of her blouse, she blindly groped for a hand towel. The cold, metallic towel rod filled her grip. There had been a towel there. She was sure of it. She had seen it before—

The soft fibers of a cloth pressed her forehead, her nose, mouth, chin and cleavage as the scent of mint filled her lungs. *Rakesh.* She snatched the towel and opened her eyes. "I can dry myself, thank you."

Rakesh pressed his body against Sheetal's back, and her navel pushed against the sink's edge. He pulled away, stepped aside and her attention flew to the streak on his T-shirt.

"I'll have that dry-cleaned, washed or..."

"No can do."

"I'll get you another."

His right cheek bulged as if he ran his tongue there. "Nope."

"I—"

He climbed the four marble steps and entered their bedroom.

She followed.

"Dinner tonight," he said.

"Who with?"

"Who do you think?"

"I don't play guessing games."

"It's a dinner for two. Me and you. Makes two."

"I don't think it's a good idea." She had no intention of going anywhere with him. She still wasn't sure what had happened on Diwali night.

He entered his open closet, pulled out a shiny red package tied with a red and black bow and gave it to her. "Here, this should help decide."

Was this a truce?

Sheetal peeled a corner of the Sellotape, uncomfortable with the press of his stare. She opened the wrapper and lifted out a red band of smocked fabric supposed to fit around her bust and a black, spandex micro-mini skirt. What was this prostitute outfit? A joke? "Where's the rest? The top has no sleeves, no strings, no—"

"No strings attached." He snatched the red garment and stretched it across her chest. "Perfect fit."

"But—"

"I was expecting this from you." He turned and reentered the closet. "So, I came prepared. Here." He handed her a black and red sparkly shawl, just broad enough to cover her shoulders. "Once you're in the car, it's off. Ditto?"

Sheetal shook her head, outraged. She refused to go anywhere in this slut outfit.

"I thought you wanted to pay me back for what you did." He pinched his T-shirt.

"I—"

"Done. I'll see you nine sharp, tonight."

"But—"

"Don't spoil the moment, baby." He leaned toward her and misted her with the scent of mint. "It's your one-way ticket. Take it or leave it."

THAT EVENING, SHEETAL PULLED GARMENTS OFF HANGERS AND SHELVES for two hours and changed from one outfit into another to see if she could substitute the slut-wear for something more decent. But a top either covered too much, had broad shoulder straps or wasn't glitzy enough and her skirts were either knee-length, ankle-length or flared like an A. By eight fifteen, it appeared a bomb had gone off in her closet. Frustrated and fed up, Sheetal looked at the piles of clothes. Arvind would never force her into anything like this or pressure her to go against her will. But Rakesh clearly had no sense of decency.

At eight thirty, Sheetal grabbed the smocked tube-top and skirt and sighed.

AT PRECISELY NINE, THE WALLS OF THE MANSION VIBRATED AND A ROAR pierced the air. Sheetal strapped on her black stilettoes, threw the shawl about her shoulders, rushed out, took the stairs two at a time and almost lost her footing. She ran across the hallway and threw open the mahogany door. Exhaust fumes stole her breath.

Parked in the porte-cochere, the Diablo thundered on full throttle with Rakesh in the driver's seat.

"I'm here," she yelled.

Rakesh's attention remained fixed on the dashboard, his body sunk deep in the seat's leather contours, like a pilot in a cockpit. He adjusted a pair of black sunglasses perched on his slick, gelled hair, his white linen suit complementing the car's tan interior and black chassis. It was obvious he couldn't hear her.

Sheetal rushed down the carpeted stairs and the Lamborghini's passenger door swiveled upright at ninety-degrees. "I'm here. Turn off the engine." She crossed her arms.

"Just testing the power of this beauty." Rakesh pressed a button and heavy metal music blasted through the speakers.

Half a dozen servants gathered in the doorway, no doubt confused by the commotion. Sheetal quickly slid into the passenger seat, embarrassed by her attire.

"What a fireball! Like you." He ran a hand along Sheetal's thigh.

She pushed his hand away and tightened the shawl around her shoulders as the servants crowded around. "Let's go."

Rakesh gripped the gear shift and pressed the accelerator. The Lamborghini roared and the tachometer arrow shot to nine thousand RPMs. Rakesh gestured to the shawl. "Off with it."

Sheetal looked at the servants. Heat spread along her shoulders as Janvi and Laal Bahadur joined the audience. She turned back to Raskesh. "Please, next time. I promise. I'll take it off later."

Rakesh depressed the accelerator. The tachometer jumped to nine thousand five hundred RPMs, and the roar of the engine caused the servants to scurry inside.

Sheetal squeezed her thighs, desperate to hide her fear, but Rakesh gestured. She yanked off the shawl and was instantly thrown backward. Wind rushed through her hair, the security guard's booth whizzed past and a sliver of concrete blurred in the headlights.

TWENTY MINUTES LATER, RAKESH PULLED UP OUTSIDE GRAFFITI, THE most affluent dance club in Raigun. Sheetal had heard about the place from friends but had never been to any nightclub because Mama and Papa believed dance clubs resulted in vices like smoking, drinking, drugs and affairs.

After the Lamborghini's doors swiveled up and Rakesh slid out, a long queue of people whistled. He tossed the car keys to a valet and led Sheetal by the hand toward the glass door. They passed palm trees that lined the sidewalk and swayed in the breeze. Red and blue neon lights blinked in alternating sequences above the club's glass door entrance. On either side of the door, water flowed from overhead outlets, trickled through side channels that paralleled the door and gushed below a see-through floor.

The wait outside was an easy half-hour, but they were escorted down a dimly lit corridor. Two ushers opened a pair of frosted glass doors and fog rolled toward Sheetal. She coughed and swept the air with a hand as a three-story dance club loomed into view.

A circular, central sunken floor was packed with dancers who gyrated amidst white fog and flashing lights. On the second and third floors, visible through the railings of circular balconies, more dancers formed shadows in the drifting fog.

Spears of white light were followed by a clap of thunder, which caused the crowd to cheer and whistle.

The drum's bass beat intensified, and Sheetal gripped Rakesh's arm. Everything about this place was so infectious, so absorbing, she didn't know where to look.

He squeezed her fingers. "It's the hot spot in Raigun. Been here?"

"No."

He led her to a VIP lounge, cordoned off with chrome posts connected by red velvet ropes. He waved to the crowd there. Several hands shot up to return his wave.

Sheetal crossed to a sofa and sat, convinced this was why he didn't come home at night. How many other clubs did he hang out at? With whom? She waited for Rakesh to take a seat, but he entered the ocean of dancing bodies on the main dance floor. She tried to follow his progress but could barely see through the semi-darkness blasted intermittently with colored lights. Then a silhouette, someone about Rakesh's size, resurfaced on the far side of the arena. Rakesh swung an arm around someone with shoulder-length hair. They hugged and kissed. Was Rakesh seeing another—

A blast of fog obscured her vision. Sheetal struggled for a better view but couldn't make out much. The music pounded, people pumped fists, jumped, raised drinks in a toast and gyrated with frenzy. Sheetal covered herself with the shawl and crossed her arms, wishing she were home.

Rakesh emerged from the human ocean and sat on her left. "Hey, sorry about that."

"Where did you go?"

He shook his head and pointed to his ear.

Sheetal cupped his ear with her hand and leaned close. "Who was she?" she yelled above the din, barely able to hear herself.

"Who?" He tapped a cigarette from its case and lit the end.

"That woman." She pointed to the other side of the dance floor. "Who was she? That other woman?"

"What woman?" He took a drag, puffed and stuck his pinky in the air. "I went to take a leak."

Sheetal tightened her jaw. She had seen him—seen *them*—kiss. The blast of heavy metal music intensified. She inched closer to Rakesh. "You seem to know a lot of people here."

"I don't, really. But they all know me. I own the place."

Her heart skipped a beat. Of course, he did. He wasn't just a CEO. Rakesh owned practically a third of Raigun, and Graffiti probably represented loose change in his pocket.

A server brought a tray with two glasses, and Rakesh thrust a cola in Sheetal's hand. Then he raised his square tumbler, brimming with a honey-colored liquid and cubes of ice, in a toast. "Bottom's up!"

Sheetal sniffed the cola and placed her glass on the table. It smelled of bitter, rotten lemons. "I'm not thirsty."

"It's all the smoke here. Take a sip. Try it."

Try on skimpy clothes. Try alcoholic drinks. Try to fit in. What next?

"Don't worry, it's a virgin. Like you. Now, hurry up."

So what really happened on Diwali night?

She looked from the glass to Rakesh and back. Now wasn't a good time to ask. But if she didn't ask now, when? If she refused to drink, he was bound to get angry. If he could make a scene at the Damani's, there was no telling what he was capable of here.

"What're you all pickled about? Just drink the fucking Coke."

Sheetal picked up the glass, closed her eyes and gulped down half. Her throat burned.

Rakesh grabbed her elbow, made for the dance floor and she followed, struggling to keep up.

The ocean of dancers parted before them and then closed, blocking retreat. Arms and elbows jabbed her back and sides as people inched for space. Sheetal tensed but was reeled into the safety of Rakesh's body as the heat of liquor, sweat and smoke closed in around them. She slid her arms around Rakesh's taut waist and could no longer feel the floor. She tipped her head back, shook her loose hair and Rakesh brushed his thumb against her navel in small, gentle strokes, sending an electric charge through her body. Sheetal raised her arms and spun on her toes. Weightless. Wild. Happy. Free.

Then the DJ spun a new release and the crowd cheered as the musical beat pulsed and raced through her veins.

She was on fire. She was fire.

22

REFLECTIONS

On Saturday morning, Sheetal decided to paint something as a parting gift for the Dhanrajs. A scene of the Dhanraj lake seemed most appropriate. She squeezed several colors onto the palette, dipped her brush in turpentine, then paint and brushed long strokes along the bottom third of the canvas. The scent of mint filled the air and she paused. *Rakesh.*

He slid an arm around her waist and pulled her back against his chest, causing the brush to fall and clatter on the floor.

Because married couples rarely expressed affection for one another in public, Sheetal twisted to release herself from Rakesh's embrace should any family member walk in. What would they say? That she was too western, too forward, too indecent and couldn't keep her hands off him?

He tightened his hold. "Another painting so soon? My, my, you are a busy little bee. Even on a weekend."

"Shouldn't you be at the cricket club or something? Hanging out with friends? At the gym? Strange you should be here on a Saturday."

"Sassy, eh?" He released her.

Sheetal picked up the fallen brush, and when she straightened and turned, he was frowning at her work.

"Too much blue there." He pointed to the bottom right of the canvas. "The tone, color. It's...all wrong."

"You don't even know what I'm painting and already an art critic?"

He walked around to the back of the easel and folded his arms along the canvas's edge. "I know about perception. And yours is wrong."

"What do you mean, wrong?"

"Believe what you see. Not what you think you see."

"What does perception have to do with— "

"You paint what you see. Correct?"

"Everyone does."

"Not everyone." His expression hardened. "You paint what all of us see. Big deal! But Pierre-Auguste Renoir. You should study that man's work."

Sheetal had learned about Renoir in college, a French painter associated with the late 1800s Impressionist movement. Renowned for celebrating beauty and feminine sensuality in his art, his still-life paintings, portraits and scenes of people dancing were world famous. He was also renowned for painting women in the nude, especially when bathing. "I have studied—"

"Don't talk when I talk." Rakesh ran the fingers of his right hand through his hair. "That man had style. His work teases your eye with deep, vibrant colors and—"

"He's dead," Sheetal cut him off.

"Ah!" Rakesh paced the studio. "He may be dead, but his work lives on. What impression will your paintings leave behind? Will people remember you or your work after you're gone?"

Did he know she planned to leave him?

Rakesh stopped at the painting of the fantasy flowers angled against a wall.

"Even this still-life thing here doesn't work. You've got to be more real than this. Like Renoir."

Sheetal crossed her arms. *So that's it. He came to insult.*

"Renoir's bathers were...beautiful. But personally, for my taste, I think the women's hips were a little too large. Imagine trying to share a queen size mattress with one." He cocked his head back and laughed. "But the 'Dance at Bougival'–I saw that in a museum in Boston, you know. And I woke up this morning with that thought."

Sheetal rolled her eyes. *Of course, he woke up with that thought. Didn't everyone wake up thinking of Renoir?*

"What is your opinion about last night?" He crept toward her.

Sheetal squirmed, uncomfortable with the narrowing distance. "It was interesting."

"So, you find my company interesting?" He breathed down her back, his voice husky and deep.

Trapped between the canvas and Rakesh, Sheetal inched left. "So, how come you know so much about painting?"

"A semester of art appreciation in Harvard. I quickly

learned that people paint when they have nothing better to do. Or when they're not capable of doing much."

How dare he? Is that all I am to him? A waste of time?

"So, what's this supposed to be, anyway?"

"How does it matter? It's all a waste of time to you."

"How about me then?"

What did he mean?

"Paint me."

"You just said painting was a waste of time."

"Precisely." He grinned. "I have an entire Saturday after-noon to kill before a game of racquetball with the guys. I challenge your talent, Madame."

"I don't need a challenge." *Or any more insults.*

"Prove it to yourself, if not me." He crossed his arms. "We'll meet here at three sharp."

She wasn't meeting him anywhere.

"Well?"

"No."

"Why?"

"Because there's no reason for me to say yes."

"You just did."

"The answer is no."

"You know you're going to do it. All in the perception." He tapped the right side of his head. "One word. Two meanings."

"No means no." Sheetal stared at the dark blue waters of the lake. Was it really too blue? Did it lack depth? She took several steps back. Were the tone and colors too strong? Too bright? She shifted weight from one foot to another, annoyed at having listened to him.

"Three sharp." He headed for the door and turned. "Wasn't

it Max Ernst who said Picasso was a genius and no one could touch him?"

Who cared what Max Ernst had said or whether Picasso was a genius? She swirled a brush in the jar of turpentine, wishing he'd leave.

"Let's see how much of a genius you are, and if you can capture me with your brush."

Sheetal wiped the bristles clean with a rag. "I said no."

"Oh, don't get me wrong. I don't want you to, either. But I have to find out if you know every inch of me the way I know every curve of you." Then he left.

At five past three, Rakesh strode into the studio carrying a sports bag. Sheetal was still working on the painting of the Dhanraj lake when Rakesh sat on a chair beside the standing lamp and tilted his face toward the light. The beam illuminated the right side of his face.

Knowing what a narcissist Rakesh was, the sooner she got this over with, the better. She switched the lake canvas for a sheet of drawing paper, then adjusted the easel so that Rakesh's face appeared parallel to the left edge of the drawing board and the size of his head at this distance was roughly the size she intended to sketch on the clipped paper. Sheetal looked from Rakesh to the board and mentally mapped the contours of his features on the sheet. Then she located charcoal and sketched an outline of his face.

"Will this take long?" he asked. "Will my face even fit on that?"

"Keep still." She completed the head and neck outlines, used curved lines to divide the face into quadrants and marked eyebrow lines. She marked the position of the nose and was about to mark the lips when he fidgeted.

"Done?" he asked.

"I'm only just starting."

"Well, get on with it." He tapped the stool's edge and shifted.

"I can, if you stop fidgeting." She carefully erased her guidelines.

"How much longer?"

"I don't know."

"I need a break."

"It's only been fifteen minutes," she said.

"You're killing me." He pouted like a spoiled child.

Something wasn't right.

Sheetal crossed to Rakesh and changed the angle of the overhead lamp so the light struck him at a forty-five-degree angle. Then she tore the paper away, clipped a new sheet to the easel and mapped out his cheeks, pencil-thin lips, the curves of his ear lobes and the vertical bridge of his nose. She stepped back to examine her work. *It wasn't even close.* She closed her eyes. *'Believe what you see. Not what you think you see.'* She replaced the sheet with another.

Rakesh jumped to his feet. "Don't tell me you're starting over!"

"Sit down, please."

He hesitated but complied.

While she sketched, she recalled the night they had supposedly made love. She'd run her fingers through his hair and down the clean-shaven slant of his jaw. Not a hair follicle had disturbed her stroke. Such a contrast to Arvind's rough stubble and rounded jaw, where the hair pricked on contact but eventually curled into submission. *Arvind's musk...Arvind's touch...*

Rakesh grumbled.

Sheetal softened the peaks of Rakesh's cheeks, lips and the sharp slant of his nose.

"Done?" Rakesh asked.

"Almost." She reworked the hair and the angle at which the light reflected off the strands. Then she lifted a speck of charcoal from the pupils' centers. "Done."

Rakesh hopped off the chair and came round the easel.

She braced for a barrage of insults.

"It's me! In fact, it's better than me. I am impressed. How —what—"

"I...I thought about what you said."

"And?"

"I looked at you in a different light."

On December first, after spending Sunday together, Sheetal prepared to return to Mama's place while Rakesh packed for a ten-day business trip to Amsterdam.

Sheetal left a finished painting of the Dhanraj mansion on her easel. When she didn't return at the end of two weeks, they'd figure out her intentions. She waited to say goodbye to Rakesh in the privacy of their bedroom, but Rakesh remained locked in his den for over an hour.

Tired of waiting, Sheetal was about to leave when the mirror-door swung open and Rakesh emerged carrying folders and loose papers. She stepped right in an attempt to catch a glimpse of the den's interior before the door locked—something she'd tried countless times before—but, the heavy door touched the wall and clicked. *No luck!*

"There's something I need to know," she said.

Rakesh tossed five folders into his black leather briefcase, which lay open on the bed. "What?"

"You promise the truth?"

"Have I ever lied?"

Sheetal took a deep breath. After two weeks of rephrasing, restructuring and rehearsing the words, she had to get this right. "What happened that night? On Diwali?"

He aligned the folders in the briefcase, his expression blank. Did he hear her? "Did...did anything happen between us?"

"Oh, that?" He grinned. "Yeah. We did the Diwali puja together. Remember?"

Mind games again. "I mean, did anything happen between us in the bedroom? Did we...did we make love that night? I've been trying to remember."

Rakesh snapped the briefcase shut, pulled her to him and brushed his lips across hers, melting the unsaid words on her tongue.

The ground seemed to give way beneath her feet, and before she could say anything, he grabbed the briefcase and headed for the door.

"See you in two." He left the room.

How could this marriage be over when his touch sent desire and an ache coursing through her body? Sheetal turned to the mirror-wall. *There was a chance, a possibility it might not have locked.* She silently crossed the room, pressed the wall, and the door inched. Light from the bedroom revealed shadow shapes in the den. She groped on the left and flicked a switch. Soft yellow lights bathed the interior of the room.

She gasped.

23
TURN BACK TIME

The black Mercedes rolled through the gates of Prasad Bhavan as koyals cooed and sparrows chirped, filling Sheetal's heart with delight. Home!

"Wait. Stop," Sheetal said to the driver. "I'll get out and you carry on." The Mercedes braked, and she hopped out. She yanked the scrunchy off her ponytail as the vehicle rolled ahead to the main entrance. She kicked off her two-inch platform sandals and ran across the front lawn. Wind rushed through her hair, blades of grass crushed beneath her feet and relief flooded her veins. Nothing had changed.

Mama halted before the front door, her pink sari pallu fluttering in the breeze. Sheetal came to a stop, caught her breath and wrapped Mama in a tight embrace. The strength and warmth of Mama's arms filled Sheetal with relief.

"Aren't you full of energy?" Mama pulled away from Sheetal and cupped her face in her hands.

"It's so good to see you. I haven't felt this free in a long time."

"You're the wife of Rakesh Dhanraj now. It will take a while, but you will get used to the lifestyle and responsibilities."

Sheetal could account for every minute of being a Dhanraj but doubted Mama wanted to hear about the problems.

Over the latter half of the morning, Sheetal chatted with the servants, asked the chef about the week's menu and bathed in puddles of sunlight streaming in through the windows. It felt good to feel sunlight run down her back, arms and face again. She called out for Preeti when Asha Prasad, her grand-mother, was rolled out in a wheelchair by one of the servants.

"What are you doing in a wheelchair?" Sheetal touched Dadi's feet, a gesture of respect, and hugged her. "Where's your walking stick?"

Dadi put a hand on Sheetal's head to bless her and embraced Sheetal. "What use do I have for a walking stick when I can't walk anymore?"

Sheetal pulled away. "What do you mean you can't walk?"

"I had a fall, shortly after your marriage, and it paralyzed me from the waist-down."

"Why didn't you tell me?"

"What's there to say? I'm an old woman. These things happen. And you should also know, Preeti doesn't work here anymore. She left some time ago."

Preeti—gone? Why hadn't anyone bothered to tell her?

After lunch, Sheetal went upstairs, running her hand along the corridor walls, content that her paintings still graced the house. She half expected to hear the hum of Shashi Behn's hair dryer, the chatter of women as they bustled in and out of her room, and the clatter of cosmetic cases clicking open and closed, but silence greeted her. She opened her bedroom door. The familiar bed, dressing table, and cupboards along the back wall caused a wave of relief. It was as if she'd never left. Sheetal crossed to the balcony, swung open the door and surveyed the lush back lawn. No changes there, either.

Mama entered and sat on her bed. "You must find this room so much smaller than what you're used to."

The room was half the size of the one she shared with Rakesh, but this was still her room. Her bed. Her cupboard. And the last time she had opened the cupboard was to give Preeti a salwar suit. "Why didn't you tell me Preeti left?"

"She was asked to leave." Mama crossed her arms. "You were just married and settling in your new home. I certainly couldn't bother you over such trivial things. That, too, a servant matter."

A servant matter? She'd been away for six months and all that time, Mama conveniently failed to mention Dadi's paralysis or Preeti's dismissal. What more would she discover?

"I'm sure the Dhanrajs have more important things to worry about than..."

Sheetal's heart sank. Preeti's absence wasn't the only empty spot around here.

On Saturday morning, the Prasads sat around a patio table in the shade of a white and green parasol as a servant poured tea from a Royal Albert teapot into Mama and Dadi's matching teacups. Sheetal and Papa shared a pot of coffee, and when Sheetal took a sip, she realized it was the only thing she and Papa had in common.

Papa peeled open the pages of *The Raigun Herald* and held the newspaper before him, blocking everyone from view, as Sheetal, at Mama and Dadi's urging, described the Japanese garden, her studio, the enormity of the estate on Barotta Hill and the effort Mummyji put into maintaining the mansion.

"Well, I'm not surprised." Dadi nodded. "To keep a house that size spic and span..."

When would this family realize the Dhanrajs were not gods? Sheetal had thought about confiding her plan to Mama in private, but Mama would guilt-trip her into returning.

"You just don't know how happy we are to see you married into such a prestigious family and settled into such a beautiful home." Dadi lazily swirled her tea with a teaspoon. "When Hemu married, we couldn't dream of giving her a fraction of the luxuries we now have. *Bichari* Hemu. Poor Hemu. Your life is any girl's dream. How times have changed."

Dream or nightmare?

Dadi turned to Papa and tapped the newspaper with her damp spoon. "I said, how times have changed!"

Papa rustled the pages and folded the newspaper.

"Why is it that you are not here even though you are here?" Dadi looked Papa squarely in the eye.

"I'm sorry, Ma. I was just reading about this catastrophe in—"

"I don't care what you're reading. Sheetal returns after six long months and instead of doting on her like every father should, you're busy reading that...that thing!"

"All right. Only Sheetal from now on." Papa flattened the sheets on the table, leaned forward, stirred his coffee, took a sip then repeated the motions. Nothing about Papa had changed. He still sat up so straight that his white golf T-shirt didn't wrinkle. He positioned his elbows on the table, leaned forward as if they were in a meeting, and glanced at everyone in turn as if waiting for an opening statement.

"As I was saying"—Dadi slapped the table— "Sheetal's happy and settled. Our princess will soon reign like a queen."

"Yes, yes." Papa nodded, his attention on *The Raigun Herald*.

Sheetal took a deep breath and fixed her gaze on the teapot. "I'm moving back—"

"You told her?" Dadi turned to Papa.

"Told her what?"

"About Hemu moving back." Dadi turned to Mama. "Well? Have you?"

"No, Maji," Mama answered. "I thought—"

"You thought if we don't tell her than perhaps it won't happen—eh?" Dadi scowled at Mama.

"Didn't you hear me?" Sheetal looked at Mama. "I said I'm planning to—"

"Not now, Sheetal," Dadi cut her short. "Hemu's obviously not wanted here and—"

"Of course not, I just..."

"Don't any of you care about what I want to say?"

"Sheetal." Mama frowned. "When elders talk, you must learn to wait your turn."

Where was the time for formalities and manner? This was about her life.

"Well, if no one else can, then I'll have to." Dadi turned to

Sheetal. "Your parents didn't think it important enough to tell you, so I will. Hemu is moving back. Vikram and Anjali are coming to live with us, as well." She glanced at Mama. "Not that all of us here are happy about it. But I don't care because bichari Hemu..."

Bichari Hemu? Sheetal's chest and throat tightened. *Aunty Hemu coming to live with them?* What was there to pity about Aunty Hemu? She knew almost everything that went on in their lives. Dadi talked to Hemu every day, if not twice a day. And even though the woman lived in Vilaspur, it was as if she lived here. "She's coming for a holiday, I guess."

"Longer. Much longer. Maybe...oh my...I'm afraid to say it out loud should I speak too soon and curse her good luck"— Dadi patted her chest and coughed— "but maybe forever."

Was Aunty Hemu separating from her husband? No, Sheetal reasoned. Women from Mama's generation stayed in their marriages until they died.

"Bichari Hemu told me how difficult a time Vikram was having in finding a decent job with a decent pay. Even though he's an engineer like his father, there are no good jobs in Vilaspur. And bichari Hemu told me how impossible it's become for Vikram to continue living on such a low salary when he's so capable. To think they've done everything possible with their limited savings and still suffer."

'Suffer,' according to Dadi, meant living paycheck to paycheck.

"And Hemu, my poor darling," she went on. "How she cried and cried on the phone last month like there was no tomorrow. So, I told her to come and live with us. Vikram can join Rana's business and..."

The air thickened. She'd been gone only six months and everything at home had turned upside down.

A servant dipped a fresh teabag into the teapot and pressed it against the side with a spoon.

If crying was all it took for Aunty Hemu and her brood to move in, then all she had to do was squeeze a few tears and Mama and Papa would surely surrender. Easy!

"Plus, there is more than enough room here for everyone. Anyway, how much longer can Rana continue alone? And eventually, your mother will need help to run this place."

"Ashwin Uncle helps." Papa's younger brother lived with his family in New Jersey, USA, with a wife and daughter, Tina. Ashwin Uncle handled the American division of Induslink Corporation.

"Yes, Ashwin is there." Dadi nodded. "All the way in Amrika. But God knows what will happen here. Your father and mother are getting old, you know. Besides, it's the least I can do for Hemu and Vikram." She clanked the cup on her saucer with conviction. "Give them a future, if nothing else."

"Family should help family," Rana said.

So, Papa agreed to all this?

"Of course." Dadi nodded. "If we couldn't give Hemu a decent past, at least we should give her and the family a decent future. We did it for you. We can do it for her."

Sheetal leaned back. She would have to wait and speak privately with Mama.

WHEN SHEETAL WOKE FROM HER AFTERNOON NAP, MAMA SAT ON THE bed's edge, caressing Sheetal's hair as if it were her wedding day all over again. "Am I still a Prasad, Mama?"

Crinkles crept around the corner of Mama's eyes. "You are special. Even the world sees it. Created by *Brahma*. Always destined to be special. You know what you are."

"I...I don't. Not anymore. I'm married but I feel different. Like I've aged twenty years in six months. I don't even know what I'm supposed to feel anymore or if what I feel is right."

Beams of sunlight streamed through the window, speckling the floor in golden yellow puddles as Mama rested a hand on Sheetal's forehead. "You will always be a Prasad. But why all these questions? Aren't you comfortable in your new home?"

"I'm confused. Marriage has changed everything. I can't make sense of time, the people around me or what I'm supposed to be doing at any moment. Everything I say or do is wrong. Everything has to be their way. There's no beginning or end to all the wrongs I do. Like I'm going in circles, chasing my tail."

Mama pulled her close and lay Sheetal's head on her lap. "Sometimes it takes a year or more to adjust."

"A year?"

"Or until you have your first baby. That gives many women a reason to settle down."

Sheetal wrinkled her nose. "You're going too far."

"Don't give me the nose, young lady." Mama teasingly pinched Sheetal's nose. "Every young woman eventually wants a baby and to start a family of her own. If not now, then later."

She could barely handle herself in that house. The thought of a baby... Rakesh's baby... She tensed. "Not me."

"You don't have to decide now. It's a decision couples eventually make over time."

They were not a couple. "Mama, there's something you need to know. I'm not going back. I...can't live there."

"What do you mean?"

"I did everything you said. Give this marriage a try. I did. But they're impossible. All of them."

"And what's so impossible?"

"They're so rude. Domineering. I'm invisible there, like I don't matter." Should she share the details of how Rakesh had publicly humiliated her at the Damani's party? "I feel—I don't belong."

"I understand." Mama ran her palm along Sheetal's hair. "Marriage is a huge transition."

"I'm serious." Sheetal sat up. "I want to move back here."

Mama inched away and lowered a hand to rest on the mattress. "What will people say? That you couldn't make your marriage last."

"I didn't marry Rakesh to prove anything. If you hadn't forced me, I wouldn't be in this mess."

"We did what was right."

"For you. But clearly it isn't for me." Her breathing grew erratic. "If Aunty Hemu can come back forever then I can, too."

"Your situation is different from hers. Besides, she's not coming back forever." Mama turned away.

"She's a Prasad daughter. So am I."

"She's moving in because of her financial situation and family problems. You don't have any. She's been married for more than twenty-five years, she's not a newlywed."

"So, because I'm a newlywed, I don't matter? I need a

number to prove my worth? I'm still a Prasad. You said so yourself."

"Why must you be so difficult?" Mama rose, her back turned.

"It's true. You don't know what it's like being stuck with someone you don't love."

"I do." Mama spun to face her. "I was married to another man before I married your father. My first husband—I lost him in a car accident."

The air stilled. "You were married to someone else before Papa? So, Papa's not my real father?" That explained why she was nothing like Papa.

"No, no." Mama shook her head. "The man I married—his name was Vishnu. But you are not his daughter. I was pregnant with a boy when I— He died in that awful accident."

Sheetal's heart skipped a beat. A brother? She had a brother? All this time, she thought she was Mama and Papa's only child. "Where is he? This boy you had?"

"Silly. Wouldn't I have told you years ago if he was still around?"

What was she supposed to believe, considering Mama had hidden this for so long? The walls and bed distanced and Sheetal felt suspended, like she was losing time, place and belonging.

"The baby died when he was three months old. We didn't have the money to cure him. We were nowhere near as comfortable as we are now. I've told you this before. Your father and I have lived a hard life. We know what it means to have little."

"Why did he die? This boy? How?"

"Pneumonia."

"What was he like?"

"I haven't thought of him in such a long time." Mama turned away.

"But you had him for three months." Sheetal fidgeted with the strand of gold around her neck and stopped at the tip of the pendant.

"He was a little dark in complexion, and he had big, brown eyes."

A bitterness crept into Sheetal's heart. Did Mama love the boy more than she loved her? "Did he look like you?" She prayed he didn't.

"Sheetal!" Mama frowned. "This is going too far."

"But I want to know. What was Vishnu like?"

"Attentive. Gentle. Caring. But we don't need to go into details. It means nothing."

Sheetal tightened her fingers into fists. "It does."

"Why?"

"Why didn't you tell me any of this?" She stood. "No one tells me anything around here."

"You didn't need to know."

"And I need to know *now* that you once had a different husband and baby?" Mama had lived a secret life before Sheetal existed, one she'd never been privy to.

"So you understand how to adjust to changes in life. Your father married me when I was a pregnant widow. I was in my second trimester when *He* died. I learned of your father through Navnit Uncle, because they were business partners."

Sheetal met Mama's older brother briefly during the wedding.

Why did Mama still refer to her ex-husband as 'He'? Out of respect, women from previous generations didn't use their husbands' names. They referred to them as 'He.' But if this Vishnu was dead, why did Mama refer to him as if he were alive?

"Your father heard what happened, felt sorry and married me despite the pregnancy. Maji never approved of our marriage because she didn't get to choose a bride for her son, which is every mother's right, and she was forced to accept the child of another in her home. But she accepted me despite everything. I guess she had to because she didn't have a choice. And for that, I'm grateful."

Is that why Dadi was unusually hard on Mama?

"I want you to know your father didn't have to marry me. He chose to do the honorable thing, for my sake."

Sheetal's knees weakened and she sank onto the bed. The proud, selfish and pompous impression she had of Papa was wrong. He had always done what was best for the family in times when they had little as he did now in times of plenty. Regret welled. She hated herself for misjudging him. The thought of buying vendors' fruits and vegetables that swarmed with flies and then crossing a road in broken sandals, arms loaded with grocery bags, caused Sheetal to turn away. Was that the life Mama and Papa had endured and the reason why they didn't want her to marry Arvind?

"All we had at the time was a one-bedroom flat in Nariyal Ka Rasta. But the past is over. Look how hard your father worked and where we are now."

It made sense, why Mama and Papa held on to their wealth with an iron grip. To think, she easily could have been poor.

She curled the fingers of her right hand, holding tight to the bond she had forged with Mama in the last twenty minutes, a bond that outweighed the last twenty-two years. Still, she wanted answers. "Did you love Vishnu?"

"What difference does it make?"

"It does to me."

Mama sighed. "At the time, yes."

"More," Sheetal hestitated to ask, "than Papa?"

"I said, *at the time*. It's over now." Mama walked across to the window, clearly annoyed. "This is getting way out of line. Nothing in life comes easy. Everything comes at a price."

"All I'm asking is if you loved him more than Papa."

"No two people are the same."

"You did. I can tell. And you can't let him go," Sheetal whispered. "So, you understand why I can't let go of Arvind."

"Forget Arvind." Mama's voice firmed. "I tried so many times to tell you, but you didn't listen. And I tried to tell him the same—"

"Who?"

"Arvind."

"He was here again, and you didn't tell me?"

"He came to say he was leaving Raigun. He came in August. About two months after you married."

"Here? He came here?" Sheetal held her breath. "And you didn't tell me?"

"Tell you what? Trivial things to upset your new life? It's finished. Over. Didn't you say so yourself?"

It was over because that's what Mama and Papa had wanted to hear. Fear gripped her. How would she leave the

Dhanrajs now? Arvind was gone, and Aunty Hemu and her brood were moving in. "Did he say where he was going?"

"What difference does it make?" Mama threw her hands in the air. "He dared to come here. Can you believe it? Here."

Which meant he still loved her. She had to find him.

"Thank God your father wasn't here, or God only knows what He would have done. It's best you forget that Arvind and that he marry some girl of his class and settle down."

Sheetal went rigid. "You're heartless."

Mama's expression hardened to stone. "There is no life without money. Even love can't survive. My first child died because we didn't have enough. But we do now, and it's best you learn how to hold on to every rupee. And understand one thing: your father is the only man in my life now. There is no other."

"You're pretending you didn't love Vishnu. But you still do. I know, Mama. I can see it."

"This stays between us. Understand? Not a word to anyone. Ever. It'll just create gossip and complications."

"And what happens to me? I can't live in that nut house with those people."

"For God's sake, grow up. You're not a child anymore. It's your decision whether you choose to be happy or not. Find happiness in what you have."

"You're not making me go back, are you?"

Mama sat beside her. "I saw your and Rakeshji's photograph in the paper the other day. The article said you two were the evening's highlight. Don't tell me you're not happy."

"It's not what it looks like."

"You have what every woman aspires to. Don't throw it away. You will learn its value and strength in time."

TWO DAYS LATER, SHEETAL PICKED UP HER RINGING CELL PHONE AND pressed it to her ear.

"Hi. Remember me?" Rakesh's deep, husky voice startled her.

"Of course, I—" Her heart skipped a beat. "When did you get back?"

"You never called once to check if I was back."

Sheetal counted the days and bit her lower lip. Rakesh must have landed four days ago, and she was scheduled to return tomorrow. "I lost track of time."

"I didn't."

"Oh."

"How have you been?"

She could almost smell the thick, sweet-sour mixture of scotch and nicotine, as if he stood in the room. "Fine."

"And everyone else?"

"Fine."

"Care to ask me?"

"Ask you what?"

"My trip. How I've been. How much I missed you."

"How was it?"

"Fine."

"How have you been?"

"Lonely."

She bit her lip. She hadn't expected that response. "H-h—"
She held her breath, daring to ask, "How much did you
miss me?"

"More than you'll ever know."

Sheetal pressed the phone against her ear, wanting the
saffron sweetness of his words to continue.

"I've been thinking of nothing but you," he went on. "The
smell of your skin, your hair, your lips, it's everywhere in our
room. Did you miss me?"

Her attention wandered to the lawn outside her balcony.
"I... I..."

"You don't have to answer. I understand." He sighed.
"There's no reason for you to miss me. But say it anyway. Did
you miss me?"

"I did think of you once or twice." She had replayed the
Diwali night and the sight of Rakesh's den like a looped tape for
the last two weeks. There was no denying the night had
happened.

"You're coming back tomorrow, right?"

She took a deep breath and exhaled. Was there any reason
to stay?

24
CHAMPAGNE DREAMS

The next morning, fifteen sterling silver trays brimming with sweet mithais, golden apples, pears, juicy tangerines, ripe pomegranates, imported boxes of biscotti and shortbread biscuits were carried into the Dhanraj mansion by servants. Sheetal, Mama and Papa followed.

Dressed in an aqua tusser silk sari and diamond jewelry chosen by Mummyji, well in advance, Sheetal made her way up the mansion's entrance stairs, the weight of high society dragging her every step.

The servants neatly arranged the trays on the glass coffee table before the Fulton Whites. Mama and Papa greeted Mummyji by pressing their hands together in namaste and bowing their heads. Mummyji thanked Mama and Papa for the gifts then called servants to whisk away the trays and bring out snacks.

A selection of savory and sweet mithais wrapped in paper-thin, edible silver *barakh* and gold-rimmed glasses of honey colored juice glittered under the bright rays of the chandelier. Mama and Papa each chose one piece from the selection offered.

Culture and tradition cautioned the bride's parents against eating or drinking anything offered at the daughter's house. The practice, one of many, helped both families keep a healthy distance to prevent the bride's family from accidentally stepping on anyone's toes, which could lead to family arguments and, in turn, disadvantage the bride.

When Mummyji gestured for Mama and Papa to have a seat, Sheetal bent to touch Mummyji's feet and seek her blessing.

Mummyji smiled broadly and sat near Mama. "Oh, you won't believe the excitement, I tell you! My Naina's wedding is less than six months away and..." She elaborated on the details of the family Naina was to marry into, their improving finances and rising status in Calkot, and how this wedding would elevate the Malhotras to the crème de la crème of society. She raved on about Naina's exquisite taste in shopping for saris and salwar suits, her ability to predict modern fashion trends, and the hope that someday she would become a role model for every modern, young Indian woman.

"Well then," Papa said, "we must meet her."

"Oh, but you can't," Mummyji said. "She's on bed rest. You see, she's been having these recurring nightmares, I tell you. Crying for days and days. It's not her fault if she was the only one affected by Ashok's death." Her voice cracked. "I mean, so what if that happened three years ago, I tell you. Naina was the favorite child, and obviously she was affected the most by his... his..."

Sheetal was convinced Mummyji was going to turn on the waterworks. Then Mama patted Mummyji's arm, and Sheetal gritted her teeth. She had taken all this trouble to return looking like a Dhanraj, in accordance with Mummyji's wishes, and Mummyji hardly cared. Even the trays of mithais were better off! At least, she had bothered to look at those.

At that moment, Rakesh sauntered downstairs, touched Mama and Papa's feet and sat before Sheetal. He nodded and smiled as Mummyji went on and on about Naina this and Naina that, his features softening under the chandelier's glow. Warmth spread within and Sheetal began to calm and relax. She tried to tune in to what Mummyji was saying but couldn't peel her attention away from Rakesh. He appeared so much more relaxed, carefree and handsome than before. And the way he scanned everyone then fixed his attention on her, Sheetal's heart skipped a beat. He really did miss her.

Then Mama and Papa rose to leave, and she followed them to the blue Maruti parked outside, with Rakesh close on her heels.

"We'll call you over as soon as we can," Mama whispered and slid into the vehicle's passenger seat. "And next time, we'll spend more time together. I promise."

The driver started the car and drove to the gate. The tail-lights blinked once, twice, and then the car turned onto Barotta Hill and the iron gates closed.

"You look stunning, and don't let anyone tell you other-wise." Rakesh enveloped her hand in his and led her back into the mansion. He stopped at the staircase landing, removed a scarf from the pocket of his chinos and blindfolded her. "I have a little surprise for you."

At first, Sheetal resisted, but the coolness of his hand on her wrist calmed her. He rested her right hand on the rail of the balustrade and let go. "You'll have to make your way up, but I'll stay close."

Sheetal raised her foot, but her toe banged the riser and she lunged forward. Rakesh caught her before she fell and helped her stand.

"Is this surprise something to be scared of?" She raised her foot again and located the first step. Rakesh's steady breathing on her left and the gentle tap of his shoes against the marble stairs meant he hadn't left her side. Not yet.

"It's in two pieces."

Another mini skirt and smocked tank top? She tightened her jaw. "What if I don't like it?"

"It's not meant to fit."

She made her way up, unsure how many steps she'd climbed, but when she couldn't find another riser, she stopped. She ran her hand along the banister. It curved right, which meant she'd reached the top.

Rakesh led her forward and spun her around three times, causing the darkness to swirl. Sheetal stretched out her arms to locate the bannister and regain her bearings but encountered a muscle-filled wall of fabric.

"This way." Rakesh raised her right hand and placed it on a hump-shaped object taller than shoulder height.

She squeezed the rounded hump. *Rakesh's shoulder.* She began walking when he did, then bumped into his back and molded against his contours when he stopped.

"Easy does it now."

She drew in long, slow breaths to quell her excitement. What could it be? A creaking filled the silence, then he started walking again. A cold breeze whooshed past, causing the hairs on her arms to stand on end.

Rakesh suddenly ducked away, and Sheetal reached out to grab something for support. A door. A wall. Anything. She found nothing within reach. "Rakesh?" No answer. "Rakesh? Where are you?" She yanked the blindfold, squinted against harsh light, and waited for her vision to adjust.

She stood in a room with beige walls. Polished brown floorboards covered the right half of the floor and the left was padded with beige carpet. An easel dominated the center of the hardwood floor. A leather sofa with a matching recliner and coffee table graced the carpeted area and the windows were draped with tan curtains. "It's beautiful. This room and the whole décor. Whose is it?"

"Yours. I renovated your studio while you were away."

"My studio. You did this?"

"At your service." Rakesh saluted playfully.

"Why?"

"Because I missed you."

"But weren't you in Amsterdam while I was at Mama's?" She headed for the easel.

"Yeah, I said that to throw you off. But I was really supervising this while you were gone. It took a whole week."

Rakesh never took time off for anyone. He had canceled their European honeymoon because of work. "You mean you redid my studio and didn't go to Amsterdam?"

"Whoa! Cool it." He raised both hands. "It was just a week. You sound as if I took a year off."

Just a week was seven precious days of Rakesh's time, which meant he cared. "Where are all my paintings?"

"I...I, uh, got rid of them."

"You what?"

"I...I thought we should start fresh, from scratch. So, I had your room redecorated for a new beginning—to your career and our relationship."

"You can't just— Those paintings were six months of hard work. My parents still decorate their house with my work and cherish what I've done. And you throw them out the moment I leave?"

He frowned. "It's not what you're thinking. I... I didn't know it meant that much to you. It looked like beginner's stuff. I thought—"

"Who cares what you thought? How dare you take my work and...and—" Anger burned through her skin and she stormed from the room.

"Wait, Sheetal!" he called after her.

Sheetal lengthened her stride, just able to see her bedroom door on the opposite wing through a mist of tears. She reached the door, took a right, careened into her room, slammed the door and locked it. Darkness engulfed her. She felt blindfolded again. Blind to trust.

"Listen, Sheetal!" He knocked on the door.

Rage tore at her heart. Sheetal pressed her back to the door and slid to the floor.

"Open the door, please."

She crossed her arms and drew in her knees, praying the

floor would crack open and swallow her.

"Listen, just listen to me."

She tucked her face into the cradle of her sari, draped between her knees. Bile rushed to her throat and burned. She didn't want to listen. She just wanted to be left alone.

"I didn't mean to hurt you."

Hurt? Is that all he thought he'd done?

"Just switch on the light and I'll go," he begged.

He was stone. He was ice. He was—

"I'm so sorry."

Sheetal rose, brushed away tears, and switched on the light. The walls had been freshly painted in a sun-burnt shade of orange, and a border of golden-brown leaves ran horizontally across the middle. Gold railings and fixtures bordered the king size bed. The sofas were no longer blue but a shade of softest peach, and the carpet had been replaced with soft, plush fibers the color of ripe papaya. A glass cabinet housed a TV.

Sheetal unlocked the door and let Rakesh in.

"I know the room was long overdue for renovations. I didn't mean to—"

She went into the bathroom and shut the door.

OVER THE NEXT TWO AND A HALF WEEKS OF FEBRUARY, RAKESH returned early from work and spent the evenings with Sheetal. Rakesh drank chai and Sheetal sipped coffee in the Japanese garden. They went out for early candlelight dinners at Chalet, IndiaFest or other posh restaurants in southern Raigun, attended movies, plays and one evening, Rakesh took Sheetal to a *ghazal* recital where a male and female singer performed ballads and love songs to a live harmonium, sitar and string quartet. They took long walks along the lake, splurged on shopping sprees and bought things they didn't need.

One evening, they lounged by the infinity pool, overlooking the lake and mountains, as a breeze rippled the water's surface, and the sun began its slow descent. Reclined on a deck chair, Rakesh laced his fingers and tucked them behind his head. "You think I'm some sort of monster, don't you? Always on edge and ready to snap."

Where was he going with this?

"I want you to know the real me." His voice remained unusually calm. "I didn't have a normal life like you. My real mother, Rashmi, she—" He paused, looked ahead at the mountains, and blinked. "Sorry, I—"

Sheetal reached out and touched his arm. "You don't have to share if you don't want to. We can talk about this later."

The side of his temple relaxed, and his brown eyes softened as rays of fading yellow and orange sunlight cast a silky net of gold on the waters. "I lit my mother's pyre when I was thirteen. Just a boy. Complications after Megha was born, and the doctors couldn't save her."

The Hindu ritual of death required the deceased person's son or closest male relative to light the funeral pyre.

"Pushpa walked in two days later. She must have been around twenty or so. Half Papa's age. I thought she was the bai hired to take care of Megha." His expression hardened. "Papa declared she was our new mother and we had to do what she said. He didn't even give us time to get over Mumma's death.

Forty-eight hours and he brings in a second wife. Obviously, he'd never cared for Mumma. She never mattered. And Pushpa, his trashy mistress, hit the jackpot with Mumma's death. I hate her. My life. Everything. That's why I'm so bitter. So angry. I...I just hate everything that happened. And the way it did."

Sheetal opened her mouth but didn't know what to say. How did anyone apologize for all the wrongs in someone's past?

"At first, I rebelled. I refused to accept her. Can you imagine someone walking into your life and taking over?"

Is that why Naina hated her? No. That wasn't possible. Sheetal went out of her way to avoid Naina.

"Papa didn't give us a choice. He said we had to accept her because they were already legally married in court."

"I remember reading, several years ago, that you'd lost your mother and your father remarried. But I didn't realize it had been so sudden. Was she ever kind? Gentle? Understanding?"

"Kind enough to give us forty-eight hours to put away all our family photos and any reminders of Mumma or our past in storage. I don't even know where those things are. We weren't allowed to look for them, and I have no idea if they're still around."

Sheetal bit her lower lip. The boxes she'd shoved back into the studio closet. Was he referring to them? She was about to say something but stopped. What if Mummyji caught wind of her discovery? Then she'd be in trouble for snooping around.

"Megha has only known Pushpa." His tone grew caustic. "She's never known a real mother's love. That's why she may come across as a little...you know...unsure. Like she's lost."

"I'm guessing Naina was affected by all this, too."

Rakesh looked at her, confused, and Sheetal's tongue felt like jelly. "I mean, she must have only been ten at the time. Probably not as strong as you were to—"

"Just leave Naina out of this," he cut her short.

"I'm sorry. I didn't mean to—"

"When Papa died, he left me the majority of the company shares with a fixed percentage for Naina, Megha and Pushpa. The business is my responsibility, and I cover the expenses to run this place. But consumer and investor confidence comes with social obligations. All those dinners, charity events, you know—are a must. The mansion and estate he left for Pushpa. But Papa didn't just leave us each our share. He slipped a caveat. If Pushpa forfeits her duties to the family or shirks them in any way, she'll be stripped of her inheritance. Her share will go to the government, and she's only left with her percentage of the company. If we lose the mansion, we lose investor confidence and—"

"So, you're tied to each other. Neither of you can walk away."

He nodded. "That's why I'm still here. Only Naina and Megha are free. It's bad enough Naina's been spoiled fucking rotten from the beginning, but forking out nine hundred million rupees for this damned wedding? Just to please her and Pushpa? It's—"

"Nine hundred million?" Sheetal shrank back. "Do you have that much? In cash?" she added, not wanting to insult him.

"I've got five hundred and fifty in liquid. I'll borrow the other three hundred and fifty from the company and return it later."

"How?"

"I don't know just yet. But I'll find a way."

"Why are you going beyond your means? If you can't afford it, just tell Mummyji."

"And let Pushpa go to the press? She'll give *The Raigun Herald* a field day. False information about me. Like I—we— just had this huge wedding—our wedding—and now I don't want to spend on Naina. She'll make me look like some kind of prick."

Whatever a prick was, didn't sound good. To think, a daughter's wedding, paid for by her father, was now Rakesh's burden. Still, something didn't make sense. Why did he hate Naina so much? She was his sister. And why wasn't Naina in any of the photographs with Rashmi, Ashok and Rakesh? Why did Mummyji openly favor Naina? Why didn't Megha and Rakesh object to the discrimination?

"I'm sorry for what I've done. How I've made you feel." His voice dropped to a murmur. "I'm always on guard, like I need to protect someone or something. I...I don't even know what I'm trying to protect. I've only been close to Megha, like a mother and father to her all my life, even when I was a child. I don't trust people the way you do. I need time to get to know you. To —" he gazed longingly into her eyes, and Sheetal's heart fisted in her throat, "give me time to come around."

The orange melted in the sky, dissolving her hatred for Rakesh with the evening. But how could she trust him after what he'd done?

THE NEXT DAY, SHEETAL SELECTED BRUSHES, FILLED A GLASS JAR WITH turpentine and was squeezing paint onto a palette when Rakesh entered and closed the studio door.

"Don't mind me, I'm just here to learn." He settled onto the sofa.

Sheetal left her workstation, reached for Rakesh's hands, pulled him to his feet, and led him to her prepared canvas. A sheet of white contact paper with a large, central oval cutout covered the canvas like a second skin. Two strips of masking tape, an inch wide, ran horizontally across the upper and lower thirds of the canvas. "You can't learn by observation."

"I can't paint," Rakesh said.

"Really? Considering how much you had to say about Renoir and Picasso?"

Sheetal positioned herself in front of Rakesh, brought his left arm around her bare midriff and leaned back against the warmth of his chest. Then she chose a brush and tested the bristles against her left palm to make sure they were dry.

"Cool." He ran his left hand down the curve of her waist, up the length of her arm and snaked her breast.

Sheetal slapped his hand. "That's irritating. Not painting." She placed his right hand atop her wrist and tightened his fingers.

"Ready."

Sheetal dipped the brush into the red paint, then pthalo blue, and swirled easy strokes of sky onto the upper third of the canvas. His grip restricted her movements. She freed her wrist, turned and instructed him to flex his fingers. "Loosen up. You're so uptight. No wonder you can't paint."

"What do you mean loosen up?" His eyes sparkled. "This is how I am."

"Then change. Let go a little."

"But I didn't ask to paint. You just grabbed me and—"

"I know. Made you paint. Now, let's do it right." She resumed her previous position and was about to dip the brush into paint when Rakesh pressed kisses along her nape. Warmth welled. "That's dangerous."

"Not as dangerous as you. But...well, I've got to do it right."

Sheetal was about to dot the center of the horizon with yellow paint when he pulled her close and hugged her.

The brush fell from her hand and clattered near her toes. "You almost spoiled the sun." Sheetal bent and grabbed the brush.

He pulled her hips to his crotch and pressed her against his bulge.

Sheetal straightened and faced him. "No more games. Promise?" She caught Rakesh's hand, dipped his index finger into a puddle of cadmium yellow, raised his finger to the canvas and dotted a ball for the sun. Then she returned Rakesh's hand to her wrist and swept the brush in long, easy strokes, left and right across the sky and around the sun. The strokes blended one hue into another. Then she scooped a little crimson, mixed it with pthalo blue and pointed to an empty spot on the canvas. "Your turn. Alone, this time."

"Look, I can't."

She forced the brush between his fingers, cupped his knuckles and tilted his hand until he held the brush at an angle. She swept the upper third of the canvas in soft, curly motions, spinning clouds in the evening sky, and pulled wisps of lilac away from the sun.

"Sexy."

"Really?"

"The painting, of course."

"Of course." She continued her lead on the lower third of the canvas, lifting waves from the ocean's surface, and again on the shoreline, filling the area with sand and shells. Paint smudged outside the contact paper's edge.

"Aren't you supposed to paint inside the cut-out?" he asked.

"Don't worry. You'll see." She peeled away the upper strip of masking tape that divided sky from ocean, and the lower one that divided ocean from coastline. Then she took the brush from Rakesh and curled his fingers around her fist. "This is where the details come in, so I'll lead because you've got to be delicate. All three parts must merge into one." Sheetal filled in the empty white horizontal spaces with just the right shades, merging horizon and ocean, then ocean and coastline.

"There. All done." She lowered the brush and tapped the bottom right corner of the contact paper's edge. "Now, I want you to peel this off like I did with the masking tape."

Rakesh peeled the contact paper, leaving a perfect, oval-shaped painting of a sunset on the beach, and took a step back. "That's stunning! Perfect."

Sheetal shook her head. "Not quite." She took a pencil-lead-thin brush and painted two tiny V-shaped objects, for seagulls, on the upper third of the canvas.

"Sweet. Life just ain't complete without chicks, right? We should give this a name."

"Like?"

"Purple sunset?"

"Too boring."

"Purple haze?"

Sheetal crossed her arms and gave him 'the look'.

"All right, all right." He raised his hands.

"How about dawn?" she suggested. "It's like the dawn—new beginning—of our marriage."

"But isn't it dusk?"

"You're right." She sighed.

"How about Dawn at Dusk?"

"Perfect."

RAKESH AND SHEETAL MADE WILD, PASSIONATE LOVE FOR THE THIRD time that evening, then lay spent in a warm Jacuzzi as sunlight streamed through the bathroom windows, casting golden, horizontal streaks across the white tiles.

Rakesh stroked Sheetal's chest with a wet sponge and squeezed water over her shoulders and neck as she relaxed against him. Bubbles frothed and popped all around them. Sheetal leaned forward and the space between their bodies filled with warm, soapy water.

Rakesh pulled Sheetal back and placed kisses along her neck.

On Thursday morning, Rakesh left the bedroom headed for the office. Seconds later, thudding footsteps entered the room.

Sheetal turned toward the door.

Rakesh caught her by the arm, startling her. "Let's get away from here. Now. Right now."

"What do you mean, get away?"

"Run away. You know...just leave and go somewhere."

"Where?"

"Anywhere. What difference does it make?"

"But that's like running away," she said.

"Don't be a spoilsport. It'll be the honeymoon we never had. We never get time alone. There's always too much going on around here."

If they dropped everything and left, Mummyji would go on and on about how irresponsible she was and how she'd broken another rule. "No."

"Grow up, Sheetal. You're an adult."

Didn't Mama say recently, 'Find happiness with what you have.' She crossed her arms. "Shouldn't we tell someone?"

"Stop being such a baby."

This had to be another of his stupid ideas. "We haven't packed."

"We don't need anything. Just each other."

To drop everything and live free of responsibilities sounded irresistible.

FIVE MINUTES LATER, SHEETAL AND RAKESH DROVE OFF TO THE Raigun Cricket Club and rented the Presidential Suite. They watched DVDs, slept in each other's arms, read dirty magazines, ordered room service and ate their meals dressed in the RCC's plush white bathrobes. At times, they didn't even bother to wear those.

On Saturday morning, Sheetal suggested they call Mummyji and let her know their whereabouts, but Rakesh suggested Sheetal chill, watch TV and leave Mummyji to him. Sheetal tried to focus on the TV screen, but her attention wandered to the wall. What if Mummyji reported them missing and their faces appeared on a newsflash? Or Mummyji somehow tracked them down and barged in?

Sheetal channel surfed to take her mind off those worries. She grabbed a magazine from a side table, flipped the pages, then resumed channel surfing—just in case. But two hours later, when the world hadn't ended, she leaned back against the sofa cushions. Is this what Mama meant by getting to know each other and giving their relationship time? Possibly. This was a side of Rakesh she'd never seen before. She wanted the weekend to pass slowly and to bask in Rakesh's attention.

On Sunday morning, the final of the four-day weekend, Sheetal's heart sank at the thought of returning to the Dhanraj mansion. She tightened the knot on her robe and was about to ask Rakesh if they could extend their stay another day when he swung open the suite's main door. Fifteen bellboys entered carrying bouquets of red and pink roses. They arranged the vases on every available surface. Then a bellboy wheeled in a trolley with a bottle of champagne in ice and two fluted crystal glasses.

Rakesh thanked the bellboys, generously tipped them, locked the door behind the last one, then approached Sheetal. "Happy Birthday!" He hugged her.

Birthday? She looked at the date and time panel on the suite's phone. February twenty-fifth. "Can you believe, I forgot my own birthday?" She laughed.

"I didn't." Rakesh uncorked the champagne, filled both glasses, handed her a glass and proposed a toast, "To your first birthday with me. And many more to come." He gulped the liquid down like water. "You haven't touched yours."

"You know I don't drink." She placed her glass on the trolley and sat on the couch.

Good Hindu women from good Hindu families didn't drink alcohol, smoke or chew tobacco, and Sheetal wasn't about to bring shame on her family.

"You can make an exception today."

"I can't."

"Everyone drinks nowadays. It's okay. Chill, Sheetal."

"I don't agree with it."

"I do." His expression hardened. "What if I say you have to drink?"

"Then I'll run away," she said.

"I'm serious."

"So am I."

"One sip. For me."

"No."

"And if I force you to?"

"What do you mean, force me?"

"Depends whether you look at this as a force or an opportunity to change."

Sheetal stared past his shoulder at the roses. Was all this, the last three days, a charade? And the flowers—what did they mean? She tossed her loose hair away from her face, stood and went into the bedroom. "This is a joke."

"One sip. Last chance." He trailed behind.

She didn't care about chances. She sat on the bed, leaned against the headboard and fanned open pages of *The Raigun Herald*.

This is a game. She caught her reflection in the mirror. *Another silly game that swings with his mood.*

Rakesh's shadow fell across her, accompanied by the scent of champagne. Sheetal lowered the newspaper. Rakesh stood there, holding her glass.

"Come on, this isn't funny." She closed the gaping neck of her robe.

He stepped closer and gestured for her to drink.

Sheetal pressed a palm against the mattress and inched away. "Why are you doing this?"

"Nothing will happen if you take a sip."

Sheetal tucked her feet under her hips and squirmed against the headboard. This stranger wasn't the Rakesh she'd known for the last three weeks.

He thrust the glass forward. "I changed for you and proved it. Now you change for me."

The headboard prevented retreat. He blocked the route to the bathroom. She reached for the glass, sipped and swallowed the bitter liquid. "There." She handed it back.

"Finish it."

"You said one sip."

"Finish it." He fidgeted with the knot of his robe.

"It tastes sick."

"I didn't ask how it tasted." He cast aside the white duvet and sat atop the sheet. "Finish it."

She raised the glass to her lips and drained the liquid. It burned. She threw the glass against the wall so he'd see her rage. This was wrong. This was not what Mama had raised her to be.

Rakesh forced her onto her back, locked her fingers in his grip and parted her lips with his tongue.

He forced her legs apart, thrust into her, and pain seared like a knife. She struggled to break free, but he crushed her with his weight.

The first night returned all over again.

Sheetal cried out, but his organ tore into her.

Then he finished, rolled off and left the room.

She caught her reflection and a cry tore from her gut. A thin stream of blood, like sindoor, trickled down from the corner of her mouth. She attempted to reach the robe on the floor, but it was too far. She stretched, fell and landed like a wasted heap on the carpet.

Fallen.

Tears coursed down her cheeks.

She'd fallen in her own eyes.

25
CAT FIGHT

When Sheetal and Rakesh pulled into the driveway on Sunday evening, Mummyji paced back and forth before the main entrance. As they climbed the stairs, Mummyji spread her arms and barricaded the doorway with her body.

"Where have you been? Do you know Sheetal's parents and her uncle from the U.S. called to wish her a happy birthday? How embarrassing, I tell you. I didn't know where you were or what time you'd be back. What to say? And you don't even pick up your phones. How irresponsible. You, Sheetal, could have at least called to let me know where you were."

Sheetal looked from Mummyji to Rakesh and back. "I told Rakesh—"

"Stay out of this," Rakesh cut her off.

"I thought about calling the police," Mummyji said. "Twice."

"Did you?"

"No. Because both of you would have made tomorrow's headlines and embarrassed the family."

Rakesh grabbed Sheetal's hand and started to drag her past Mummyji. "Come with me."

Sheetal shook free, and Rakesh left without her. If she ignored Mummyji, she would be labeled rude and disrespect-ful. If she ignored her husband, she'd be going against his will. There was no pleasing both. Sheetal brushed past Mummyji and entered the mansion.

THE FOLLOWING SATURDAY, SHEETAL WAS AT WORK IN HER STUDIO when the odor of stale chutney permeated the room. Naina, out of hibernation, had spent most afternoons on the Bradford Browns, combing through fashion magazines. So, Sheetal was a little surprised to see Naina storm in, considering she had care-fully avoided her sister-in-law.

"You bitch! How dare you act as if you own the place? First you brainwash Rakesh and then trap Megha into liking you. You trample all over my mother as if you're in charge. But who gave you the right to control the servants?"

"I don't control anyone." Sheetal calmly put down the brush. She could barely get past what Rakesh had done on her birthday. The last thing she needed was Naina creating more chaos.

"You do, and you know it. Or why would Laal Bahadur cook your favorite meals every day, na?"

All she had done was appreciate Laal Bahadur's cooking

instead of complaining. "Where's the question of planning anything when Mummyji gives me the week's menu every Monday?"

"You know that's not true. Mummy thinks she decides everything, but you're secretly taking over, na. Maybe no one else can see it, but I do. I grew up here. This is my home and you can't take it away from me." Her loose hair fell in cobwebs around her face, and her eyes sparked with vengeance. She grabbed Sheetal's wrist and squeezed the glass bangles, causing them to crack and scrape Sheetal's skin.

"Let me go." Sheetal struggled to break free.

"Admit it." Naina tightened her grip. "Tell everyone you're trying to take over."

"I don't—"

"What on— Oh my G-God!" Megha rushed in and tried to free Sheetal from Naina, but the harder Megha pulled, the tighter Naina gripped.

"L-Let B-Bhabhi g-go!" Megha screamed as blood trickled from the cuts on Sheetal's wrist.

Sheetal relaxed for a second, saw confusion etch lines on Naina's face and then lunged forward, hurling Naina across the floor.

Naina landed on her bottom and howled. At that moment, Mummyji rushed in, cast her arms like a net around Naina, slipped and fell on her back.

She scowled at them. "How dare you gang up on Naina?"

"We d-didn't d-do anything. N-Naina g-got what she d-deserved." Megha pulled shrapnels of glass from Sheetal's wrist.

"What's all the noise?" Rakesh rushed in. "Fucking hell. Janvi!" he hollered. "First aid box, now."

"She...she hates me," Naina sobbed.

"Who wouldn't after what you d-did?" Megha used the end of her T-shirt to staunch the bleeding.

"She doesn't belong here and shouldn't have come in the first place," Naina yelled. "She should be grateful she's a Dhan-raj. But that's not enough, is it? You can't just marry into a family and expect to worm your way into people's hearts."

"The only worm around here is you," Megha shouted.

"Watch your tongue," Mummyji yelled.

"You watch yours," Megha fired back. "I've b-been holding b-back all m-my l-life. B-but n-no more."

Silence filled the room. All eyes were fixed on Megha. Mummyji's chest heaved and her eyebrows almost touched her hairline. Clearly, Megha had never talked back to anyone until now.

"Come on, ladies, let's get out of here." Rakesh led Sheetal and Megha out.

RAKESH CLEANED AND BANDAGED SHEETAL'S WRIST AND FORCED HER to lie down and rest even though Sheetal insisted the cuts were minor injuries. He had meals wheeled up to their bedroom and five servants on stand-by to do Sheetal's bidding.

However, after three days of being pampered and fussed over, Sheetal couldn't take it anymore. How could Rakesh be so cold and calculating one minute and so caring the next? How did he expect to heal wounds inflicted by Naina when he hadn't apologized for those he'd inflicted on her? "Rakesh."

He looked up from a pile of paperwork spread across the sofa in their bedroom.

"Look, you defended me when I needed you, and I'm grateful. But I don't need all this sick-patient treatment."

He stood and made his way toward her. "No one treats you that way. You're my wife."

Her jaw tightened. What about last week on her birthday? Wasn't she his wife then? "So?"

Rakesh tucked the upper edge of the quilt below her chin and along the sides. "Naina crossed all lines of decency this time. Damn her."

What about his language and behavior? Was his birthday gift to her in any way decent?

"No one messes with my wife. My..."

Her chest tightened, ready to explode. This wasn't about her wounds. It was about the damage done to one of Rakesh's properties. Apparently, he was the only one who had a right to hurt her.

THE FOLLOWING WEEK, SHEETAL WORKED LATE IN HER STUDIO, ADDING the final touches on a painting, when she realized it was eleven. Time to go to bed. She cleaned her tools, turned off the light then heard footsteps headed along the south wing. She opened the door ever so slowly. Who could be about at this hour? A faint beam of yellow light spilled from the hall into the room, casting a slash across the wall. Harsh whispers made her draw closer.

"I told you not to call me at home or on my mobile. No. Impossible! You have to understand—"

The click-clack of footsteps stopped, and from the clarity of Rakesh's voice, Sheetal guessed he must be three feet away.

"That's a lie and you know it. Fuck you." A shadow cut the sliver of light, and Sheetal hid behind the door.

"Don't do anything. I'll be there in fifteen minutes... Yes, yes." His voice softened. "Promise. Come on, don't make me say it. All right. Just once. I...I love you." Footfalls headed away down the hall.

The room spun, and Sheetal's knees buckled. She grabbed the doorknob for support. Silence lapped the corridor. She poked her head around the door. The ghostly balcony railings and closed doors were discernable in the light of a dimly lit chandelier and a moonbeam, spilling through the windows on the right. Sheetal edged toward the balcony, soaking in the eerie chill of the cold mansion.

The silhouette of someone in a hurry cut down the stairs ahead. When the figure sliced the silver moonbeam, Sheetal could just make out a pair of jeans and white T-shirt. She ducked behind a pillar. *Where was Rakesh going at this hour?* She peered around the pillar's edge once more for a clearer view. A tink-tink came from the kitchen, tucked on the far left. *Laal Bahadur was probably still cleaning up after dinner.* A chunk of white light cut across the hallway like a knife's blade, its tip resting on the kitchen door.

Rakesh paused mid-way, looked up, and Sheetal ducked behind the pillar, her heart pounding. Her breaths came in quick, short spurts and her head throbbed. *Who was he going to meet? And why?*

The rev of the Lamborghini thrummed the air. She headed back into the studio to see Rakesh's car pull out of the driveway.

Blackness shrouded her vision, and the floor beneath gave way.

26

JIGSAW

Dr. Joshi slipped Sheetal's papers into a folder, and Mummyji repeatedly flicked her thumb on her purse's lock, breaking the silence of the doctor's office. Mummyji slid a pair of rimless eyeglasses up the bridge of her nose as Sheetal fidgeted with the ring on her finger.

"There's absolutely no need to worry, Mrs. Dhanraj," Dr. Joshi said. "The dizzy spells, nausea, general discomfort and your test results—all signs of a normal pregnancy. Congratulations."

Sheetal's stomach clenched.

"A baby?" Mummyji clapped her hands. "Why, this is just wonderful, I tell you. Simply wonderful."

"According to my calculations, you are due on..." Dr. Joshi consulted a calendar. "Let's see... October the fourteenth."

"No."

Dr. Joshi stared at her.

Sheetal didn't realize she'd spoken aloud.

"Is something wrong?" the doctor asked.

"A baby?" In seven months' time?

"Oh my, my, my!" Mummyji beamed. "How wonderful! A baby in the house. I can't believe it."

All the way home, Mummyji pampered and fussed over Sheetal. She insisted Sheetal make lifestyle changes, like going to bed early, not working too hard, making healthier food choices and on and on. At home, she forced Sheetal into bed, propped her feet on two pillows, dragged the bedcovers up to her chin and debated when to share the good news with everyone. "I'll wait until after your first trimester, I tell you. It's safer. Better—no?"

The first trimester was considered the most crucial for an expectant mother, the delicate phase when things could go wrong.

"Well, what do you think?" she asked.

What was she supposed to think? She was going to be a mother. Rakesh was going to be a father. They were going to be a family. A broken family.

LATER THAT EVENING, IN THE COMFORT OF THE TV LOUNGE, SHEETAL watched a Bollywood *masala* movie after a failed attempt to take her mind off the day's revelation. Rakesh entered and sat on the coffee table, blocking her view of the TV. Sheetal looked past his shoulder to the upper edge of the screen, where a kaleidoscope of colors and muffled voices fused with the pandemonium in her heart. It was easier to keep quiet and hope the moment passed than deal with him.

He placed a hand on hers and looked into her eyes. "Is it true? We're having a baby?"

She blinked and took a deep breath. "That's what Dr. Joshi said."

"Is...is something wrong? I know we didn't plan on it. It... Things happen. But it's okay."

Okay? Is that what this is? Okay? First the marriage. Then the brief romance. And now a baby. All in the right order. "I don't know."

"It's what I've been waiting for. I...I mean, it's what *we've*— any man— I mean, any *couple* wants, right?"

If he was so sure about this baby, why was he fumbling for words? Like he wasn't sure if he'd say the right thing or say it right? Sheetal rose, walked to the patio, slid open the glass door and stepped outside. She took a right on the cobblestone pathway lit by garden lights and sat on her favorite bench before the pond of koi. The fish darted in and out of rocks and plants, mimicking the thoughts racing through her mind. How on earth was she going to raise a baby here?

"You're still pickled about the birthday, aren't you? Still angry." Rakesh sat beside her.

Angry? Sheetal cringed. Anger was just the leftovers. A month had passed since the episode, but it hurt like a raw and infected wound.

"I never...meant it to go that way," he whispered. "It was... just...a test."

"A test?" Blood rushed to her head. "Did I pass with flying colors?"

"You're not going to make this easy, are you?"

"You never did. Why should I?"

"I admit what I did was wrong. And I promise things will be different from now on."

"You said that before. Nothing changed."

"I've changed, haven't I?"

"I'm paying for it. Aren't I?"

"Look, you're tired."

"I am, as a matter of fact. Tired of you. Wouldn't you feel the same way if you were me?"

"Look." He put an arm around her shoulders.

Sheetal shrugged off the embrace.

"It just happened in the heat of the moment. I didn't mean it to—"

"What else didn't you mean? This marriage? Mummyji made that clear. This baby? I heard you on the phone last night. I know everything, Rakesh."

"I don't know what you're talking about." The lines on his forehead deepened.

"Stop lying. It was around eleven. You left the house after talking to *her* on the phone. I saw you run down the stairs in jeans and a white T-shirt."

He crossed his arms. "I wasn't on any call with anyone outside your studio. I never changed into a T-shirt and jeans, and I...I was looking for you. You weren't in the room, so I went downstairs thinking you might be in the kitchen. But later, when I saw the studio door open, I figured you might still be there. So, I ran back up and found you unconscious."

"I heard you tell her you would meet her in fifteen minutes. You said you loved her. I heard you. Who is she?"

"I don't know what the fucking hell you heard or saw," he snapped. "I wasn't on the phone last night with anyone. I was home the entire evening, dammit!" He raked his fingers through his hair. "Why is everything so difficult with you? I think you're tired with all of it. The pregnancy. Naina's wedding…"

Naina's wedding was three months away, and Mummyji had been handling the preparations. The only thing she was tired of was him.

"I think your imagination is overworked."

"My imagination?" Her chest tightened. "So, now you're telling me I'm imagining things?"

"What you saw last night was me looking for you." He loosened his tie. "You should rest."

"I don't need rest." She took a deep breath, holding back tears. Was this another 'believe what you see, not what you think you see'? Why did everyone keep shoving her aside? Like forcing her to lie down. Insisting she didn't know what was good for her. And now claiming she imagined things. "How do I know you were looking for me?"

"You want proof?" Rakesh pulled his wallet from a back trouser pocket, flipped it open and handed her a white envelope the size of her palm. "I've been carrying this for weeks. I wanted to give it to you earlier, to apologize for what happened on your birthday. But there's just never a right time with you."

Sheetal peeled open the envelope's flap and removed a card. A picture of a single red rose graced the cover with a handwritten message inside. *I'm sorry for the trouble I've caused between us. Look forward to your art exhibition from December fifth to tenth.*

"What exhibition?"

"I booked the Crowning Galleria for five days in December."

Sheetal's heart skipped a beat. Crowning Galleria was the best art gallery in Raigun, where local and internationally renowned artists displayed their work. "The Crowning Galleria?" she repeated, to make sure she'd heard right.

"That's right. Your exhibition. Precisely why I was looking for you. Now you have all the proof."

Her heart grated the pit of her stomach in guilt. "But you never told me. We never even discussed—"

"It was a surprise! What more can a man do to make up? I take the trouble to arrange an exhibition for you. And what do you do? Blow it off with some silly story about a phone conversation I never had with some...some other woman?" His attention shifted to the pond.

Here, she'd been thinking negatively about him while he'd been working to advance her career. She read the card again to make sure, and each word weighed like lead. The proof was here in black and white, like the sonogram of the fetus she'd seen that afternoon, evidence of supposedly good things to come. And what about the phone call? And the rev of the car engine? She had heard them.

"Well, what do you say?"

"I've never done anything like this before, putting my work on display. I'm— I don't think I'm ready."

"You've never had a baby, either. How do we know we're ready? There's always a first time."

"But—"

"You'll need fifty paintings ready by then. I signed the contract papers. You are up to it, aren't you?"

Three months until Naina's wedding. Seven months until the baby's arrival. Nine months until her exhibition. Sheetal bit her lip.

"You are ready," Rakesh said. "Let the public decide about your work."

There was so much to do and so little time. "I—"

"I came here to celebrate. Don't spoil the moment."

THE FOLLOWING SATURDAY AFTERNOON, RAKESH, SHEETAL AND Megha returned from a luncheon to celebrate the baby and found Naina and Mummyji in the main hall surrounded by clothes, velvet jewelry cases and a plethora of saris.

Shortly after Naina had attacked Sheetal, Naina confined herself to her room and Mummyji blamed all three of them for Naina's relapse. Now, Naina perched on the Fulton Whites and Mummyji stood amidst the clutter. Streams of colorful saris cascaded like waterfalls from the bulges of Mummyji's arms. Naina pulled chiffons and silks from shopping bags and draped each one over Mummyji's arms.

When Sheetal, Rakesh and Megha entered the main hall, Mummyji lowered her arms and the saris clumped on the floor. Then she hopscotched through pools of fabric toward Sheetal and clapped her hands.

"Good you are here, I tell you! Naina's putting together everything she'll need, as you can see, and she's fallen in love with your Cartier set."

Most of Sheetal's jewelry sets were tucked safely in bank

lockers, but Mummyji had insisted they keep a few at home, giving Sheetal immediate access to them. However, the Cartier, and the Jaipur *Kundan* set Sheetal had worn on Diwali, were kept in Mummyji's personal locker.

"She didn't just take it. Oh no!" Mummyji slapped her chest. "Naina asked if she could have it, I tell you. And I knew you wouldn't mind. But first things first, you haven't worn that, by any chance, have you?" She gestured to the Cartier set on the coffee table.

Sheetal plowed through the mess. The chunky gold necklace, about four inches wide, embellished with rubies, emeralds and sapphires, and matched with a bracelet and earrings, was left in the open for everyone to view.

What more would they take from her?

"So?" Mummyji hopscotched back to Sheetal. "Have you worn that?"

"No."

"Perfect! That means it's still brand new. And I'll make sure everyone knows you took such an expensive set from your collection to give Naina as a wedding gift." She grabbed the necklace and held it up to the chandelier. "Even the best Indian craftsman could never get a finish like this."

Rakesh coughed. "Shouldn't you have asked Sheetal first?"

Naina cast aside two saris and jumped to her feet. "I knew this would happen. All you or anyone cares about is Sheetal. She-e-etal, *Sheetal!*"

Sheetal sensed a repeat performance ahead.

"Naina," Mummyji intervened. "Show Sheetal some respect. She is, after all, giving it to you."

"You hate me. All of you hate me. But when I'm gone, you'll

all be sorry, and then you'll realize what she"—she pointed at Sheetal—"did. But it'll be too late by then." She tossed back her hair, spun on her toes, and stormed upstairs.

"*Hai Ishwar!* Did you have to say that?" Mummyji tossed the necklace back in the case. "Poor girl's just come out of her bedridden phase today, I tell you. And what do you do? Upset her all over again."

The slam of an upstairs door echoed through the house.

Mummyji turned to Rakesh. "I will have another set made for Sheetal. Bigger. Better. By the best craftsman in Raigun, I tell you. But you don't want Naina to be happy, even on her wedding day. And you," she turned to Sheetal, "didn't even apologize after what you did to her in that studio of yours. That necklace would have sorted out all your personal differences and made her happy. Ask me! I know what it's like, I tell you, to live without all...all this. I've lived the unthinkable life. But none of you would understand what it means to have so little."

"Even if we did," Megha said, "is Naina ever happy?"

"Enough!" Pushpa turned and trudged upstairs, no doubt to console Naina.

A lump formed in Sheetal's throat. She swallowed. The necklace would make Naina happy for now. But what about next time Naina was unhappy? What bone would the Dhanrajs dole out to the family pet then?

"Go on, take it." Rakesh offered her the Cartier box. "It's yours."

Sheetal walked away.

Two weeks later, Mummyji and Naina left on another shopping spree. Megha was at college, Rakesh at work. Taking advantage of the perfect opportunity, Sheetal stole into the dining room. "Laal Bahadur?"

Laal Bahadur emerged from the kitchen, wiping his hands on a white cotton tea towel. "Some chai, Choti Sahiba?"

"No, thank you." Sheetal pulled a chair for herself and lowered her voice to a whisper. "I need to ask you something, and I want the truth."

His round eyes shrunk back into the soft, dough-like texture of his face. "Badhi Memsahib leave clear instructions, not chat with anyone."

'Anyone' meant her.

"I understand. And she's not here. She's out shopping with Naina."

"But..." He twirled the frayed end of the towel. "If anyone find out? My job. I will—"

"How about this? Don't talk. Just nod or shake your head. That way, you're not breaking Her house rules."

"I..."

Sheetal took a deep breath and rested both hands on the white, embroidered tablecloth. "The night I fainted in my studio. It was about eleven, if I remember correctly. You were in the kitchen." She quickly added, "I heard you."

He shifted uneasily from one foot to the other. "I don't know. Just let me go, Choti Sahiba."

Sheetal locked her fingers into a fist. "You're the only one who can help me. Did Rakesh leave that night and go out?"

"I...I no see anything, Choti Sahiba. I in kitchen whole time." His expression tensed.

This was not going to be easy. "Yes or no. Did you hear Rakesh's car that night?"

Silence.

"Come on, Laal Bahadur."

"I know so little about cars, only kitchen chores."

"Did. You. See. Rakesh. Leave. The. Mansion. Late. That. Night? Around eleven? Eleven-fifteen?"

He scratched his left ear then twisted an end of the towel into a knot. He nodded.

"So, you saw Rakesh leave?"

Laal Bahadur nodded.

"So, if he left the house, that means he wasn't here. Then, who found me upstairs?"

Laal Bahadur shuffled forward. "The studio door open, little bit. I go up see if you need anything before I close kitchen for night. But then you are unconscious on floor."

Sheetal swallowed. "Then?"

"I yell for help. Chotte Sahib"—he referred to Rakesh— "behind me. He come back in house."

Sheetal bit her lip. So, Rakesh was lying. "Then?"

"He make me tell everyone he find you. Not me."

"And?"

"He take you to room and tell me to wake up Badhi Memsahib."

Sheetal straightened her posture. Her imagination was not at work. Rakesh was at work.

LATER THAT EVENING, SHEETAL MADE HER WAY TO RAKESH'S BEDROOM, determined to get answers. "Rakesh?" she called. "Rakesh?" She checked the bathroom and walk-in closet, but both were empty. She walked across the room and pushed the mirror-door. It surrendered to her weight.

The den was dimly lit. A cigarette burned on an ashtray in the center of the oak desk, near a glass of scotch beaded with drops of water. "Rakesh?" She picked up several colored slips of paper, scattered on the desk's surface. They were bills, invoices and receipts.

Escape, Amsterdam...a bill for fifty euros. Bep Bar, Amsterdam...sixty-three euros. De Kroon, Amsterdam...tickets for two, Mazzo, Panama...another bill. The names went on and on. The Twilight Zone Coffee Shop, Erotic Museum... A hotel bill, the Park Plaza, Berlin, for a one-bedroom suite for two thousand euros. A second bill for the same dates of stay in another room at the same hotel for eight hundred euros. Two KLM tickets—Raigun to Amsterdam and back, both bills in Rakesh's name, stating departure dates on December the first and arrival in Raigun on December the eleventh.

She was at Mama's place at the time. Didn't Rakesh first claim he was in Amsterdam during her absence and then later deny it on the pretext of having secretly stayed home to supervise the renovations of their bedroom and her studio? Sheetal shuffled through more receipts and double purchases. *What was Rakesh up to now?*

"What are you doing here?"

Sheetal spun around as Rakesh kicked the door closed with his heel.

"I... I was looking for you. Where were you?"

He walked toward her. "Downstairs."

"I mean, in the first week of December." She held up the receipts. "When I was visiting Mama."

"None of your business."

"You told me you were here. That you cancelled the trip to renovate our room. But these receipts say you were in Holland with someone else."

He slid both hands into his trouser pockets. "What difference does that make? I'm never alone when I'm on business. Clients."

"What business, exactly?"

"I don't answer bullshit. You entered without my permission. You should be the one answering questions. Not me."

"You lied." She raised her voice to show she wasn't scared. "I want the truth."

He was two feet away and closing.

"There's another woman, isn't there?"

The left corner of his lips curled into a sneer. "And what if there is?"

Her fingers numbed, and the receipts fell onto the desk.

"All this pregnancy and snooping around like some silly detective is plain stupid. You're losing it." He gathered the sheets, walked around the desk and sat in his chair, causing it to creak. "What will you do if there is someone else?"

Fear crept through her veins. "You're lying. You're—"

"Get out."

"I won't leave until you—"

"Vipul Sahib was with me if you must know. Does that explain two of everything?"

Vipul Swampat, the oldest employee at Dhanraj & Son, had

worked with the late Ashok Dhanraj for a good twenty years. After Ashok's death, Vipul was made CFO under Rakesh's leadership.

"There's only one way to solve this. We have to stop interfering in each other's lives and start living our own."

Weren't they already leading separate lives? What did this mean? A divorce? The baby. Panic gripped her. What about the baby? It was too late to consider abortion. Where would she go at the end of her first trimester?

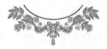

ALL FIVE DHANRAJS WERE SEATED AT THE DINNER TABLE THAT EVENING when Rakesh announced that Sheetal would move to a different room on the east wing, close to Mummyji. Sheetal would no longer have to put up with his smoking or unpredictable hours, and the move would be good for the baby.

THAT NIGHT, SHEETAL SAT AT HER DRESSING ROOM VANITY AND STARED at her reflection in the mirror. Was Rakesh moving her out because he expected her to become bloated and ugly? Is this what Shashi Behn meant when she talked about love dying? Was love based on appearance? Or—a pain fisted in her heart —had there been no love to begin with? What he'd done on her birthday was certainly no expression of love.

She threw her hairbrush on the table's surface. The prongs

hit the mirror and bounced off. Tears rolled down the sides of her face. She was in this mess because of them. All of them. She swiped an arm across the dresser, hurling bottles of perfume onto the carpet. She cupped her face and propped both elbows on the vanity's surface. She was losing her mind. Her sanity. She had to do something before she lost everything.

Sheetal picked up the phone and called Mama. She was going home for good.

Dadi picked up the phone. "Hello, Sheetal? You won't believe the good news."

Sheetal resisted the urge to raise her voice. "Can I speak to—"

"Anjali's pregnant!"

Anjali, Aunty Hemu's daughter-in-law, had moved into Mama's house two months ago with Hemu's son, Vikram.

"She's due in three months, just a little ahead of you. Which is why Hemu and I decided she should have the baby here in Raigun. And the best part is, now Hemu will get to stay even longer."

A knot formed in Sheetal's throat.

"A baby! So much excitement. So much for Hemu to do, to manage," Dadi went on. "So much responsibility once the baby arrives. And after all that is out of the way, we'll see about Hemu's return to Vilaspur."

'We'll see' meant 'we'll try and postpone.' And because Dadi was using 'we,' she was banding the Prasads and Choudharys together as one family.

"Until then...oh...oh...so much to look forward to. Now," she paused, "you called to speak to Indu?"

Sheetal couldn't breathe. What would she go home to now? Give birth to a fatherless baby and fall in everyone's eyes?

"Hello? You still there, Sheetal?" Dadi coughed. "Say something. Are you there?"

Sheetal put down the receiver. She didn't know where she was anymore.

27

THE GOOD HUSBAND

The next morning, as Rakesh headed out for work, Pushpa called to him from behind the stairs, "It's an emergency, I tell you. Meet me in the TV lounge."

Rakesh looked at his watch. He had a nine o'clock meeting with Vipul Sahib and it would take more than half an hour to get there. "I'm running late."

"I don't care. Now."

With no alternative, Rakesh headed to the TV lounge.

"I just don't understand." Pushpa shook her head. "You were supposed to get along with her, I tell you. Not kick her out the room."

"She snoops around my stuff. It's impossible!"

"I don't care how impossible," Pushpa hissed. "You shouldn't leave her alone at a time like this, I tell you. *Hai Ishwar!* What will people say? She's carrying your child. What if the Malhotras find out? What impression will they have of you? Of me? Of Naina? It's not like the old days when a woman was stuck to her husband until she died. Ask me. I know how impossible it was to find a reliable man in my time. My parents couldn't afford much, barely two meals a day. But the Prasads can afford anything they want. And they'll have Sheetal back if that's what she wants. But in my time—"

"In your time, you latched on to Papa." His voice cracked at the memory of how ruthless Pushpa'd been when she set foot in their home. Only thirteen, Rakesh was grieving Mumma's death when Papa introduced Pushpa as their new mother. Servants scurried to obey her crack-like whip-commands. Rakesh had hoped she would, at least, be gentle and caring toward newborn Megha. But kindness didn't exist in Pushpa's dictionary. "You forced your way into our home and took away—"

"I didn't force my way into anything. It was all legal, I tell you."

Rakesh took a deep breath and maintained calm. "Legally wrong. You tore my family apart."

"Your family was falling apart until I came." Pushpa's face swelled with rage. "I put everything and everyone in order. So much chaos—"

"We were doing fine. Just fine, without you." Anger clawed his heart. "You took away Mumma's memories. Every last one."

"I did what any sensible woman would, I tell you. Did what it takes to keep this family together and move everyone forward. It was my promise to Ashok. He made me swear on my dead mother's grave. But how would you know any of this when no one ever told you?" The freckles on her face darkened. "If I failed, Ashok promised to send me back to my parents' home. Penniless. Poor. With just the clothes on my back. Three years since your father died and still, every day, I keep my promise."

"He's dead. Gone." Rakesh's chest tightened. "But what about me and Megha? You keep screwing up our lives."

"I am not ruining anything. You have to live according to society. First your marriage. Then Naina's. Then Megha's."

Like she'd ever take an interest in Megha's life.

"I won't let your life fall apart for Naina's sake. I was here when you all needed me. And I am still sacrificing, managing all your lives."

Managing? Rakesh worked to calm his rage. "You're like a fucking Hitler."

"Ai-ee! Call me what you want. But one thing I've never done is run away like you and Sheetal. Or defamed the Dhanraj name. I've been loyal, faithful to this family for seventeen years, I tell you. But that doesn't mean Sheetal will be loyal. And Rana will call her back if he's the slightest bit suspicious that you are up to no good."

"He's a coward. The embarrassment will kill him. Especially now that Sheetal is—"

"Pregnant—no? I don't like this attitude of yours. You should be taking care of her. Be a good husband. Spend time with her."

And have her discover something that could give her a nervous breakdown? Then he'd risk losing her and the baby. Saliva lodged in his throat and he swallowed.

"Wait." Pushpa raised a hand. "I think I hear something." She maneuvered to the patio door, slid it open and peered outside.

The yard was empty.

28

GOING SOLO

Before Mummyji had the opportunity to assign Sheetal new accommodation, Sheetal had the servants dust and aerate a room on the south wing, two doors away from her studio. She discarded the old furniture, had the room painted pastel green and fresh beige carpet laid, bought new furniture with floral-green upholstery, bookshelves, a twenty-four-inch TV, a Sony boom box, a new wall clock, matching bed linens and several knick-knacks to spruce up the décor.

Mummyji appeared at the doorway and pumped both hands on her hips. "Didn't Rakesh say you are to move two days from now into a room close to mine?"

"With twenty-two bedrooms, surely I can choose one that I like."

"But Rakesh left instructions for—"

"I just need enough help to get set up." She was firm. "Nothing more."

"Oh yes, of course," Mummyji's voice hinted at panic, "but what will Rakesh say?"

"I'll deal with Rakesh."

Sheetal's heart swelled with pride over her new room. It was warm, beautiful, comfy, and the first time she had accomplished something on her own at the Dhanraj's. When everything was in order, she left the bills on Rakesh's desk in the den, precisely where she'd found the others. However, when she tried to sleep that night, she tossed and turned on the queen mattress. A knock on the door startled her.

"Sheetal?" Rakesh called.

Was he here to force her into a room of his choosing?

"Hey, it's me. Are you okay in there?"

She stayed put. The old Sheetal would have gone running to the door in the hope he came to make peace and beg her to return. But she knew better. Rakesh was not the type to ask forgiveness. Arvind was. Arvind would never have left her alone at a time like this or let her out of his sight. Arvind...

The name reverberated with loneliness in her heart. It had been so long since she'd thought of him. She closed her eyes to remember his face, but his image blurred.

Five more knocks followed.

Maybe he came to apologize.

Desperation filled her heart. Maybe he waited for her to open the unlocked door. All he had to do was turn the knob.

Retreating footsteps click-clacked on the marble floor.

He was gone.

Twenty-two bedrooms and not one close to home.

THE DHANRAJ MANSION BUZZED WITH ACTIVITY OVER THE NEXT MONTH as wedding planners, caterers, florists, professional sari packers, architects, beauticians and musicians arrived to meet Mummyji and finalize details for Naina's wedding.

According to Raigun rumor, Rakesh was putting together a wedding the world had never seen. Sheetal worried how much more stress this would put on her marriage, and the effect that strain would have on her and the baby.

Naina's wedding card, the first clue of what lay in store, took Sheetal's breath away. Tiny Swarovski crystals dotted the forehead of Lord Ganesh on each of the two thousand four hundred silver-embossed, silk wedding invitations. The cards were mailed by post, except for two hundred that, in accordance with custom, had to be hand delivered to family, relatives and close friends.

Away on a two-week vacation with college friends, Megha was to return a week before the wedding. With less than a month to go and two hundred invitations to deliver by hand, Rakesh, Mummyji and Sheetal were hard-pressed for time. Sheetal agreed to accompany Rakesh to several relatives' homes, including Vipul Swampat's the following Saturday.

THE SWAMPATS' FRONT DOOR SWUNG OPEN AND THE ODOR OF BURNT oil, overcooked *masalas* and garlic caused Sheetal to wrinkle her nose, turn away and cough. According to Rakesh, the Swampats maintained a decent standard of living compared with most upper middle-class families, and Rakesh had warned Sheetal to hide any signs of discomfort so as not to offend their host.

"What an honor to have you both here. Please, do come in." A gentleman in his late forties greeted Sheetal and Rakesh. The thick hairs of his gray moustache sparkled under the harsh florescent light.

"Vipul Sahib," Rakesh introduced Sheetal to the gentleman. "My wife, Sheetal."

The walls of Vipul Sahib's flat stood fifty feet apart, crowded with two double-seater sofas, a wooden coffee table and two rattan chairs. A dining table for four fit snugly against the far-right wall. Sheetal looked around and sighed, unsure how to make her way through the tiny channels between the furniture.

"Please have a seat." Vipul Sahib gestured to a sofa. "It is a tiny but humble abode," he added. "Nothing compared to what you must be used to."

Rakesh stared at Sheetal, and Sheetal lowered her gaze to the floor. She hadn't meant to be rude. But how was she to move around or sit in the cramped space without knocking into something?

"Your home is as big as your heart," Rakesh filled in the awkward silence. "Whether we sit together at Dhanraj Towers or here, you are always family."

Really? Sheetal hated herself for the thought, but their differences were striking. She took a seat, and the sofa cushion sank under her weight. She grabbed the right armrest for support, to prevent further sinking. Vipul Sahib sat opposite, and she peered past his shoulder to a corridor behind that ran for maybe ten or fifteen feet and ended at a wall. A door on each side of the hall had been left ajar. A window on the living room's left wall opened to a view of concrete pavement and several trees. The flat was like being boxed in a Rubik's Cube with a few squares knocked out for breathing space. It was all so cozy. Too cozy. Like, no matter where you sat, you'd still be cramped.

Was this the carefree life she would have shared with Arvind? A cozy nest with no frills? No trimmings? No conflict? With only two feet of space between her and Rakesh and five feet between her and Vipul Sahib, and a table squeezed between all three. Wouldn't she and Arvind have fallen short of breathing space in a home this size? She sank deeper into the cushion and squirmed to right herself, worried the sofa would swallow her. Her extra weight was probably because of the baby, she reasoned as the stench of burning spices made her insides curdle. She wanted to stand by the open window and take a breath of fresh air.

Rakesh watched her from the corner of his eye while making small talk. He leaned across the table and handed Vipul Sahib the wedding card. "I hope you and your family will come to bless the couple and grace the occasion."

"Why, of course!" Vipul Sahib nodded. "I wouldn't miss Nainaji's wedding for the world. In fact, I hear it's to be the biggest bash."

"All media hype. Nothing else." Rakesh waved a hand and crossed one leg over the other. "You know those reporters. Always need something to talk about."

Vipul Sahib thumbed open the envelope and removed the card. "It's beautiful."

A woman in an indigo sari with a red bindi the size of a marble emerged from the kitchen, and the aroma of cloves and cinnamon arrived with her. "Oh my! Such distinguished guests at our home. Namaste. What a privilege!" She pressed her hands together, bowed slightly and sat beside her husband. She fanned the pleats of her sari across her toes, her fingers tainted with turmeric, and turned to Sheetal. "Are you all right? You don't look well."

"My wife, Bina," Vipul Sahib introduced her.

"I'm fine," Sheetal said. "I... I just get bouts of morning sickness. That's all," she lied.

"Oh, yes, yes. Congratulations! Vipul told me and I read about the good news in the papers."

Apparently, everything they did appeared in the papers.

"When's the baby due?"

"Mid-October."

"Pregnancy is such a difficult time. Both our sons are all grown up now. In their twenties. But how I vaguely remember that awful morning sickness." She snatched the wedding invitation from Vipul Sahib, smudging the silk with yellow fingerprints of turmeric. "What a pretty card. So delicate and...and... Oh, my manners. I forgot to ask. Would you like some chai? Coffee or juice, perhaps?"

Her throat parched, Sheetal desperately wanted something to drink and was about to agree to a glass of juice when Rakesh rose to his feet.

"We're running late. We still have several families to visit. But thank you for the offer."

"Surely you can spare five more minutes," Vipul Sahib said. "Sheetal must be tired from being on her feet all morning with so much of the wedding responsibilities on her shoulders at such a delicate time."

Her legs ached and her feet hurt. Rakesh had his supply of cigarettes to keep him going. If she didn't speak up for herself, no one else would. "I am a little tired."

"Well then, that's settled." Vipul Sahib smiled. "Light snacks and refreshments for everyone."

"Is there a bathroom I can use?" Rakesh asked.

"Yes, of course. Here, let me show you." Bina jumped to her feet and led Rakesh through the corridor to a door on the right. Then she returned to the kitchen.

Sheetal turned to Vipul Sahib, unsure what small talk to initiate since she hardly knew him. But she had to say something; otherwise, he was bound to consider her rude and snobbish. "How was your trip to Amsterdam?"

Vipul Sahib raised his eyebrows. "Amsterdam? I've never been."

"You went in early December last year. Rakesh mentioned you had gone on a business trip together."

He frowned and shook his head. "I think you're mistaken. I was in Goa with my family, on holiday."

"I'm talking about this last December," she repeated, aware of the intensity of her tone.

"Yes, I'm sure. Absolutely sure. You look unwell, is it that morning sickness, perhaps, you were talking about?"

Sheetal bit her lip. "I must have confused you with someone else. I'm so sorry."

"Not to worry. No problem."

He was right. There wasn't a problem. There were many.
Her biggest: Rakesh Dhanraj.

WITH MEGHA DUE TO RETURN HOME ANY MOMENT, SHEETAL DARTED
to the studio window every five minutes in anticipation of the
Lamborghini's arrival. Disappointed by the vacant drive, she'd
return to her easel, pick up the brush and resume work on a
painting of a squirrel holding a nut—one in the line-up of fifty
for the December exhibition. However, she found herself
listening for the vehicle's honk or the rev of its engine, and realized her brush remained poised in mid-air.

While Mummyji and Naina had spent April and May raking
in Naina's dowry, Sheetal had helped Megha shop for a new
wardrobe, enroll in a grooming course, and decide upon a new
hair style. Megha discarded her eyeglasses in favor of contact
lenses and switched to smaller size clothing that flattered her
petit frame. Sheetal loved how Megha looked to her for guid-
ance and asked for her opinions.

The crunch of tires against gravel made Sheetal drop the
brush, rush out the door and make her way carefully downstairs.
Megha ran into her arms and the overwhelming fragrance of
lilies made Sheetal's head spin. *How much perfume did she spray?*

Megha hugged Sheetal from the side, avoiding the bulge of
her tummy. "It's so good to come home to you, Bhabhi."

Megha's aqua knitted T-shirt neatly hugged her curves, her
jeans contoured the slim length of her long legs and the stilet-

toes added two inches to her height, making her taller than Sheetal.

Sheetal pulled back and cupped Megha's cheek. Her sister-in-law's face glowed with more than make-up. A spark of joy glittered within her eyes.

"You won't believe how much fun we had! It was the most amazing..." She went on in coherent sentences with appropriate pauses and cadences.

Megha is a whole new person.

Sheetal kissed her lightly on the forehead and caught her shoulders. "You look absolutely gorgeous."

"All thanks to you," Megha whispered. "You should have seen Bhaiya at the airport. He didn't recognize me."

Mummyji emerged from the TV room minutes later followed by Naina, who carried an imported copy of *Elle Bride*, just as Rakesh entered through the front door.

"Oh, you're back." Naina smirked. "So soon and so"—she wrinkled her lips—"changed."

"Any later and I'd miss getting rid of you," Megha replied tartly.

"Now everyone come sit down for a family meeting, I tell you." Mummyji waved a hand toward the Fulton Whites and handed each person a sheet of paper as they sat down. "You all have your to-do list for the wedding, and I want to make sure we go through it together so nothing's left out."

The last two months had been all about Naina's wedding. What could possibly be left out?

"Rakesh has agreed to take a week off work to supervise the layout of the wedding ground and décor. Yes?" She turned to

Rakesh, who sat relaxed in a single seater, his elbow perched on the arm rest and a cigarette in hand.

"Hmmm." He took a drag off the Marlboro, arched his hand away, and tapped the cigarette ashes onto the floor. "I've been supervising the project since the day after our wedding. How much more do you want me to supervise the fucking ground?"

"You, Megha," Mummyji ignored the question, "are to try on your ghagra, check the fitting, and go through the guest list to make sure no one is left out."

Megha raised her eyebrows and let out a sigh. "Okay."

"That attitude, I tell you, is not okay. The little vacation you had is over and it's time to get to work," Mummyji snapped. "And you, Sheetal, are to supervise the packing of Naina's dowry. One hundred and fifty-one saris. Fifty-one salwar kameezes and thirty jewelry sets. Nothing should go missing."

Did the thirty include the Cartier set? Sheetal wanted to ask but decided it wasn't worth igniting another family argument. The sooner Naina was gone, the better.

A team of professional sari packers was expected to fly in from Mumbai the following week, and Sheetal was to supervise every garment's arrangement for the display in the dowry room. She hardly dared imagine what would happen if a jewelry set went missing. Pandemonium was an understatement. Mummyji would probably suffer a breakdown.

"And I've hired another landscaping company to turn the front lawn into a paradise. With so many guests dropping in to visit Naina, why, we must create the whole feel of a wedding, I tell you. And Sheetal, of course, you will host and manage them all."

As a way to display their affection, custom required friends and family to pamper the bride and groom-to-be with gifts of their favorite food and drink.

Sheetal pressed a hand against her tummy. *How on earth am I going to entertain a flood of guests in this condition?*

"Well?" Mummyji crossed her arms. "Won't you?"

Sheetal seethed. "Yes."

"Good." Then Mummyjii went on and on about how Naina's wedding was going to be an event people would remember for the rest of their lives and no expense should be spared.

Sheetal thought back to how excited Mama and Papa had been before her wedding. How many lists had they drawn up and distributed? How they must have planned and anguished over every tiny detail. For Mama, it was the day she'd been waiting for all her life. Papa's anxieties had focused on a determination that everything should run like clockwork. Even Preeti had been obsessed with the color and flair and a chance to be on TV. And what had she obsessed about? Arvind. Guilt grated her heart. Had she selfishly stolen the anticipation of the moment from her deserving parents?

Rakesh took a drag and blew a gray mist into the air.

Despite all the work required to put together a marriage of this magnitude, had their first year together simply gone up in smoke?

29
BLACK PAGODA

Pushpa privately confronted Rakesh that evening in the dining room. "I don't like this idea, I tell you."

Rakesh thumped his briefcase on the dining table. "What now?"

"That Black Pagoda, I tell you. It's unlucky, I am hearing. Proven to bring bad luck and—"

"It's superstition, for God's sake! Think logically. How can a monument cause bad luck? Plus, ours is only an imitation."

A blend of legend and history had led people to believe that the Konark Sun Temple, also known as the Black Pagoda, built in the thirteenth century and situated on the Bengal coastline, was the cause of every shipwreck that occurred in the region. The magnificent original, two hundred and twenty-nine feet tall structure, a golden chariot with twelve pairs of wheels pulled by seven pairs of horses, was crowned with a golden dome. This cursed magnetic dome, believed to be the cause of the tragedies, gave the structure the nickname The Black

Pagoda. Even after the dome was replaced many years later, the Sun Temple still retained its inauspicious reputation.

Because it was impossible to recreate the Konark Sun Temple, Rakesh had rented a large building at Lake Pyasi prior to his wedding and had the façade constructed and painted to replicate the majestic structure. Sheets of tarpaulin and scaffolding still skirted the temple's façade, concealing it from public view.

"I don't know. I've been hearing things and—"

"From who?"

"The servants. Everyone. They're all talking about it."

"Let them talk." Rakesh loosened the tie around his neck. *Women! Five days to go and now she gets the jitters.* "Look, people want something to talk about. It's human nature. You should be happy with all the media attention. You're getting everything you wanted."

"Choose something else, I tell you." She paced the length of the dining table. "Something safe, with no bad luck. Or harm or chance, I tell you, of—"

"You're overreacting. If I had any doubts, do you think I would have gone ahead? Just wait and see it unveiled and then you'll agree."

ALONE IN THE BEDROOM WITH A BURNING CIGARETTE IN HAND, RAKESH flopped his head back against the sofa's headrest and propped his feet on the coffee table. He had been on his feet all day, monitoring the wedding preparations. His head throbbed. He massaged his temples. *Five more days till all this shit is over.* He added pressure and his jaw relaxed with the soothing effect. The bank loan of three hundred and fifty million had been approved without a hitch. Everything progressed as planned.

The door swung open and Sheetal walked in, her gait uneven due to the weight of the baby. If she was here to talk, he didn't want to listen and end up in another argument. The last thing he wanted was to hurt her or the baby.

He faintly remembered how Mumma had ballooned in size when she carried Megha, and she had struggled to do simple things that he took for granted. He remembered ever so gently resting his head on Mumma's tummy and waiting for a tap, a kick or a sliding movement from the growing baby.

He ground his cigarette in the ashtray on the end table as Sheetal took a seat on the other end of the sofa and faced him. He closed his eyes. Maybe she'd get the hint and leave.

"I... We need to talk, and I want you to be honest."

"What now?"

"Is there another woman?"

"I really don't have time for this shit."

"I'm not leaving until I have an answer."

He slid his feet off the table, opened his eyes and sat up. "What do you think?"

"I honestly don't know. That's why I'm asking."

"Look, I don't want you getting all upset over nothing. It's for your own good."

"I know what to do for my own good. I need answers so I can stop guessing...thinking...winding myself up with the same question every night. I need to get on with my life."

So did he, and her persistence didn't help. "I've done everything possible to make it easy so you don't have to worry. Just hold tight for another week. The wedding will be over and then—"

"What were all those hotel receipts?" She gripped the sofa cushion. "Why did you lie about the whole Amsterdam trip? Why do you keep"—her expression tightened— "vanishing at night?"

Why couldn't she let it go? Why did she have to be such a snoop? Doesn't she understand the pressure I'm under? The throbbing intensified and he buried his face in his hands. *There was a fucking wedding ahead, but she just wouldn't give up.*

"Why did you really renovate my studio and the bedroom? Why did you say Vipul Sahib—"

He winced at the pressure of molar against molar. "Who the fuck do you think you are, demanding answers like you're the boss of me?"

She crossed her arms over her belly, and Rakesh swallowed. *Fuck!* He'd done it again. Let loose like a cannon. "I'm— That's not what I meant." He touched her hand, but she withdrew. "I'm under so much pressure with the loan, the wedding. And now, it's beginning to... I—"

"It's not my fault. You should have gone with something simpler. Taken out a smaller loan."

"Do you know what that would have done to Pushpa and Naina?"

"I'm so sick and tired of Naina." She was breathing hard. "Why is everything always about her? What did Mummyji mean that day when she said, knowing what it's like to have nothing? Was she from some poor family? Or—"

Rakesh shook his head. What was the point of this discussion? It could only make things worse. "Just forget about every-thing else. Focus on you, the baby, this wedding. Whatever you must to keep going." Maybe she needed to see a doctor or get help. "When's the next doctor's appointment?"

"After the wedding."

"I can go with you if—"

"I'll manage." Sheetal rose and started for the door.

An emptiness tore at his gut. "Call if you need me."

"I have. So many times. Didn't you hear?"

30
SUMMER WEDDING

On May twenty-fifth at four-thirty in the afternoon, the local TV stations interrupted their daily broadcasts to relay the unveiling of 'Typhoon Tycoon's Loudest Thunder.'

Sheets of tarpaulin slithered off scaffolding and pooled like silk around the building's perimeter. Reporters in helicopters took aerial shots of the monument. Spectators and journalists gaped at the two hundred and twenty-seven feet tall golden chariot with twenty-four wheels drawn by fourteen golden horses. Sprawled over two hundred acres of land, the Sun Temple sparkled in the afternoon sun as artificial waves lapped the lakeshore, leaving diamond-like specks glittering along the sand.

An army of guards manned the grounds of the Sun Temple, hired to prevent members of the public and media from sneaking through a corridor or past a pair of majestic golden stone lions. The public pleaded for a glimpse of one of the three inner halls—the reception, dining or dowry room—but were asked to enjoy the outside view because the wedding could be attended by invitees only.

The media photographed the three-tier, pyramidal roof and the spire crowning the monument, then focused their lenses on capturing the delicately painted, three dimensional "carvings" of animals, dancers and couples in erotic poses that comprised the exterior.

On June fifth at six-thirty in the evening, Sheetal stood at the base of the stage stairs and watched Mummyji, dressed in a white silk sari embellished with fifteen hundred Swarovski diamonds, approach the main entrance and formally greet the groom and his procession. Ajay Malhotra dismounted from a mare, straightened his gold trimmed, bronze sherwani, and stepped onto a golden footstool that faced the Sun Temple. Ajay clasped his hands together and stood tall and proud at five feet ten, his burnt-clay complexion glowing like a sunset in the cameraman's light. The entourage of Dhanrajs, Prasads, Choudharys and extended family members assembled behind Mummyji, murmured approval of the austere manner in which Mummyji applied a vertical streak of vermilion between Ajay's eyebrows, dotted the mark with dry rice and tactfully avoided bumping his beak-like nose. She then circled the puja thali clockwise to officially welcome Ajay into the family.

With the formal welcome completed, Ajay stepped off the stool and entered the Sun Temple. Mummyji followed him, then broke away and hurried to reach the audience hall's main stage. Banners of Naina and Ajay hung from the ceiling and sparkled in the chandelier's light. Twenty-feet tall windows provided a view of the courtyard, where guests aimed cameras at the walls.

At exactly eight o'clock, Naina coyly made her way up the dais dressed in a red and gold ghagra and gold jewelry studded with rubies. A dozen women followed, bearing a tray with a garland for the Varmala Ceremony.

Ajay approached from the opposite staircase, accompanied by a best man and friends who bore a matching garland on a golden tray. They joined Naina and her bridesmaids center stage. While the couple garlanded each other, guests photographed the room's interior.

When Naina's attention left Ajay, she turned toward the wedding guests, pumped her hands on her hips and marched toward the audience. Images projected onto two huge screens, to the left and right of the stage, zoomed in on her face.

Standing at the foot of the dais stairs, Sheetal half expected Naina to throw a fit. With Mummyji and Rakesh nowhere in sight, Sheetal started up the stairs, her mind racing with a barrage of excuses. *'I'm so sorry, ladies and gentleman, for that outburst,'* she could almost hear her announcement, *'but Naina's a little eccentric.'* No. Spoiled? *'Used to being the center of attention and throws tantrums when she doesn't get her way?'* Oh God, no.

At that moment, Mummyji rushed center-stage, cleared her throat and grabbed the microphone. "Your attention, please! Thank you all, I tell you, for coming." Her voice boomed between the walls draped in red and gold silk, followed by an ear-piercing electronic screech. People covered their ears. "As you can see, we are all here to celebrate the wedding of my daughter, Naina, with Ajay Malhotra." The crowd whistled as Mummyji put an arm around Naina's shoulder, whispered something in her ear and signaled for her to rejoin Ajay. "Now, as you all know, the Malhotras are well established in Calkot, and we are so happy to welcome Ajay to our family. But I've been congratulated again and again over how lucky Ajay and the Malhotras are to have Naina in their family. And who would dare to question that? After all, Naina is a Dhanraj and the name speaks for itself." She looked at the sea of people and waited. "I said, the Dhranraj name speaks—"

The crowd cheered and raised their glasses.

"Now, I know Naina will require a while to adjust to her new surroundings, like all newlyweds do. She'll make do with a home that's a fraction of the size she's been used to and, of course, that shouldn't pose any problems since I've taught her well."

The crowed murmured and shifted uneasily.

A camera zoomed in on Mummyji's face. The arches of her eyebrows almost touched her hairline, and her eyes sparkled with the ferocity of her diamond earrings. "I said, I've taught her well. And now, applause for the couple." She swept her arm to direct the audience's attention to Naina and Ajay, but accidentally whacked Naina, who hadn't yet moved. "And for your dining pleasure, I tell you, we have twenty-one types of cuisine..."

Swarms of people broke away and rushed toward the banquet hall's massive doorway before Mummyji finished.

For the grand reception, Sheetal and Rakesh took positions on the stage beside Naina while the Malhotras assembled beside Ajay. Guests formed a queue and made their way up to congratulate the newlyweds, to present their gifts and to be photographed with the couple.

Vipul and Bina Swampat joined the bride and groom, and Bina clasped Sheetal's hand. "Magnificent!" Bina looked as if she were about to explode with excitement. "It shows, it truly shows! All the love and affection you two have for Naina. What a lucky girl to have such a loving brother and Bhabhi! And you are both so modest about all you do for her."

"It was all Rakesh's efforts, planning and execution," Sheetal said.

"We did what was in our hands," Rakesh said. "Nothing more."

We? Sheetal looked at him. Was Rakesh referring to them as 'we'?

Mummyji squeezed between Sheetal and Naina and gestured for the photographer to focus on her.

Rakesh gently nudged Sheetal aside and leaned close to Mummyji. "Perhaps you should mingle with the others off-stage and spend some time with the guests."

"What for, I tell you?" she snapped. "I'm the bride's mother. I should be here."

"And shadow Naina with your bad luck?" Rakesh hissed. "Last thing we need is for something to happen to Ajay."

"Smile!" the photographer called.

Mummyji smiled broadly and held the expression until a flash lit her face. Then she whirled and strode off stage.

"You did far more than any brother would in today's time." Vipul Sahib's statement redirected their attention. "You went above and beyond, as always. Whether at home or Dhanraj Towers, you always excel."

After Vipul and Bina stepped away, Aradhna Damani approached on the arm of her husband, Akshay. A tide of guests trailed behind the pallu of her sequins-sparkling, yellow chiffon sari. The fabric clung to her voluptuous curves and fluttered as she sashayed.

Sheetal turned away and fanned the pleats of her turquoise ghagra over the bulge of her tummy as if she hadn't noticed Aradhna's approach.

"The décor. The colors," Aradhna squealed. "So fantastic! So just...wow!" She let go of Akshay's arm and grabbed Rakesh's wrist. The photographer asked them to smile, and she pressed close to Rakesh.

Fury coursed through Sheetal. Had Aradhna accompanied Rakesh to Amsterdam? Sheetal was about to pull Aradhna away when Rakesh plucked Aradhna's fingers off his wrist and stepped aside.

"I'm just glad it all came together in the end. Now, if you'll excuse me." Rakesh turned toward Akshay and made light conversation.

"And shame on you, Sheets"—Aradhna wagged a finger in the air—"for not telling anyone about this. Not even..."

Sheets? A new nickname? "I didn't know the details myself."

"So like Rakesh to handle everything on his own, considering you must be tied up with the pregnancy and all. And you didn't wait too long, did you?" She winked as the queue of people grew longer. "But you're looking happy, healthy." She scanned Sheetal from head to toe and raised an eyebrow.

Sheetal winced. Just because she was double Aradhna's size didn't give her or anyone the right to pass insults. "Look, Rakesh." She diverted Rakesh's attention to a group of ten who waited behind Aradhna and leaned close to whisper, "The Malhotra's relatives. We should invite them on stage."

"Oh yes, of course. Excuse me." Rakesh turned to the incoming tide of people, and Sheetal straightened with pride. This is what good wives did: steered their husbands in the right direction.

She searched the crowd for Mama and Papa, but her attention fell on a woman in an orange and silver ghagra.

The young woman appeared to be in her early twenties and flitted across the open floor like a butterfly. From the manner in which she attended to guests, it appeared she had hosted parties her entire life. At first, Sheetal couldn't catch a glimpse of her face, and when she did, her heart skipped a beat. *Was that really Megha?* A pang of pride and guilt washed over her. With all the focus on Naina, she hadn't had a chance to help Megha with her clothes, accessories or makeup. But from the looks of her, she didn't think Megha needed her advice anymore.

"Sheetal," Rakesh whispered, "you're ignoring the Malhotras."

Sheetal turned to a woman in a bright green sari, Ajay's older sister, and apologized.

Rakesh nudged Sheetal's elbow. "You look tired. Perhaps you should sit down."

"I can't leave with so many guests to attend. I'll be okay."

While Rakesh made conversation with Ajay's sister, Sheetal's attention drifted to several young men in the crowd. She mentally sized up several as potential suitors for Megha. The young man in the brown suit with wavy black hair? No. Too tall. What about the man in the light blue silk kurta pajama? She tiptoed for a better view. Too short. A man in a black suit and red tie with a mischievous grin wove through the crowd.

Too old. Married, perhaps? And he didn't convey the impression of a responsible husband.

Her breath caught. Is this what Mama and Papa thought with their dream that she marry a *Rajkumar*?

At that moment, Papa, Mama and Dadi arrived center stage. Dadi congratulated and blessed the couple, and a servant positioned her wheelchair between Naina and Sheetal for a photograph.

"I heard you supervised all the dowry packing," Dadi whispered.

"I had to keep a close watch," Sheetal said, "so there wasn't any chance of the jewelry—"

"Please, everyone!" the photographer called. "Look this way."

"You understand then," Dadi continued, "what it means and how hard it is to put together a life for someone and give them a new start. To bear the responsibility of their actions even though you are not responsible."

Sheetal nodded. Just last year, her dowry had meant little because she had done nothing to earn it. It simply followed and went straight into Mummyji's hands. But Naina's dowry represented Rakesh's and Ashok's hard-earned money, and hours and hours of precious time robbed from her prospective career. It was just one of the numerous expenses for which Rakesh had to pay out five hundred and fifty million rupees and take a three hundred and fifty million rupee bank loan.

The photographer gestured for everyone to stand closer. "Smile, now."

Squeezed between Rakesh and Naina, the zardozi work on Naina's ghagra pricked Sheetal's elbow. She cringed. So much glitter. So many lights. So much glamor. For what? A flash of light blinded Sheetal. She blinked, but the spots of light that interfered with her vision persisted, much like the game of deception in which they all shared blame.

AFTER THE RECEPTION, SHEETAL AND RAKESH LED NAINA AND AJAY TO their seats in an area of the dining hall cordoned off with pink ribbons. The Malhotra family and their closest friends, the Dhanraj's extended family, and the Prasads were already seated at round tables. Golden tablecloths laid with sterling silver place settings had been crowned with silver swan centerpieces. Pink roses descended the backs of the swans, and matching pink ribbons encircled the backs of silver-cloth-draped chairs.

A table for two, set atop a miniature dais, faced the guests. A pair of golden chairs plumped with pink cushions provided seating for the bride and groom. Once Naina and Ajay were comfortably seated at their table, waiters served the first course.

As immediate members of the bride's family, Sheetal, Rakesh, Megha and several other Dhanrajs were expected to ensure all VIP guests received personal attention. Sheetal left the bridal couple, lifted the skirt of her ghagra an inch so she wouldn't trip over the hem, and led a server bearing a tray of sweets toward the Malhotras' table. When she reached Mrs. Malhotra's chair, she turned to the server's tray and chose a yellow, soft buttery saffron sweet in the shape of a round pot coated on the outside with sparkling edible silver filled with gelatinous syrup and decorated with a sprig of mint. Sheetal placed the treat on Mrs. Malhotra's golden plate and waited for her to take a bite. "I hope you like the *kesar matki barfi*. We had this sweet made specially for your family."

Mrs. Malhotra looked over her left shoulder and up at Sheetal. She raised her eyebrows. Her tiny sparrow face appeared small in comparison to Mr. Malhotra's, who was seated on her right. "That's very kind of you. I hope Naina can cook a fraction of the menu. Perhaps one cuisine of the twenty-five being served tonight."

Sheetal's mind raced. "I... I think you'll be surprised by all she knows." Then she quickly inched away before Mrs. Malhotra could say more.

"I do hope you've taught her a thing or two," Mrs. Malhotra said past her husband's head.

Sheetal smiled and nodded, placed a *kesar matki barfi* on Mr. Malhotra's plate, and proceeded to make small talk with others seated at their table.

After all the VIP guests had been personally attended, Sheetal, Rakesh and Megha joined the Prasads and ate their dinner.

TWO HOURS LATER, AS SHEETAL MINGLED AMONG GUESTS ON THE OPEN grounds, a whiff of stale fish tickled her nose.

"*Hambe*. How are you?"

"Aunty Hemu. How are you?"

"I asked first. But in any case, you know me. Busy. Always busy. Sorting things for Anjali's baby and all. And you?" Her attention fixed on the baby bump. *"Hambe,* you hardly look pregnant. Can barely tell. Still, looking rather decent." Then her attention flew to Sheetal's gold and diamond choker. "Not wearing the Cartier? What a shame. I guess it was below your in-laws' standards."

Sheetal tensed. Just because they had both been Prasad daughters didn't give Aunty Hemu the right to talk down to her. If Aunty Hemu couldn't digest the family Sheetal had married into and the lavish lifestyle she now led, that was her problem. "Actually, Naina liked the Cartier so much I gave it to her as a wedding gift. It's in the dowry room. You should hurry before they close it. Unless, of course, they don't allow you in."

Aunty Hemu's posture slackened, her jaw dropped and Sheetal savored the moment. It felt good to get even.

AT THE AUSPICIOUS HOUR OF TWO IN THE MORNING, NAINA AND AJAY took their pheras under a mandap of the finest ruby-red silk, beneath a clear sky of glittering stars. They perambulated the havan seven times as priests chanted one vow in Sanskrit for each phera: to earn a living and respect their abundance...to live for each other...to be concerned for the other's happiness. Naina led Ajay, while the swirls of embroidery decorating the lower third of her ghagra sparkled in the firelight with each addition of ghee. On the seventh and final round, the couple switched places and vowed to love each other forever.

Seated on Rakesh's left, Sheetal nudged his elbow. "We

took those pheras just a year ago." And then he'd raped her. "Ten days until our anniversary."

His attention remained angled toward his right knee.

Sheetal leaned close to see what held his attention and a flutter, like the gentle stroke of a brush on canvas, pushed outward against the wall of her tummy.

The baby kicked!

"Rakesh, you hear me?" She saw the Blackberry in his hand and her chest tightened. "The baby kicked again. Just now."

"What?" He shifted the phone from view as if he hid something.

Her throat tightened. Oh, they were blessed with abundance, all right. Servants, chauffeurs, wealth beyond belief...and an abundance of lies and deceit.

AN HOUR LATER, NAINA AND AJAY MALHOTRA WERE DRIVEN TO THE Plaza, Raigun's most classy hotel, where the Malhotras and their entourage of five hundred had been accommodated at the Dhanraj's expense. Both relatives and newlyweds were scheduled to fly to Calkot tomorrow morning aboard a private jet.

Per Mummyji's instructions, Sheetal arrived at Naina and Ajay's hotel room promptly at seven the next morning ready to help Naina dress, but muffled bickering between Mummyji and Naina's elderly mother-in-law wafted through the closed door. Before Sheetal could knock, the hall door swung open. Mrs. Malhotra bolted out and slammed the door, her sparrow face tight.

"Is everything all right?" Sheetal asked.

At four feet nine, dressed in a magenta *sari*, Mrs. Malhotra, a frail, bony woman crossed her wiry arms and paced the corridor. "Exactly why I went in to check in the first place. Naina's been in bed all morning, and Ajay can't get the girl on her feet. Ajay thought she was sleeping but then realized she wasn't responding. I told Pushpaji to call a doctor, but she went on about how Naina's exhausted from the wedding. Well, so are we." She spun on her heels and reversed direction. "Everyone's been on their feet. But then Pushpaji went on about how Naina goes into these quiet phases because she's still grieving her dead father or something. You're Naina's Bhabhi. What do you know about all this?"

Sheetal pressed her tongue against her cheek. What was she supposed to say without jeopardizing everything when Naina had relapsed thrice in the last year?

"Well?" Mrs. Malhotra pressed.

"I haven't seen her act in this manner." The lie rolled off her tongue with ease, and mimicked Mummyji's voice. "I guess this wedding really has been too much for Naina. She's very delicate, you know. All of us are used to peace and calm. Poor girl's probably collapsed from fatigue."

Mrs. Malhotra's jaw dropped, and she frowned. Her posture slackened.

It worked!

Bacause Naina was moving to another state and city, the formality of Rakesh bringing Naina home after the wedding had to be dispensed with. So, seven hours later, Naina was carried aboard the chartered flight on a stretcher as Mummyji handed Mrs. Malhotra a brown medical bag. Mrs. Malhotra opened the zipper, glanced inside, then sealed the bag shut again.

"Nothing to worry about, I tell you. It's a bag of vitamins. Naina takes three every night. Just make sure she gets lots of rest and relaxation to recover. It could easily be several weeks before she's on her feet."

Mrs. Malhotra turned to Sheetal in shock, and Sheetal turned away.

Two hours later, after everyone had boarded, the airplane raced down the runway, sliced through the afternoon sky, and disappeared into the clouds.

Sheetal took a deep breath and exhaled. At last! Naina was gone for good.

31
WATERWORKS

After the wedding, Sheetal was delegated to clean Naina's room because Janvi, the only servant allowed into the families' bedrooms, was busy with post-wedding duties.

When Sheetal entered Naina's room, the stench of insect repellant caused her to take a step back. Crushed dupattas and salwar suits lay tossed on the bed. Cases of blush-on, lipsticks, eyeshadows, colorful hair pins, butterfly clips and crumpled wads of tissue littered the carpet. The duvet lay rolled up in a corner beside the sofa.

Sheetal opened Naina's closet door, hoping to find some sense of order. However, virtually every hanger had been stripped of clothing and garments littered the lowest shelf.

Sheetal's head spun. She leaned against the door jamb. How was she supposed to rearrange a chaos of this magnitude with a tummy the size of a watermelon? Did Mummyji know what a mess this room was before she added it to Sheetal's list?

Sheetal sighed, half-sank into a crouch and picked up litters of tissue, hairclips and cosmetics strewn over the floor. She mounded them on the dresser until the carpet was clear. Then she separated the tangle of dupattas and organized them into piles, folded salwar suits, straightened the bedsheets and spread the duvet. She was about to tuck in the sides when an ache in her feet shot up to her calves and thighs. Exhausted, she sat on the mattress's edge and looked at her feet, puffed like two bread rolls. A shiny orange pill on the carpet caught her attention. She knelt, grabbed it and placed it on her palm. 'Elavil-40' was printed in white letters on one side.

Sheetal tossed it into a waste basket, then replaced clothes on hangers and organized the cupboard. She opened a drawer to stash the hair clips when another orange tablet rolled to the front right corner. Curious, she opened the drawer wider. Four white plastic bottles labeled 'Elavil' stood at the back. Sheetal picked up one and read the directions. 'Take three every night after dinner.' Was this what Mummyji referred to when she handed Naina's bag of vitamins to Mrs. Malhotra?

THAT EVENING, SHEETAL ASKED RAKESH ABOUT THE ELAVIL, BUT HE shrugged and suggested it was probably some diet fad. Megha said she wasn't aware Naina was on medication and suggested she might have started birth control pills. Finally, Sheetal asked Mummyji.

"Orange pills? Oh, yes, yes. I...well..." Her face filled with crinkles. "Vitamins. That's right! For Naina's health. So weak she is, I tell you. But you shouldn't waste your time on such trivial things."

That night, Sheetal did a quick google search on Rakesh's laptop in the den.

TEN DAYS LATER, ON JUNE FIFTEENTH, SHEETAL WOKE AT SUNRISE AND began her day earlier than usual. She wanted to keep the evening free so she and Rakesh could celebrate their first wedding anniversary. Though Rakesh hadn't mentioned dinner reservations, Sheetal suspected he planned a surprise dinner at Chalet, their favorite restaurant. For certain, Rakesh had something up his sleeve—he always had something up his sleeve—especially considering he'd surprised her with the art exhibition. Which is why she'd secretly bought a new, western-style maternity dress for the occasion.

In her studio, Sheetal surveyed paintings of still-lifes, waterfalls, snow-covered lodges in the Himalayan foothills, lush forests of flora and fauna and wave-crested seashores left to dry against a wall. The works were the best she'd done so far, but what if they weren't good enough for the exhibition? *Believe what you see, not what you think you see*, Rakesh's words filled her thoughts. Right.

She reached for a white canvas, centered it on the easel and took a deep breath. No more worrying about what was done. She had to get on with what lay ahead. She dabbed a brush into green and brown paint and raised the loaded bristles to the upper third of the canvas. Mountains? No. Not today. A lake? She lowered the brush. Tomorrow, perhaps.

She'd settled on a scene she'd been thinking about for several days now when Mummyji halted in the doorway, panting.

"Happy Anniversary! I'll be at the club if you need me, I tell you." She waved her fingers and dashed off, the trail of her white sari sparkling in the light.

Well, that didn't take long.

Sheetal shook her head, mentally positioned a deer and fawn on the blank canvas and began painting. An hour later, the phone rang. Her heart flipped. *Rakesh?*

"Happy Anniversary, Beti!"

It was Papa.

"Thank you," Sheetal replied before Mama's voice filled the speaker.

Sheetal still talked to Mama two or three times a week, and though Mama had invited her to visit on several occasions, Sheetal refused, reasoning that she must have all fifty paintings ready before she gave birth.

"So, how are you planning to celebrate?" Mama asked.

"I don't know."

"Perhaps Rakeshji has planned a surprise party."

Normally, Sheetal would have been thrilled at the idea, but the thought of waddling about like a duck while other women flitted around Rakesh like butterflies soured her mood. She could barely stand for more than half an hour and had to take frequent breaks to ease the pressure on her feet. She imagined sitting with her feet propped up all evening while Rakesh danced with other women. What if Aradhna came? Bile rose in her throat and she swallowed. How could she expect a man as stunning as Rakesh to like her, to want to be with her, when she couldn't stand herself?

The phone rang at five that evening, and Sheetal answered before the second ring. *It had to be Rakesh.* She had enough time to shower, change and meet him at six. "Hello?"

"Happy Anniversary!" It was Uncle Ashwin from New Jersey, U.S.A.

"Thank you." Sheetal calculated the time difference. "It must be early morning for you."

"Very early. But any later and we'd miss wishing you because I'm sure you'll be tied up with a party or some sort of celebration."

"We're going out for dinner with friends," she lied.

Around seven, Sheetal was about to begin work on a second painting when the phone rang. She stiffened. *What was the point in answering?*

What if Rakesh had got held up in a meeting and was finally able to call? She pushed the answer button just as the ringing stopped. Caller ID showed an unknown number.

Did Rakesh not remember? How could he have forgotten when she'd reminded him at Naina's wedding? And where was he? At dinner with clients? At a bar? Graffiti's? She gulped and brushed away the thought.

At ten-thirty, Sheetal couldn't take the loneliness anymore. She called Mama. Naina's wedding fanfare was over. She was going home tomorrow whether Mummyji agreed or not.

THE FRAGRANCE OF FLOWERS BLOOMING IN MAMA'S LAWN HELPED calm Sheetal's anger, but something about home had changed. She ran her fingers along the frames of paintings mounted on the walls of the Prasad mansion. The wood felt rough and chipped, and the odor of stale fish lingered in the corridor.

Sheetal took a deep breath and hurried to escape the smell, but the odor seemed to grow stronger as she neared her bedroom. Was something rotting inside? She swung open the door just as Mama appeared at the corridor's end.

"You can't go in, Sheetal!" Mama called. "It's—"

"How dare you barge in?" A mousy-looking woman with a sharp nose, pinched lips and a scarf around her head looked up in shock. Anjali rocked an infant in her arms while seated on a king-size bed. A baby changing station and crib filled the area where her workstation used to stand. Huge black cupboards blocked the balcony door, and several chairs had replaced her dresser. "Where's my stuff?"

"It's my room," Anjali yelled.

The baby startled and cried.

Sheetal looked around, convinced she'd entered the wrong room, but she'd made no mistake. This was all Aunty Hemu's doing!

"How dare you take my room?" She raised her voice.

"Look, you've upset her now." Anjali rocked the baby and gave Sheetal a look of warning.

"I'm so sorry, Anjali." Mama touched Sheetal's arm, ushered her out, closed the door then led Sheetal down the corridor. "I was going to tell you, but—"

"Tell me what?" Sheetal snapped.

"Vikram and Anjali preferred your room over the others and moved in after Naina's wedding."

"Why didn't you tell me?"

"I didn't want to upset you."

"And this isn't upsetting me now? There are so many rooms. Why mine?"

"It's what they liked best."

Anger surged anew. "This isn't a hotel, Mama. You can't just let people walk in and choose whatever room they want."

"I tried. I showed them others, but they insisted on yours."

"You mean it's what Aunty Hemu wanted." *Was this Aunty Hemu's way of getting even for the comment at Naina's wedding?*

"Your grandmother finalized it all. She—"

Sheetal didn't want to hear any more and was about to leave but hesitated. Where would she go? How did this happen again? First kicked out of her bedroom at the Dhanrajs's and now here. She stormed out and made her way down the corridor, unsure where she was going. She just needed to be alone for a while to make sense of it all.

"I tried to reason with your grandmother"—Mama followed—"but there was no changing her mind."

The weight of the baby and the ache in Sheetal's feet forced her to slow.

"It wasn't my fault. You know your grandmother is in charge here."

Twenty-three years later and Dadi was still in charge. Would anything ever change?

"I even told them you might be coming to stay if you have the baby here...but you have to understand—"

"What more do I have to understand?" Her throat choked

with hot breath. "That I'm a liability because of how much you had to spend on my wedding? That even when you didn't have money ten—fifteen years ago, you still spent it on some coloring book I wanted? And you didn't have the heart to tell me no then. But you and everyone can say and get away with whatever you want now?"

Mama's face paled. "That was a lie."

Sheetal leaned against a wall for support. "What? What's a lie? Rakesh? The Dhanrajs?"

"That we went hungry one night because of the coloring book. I made that up, and I know I shouldn't have."

Sheetal stared at Mama in disbelief. "So, you didn't starve. You lied?"

"To... I had to say something, anything, to keep you at your in-laws and maintain the peace."

Mama chose peace over her?

"I love you, Sheetal. I care and worry about you all the time. But you have to understand, you don't live here anymore."

The words cut through her heart. "Well, that explains everything. Those who live here are the ones that count."

"It's got nothing to do with—"

"All you had to do was take my side and say no."

The pointed tip of Aunty Hemu's head appeared at the landing, and Mama ushered Sheetal into a nearby room. The white walls bore scratches and scrapes from the corners of furniture. Cobwebs draped a ceiling fan, and a panel of windows overlooked the front lawn and Rosewood Street. "They could have easily managed with this room. Or the one next door."

"What could I say to Hemuji when—"

"It's because you say nothing that the Choudharys moved in and nobody lets you say anything. It's precisely why I'm stuck in that family with Rakesh."

The crinkles around Mama's eyes tightened and she closed the door. "You're stuck there because of your own stupidity. You sneaked out to meet Arvind when we specifically told you not to. At the Broken Fort."

How did Mama know?

"Rakesh saw you that day with Arvind."

"Rakesh?" *How was that possible?*

"Yes, and he told us everything."

"You believed him? And you knew all along the Dhanrajs were—were..." She couldn't think of a word to describe them. "And you still married me to—"

"Consider this. After you met Arvind, Rakesh was still gracious enough to take you as his wife. Be grateful."

Like Mama was because Papa had married and rescued her? Was Rakesh now a savior?

Sheetal's head throbbed. She was going to be sick. Why had Rakesh been spying on her in the first place? "We were just friends. Good friends. I've told you—"

"Rakesh saw everything, and he still married you."

"Why do you think he did?"

"To save you."

"From what?"

"Yourself. Your own foolishness. He saw a chance to give you a future. A home. A family. Stability."

Her insides felt like jelly. Just because a girl married didn't mean she acquired stability. Helping to groom Megha, that was helping a woman find independence and blossom. Besides, this wasn't about saving her. It was about Mama and Papa saving themselves from the shame of a crime she hadn't committed. It was a kiss. One harmless kiss. But according to them, one kiss apparently meant she was tainted. Damaged goods. "I can't believe you chose to believe him over me."

"What else were we supposed to believe?"

"You could have asked me."

"Asked you what? You disobeyed us despite everything. Rakesh offered to marry you. What choice did we have but to agree?"

"And you agreed, knowing the Dhanrajs were messed up?"

"You left us no choice."

"Everyone has choices. It just depends on the ones you make. Now I understand why nothing's ever right. Because it was never right to begin with." She stared at her reflection in the pools of Mama's eyes. "Whenever I try and tell you my life is complicated and I'm not happy, you say happiness is a state of mind. How I choose to feel. You put me in this state, Mama. You chose your happiness over mine and now expect me to find happiness in this mess? How am I supposed to love a husband who's working against me?" A secret. Isn't that what he'd used against her on the first night?

"Rakeshji put together an exhibition for you. You're having his baby. Doesn't that mean you love him and things are fine between you?"

Having a baby didn't incubate time for relationships to stabilize. "He had me moved to another room. I'm alone."

"What?" Mama blinked. "Why didn't you tell me?"

"According to you and Papa, he saved me from myself. The Dhanrajs are mad. All of them. I tried to tell you so many times and called you for help. But you didn't listen. You plugged me there. You lied, Mama."

Mama gulped and leaned against the wall. "I'm so...sorry. I don't know what to say." Tears coursed down her cheeks. "I'll do whatever you want. I'll call Pushpaji and speak to her. Or Rakeshji and—"

"It's too late. Just because Papa saved you doesn't mean Rakesh saved me. He hurt me. But that's not all. He's using us for something. I need to find out what."

Dr. Joshi unplugged the stethoscope from her ears and helped Sheetal sit up. "Everything seems normal. You should prepare for the baby any day now."

Sheetal swiveled until her feet dangled above the footstool and pressed both hands against the sides of her tummy. "This weighs a ton! I wish it was out."

Over the last two months, Sheetal was surprised at her body's ability to balloon beyond comprehension and was convinced that if she expanded another inch, she'd explode.

The nurse drew aside the curtains that separated the examination area from the office.

Sheetal slid off the examination table, sat opposite Dr. Joshi, rummaged in her purse, and pulled out a small, transparent polythene bag. "Can you tell me what these are?"

Dr. Joshi took the bag, slipped on her glasses and examined the contents. "Are you on them?"

"Oh no! They dropped from a friend's purse," she lied. "I was just wondering."

"They're anti-depressants. Does your *friend* have a history of clinical depression?"

"Not that I know of." Naina wasn't on a diet; she was chronically sick. "What exactly is clinical depression? What's the cause?"

"A persistent low mood that affects your everyday life. A number of factors are believed to increase the risk of getting it, such as an imbalance of chemicals or hormones in the brain. Genetic factors are possible causes. In most cases, it's triggered by life-changing events like bereavement or separation due to loss of a loved one. Sometimes it's the effect of another illness, stress or an unstable home environment."

Perhaps Mummyji was right about Ashok's death affecting Naina. "How can you tell if someone has depression?"

Dr. Joshi handed Sheetal the bag. "There are a variety of symptoms. The most common is a persistent low mood. Feelings of worthlessness. Patients often lose interest in life. They no longer seem to enjoy things they once did, like hobbies and recreation. They may become irritable." She removed her glasses and lay them on the table. "Physical symptoms like poor sleep, impaired memory and an inability to concentrate are common, along with drastic changes in appetite and weight gain or weight loss."

Naina was underweight, for sure. Irritable. And always in a foul mood. And she'd never shown an interest in anything besides marriage and her dowry. "Some of what you said describes my friend. Does that mean, if she still has the symptoms, that the medication isn't working? Or should she consider other types of treatment?"

"Mmmm..." Dr. Joshi tapped a thumb on the desktop. "It's possible the dose is wrong. Another drug might be more suitable for her. Or perhaps she's not taking her medication regularly. Many people stop treatment after a few weeks or months because they think they're fine. They appear fine. But then they relapse and fall into depression again."

Phases. Isn't that what Mummyji called them? Perhaps Naina was fine when she was on Elavil but fell into depression when she went off.

"Many patients find counseling helpful because medication alone isn't enough. Is your friend consulting a psychiatrist or counselor?"

"I don't think so. I don't know. How serious can it get?"

"It's beyond my expertise, but psychological and social support management can help stabilize the patient. But the feeling of sadness, it's like a sinking feeling, from what I've heard. It can be so severe, the patient contemplates or has recurring thoughts of suicide or death." She looked at Sheetal warily. "Does that sound like your *friend*?"

"She keeps to herself a lot, so I can't really say."

"Unfortunately, in our society, having any type of mental illness is a stigma. People do what they can to hide it. Maybe that's why she's never brought it up."

"Maybe." *Did that mean Mummyji had lied to the Malhotras and the world about Naina? How long could the charade continue?*

"You're sure you're not on these?"

"No, but thank you."

"No problem." Dr. Joshi appeared slightly relieved. "Take

care. The baby can come any day now. Remember to call my mobile if you can't reach me at the office."

THE NEXT DAY, SHEETAL WAS AT WORK ON HER FORTY-SEVENTH painting when a wave of pain rode up her lower back. The pain had begun as a tiny ache and persisted for an hour, but Sheetal had been uncomfortable for weeks. Now, however, it felt as if someone had rammed a doorknob into her back and twisted the handle tighter with every passing minute.

Megha walked in. "Have a minute to talk?"

Sheetal didn't have a spare minute. She needed to finish three more paintings. Once the baby was born and the forty-day confinement that followed ended, she'd have less than a week before the paintings had to be delivered to the exhibition hall. The last thing she wanted was Rakesh thinking she'd failed to meet his expectations yet again. This opportunity was her one chance to prove her worth.

"It's urgent." Megha sat on the sofa and patted a cushion.

Sheetal put down the brush and joined Megha. "Go ahead."

"Something's been nagging at me for days." Megha knotted the end of her T-shirt. "It's personal and I...I haven't told anyone."

A torque, like an electric shock, rode up her back and around her belly. Sheetal squeezed her fingers into fists and locked them by her side, taking deep breaths.

"Bhabhi? You listening?"

Sheetal cradled the underside of her belly, but another

spasm worked its way up. They were coming faster, harder and driving deeper, burning her insides. She gasped and grabbed the sofa's edge.

"There's this...at college...and I think I—"

"Go on, I'm listening." She took a deep breath, but now the pain was a knife slicing her apart.

"I think I'm—"

A sear-wrenching pain tore at her gut. She squeezed the cushion and grabbed Megha's hand. "Get me to the hospital now. My water broke."

32
BABY BABY

At seven twenty-five in the morning, on October tenth, Dr. Joshi emerged from the delivery room and joined the Prasads and Dhanrajs in the hospital lounge. "Congratulations, everyone! It's a boy."

"A boy." Pushpa smiled from ear to ear. "A boy! Why, I tell you, a boy."

Rana put a hand on Rakesh's shoulder. "Congratulations! You're a father, my son. A father."

Warmth spread through Rakesh's body as both families congratulated each other, filling the waiting room with cheers and excitement. He couldn't believe it. He was a father. Father to a baby boy. His baby. His boy. His heart melted. "How is Sheetal? Can I see her?" he asked Dr. Joshi. "And the baby? Can I see the baby?"

"Soon enough. She's being taken to her room now so it might be another hour or so. The nurses are on their way to the nursery to weigh and clean the baby."

Rakesh remembered like it was yesterday. He had visited Mumma at the hospital and peeked through folds of the pink blanket in her arms. Megha's face was scrunched up like a delicate sponge ball of wrinkled skin, and she looked like an old man. Mumma laughed and said the baby's skin would smooth out in a day or two. Then Mumma had promised to come home soon, but she never did.

"How long before I can see her?" he asked, and instantly regretted doing so. What if he visited Sheetal and lost her, too? Fear clawed at his heart. He couldn't live knowing he'd hurt Sheetal. And the baby? He numbed. The baby would have no mother and he would be at Pushpa's mercy. Saliva lodged in his throat and he swallowed. He couldn't do this to them.

33
BABY BLUES

A gentle bleating filled the air. Sheetal squeezed her eyes shut, but the crying persisted. She rolled onto her side, away from the noise, but spasms of pain shot across her lower back and spread to her pelvis.

"Mrs. Dhanraj?" a woman, a stranger, called. "Your baby is hungry."

Sheetal rolled onto her back again, rubbed her eyes, and a metal trolley crystallized in her vision. A nurse in a white uniform approached with a blue bundle in her arms. "Would you like to try nursing him now?"

She raised onto her elbows, but a blanket of pain pressed against her chest and pelvis, and her thighs burned as if on fire.

"Here, let me help."

A buzzing sounded, followed by several clicks, and Sheetal's upper torso inclined with the rising mattress. The nurse placed the bundle in the crook of Sheetal's elbow and helped adjust its position until Sheetal was comfortable. Carefully, Sheetal lifted away the fabric from the baby's face and her heart leapt at the heart-shape ball of dough, the size of a clenched fist. Two tiny slits for eyes. A thumbnail-sized knob for a nose. A pair of pastel-pink threads for lips. The baby opened his eyes and two dots of black, like bindis, looked straight at her. His lips parted, and a cry lifted from the soft petal-pink curves, causing an ache to well in Sheetal's chest. She rocked him. She parted the overlapping folds of fabric and counted his fingers and toes that jutted like minute strings of dough. Five. Five. Ten. Perfect. She measured his thumb against hers, a fraction. The cuticle alone was equivalent to a beauty spot on her hand. Sheetal traced the side of his face and the curve of his shoulder, just visible behind peaks of his white one-piece, overcome with an instinct to shield him. She snugged her hold and inhaled the milky-soft fragrance seeping from the blanket. He was perfect! Perfect in every way.

The baby sucked on his fist and, worried, Sheetal turned to the nurse.

"I think you're ready. Do you want to try?"

Like most Indian mothers, Sheetal had decided to breast-feed her child. "I don't know how to."

"Not to worry, that's why I'm here." The nurse helped Sheetal release the top buttons of her nighty, peeled back her collar and nudged Sheetal to raise her elbows, thus bringing the infant closer to her breast.

The infant turned his face toward her, mouth open, and Sheetal plunged the aureole between his petal soft lips. A warm tingle filled her chest. An inner tsunami spilled as his tiny cheeks pumped furiously, and a pearly white drop seeped from the corner of his lips.

Sheetal finished nursing the baby, buttoned her nighty and visitors, who had been waiting outside, flooded the room with flowers, balloons, laughter and a tirade of congratulations. The door opened and closed for the next two hours as friends and family walked in and out. Sheetal peered through the gaps of moving bodies for a glimpse of the outside corridor. Rakesh was nowhere in sight.

TWO HOURS LATER, THE CROWD DWINDLED TO A TRICKLE AND dispersed. Sheetal asked the nurse to leave the sleeping baby in the bassinet with her for the afternoon before the nurse had a chance to whisk him off to the nursery.

Sheetal was about to relax against the mattress when a light knock on the door made her sit up. "Come in."

The door swung open bringing in a gust of mint and tobacco. Rakesh stood in the open doorway.

So, it took half a day for him to finally visit? Sheetal crossed her arms. From the stench, he must have smoked an entire pack of cigarettes just to ramp up the courage.

His shoulders hunched and one hand rammed into the pocket of his Chinos. He entered. "How are you feeling?"

Is that all he had to say after nine hours? How was a woman supposed to feel after carrying a child for nine months, followed by fifteen hours of labor, knowing all too well her husband could be out flirting with some other woman? A rush of heat spiraled up her gut. She was ready to explode.

"May I?" He pulled a chair from the opposite wall, dragged

it around the medicine trolley, scraping metal against floor and caused a loud screech.

Sheetal winced, and the baby stirred. "Sit wherever you want. You're paying for all this."

Rakesh circled the bed and examined the baby as if he were a finished product. He nodded and returned to the chair. "He's beautiful. Our son." He wrapped his fingers around Sheetal's hand, but she pulled away.

"What's pickling you now? Every time I come near or try to be nice, you back off."

"Every time?" She stared. "How many times have you tried to come near me in the last six months?"

He shook his head. "You're impossible."

"Impossible when I'm kicked out of my room. Forced to live somewhere else. Impossible when I give birth to another human being and don't know where the father is."

"I was outside with the others in the waiting room."

"I'm talking about the last nine months, not the last nine hours."

"There were reasons."

"Of course, there's a reason. There's always a reason for everything."

"If you didn't snoop around my den or—"

"I wasn't snooping."

His fingers tapped the chair's armrest in waves. "Looking for evidence to hold against me. Is that it?"

"People look for evidence when they're suspicious. I was simply trying to find you. Talk to you. But you're so wrapped up in hiding this...this affair of yours—"

His expression stiffened. "I don't know what you're talking about."

"Your trip to Amsterdam with Vipul Sahib. He was never with you. He told me himself. He was in Goa with family, on holiday. I checked—"

"You what?" Rakesh jumped to his feet and the chair screeched against the floor. The baby cried. "You dared to question him about me? *Besharam!* Do you even know what a fool you've—"

"I didn't mean to. It's not like I was trying to find evidence against you. We're married. I trusted you—or, at least, I tried to."

"Sweet! I organize an art exhibition. I step in and take your side when Naina insults you. Tell me, what man protects his wife the way I do?"

Her insides boiled. "You're not protecting anyone. You didn't think I'd find out about Vipul Sahib, but I did."

"You know nothing."

Sheetal reached across to the bassinet, scooped the baby into her arms and rocked him. "You should leave."

"You deserve to be alone." His tone was hard. "You've turned my life into a fucking hell!"

"And you spend all your time hiding. Isn't that why you moved me out of the room? Because you're hiding—"

"You want the truth? All right, have it then. I am. On purpose. Want to know why?"

Sheetal held her breath and tightened her grip on the baby as the medicine trolley blurred. "It's not true. You don't mean it." Hot tears rolled down her cheeks.

"It's what you wanted, right? Maybe now you'll fuck off!"

Sheetal gulped. "That night on Diwali when we made love. The painting, Dawn at Dusk, and all those evenings we spent together. Doesn't that mean anything?"

He made for the door. "You've left nothing between us."

"Who is this other woman?"

The hospital door opened and Mummyji rushed in. "Is everything all right? I heard the two of you— *Hai Ishwar!*" She grabbed the crying infant from Sheetal and turned to Rakesh. "Just look at what you've done. A woman gives you the perfect family. A son. And what do you do? Make a mess of it all."

"She gets worked up over nothing."

"You should leave." Mummyji circled the bed to reach the bassinet.

"I shouldn't have come in the first place." Rakesh left and slammed the door.

"These men, I tell you," Mummyji said. "They just don't understand. At least Anand will grow up to be better than him."

"Who's Anand?"

"Why, the baby, of course." Mummyji lay the infant in the bassinet and rocked it gently.

"I didn't know you had decided on a name."

"I called the pundit a few hours ago."

It was considered inauspicious to decide on a baby's name until after birth. Mummyji had obviously consulted the family priest—who used the configuration of stars and planets at the time of birth to determine the newborn's initials.

"Isn't that what the two of you were arguing about, I tell you? The name? I filled the birth certificate an hour ago."

Sheetal raised her eyebrows. "Who decided on Anand?"

"Why me, of course." Mummyji beamed. "The pundit said his name must begin with 'A,' I tell you. And I thought, Anand, a little happiness, would do you both some good."

"And you didn't think to ask me?"

"Why, I didn't think you'd mind."

"Well, I do."

Two days later, Sheetal had a new birth certificate drawn up for the baby with the name 'Yash,' meaning success.

ON OCTOBER FIFTEENTH, SHEETAL RETURNED HOME WITH YASH AND was welcomed by the family and additional maids, hired to cater to hers and Yash's needs.

A newborn and mother were considered unclean and impure for forty days after the birth and were forced to adhere to a strict set of rules. Anyone who touched their utensils, bed sheets or clothing were considered unclean and had to bathe before touching anything in the house. Sheetal and Yash, quarantined in Sheetal's new room on the south wing, limited the post-partum filth that would otherwise have spread in the vicinity.

It was hard to believe that the room she had cleaned and redecorated was now a prison. Her books and magazines had been removed from the shelves along with the TV because any activity that required a new mother to focus and concentrate immediately after childbirth was believed to tax the brain and slow down her recovery at a time when she was considered to be at her weakest and most vulnerable. Hot, fluffy chapatis and curries were replaced with porridge and herbal remedies flavored with dry turmeric, ginger, and loaded with saturated fats, thought to help the new mother with the production of milk and to ward off infections.

Morning sunlight spilled through the windows, stretched across the carpet and bed, and Sheetal couldn't believe the celebration of motherhood, a new chapter in her life, could curdle like sour milk so soon. She nursed Yash, then showered and changed into fresh clothes. A maid massaged Yash with warm olive oil, bathed and changed him, then Sheetal nursed Yash again until he fell asleep.

Lunch was wheeled up to her room, followed by another round of nursing, after which Sheetal took her afternoon nap. She spent her evenings talking to Mama on the phone, playing with Yash and listening to Megha waffle about her day at college. Occasionally, Mummyji's friends visited and clogged the remainder of her day with gossip she didn't want to hear. The latest, according to Mrs. Damani, was news of Aradhna's pregnancy. Aradhna was in her first trimester, and Sheetal hoped the woman ballooned to triple her size and stayed like that forever.

Sheetal marked each passing day on her calendar with a red X. In mid-November, she marked Diwali with a bolder X because she was still under house arrest, unable to join the family celebrations. Yash's first Diwali and, aside from several shiny wrapped gifts, all they got was a *diya* on the windowsill to commemorate the day.

After X-ing out the twenty-eighth day of confinement, Sheetal threw the red marker on the floor. It had been four weeks since her imprisonment and Rakesh hadn't visited once.

She was in this position because of him. In confinement because of him, and he was free!

Sheetal sat on the bed's edge and the mattress sank beneath her weight. She straightened and the foam padding dipped deeper as if dropping her into an abyss.

Then Yash cried. Sheetal turned to look at him. His hands flailed the air above a sea of cushions and bolsters that padded him on all sides, and her screams bounced off a vacuum insulated panel blocking her mind. Her heart fisted in her throat, and pins and needles pricked her gut. *Pick up the baby*, a voice said, but she couldn't.

Moushmi Kaki, a nanny, rushed in, picked up Yash and swung him gently. She cooed and whispered, rocking him to sleep while pacing the corridor outside.

Sheetal's heart sank as the crying subsided. Yash was fine and didn't need her. Mummyji was fine, too, and didn't need her, either. Rakesh had never wanted her. Even Arvind had moved on with his life, just like Mama and Papa and Megha and Naina. They were all moving forward while she had reached a stand-still. The ticking of the wall clock deafened her. Nothing mattered. She didn't matter.

She rose to her feet, removed her purse from a cupboard and fished for a bottle of Elavil she had secretly taken from Naina's drawer. She spilled several tablets into her palm, ran her thumb over the orange-coated skins and savored the slick, hard shells. Didn't Naina spend weeks on bedrest, confined to her room? Weren't meals wheeled up on a metal trolley? If three a night was good enough for Naina, perhaps four or five would do the trick.

Sheetal spread her fingers apart and the tablets fell and

bounced on the carpet. She looked at her hands, her fingers, her cuticles, and touched herself. No one had touched her in almost a month. Maybe they couldn't see her. Maybe she was invisible. What if—her gut tore from within—what if she *didn't* exist?

She pinched herself and a sharp sting travelled up the length of her arm. She felt it. She must be real. Alive. She picked up the tablets, dropped them back in their bottle and took a small breath. She didn't need Elavils.

She just needed to die.

THE FOLLOWING AFTERNOON, THE CREAK OF THE OPENING DOOR caused Sheetal to look up. Breath caught in her throat.

Rakesh coughed and turned away. Sheetal wasn't surprised. It must be hard to inhale the odor of vomit, poop and milk she had grown accustomed to. She didn't want to look at him, but it was hard not to. He looked so young, so vibrant in a blue T-shirt and khakis, his tousled hair adding a carefree touch. It seemed like they had last met a lifetime ago.

He walked over to the food trolley, laden with containers and Tupperware boxes, and unscrewed the lid off a thermos flask. "You didn't eat lunch?"

"I'm not hungry." She slid beneath the covers, feeling like a carrier of some contagious disease. "What are you doing at home in the afternoon?"

"It's Saturday."

"Oh." Saturday. Sunday. Monday. What difference did it make?

"Are you okay?"

"Fine."

"Eleven more days, then you'll be free."

Had he been counting the days? "First nine months. Then forty days. Now eleven." She held back the urge to raise her voice and vent frustration. The last thing she needed was another argument. "What after this? Where do I go from here?"

Rakesh sat on the edge of the bed, causing the mattress to sag. "It's just how Pushpa runs things. This is her domain. It's always been that way and there's nothing I can do."

Since Naina's wedding, she hadn't heard Rakesh or Mummyji argue, which meant they were either steering clear of each other or she really was in the dark about the goings-on in the family. Rakesh laid a hand on her arm and she melted at his touch. "Just go along with whatever she says. It's easier that way."

Easier? Sheetal winced and withdrew. *Had Rakesh compromised with Mummyji in the last month and reached some sort of truce?*

Rakesh leaned across Sheetal and ran his palm along the blanket that swaddled Yash. "Can I hold him?"

"You'll become unclean, like us."

"Bullshit."

Yash wrinkled his petal lips. Sheetal slid her hands under the cocoon of his frame, lifted him, and propped him upright against her left shoulder. She rocked, patting him gently. "Why can't you stand up for me like a real husband?"

"Here, give him to me." Rakesh spread his fingers apart and held out both hands. "I can—"

"You'll drop him."

"Look, I've just managed to make peace with Pushpa after Naina's wedding. Speaking up for you will complicate—"

"That's right. Standing up to Mummyji will complicate everything but standing up to me is fine because I always compromise. It doesn't matter what I say because this is her house. Her room. Her—"

Rakesh gripped her shoulder and dug his fingers into her flesh. "What's wrong with you?"

Her heart welled in her throat. "I'm stuck between four walls like some caged animal. No TV, nothing to read. I do nothing all day but talk to the servants and myself like some mad woman. Even prisoners are treated—" Tears ran down her cheeks. "I can't take it anymore." She collapsed against his chest.

His arms encircled her. "You're strong. You just need to get back on your feet."

"All I did was have a baby. Your baby. And now I'm unclean? Filthy, like some stray animal off the street? It's crazy."

Rakesh let go and took a deep breath. "I agree. It is. The whole thing." He bent his arms at the elbows and joined the palms of both hands into a makeshift cradle. "Now, should I hold him like this?"

Anger filled her gut. How dare he ask to hold Yash when he hadn't bothered to visit?

Rakesh leaned forward, waiting for Sheetal to lay Yash in his arms.

She gulped. How could she deny Rakesh his son? He had as much right as she did.

She positioned Yash in the cradle of Rakesh's arms then

gently pushed his elbows toward each other and his hands in toward his chest.

The door swung open, startling her, and Mummyji marched in. "Oh, how nice, I tell you. The picture-perfect family. Good to see you have made up." She narrowed her attention on Rakesh. "Make sure you shower before dinner. You've touched them, and now you're just as unclean."

"No." Rakesh was firm.

The freckles on Mummyji's face squeezed against each other, threatening to pop.

"What if I don't?"

"You will join us when you are clean."

Yash wriggled in Rakesh's arms and Rakesh handed him back. "Isn't it time you cut out your old-fashioned mumbo jumbo?"

"You are calling my faith nonsense? There's no reason why your wife should be excused. In my time—"

"It's the twenty-first century, for God's sake!"

Mummyji wagged a finger at him. "Don't you tell me what century it is, I tell you. Forty days. After that, do what you want."

"Be reasonable." He softened his tone. "It's insane to lock someone up like this."

"Dinner only when you are clean." Then she left.

"I'm sorry." Rakesh turned to Sheetal, his attention on the duvet. "I tried, but..."

Her attention drifted to the Xs on the calendar. Perhaps none of the Xs mattered. Only Rakesh mattered.

THE FOLLOWING AFTERNOON, MEGHA SAUNTERED IN, WEARING A tight-fitting, yellow knitted T-shirt and a pair of skinny, faded blue jeans. She waltzed around with an air of confidence, her bright red toenails peeking out from the pointed ends of a pair of golden sandals. She played with Yash for a while, then sang lullabies, and cooed and chatted with him.

"Nice sandals," Sheetal complimented her. They were such a contrast to the thick, clumpy hiking boots Megha used to stomp around in. It felt like yesterday that Megha was a clue-less tomboy. She'd transitioned with almost no resistance into a chic, young Tommy Girl.

"Recognize them?" Megha asked.

Sheetal shook her head as Megha fanned her arms, stood on tiptoes and spun. Streaks of plum-colored highlights in her hair waved across her face, and Sheetal remembered how young and carefree she had once been. Then Megha pinched the air on either side of her hips and curtsied as if to a make-believe audience. She wasn't just happy about something. She was ecstatic.

Conscious of her feet, Sheetal wiggled her toes under the bedcovers, relieved they were no longer fat and swollen. However, an additional forty pounds of weight waterlogged her, a huge portion, the potato sack on her belly. Cellulite padded her hips, waist and breasts like an outer body that she could feel but didn't feel a part of. Then Sheetal noticed several golden straps criss-crossing the front of Megha's sandals. "They remind me of my wedding sandals."

"They are."

The words punched her in the gut. "You're wearing my sandals? You didn't even ask."

"I didn't think you'd mind. Besides, you haven't worn them all year."

First Naina with the Cartier set. Now Megha. Sheetal struggled to pull herself upright, dragged down by the extra weight. "You could have at least asked before trying them on."

"Chill, yaar Bhabhi. I'm not taking them like Naina did. I just wanted to see if they fit."

Well, they obviously did. And from the ease with which she confidently flitted around like a butterfly, they appeared to suit her better. A bitterness roiled in her heart. How dare Megha tell her to chill when she was tied to this baby like a cow, imprisoned for the last month?

"Bhabhi... Bhabhi?"

"What?" she snapped. "Sorry, I was lost. Just thinking of when I was younger, like you."

"Bet you weren't a chatterbox. Bhaiya told me to watch my tongue when they came over two days ago. He told me not to talk so much."

"Who?"

"Prakash Goyal and his family." Megha sat on a chair, keeping a distance.

"Who is Prakash Goyal?"

"You don't know?"

"No."

"Didn't Bhaiya or anyone tell you?"

Rakesh had come to visit yesterday, but he hadn't

mentioned a thing. Mummyji popped in and out of the room several times, but no word, either.

"Bhaiya tried to fix me up with a boy. He invited the family over for dinner two nights ago. He didn't tell me beforehand what they were here for. No one did. This guy, his parents, and some aunts, like five of them, just turned up to see me."

"As in marriage?"

"Can you believe it?" Megha bolted out of the chair and paced back and forth. "Bhaiya assumed I would agree to marry someone of his choosing, just like that. He didn't even think to check with me first."

According to custom, brides and grooms were carefully selected for one another only after the heads of both families met and the girl's parents visited the prospective groom's home to better understand their daughter's prospective living condition and lifestyle. Only after the prospective couple met and felt they were suitable for one another did the families initiate the engagement and proceed with the wedding preparations.

Which meant Rakesh had visited the Goyals' place and approved. But then why didn't he mention anything yesterday? "So, what happened? What did you say?"

"Go to hell."

"You told Rakesh to go to hell?" *No one told Rakesh to go to hell.*

"No, that Prakash twit. He has the darkest complexion ever. The biggest nose, and hair oiled to his scalp like glue. I don't care if he's rolling in money. I told him I don't plan to marry anyone. Especially him."

"You really said that?"

"You bet. I told him marriage was completely out of the question."

Sheetal sat in awe of Megha's courage. "So, you're not planning to marry anyone?"

Megha stopped pacing. "There is this boy at college I like. Raj Saxena. I wanted to tell you about him the other day, but then we had to rush you to the hospital and..."

"I'm... I remember, and it's my fault. I never even asked again. But tell me everything. I'm listening."

"There's no point. Bhaiya doesn't believe in love. He calls it nonsense. A waste of time. If I tell him about Raj, he'll think Raj is only after me for the money."

What if Rakesh was right? What if this man was only interested in Megha for the money? They knew nothing about him or his family or background. "So, you love Raj?"

"Is something wrong?"

"I thought you said you liked him as a friend."

"No, I meant like as in love. I want to marry him."

Sheetal took a small breath and tried to hold back surprise. "Aren't you a bit young? And we don't know anything about him, like where he lives, his parents, his qualifications. You're only—"

"What difference does any of that make? We love each other. That's what counts. We've already decided—"

"Shouldn't we meet him first?" She could imagine Rakesh's expression if he found out. But then, he had a soft spot for Megha, so perhaps he wouldn't lose his temper.

"How can you, when Bhaiya invites all these other boys and their families to meet me, without asking?"

"He's doing it for your own good." *Wasn't that Mama's voice?*

Mama's words? And why did she feel like she was talking to herself?

"And how do you know what's for my own good?"

If Mummyji could play favorites with Naina, she could certainly do so with Megha. After all, she'd been taking care of Megha like a mother in many ways. "We do know a little more than you. And better than you. Marriage is not a game. Everything has to be thought through carefully." So akin to Mama's words. *Go easier. Be gentle on Megha,* a voice inside said. "I'll talk to Rakesh and see if he's willing to listen. I'll handle it from here. Trust me."

"Trust you? How can I when Bhaiya doesn't? If Bhaiya trusted you, he would have stuck by your side and not kicked you out of the room. So maybe you're the one who needs advice, not me. I know my brother very well, thank you." She spun on her heel and left.

34
KINDLE

Sheetal's confinement ended exactly ten days before the start of her exhibition. Rakesh had shipped forty-seven paintings to the gallery, but she still lacked a forest, a lake and a still-life. Determined to have all fifty paintings ready in time, she entered her studio, positioned a canvas on the easel and prepared a palette with a selection of summer lake colors. She loaded paint on a paintbrush and swept a long stroke of blue. The paint scratched and clumped across the textured surface. She brought her hand back, accidentally knocked a jar of turpentine and the pungent liquid spilled onto the floor. She grabbed a rag and bent to clean up the mess, but the room began to spin. She straightened, dropped her brush on the workstation, stumbled to the sofa, collapsed in a heap of dismay and rubbed her knees. They ached from the pressure of her weight. Too much weight and lack of muscle strength. How on earth was she going to manage three paintings when she didn't have the muscle control and stamina to paint one?

Needing to escape her misery, she telephoned Mama.

Before lunch, Sheetal signed up for Pilates, and on the first visit to the gym her private instructor, Amita, directed her to lay on her back atop a rubber mat.

Amita's black hair, tied in a ponytail, emphasized her wide-set eyes and full lips. Her olive-tan complexion, broad shoulders, slim waist, tight hips and muscled frame contrasted with Sheetal who felt like she was encased in an extra-large body suit pumped with air. That wasn't the only problem. Amita, who appeared to be in her mid-twenties exuded a confidence, control and determination that made Sheetal squirm with embarrassment over her own physique.

Amita knelt beside her. "Palms flat on the floor. Breathe. Control. Concentrate. Look at the ceiling, find a spot to focus on and fix your attention there."

Sheetal searched for an imperfection on the white ceiling panels, but the uniform black holes offered no distinctive mark on which to focus

"Flow of movement, range of motion and stability are what you will begin with." Amita tapped an index finger on the lower half of Sheetal's breastbone. "The xiphoid, let's call it button one." She slid her index and second fingers down Sheetal's chest in a straight line, fanned them apart and stopped at two imaginary points over Sheetal's rib cage. "Button two." She continued south and halted on Sheetal's belly button. "Button three." At her pelvis, "Button four. And the last one..."—she

halted at the pubic bone—"is button five." Amita tapped Sheetal's xiphoid. "Imagine my finger is constantly pushing down
on button one. Suck your chest in here."

Sheetal took a deep breath.

"Not hold your breath. Suck this portion of your body in.
Root it to the mat."

Sheetal exhaled, curled her shoulders and sucked in her
torso until her spine pressed the rubber mat.

"Good, we call this closing button one. Remember, don't
hold your breath. Just hold your position and breathe. You
should feel like you're anchored to a bed of concrete."

More like a frog pegged for dissection.

Sheetal looked toward her toes. The flab at her waist curved
like a jelly half-moon across her horizon. Helplessness lodged
in her throat. She'd been zipped into a tight-fitting wedding
gown all over again. Only, this time, she wasn't padlocked
behind folds of fabric, but trapped in her own skin. She gulped,
resisting an urge to cry.

"What happened?" Amita asked.

"I...I can't do this. I've just come out from forty days of
confinement and now this? I signed up to lose weight, not trap
myself all over again."

"Don't think of it as a trap. Think of it as gaining control.
Finding parts of yourself you didn't know existed. Shall we
begin now?"

"Begin what?" Her body longed to spring into its natural
position, but she kept her spine pressed against the mat.

"The exercises."

"I can only just breathe and you expect me to move?" Anger
filled her heart. She shouldn't have eaten all that fat-laden

food. Maybe if she'd protested, she would have gotten her way and not ended up with a barrel for a body. "This is impossible. I just had a baby. Maybe it's easy for skinny instructors like—"

"I'm a mother of three, Mrs. Dhanraj. And each birth doesn't get any easier."

"Three children?" The woman didn't look like she had one!

"Six, four and two years old," she said as if reading Sheetal's mind. "Look, I know it's hard, but after a few sessions and practice, it'll become second nature." Amita placed the edge of her left hand across Sheetal's collar bone and the right across Sheetal's thighs. "Your central focus, the area between my hands, is your powerhouse. The inner core of your being. Your deepest level of inner strength. Once you learn to anchor your body before any movement and navigate so that your arms and legs work together and in opposition, you'll begin to feel and find a strength you never knew you had. Slow and steady movements paired with breathing is how we begin. I know it's going to take a while to get used to, but our aim is to help you achieve balance, alignment, inner strength and core stability."

Our aim. Sheetal allowed the words to sink in. She was not alone.

Later that day, Dr. Banerjee, a dietician, drew up Sheetal's meal plan with restrictions on her calorie intake. He encouraged Sheetal to incorporate a cardio program with Pilates and to set a goal to lose fifty pounds over the next six months.

Sheetal skimmed the timetable, folded the sheet and slipped it into her handbag. She could do this. She *would* do this. For herself and Yash.

35

THE GOOD FATHER

Rakesh returned from work and was heading upstairs when Yash's wails pealed the air. Expecting one of the nannies, on round-the-clock shifts, to attend to Yash, Rakesh headed toward his room when his son's cries intensified into a full-pitched scream. Rakesh's heart raced. Where was everyone? Sheetal? Pushpa? Megha? Surely someone was around. He headed for the south wing while memory replayed its looped tape.

He had arrived home from school and Megha's cries filled the air. He waited for Pushpa to attend to her, but learned, from the servants, that Pushpa had gone out for afternoon tea.

Rakesh headed straight to Yash's nursery, adjacent to Sheetal's room, and found Moushmi Kaki, the older of the two nannies, in her sixties, bent over the railing of the crib. A breeze from the open window flapped panels of Thomas the Train curtains just above her head.

"What's going on?"

Moushmi Kaki jumped, startled. "He no stop crying, Sahib. I not know what wrong. I try everything. Change diaper. Give bottle, but no stop."

"You've probably forgotten something." Rakesh set his briefcase on the blue carpet and peered at Yash, who had balled his fingers into two tiny fists. Eyes squeezed close, tears coursing down his cheeks, Yash pumped his legs back and forth. "Where is Sheetal?"

"Go to gym, Sahib." Moushmi Kaki lifted Yash and propped him upright against her shoulder.

"The gym? At this hour? What was she doing all morning?"

"Busy, with *Chotte Baba*"—Little Master—"all morning and afternoon. Little bit sleeping. Play with him, then she do her work. Just now she go. About one hour ago." Moushmi Kaki paced the nursery, patting Yash on the back, gently bobbing with each step. However, her efforts did little to soothe Yash's cries.

Like the time he was thirteen and Papa, Pushpa, Naina and he sat down for dinner in the Marquette Dining Room when Megha's cries came through the speakers of the baby monitor. He turned toward Pushpa, expecting her to rush off and quiet his baby sister in the nursery upstairs, but she simply hollered for a servant to attend to Megha.

Megha's cries grew louder, echoing between the walls. Rakesh's insides crumbled. Unable to take Megha's wails any longer, he jumped to his feet to take care of her, but Pushpa grabbed him by the arm, dug in her nails, and sat him down.

"Nothing will happen if she cries a little longer, I tell you. Now sit down and eat. She's not the only baby on earth." Then she switched off the white monitor and an ominous silence filled the room.

Rakesh turned to Papa, but Papa was helping himself to another serving of curry. Naina, three, in a booster seat, played with her food. Panic gripped him. What if Megha choked? They'd never know.

He broke free and ran as fast as he could while Pushpa yelled for him to come back. He bounded up the stairs two at a time. Megha's cries tore at his heart. He rushed into the nursery and peered over the raised bars of the crib.

"Bai!" he called for the nanny while standing on tiptoes. He reached over the bars of the crib but wasn't able to reach her. Megha sucked furiously on her fist.

He pulled a chair from the corner, climbed onto the seat and scooped Megha into his arms. "Bai!" he called again, and the nanny rushed in with a bottle of milk. She slid the teat into Megha's mouth and Megha's pink lips curved around the nipple and sucked hard. Rakesh held her until she finished every drop, his heart bleeding. If Mumma had been alive, this wouldn't have happened.

Rakesh reached out to hold Yash, but then withdrew. What if Yash squirmed out of his arms? Or he squeezed too hard and Yash asphyxiated or died of a heart attack? No. A shiver ran up his spine. "Do something!"

"Maybe colic, Sahib." Moushmi Kaki spoke above Yash's cries. "Tummy aching. Many babies have. Choti Sahiba always knowing what do."

"Call her, then."

"I no knowing phone number of gym, Sahib."

How irresponsible! "Here. Give him to me."

Rakesh locked the fingers of his hands into a fist and raised his arm to chest level in the shape of a cradle, like Sheetal had taught him.

"Too big, Sahib." Moushmi Kaki gestured for Rakesh to cup the opposite elbow in each palm, then she laid Yash horizontally across and helped Rakesh adjust position to mold to Yash's contours.

"It's all right, Papa's here," Rakesh cooed and paced the room, but that didn't help. "Shhh...calm down my *Beta*." He rocked his son like he'd seen Sheetal do, but that didn't help, either. How on earth could an infant this tiny scream with such force? Rakesh turned to Moushmi Kaki for help. How dry his little throat must— That's it! "Kaki!" He gestured to an army of baby bottles on a trolley. "Give me that bottle."

She rushed over and picked up one. "This?"

"No. The blue lid." He pointed.

Moushmi Kaki slid the teat into Yash's mouth and Yash sucked hard. Air bubbles streamed up through the bottled water. Relief calmed Rakesh's nerves. He did it! He took care of his baby. His son.

"Very good, Sahib." Moushmi Kaki smiled.

Yes, life was good. Very good. Maybe he could learn to let go a little and love again.

36
CROWNING GALLERIA

A t nine-thirty in the morning on December fifth, half an hour before the opening of the exhibition at Crowning Galleria, Sheetal walked past a marble fountain in the center of the lobby. Shifting silhouettes of people on the other side of the frosted glass doors caught her attention. She stopped and turned toward the doors.

Jewel-toned, stained-glass vines and fruits spiraled up the frosted glass, and Ravi Shankar's instrumental swept through the room. The soft plucking of the sitar's strings and gentle drumming of the tabla peaked and plateaued with the shift of shadows beyond the door. The first two days were for VIP guests by invitation only and Sheetal hadn't expected anyone to arrive until after lunch. Her heart stirred with unease. She gulped. Surely they weren't all here for her exhibition. There had to be another event happening simultaneously.

Rakesh strode past two guards in beige uniforms and across the lobby toward the main showroom door. He had taken a week off work to organize the event, making sure every painting was mounted correctly, educating the staff about Sheetal's work, and ensuring the right combination of wines, cheeses and fruit graced the buffet. He looked stunning, as always, in a beige crepe linen suit, a Burberry tie and ochre shirt. So calm and composed, while Sheetal could hardly contain the butterflies in her stomach. Rakesh paused and glanced in her direction, a look of concern on his face. Then he signaled Pamela, the curator, and Mukesh, the gallery manager, and they followed him down a corridor.

In her late twenties, Pamela had been with the gallery for five years and answered potential buyers' questions concerning an artist's work. Mukesh handled sales, and the gallery retained a thirty percent share of any painting sold.

The central lobby fanned out into five corridors, like fingers on a hand, that linked to five unique showrooms. Each display room housed a different collection of work, from 'Antiques' and 'Still Lifes' to 'Falling Forests' and 'Running Waters.' However, 'Sunset Boulevard' was expected to attract the largest crowd.

Sheetal glanced at her Chopard watch. Nine-forty. Twenty minutes to go. She shifted from foot to foot. The rising tempo of the music didn't help to calm her nerves, and the crowd beyond the door continued to grow. There must be twenty, no, thirty people outside.

Sheetal loosened the hand-painted scarf around her collar. Drops of sweat rolled from her chignon down her nape. She fiddled with her diamond solitaire earrings, straightened the cuffs of her shirtsleeves and fished in her handbag for the phone. Should she call Moushmi Kaki to see if Yash was okay? *No, he must be fine,* she reasoned.

Murmurs of the waiting crowd floated like a storm cloud, ready to burst. An art critic from *The Raigun Herald* was expected to attend today's premiere, and he had a reputation for ruthlessness that had ended careers before they had a chance to bud.

What if he hates everything? What if he declares me an amateur? What if...

One of the guards unlocked the glass doors.

Men and women in formal black and white business attire, with gold name tags pinned to their shirt pockets, entered and zigzagged across the lobby, blurring her thoughts.

Rakesh nudged her hand. "Hey, what's wrong?"

Sheetal flexed her fingers, aware of her nails biting into her palms. "Is the gallery hosting another event today?"

"No, why?"

"So many people. I don't think I can do this." Her knees weakened, but Rakesh held her hand and tightened his grip. Warmth surged through her veins and calm dispelled fear.

"You're going to be fine. Just fine."

She had to be fine. She took a deep breath and collected herself. She was ready.

Five hours into the exhibition, Mummyji cruised up and down the buffet table, attending to friends, relatives and members of the ladies' club. Sheetal happened to overhear Mummyji complain how Sheetal had shirked the responsibilities of Naina's wedding to work on her paintings. Sheetal was about to refute the false accusation when a middle-aged gentleman in a dark business suit and thick silver lasses headed straight for 'Sunset Boulevard.' Sheetal recognized him from the thumbnail photograph that accompanied the "Art and Aesthetics" column in *The Raigun Herald*. Naidu Sahib.

Sheetal broke away from the attendees and followed Naidu Sahib, maintaining a ten-feet distance. She prayed he consider at least one of her works adequate and give her a chance, but from the way he paused before a canvas, shook his head and moved on to the next, it didn't appear as though she'd make the cut.

Then he stopped before Dawn at Dusk, and Sheetal's heart skipped a beat.

He slipped a hand into his trouser pocket, pulled out a pen and notebook and scribbled something.

Her throat parched. Should she ask if he had questions, or wanted an explanation, or—

He took several steps back, slid his glasses up the bridge of his nose, and jotted more notes.

Was something wrong? Had he somehow guessed she hadn't done the painting alone? Impossible, she reasoned. It was just like any other painting. But then, why was he focused, like he'd discovered some secret?

'Believe what you see, not what you think you see.'

She had to stop second guessing and making more of his observation than existed. He was simply observing her work. Nothing more.

Sheetal stepped closer.

When she was three feet away, Naidu Sahib snapped shut the notebook and frowned.

Guests milled about blurred in her vision. Sheetal held her breath. *My career is over.*

"Interesting work." Naidu Sahib folded his hands together in namaste and made for the lobby door.

THE FOLLOWING DAY, AN EVEN LARGER CROWD ATTENDED THE EVENT. People complimented Sheetal's work with phrases like, 'such talent,' 'amazing blend of colors,' 'such fine details,' and 'budding artist.' However, the comments meant little because Rakesh measured success by net worth, and no painting had sold.

Sheetal was in the hall of 'Sunset Boulevard' when Rakesh approached.

"Hey, all okay?"

"Fine."

"I don't think so."

"Really, I'm fine." She lowered her gaze, and the cracks running across her Italian leather pumps seared her heart. *What sarcastic comment was he going to come up with this time? Budding failure?*

"Did you see that?" He pointed to a wall behind.

Sheetal turned. A 'SOLD' tag was pinned beside one of her paintings. Not just any painting. Beside Dawn at Dusk.

LATER THAT EVENING, SEVERAL MORE 'SOLD' SIGNS POPPED UP ON walls, but Sheetal didn't have time to ask Mukesh the buyers' details. When she had a free moment, she crossed the lobby to Pamela, hoping she'd have some information.

Pamela flipped through the register of sales and shrugged. "No names here. Seems like the last few were purchased by anonymous buyers."

"There must be a check somewhere."

Pamela drew an imaginary line down the sheet with her index finger. "Says here, cash...cash...and cash."

Who walked around with ninety-five thousand rupees in cash?

"I was out for lunch when Mukesh was on duty. He handled all the sales. Look, his signature here...and here and here." She tapped several identical signatures.

"Where is he now?"

"Off duty. But he'll be back tomorrow."

"Is there an address or some location we can track to find where the paintings are headed?"

"It just says personal pick up."

"Well." Sheetal crossed her arms. "Whoever Mr. Anonymous is, he sure knows how to stay anonymous."

MEGHA ATTENDED THE EXHIBITION EVERY EVENING AFTER COLLEGE, and each time brought a different group of friends. She began her tours by introducing her friends to Rakesh and Sheetal, then led them through the five halls. However, one friend, a tall, lanky young man, accompanied Megha every day. He walked with one arm around Megha's shoulders or waist and lingered on late in the evening, well after others had gone home. He smiled at Rakesh and Sheetal from a distance but walked away if either approached.

Mr. Anonymous? No, Sheetal reasoned. How could a college student possibly have that much cash on him? *Perhaps he was Raj, the young man Megha loved.* Sheetal was about to ask Megha and then stopped. This was not her problem, and she didn't need to get involved.

Over the next two days, more 'SOLD' labels appeared around the gallery, as if the sale of Dawn at Dusk had triggered a buying spree. Sheetal could no longer contain her smile and felt alive in a way she'd never experienced before.

That evening, Mukesh informed her that an elderly gentleman with gray hair had paid cash for Dawn at Dusk and then left with several more pieces.

ON THE FIFTH AND FINAL DAY, AUNTY HEMU, VIKRAM AND ANJALI accompanied Mama and Papa—who'd attended every day of the exhibition.

The pallu of Aunty Hemu's sari cascaded along the length of her left arm and swept the floor as she struggled to balance on a pair of stilettoes. Her hair was coiled in a bun and her face gleamed in the chandelier's yellow light as thick drops of sweat oozed down the sides of her face, streaking a layer of foundation. The scent of air freshener wafted from her skin as she struck a pose.

"*Hambe*! Here, here, photo *wallah*!" she called out to the photographer. "*Mera photo aisa hi laina.*" She swept her left arm toward her chest, fanned the sash of green fabric that cascaded like a waterfall, and insisted the photographer shoot her in this pose.

Sheetal grabbed Mama by the hand and pulled her aside. "If you hadn't pulled those paintings off the walls at home," she whispered, "I'd never have met my quota."

"Lucky I remembered."

"You've done us proud." Papa patted her shoulder.

"Of course, of course," Aunty Hemu intervened. "All of us are proud, I tell you. Now, don't get me wrong"—she turned to Vikram, who stood behind and waved the photographer away — "I heard Sheetal's been secretly working on this exhibition for months. Behind everyone's back. I even heard the Dhanrajs had to sacrifice Sheetal's duties at the office and some of Naina's wedding preparations so she could pursue her career."

The lies!

Sheetal wanted to grab Aunty Hemu and wring her neck. She locked both hands into one fist behind her back to refrain from doing so and searched the crowd for Rakesh. There was only one way to shut down Aunty Hemu. She spotted Rakesh heading for the corridor toward 'Still Waters' and called for him to join them. "Why not discuss your worries with Rakesh, Aunty Hemu, since he knows all the secrets around here?"

"Oh!" Aunty Hemu coughed. "It's not necessary, really."

"You wanted something?" Rakesh joined them.

"Aunty Hemu was just sharing with everyone," Sheetal said, "how I had to give up work at the office and some of my duties at Naina's wedding so that I could put all this together. I thought we should hear it from you."

"What responsibilities?" Rakesh turned to Aunty Hemu. "She doesn't work for me or my company. And none of her paintings interfered with Naina's wedding."

"Oh, I—" Aunty Hemu looked from Rakesh to Papa and back. "I was just telling what I heard and—"

"Talent of any kind is God's gift," Rakesh cut her off. "It's precisely why I booked this gallery and had the studio at home renovated. Anything else you've heard is just gossip. Besides" —he slipped his hands into the side pockets of his trousers— "what would my wife do in the office anyway when I have thousands of people working for me? Shouldn't she pursue her own career when she's obviously so talented?"

Sheetal's heart skipped a beat. *Did Rakesh really mean this?*

"As for Naina's wedding," he continued, "I don't think any woman in her second trimester could be or should be doing more than what Sheetal managed. You would know, Aunty Hemu. Anjali just had a baby, right?"

"Oh... I...uh–the bathroom, *hambe*. Where is it?" She slipped away, and Sheetal straightened her posture with pride.

AT FIVE O'CLOCK, NEAR CLOSING TIME, PAMELA CONGRATULATED Sheetal. "This is the most successful exhibition I've seen for a first-time exhibitor, Mrs. Dhanraj. Raigun loves you."

Sheetal's heart soared. She felt as if her head would touch the ceiling. "I can't believe fifty paintings sold in five days."

Rakesh joined them. "This calls for a celebration. I'll find Megha and we can go out for a celebration dinner."

"A double celebration," Pamela joined in. "A first for us, too, and a success we're going to remember for a long time."

SHEETAL SWUNG OPEN THE GALLERY DOOR AND STEPPED OUTSIDE. Storm clouds roiled overhead.

Rain in December? Unheard of.

Wind whipped tendrils of hair from behind her ears, lashing each strand against her cheeks as streaks of lightning flashed across the sky. A boom of thunder caused her to jump. All hell was about to break loose, for sure.

Sheetal tore down the gallery's stone steps to the black Mercedes parked at the curb as plastic bags, dried leaves and shreds of paper whirled around. The chauffeur swung open the door. Sheetal slid into the vehicle before he slammed the door shut and he resumed his position in the driver's seat. Then the heavens cracked open and raindrops bounced off the windshield and windows like popcorn.

Rakesh rushed out, taking the steps two at a time. He tapped on Sheetal's window and hoisted a blazer above his head for a makeshift umbrella as water plopped on his slick, black hair and trickled down his collar.

Sheetal rolled down the glass and pulled away from the icy drops that splashed in.

"Where's Megha?"

The last time she had seen Megha was half an hour ago with that young man. *Had they gone off somewhere together?*

Rakesh stared past her shoulder and blinked. "Did she say

anything about plans to go out for the evening?"

Sheetal bit her tongue. How much could she tell him? And how much did she really know? Sheetal pressed her lips together. This was not her problem. "She promised to meet us after the exhibition was over. Near the fountain," she yelled above the roll of thunder.

"Something's wrong."

Sheetal turned away before her expression gave her away.

"That tall college student. The guy with the glasses. He was with her, right?"

"You're worrying too much. The last time I saw Megha, she was with a group of friends."

"There was no group at four-thirty. It was just the two of them. Alone. Remember?"

They walked hand in hand, unconcerned with what anyone might say.

Rakesh fished his Blackberry from a trouser pocket. "Hello, Janvi?"

Tell him, an inner voice said. Sheetal looked past Rakesh's shoulder to a flash of lightning tearing across the sky.

He switched off the phone and tucked it inside the pocket. "Megha's not home. Janvi said she left this morning carrying a large sports bag."

"Oh." She numbed.

A deafening boom shook the air. The storm raged overhead. Thick, grey clouds—the meaning of Megha's name—pregnant with rain, scudded across the sky. Lightning blazed, melting the success of Sheetal's exhibition with the downpour. Thunder rumbled again and again, all night long, but neither heaven nor hell knew where Megha had gone.

37
MISSING MEGHA

Rakesh spent the night reaching out to every contact in Megha's phone book, but twenty-four hours later, there was no news of her whereabouts. He called the police, declared her a missing person, and the Raigun authorities began an investigation advising him to wait for further news.

Wait? Rakesh numbed. He couldn't just sit and wait. *What if Megha had been kidnapped for ransom and her life endangered?* He located a recent photograph of Megha and drove off in the Lamborghini. He cruised the streets surrounding the college campus, pulled up at cafes, restaurants and venues where young people hung out and held up Megha's photo, but none of the students had seen her. He turned to shop owners and residents, but no luck. Frantic, he approached pedestrians and offered a hundred-thousand-rupee reward to anyone who could help find her, but no one, not even beggars, had the time.

Rakesh raked his fingers through his hair as never-ending

streams of rush-hour traffic, smog and pedestrians fogged his thinking. *Where could she be? Or have gone?* He held up Megha's photo like a placard to every passerby, but no one took notice. His head pounded as desperation mounted. When he wiped sweat from his temple, his fingers came away slimed with dirt. To think, he'd never given any beggar so much as a *paisa,* and now he begged every street urchin and roadside peddler for information.

If she'd run away, was it to escape him? Why? He was only doing what Papa would have done had he been around. He'd stood up for Megha, been her rock since she was a baby, and she returned the favor by abandoning him? His heart ached and his chest constricted with guilt.

ON THE THIRD DAY, RAKESH WOKE BEFORE DAWN TO CRUISE THE streets, this time west of campus—a maze of open-air food stalls and kiosks. He drove down roach-infested back alleys, hit dead-ends, and almost struck a lamp post. He squinted in an effort to discern the divide between sidewalk and road, convinced he was going in circles. Twelve hours later, his throat raw and full of cacti needles, he searched for a bar, located one, and parked the Lamborghini. He sat for a moment, pounding head pressed against the headrest, eyes closed, then summoned the strength to step from the car. He reached for the door of the bar when someone in the distance with Megha's neck-length hair and petite frame caught his attention. The young woman, dressed in a pair of skinny jeans and a tight-fit, green T-shirt stood on the curb with her back to him.

"Megha!" he yelled. "Megha!"

The girl hitched her purse on her left shoulder, stepped off the pavement and zigzagged between six lanes thick with traffic.

"Wait!" Rakesh took off after her. He dodged hawkers, fruit carts and open-air food stalls in a rush to catch up, but she vanished amid swarms of bodies on the far side of the road.

He stepped off the pavement, but a man on a bicycle with two huge aluminum milk containers hanging on either side of the bicycle like lop ears almost knocked him over.

"Arrey, sambhal ke challo!" the milkman yelled for him to watch where he went as the rattle of aluminum against wheel-spokes grated the air. A lorry passed by in the second lane, blasting diesel fumes that made Rakesh's eyes water. Then headlights caught him in a glare of blinding light. A horn blared. He closed his eyes and braced for impact. Someone yanked him aside. Wind whooshed. The hairs on his body stood on end.

"Why you try to die?" yelled a beggar in tattered brown clothing who reeked of fish, sweat and stale alcohol. "People like you have everything and want to die, while people who have nothing, like me, should be dead but continue to live."

Rakesh pried the beggar's fingers off his suit and stuffed several rupee notes in his half-open palm. Then he staggered across the road, weaving in and out of human and vehicular traffic. *Megha,* he remembered. *Find her.* On the crowded far pavement, he waded through the stench of sweat-filled bodies, looked up and saw the girl again. He lengthened his stride, but she rushed ahead. "Wait! Megha!" He elbowed past people and swept them aside. "Megha!"

The girl leapt into the arms of a young man and kissed him on the lips.

"Don't touch her," he yelled.

The young man let go. The girl turned and the breath caught in Rakesh's throat. She wasn't Megha.

38
DÉJÀ VU

Sheetal sat beside Rakesh in the TV lounge as the overwhelming odor of scotch, burnt cigarettes and stale deodrant enveloped her. If she didn't speak up now, she'd regret it later. "I...I think I know where Megha might be."

Rakesh placed his glass on the coffee table. "You think you know, or you know?"

"There's this boy she likes in college. Raj. She mentioned—"

Rakesh turned to her in disbelief. "She what?"

"A while back."

"And you...she...none of you told me? The guy with her in the exhibition. That was him, right?"

"I don't know."

"What do you know? What else did she tell you that I should know?"

"She said you were trying to fix her up with someone. Prakash Goyal."

He flinched.

"You invited the family over to meet Megha, and you didn't tell her they were coming or why. You didn't even tell me."

"She's eighteen. I figured I had to start—"

"She's only eighteen! That doesn't give you the right to decide her life."

"I wasn't fixing anything. The Goyals had come to meet, talk and get to know her. That's all."

Wasn't that how Mama and Papa had arranged her marriage? First meet Rakesh at a party, then over lunch. "But did you ask? Did you talk to Megha beforehand?"

"Papa would have done the same if he'd been alive."

Anger surged through her veins. "That doesn't give you the right to decide Megha's future."

"This...this—what's his name? That fellow—"

"Raj." First 'that Arvind', now 'that Raj'. *Why couldn't love be accepted? Why did love have to carry a label like a taboo?*

"I'm guessing he's probably some punk off the—"

"He's not off the street and this is your fault. All of it."

"Me?"

"Yes, you. You were trying to fix her up with someone she hates. Someone she didn't want to—"

"That bastard," he cut her off.

If Raj was wealthy and from a decent family, Megha stood a chance of marrying him. 'Decent' meant Raj's family should own a bungalow, a few estates, membership in the Raigun Cricket Club and a successful family business.

"At least find out who he is before calling him names."

LATER THAT AFTERNOON, SHEETAL AND RAKESH LEARNED THAT RAJ Saxena was Raigun University's top medical student in the final year of his M.B.B.S. and held no criminal record.

The Saxenas, a family of four, owned a two-bedroom apartment in a mediocre section of Raigun and Raj was the older of two siblings. Mr. Saxena was a manger for Nokia, the country's leading mobile phone supplier and telecom network service provider, and Mrs. Saxena was a primary teacher in a private school. The Saxenas had also reported Raj 'missing' around the same time Megha's case had been filed and they hadn't heard from their son since.

"I'll buy out Nokia. Shut down the damn school!" Rakesh shouted against the din of a soap commercial while pacing the lounge. "I'll put them on the streets so no one will give him or his two dogs a job for life."

"You put the Saxenas on the streets and that's precisely where Megha will be." Sheetal lowered the TV volume with the remote. "She's not coming back."

"How do you know?"

"Because she loves him. There's nothing more powerful than love. So what if Raj is not like—up to our standards? Give him a chance." *A chance was all Arvind needed.*

"It's your fault. If you had kept your womanly advice to yourself, none of this would have happened."

The blood rushed to her head. First Mummyji. Then Naina. Then Megha. Now Rakesh. How convenient for everyone to blame her when things went wrong. "Megha came to me for help. Not once, but twice. I was the only person she could talk to, and I suggested she tell you about Raj, but she obviously chose not to. I even suggested that you'd eventually turn around, but she was scared. I see why now. You're stone, Rakesh. And she's petrified of you. We all are."

"Do I look like some kind of—" He swiped the air with a hand. "You sold her all that how-pretty-you-are shit. *Brahma-*created-you rubbish. She obviously soaked it up and flaunted herself to hook a man. She was fine until you came along. You screwed us all and turned Megha into a God knows what!"

Sheetal curled her fingers into fists. "She was lost. She didn't know who she was. I helped her discover her potential. But you're too blind to see that."

Rakesh sat down and cupped his forehead in his hands. "You turned her into a slut in those tight-fitting clothes."

"The same tight-fitting clothes you forced me to wear not so long ago? Remember Graffiti? Those clothes hardly covered me." Her attention fixed on Rakesh, and his expression blanked. "I did what any woman with a heart would have done. I gave Megha confidence to escape her shell and be a woman. Clothes are just the outside, it's what you are inside that matters."

"She's only eighteen." He looked up. "A girl, dammit. Just a girl."

Sheetal almost choked. "My grandmother had a child by the time she was eighteen. Megha's just a girl to you because that's how you choose to see her. What's that you said the other day? Believe what you see, not what you think you see. You see every woman as a sitting target. Aim. Shoot. Fire. Because you choose to see all women that way. Except Megha."

"You have no fucking right to put yourself between me and my sister."

Sheetal anchored her spine against the sofa's backrest. "Do you know why Megha ran away?"

Rakesh's attention narrowed on the carpet.

"Because of you."

"How dare—"

"If you don't want me in your life, you shove me off to a room on another wing. Is that your answer to our problems?" Adrenaline rushed to her head and she didn't give him a chance to answer. "But if I don't want you in my life, where do I go? Do I have a choice? Husbands and wives don't hide things from each other. They share their lives. They live with one another. And do you know what the worst part is?" She rose and towered two feet above him. "Even if I want, I can't run away from you."

SHEETAL WAS ABOUT TO SIP HER COFFEE ALONE IN THE DINING ROOM late that evening when Laal Bahadur emerged from the kitchen, fidgeting with the ends of a white tea towel. "There's something I come to tell you." He shifted weight from one foot to the other. "Some time ago…"

Sheetal listened, her heart cracking with every word. When Laal Bahadur finished, she blew across the surface of the coffee. Then she looked up. "Are you sure?"

He nodded.

"This stays between us. Understand?"

39
AWAKENING

Sitting on Megha's bed, Rakesh scrunched the duvet between his fingers and ran his hand along the surface of Megha's pillow. Six days had passed and still no news. Was she alone? Was she with someone? The image of Raj with his arms around Megha filled him with a fury that spread like hot metal. *What if Raj had left her in a ditch somewhere? Or she had been attacked by—*

No. He cut short the thought before another image came to mind. Then warmth spread along his right shoulder and he turned to look behind. *Sheetal.* He searched the browns of her eyes and his heart ached. She was right. He wasn't a brother. He was a monster. "I—"

Sheetal pressed a finger to his lips. "She'll come back. I know she will."

LATER THAT EVENING, RAKESH SAT ALONE IN HIS BEDROOM SEARCHING for any news of Megha in *The Raigun Herald*. The police still didn't have any information on her whereabouts, and he had reached his wits' end.

Pushpa marched in and sat down on a sofa. "We need to discuss something."

Rakesh raised the paper to create a wall between them. "What now?"

"Sheetal is getting a little out of hand. I couldn't help but overhear you two arguing in the TV room the other day. *Hai Ishwar*! I think we should speak to her parents about her behavior. This bellowing, screaming, just won't do. Not in my house, I tell you. Today, you. Tomorrow, me."

"Better late than never," Rakesh mumbled.

"What's that? Did you say something?"

Rakesh lowered the paper. "Sheetal is my wife. What I do is my business."

"Yes, yes. I know all that. But what are we going to— How are we— I don't understand what we're going to do with her."

"Do? Nothing."

"But—"

"The question is, when Sheetal takes over, what are we going to do with you? I married to build my image. But you know what? She's the one thing I've done right. She knows me. She wants to understand me. She's with me night and day when no one else is. My father was photographed for meeting prime ministers and presidents. In thirty years, not once did he tarnish our family name. Just look at what you've done. Created a media circus when you married him. Mistress becomes millionaire. At least live up to my father's name, if nothing else."

"I am not your father," Pushpa bellowed.

"I can see that."

"What I do is my business."

"Your business, to waltz in and ruin our lives."

Pushpa was about to say something, but Rakesh didn't give her a chance.

"You are the reason I hate women. You ruined my life, but I won't let you ruin my marriage."

40
DAWN AT DUSK

When Sheetal returned from the gym, Mummyji paced beside the Fulton Whites, the telephone pressed to her ear.

"I see...well...yes... I tell you, that's just how she was raised. Right from day one. Yes." She nodded. "You know, servants at her beck and call."

Seven days, and still no news of Megha. Sheetal sat down, unable to resist eavesdropping in case some information had finally come.

Mummyji raised her voice, "I understand, but you must calm down. Speaking to Naina won't make a difference, I tell you. I know my daughter." She paused. "How can you expect me to explain things to her about your family, I tell you, when I hardly know your ways myself? Your family, your problems. You'll just have to help Naina fit in." She fanned her fingers against rays of golden light from the chandelier. "And if she can't...well...then you'll have to adjust. I've taught her well."

Sheetal crossed one leg over the other. Who was she supposed to feel sorry for? Naina or the Malhotras?

Mummyji beeped off the phone and turned to Sheetal. "That was from Calkot. Mrs. Malhotra was calling to complain that Naina has made no attempt to fit in with their family. Really!" she huffed. "They say she's over-pampered. Over-fussed. Used to too much luxury. But is it our fault, I tell you, if this is the life we lead? If I have been lucky to provide well for my family? Because I know what it's like to have little."

"You mean, poor? Is that it?" Sheetal asked. "Were you poor before you married Rakesh's father?" Then the unthinkable rolled off her tongue, "Did you marry him for money?"

"How dare you?" Mummyji pumped a hand on her hip. "Who told you such a thing?"

If Mummyji had come from a poor family and was able to stake her claim on this turf, then there was no reason to live in fear.

"We married for love, I tell you. So what, if I had little at the time? He left me all this and the estate. But He was smart, I tell you. Way too smart. Made it clear in the will that should I turn away from my duties to this family, I lose everything. Which is why I'm stuck, I tell you. Stuck looking after all of you."

Sheetal fished in her purse and handed Mummyji several sheets of folded paper. "Then you need to take care of my menu for the week. I'll be giving you and Laal Bahadur one every Monday. Dr. Banerjee drew it up." She handed Mummyji another sheet. "And this is a list of all the foods crossed off my diet."

Mummyji ran her Kit Kat thick fingers down the page. "Aaee! No cream. No cheese. No paneer. No white flour. No white bread. *Hai Ishwar!* What will that poor man cook, I tell you?"

Sheetal crossed her arms. "He's the chef, he can figure that out. It's his job, isn't it?"

Mummyji tossed Sheetal's papers on the coffee table and placed both hands on her hips just as a servant entered the great hall.

"Memsahib, koi aaya hai," he announced someone's arrival.

"Who is it now?"

"A young man wear glasses," the servant replied. "With short, black hair and—"

"I didn't ask what he looked like! *Hai Ishwar!* Who is he? His name? What's his name?"

"Oh, I not know. I no ask. But I no see him before."

"Isn't that helpful, I tell you." Mummyji rolled her eyes.

Could it be Raj? Sheetal's heart flipped. *Was Megha with him? Had they decided to come home?* She raced to the door.

"Stop, I tell you," Mummyji called after her. "Those manners just won't do. You can't run around the house attending to strangers and doing the servants' jobs."

Sheetal turned the knob, pulled open the door and took a step back.

"Mrs. Dhanraj?" The stranger smiled. "I have a delivery."

Sheetal's heart sank. "Which Mrs. Dhanraj? There are two of us."

"It's from the Crowning Galleria."

"Then it's for me." It was probably a check from the Crowning Galleria for the seventy percent balance amount due.

Another delivery boy unloaded a large rectangular package from a truck parked outside and carried it to the front door.

Sheetal signaled for him to bring it in, signed the topmost sheet of paper on the clipboard and stepped aside.

"Oh! A package. Well, go on, open it," Mummyji ordered the servant. "Hurry up, now, I tell you. I'm getting late for dinner."

The servant opened the flaps, pulled out layers of packaging and Styrofoam, hauled out a canvas in a bronze frame, and turned it around.

Sheetal's heart skipped a beat. It was Dawn at Dusk. *Did the buyer suddenly decide he didn't want it?*

"It was sent for delivery to this address." The young man ran his finger down the sheet of paper, "Signed by V. Swampat."

Sheetal swallowed. *Mukesh did mention that a gentleman had paid for the painting in cash and then left. But how did Vipul Sahib have the kind of money to buy her work? And why would he have it delivered here? Unless...Rakesh?* She bit her lip. *Did he secretly buy this through Vipul Sahib to commemorate their love? Was this his way of showing he cared?*

"Now, isn't that interesting, I tell you." Mummyji grabbed the list. Rakesh pays fifty-five thousand for a painting he could have kept for free. Imagine!" She handed the clipboard back to the delivery boy. "Paid for by the pocket that funded its creation in the first place. *Hai Ishwar!*" She threw her hands in the air. "It's because we are so blessed that you young people take all the liberties you want." She turned and trudged upstairs.

Sheetal secretly smiled. Mummyji would never understand. This wasn't just a painting, it was Rakesh's way of saying he loved her.

"And the other packages, Mrs. Dhanraj?"

"What other packages?"

"We have twenty-four more in the truck. All to be delivered here." The delivery boy flipped to the next sheet and held it up for Sheetal to see.

All twenty-four had been signed for in Vipul's handwriting. Clearly, the man didn't have the money to buy one, let alone twenty-four. This had to be Rakesh at work. Blood rushed to her head. "Bring them in."

Sheetal had every painting removed from its box, unwrapped and lined up against the Fulton Whites. A squirrel chewing on a nut. A deer in a forest. A waterfall running down the slopes of a mountain. Porcelain vases partially draped in sheets of white satin. Defined by her imagination and crafted by her hand, each painting was like her child, her true assets.

Sheetal gave the delivery boy a hundred-rupee tip, dismissed him and paced the hall. *What was Rakesh trying to prove by purchasing half the collection? And why? And what about the other twenty-five? Were they real sales? Or fictitious?* Her head spun and the air thickened. To think she had trusted Rakesh and believed he was doing this for her. For them.

Her attention fell to Dawn at Dusk and she took a deep breath. "Janvi!"

Janvi hurried into the hall.

"I want every one of these paintings taken out back into the clearing. Tell Maali Kaka to get firewood and kerosene ready."

"But Choti Sahiba—"

"Do it," Sheetal commanded. "I'm coming in fifteen minutes." Sheetal went up to the room she and Rakesh shared and made straight for his walk-in closet. She opened Rakesh's vault, yanked the princess-cut diamond ring off her finger and tossed it in. The ring rolled into a corner and clanked against the back wall. Sheetal peered in, and a long, slithering item of jewelry caught her attention. She reached for it, and her heart skipped a beat. It was the Belgium diamond-drop necklace from her wedding dowry.

Precisely fifteen minutes later, Sheetal marched to the clearing at the back of the Japanese Garden. Maali Kaka had stacked a pile of dry branches, left a can of kerosene, and placed a match box to one side. Sheetal poured kerosene on the pile of kindling, struck a match and threw it atop the branches. Flames danced on thin, wooden sticks and spread in yellow waves.

Sheetal turned to several servants lined on the left holding her works. "Bring that here." She pointed to one of a waterfall.

A servant stepped forward and flinched as a breeze blew the flames in his direction. "Choti Sahiba, what are you doing?"

Sheetal wound her orange sari pallu, tucked it at the waist and grabbed the painting. Then she marched toward the flames, swung her arms back and tossed the waterfall atop the fire. The fire hissed. Sheets of black smoke rose from the bed. Sheetal tossed in painting after painting, scenes of waterfalls, forests and wild animals. Snaps and crackles whipped the air as nine months of labor turned to ash. The servants begged her to stop, but Sheetal called for Dawn at Dusk.

"She-e-e-tal!"

Rakesh? Was this how he'd intended to get rid of all her

work, without leaving a trace of evidence? She grabbed *Dawn at Dusk* from Janvi and approached the flames. This time she was going to burn every stroke, every detail of their relationship.

"She-e-e-tal!" Rakesh's voice floated toward her on a cloud of smoke.

She pulled her arms back and was about to throw the painting in when she noticed Rakesh from the corner of her eye and gritted her teeth. Just because he'd organized an exhibition didn't give him the right to organize her life.

"Holy shit!" he screamed. "What's wrong with you?"

She turned her back to the fire, lost footing, staggered, and stumbled on stones and broken twigs that snapped under her sandals. Heat pricked her skin and beads of sweat oozed down her back. Rakesh reached out, but she shoved his hand aside. "Your money can buy you everything, but it can't buy you me." She backed away, toward the flames.

He inched in her direction, but every step made Sheetal move closer to the fire. "It's the painting we did together. Remember?"

"You asked what impression my paintings will leave behind. How people will remember my work." She grew closer to the bed of coals and flames. "I'm going to erase it all just like you did. Give no one reason to remember me."

"Let's talk—" He coughed and turned away from the blast of heat and smoke.

Rage burned her heart. *That's all anyone ever did. Talk.* She inched farther away. She tripped once, lost balance, but staggered to her feet, determined to end it all. Right here. Right now.

"Stop, Sheetal!" Rakesh lunged, but Sheetal swung the painting away from his reach. The sari pallu slipped from her waist and fanned open like a tail.

Then a scream like the cry of a dying animal escaped Rakesh's lips. He was peeling off his blazer. But there was no turning back. A surge of heat erupted like a volcano behind her.

"You're on—"

A matching fury erupted within. "Get out of my life!"

And then everything went black.

41
SHANTI (PEACE)

A speck of light beckoned Sheetal. Wrapped in a cocoon of silky innocence, she rose weightless, like a cloud. Then a shard of light sliced the silence. "Sheetal...Sheetal."

She parted her lips, but a torrent of water gushed down her throat. She was drowning once again.

42
PARAJAY (LOSS)

Her hair fanned the pillow like broken cobwebs and soot smeared her face. She lay on the bed, draped in a white sheet, like an angel.

Dr. Pratik, a gentleman in his late forties with a toothbrush mustache, gave Sheetal a tetanus shot, then disposed of the syringe in a seal-lock plastic bag. He adjusted the thin rubber tube that snaked out of Sheetal's arm to a bag of glucose, clipped to a drip stand, as Nandita, a nurse, monitored the flow of liquid. "I'll prescribe antibiotics which you should start her on tomorrow. I've already administered some through I.V. Make sure she takes it with food and she drinks plenty of fluids and stays hydrated."

Rakesh nodded, unable to peel his attention from the orange sari discarded in a corner of the room. Holes gaped through the fabric, rimmed in charcoal black. He closed his eyes, and the image of Sheetal gripping Dawn at Dusk haunted like a still-life, bright yellow flames dancing on the pallu's end, clambering and chewing it to ashes. His screams still echoed in his head. He'd lunged to pull her away from the bedrock of burning logs and then the flames flared like a cobra on fire.

He peeled his jacket and took a step forward, but she inched away. The servants yelled and screamed at her to stop. He froze, the flames like an aura behind her. "You're on—"

"Get out of my life!" She swung her arms to catapult Dawn at Dusk when he leapt and took her to the ground.

"*Bachao! Bachao!*" He rolled her on the grass, beating the flames with the jacket, as servants rushed to aid. "*Doctor ko bulao,*" he ordered the servants to call the doctor, then scooped her into his arms and carried her inside. The odor of burnt flesh, fabric and wood cindered his lungs.

"Rakesh, are you okay?" Dr. Pratik asked.

"She..." His tongue felt like jelly. "She will be all right? I mean, she'll—"

"She's in shock. It's obviously been traumatic and taken a toll. Just thank *Ishwar* you were able to put out the fire before it did more damage."

The memory of Janvi cutting open the remainder of Sheetal's blouse and petticoat made his insides curdle. Blistered skin covered her back like a broken map of welts. Janvi and Pushpa soaked white towels in cool water and positioned them on Sheetal's back, shoulders, arms and legs to bring down the swelling, as per Laal Bahadur's instructions. They peeled off her bangles, removed her jewelry, and continued to apply cool compresses while waiting for the doctor.

Rakesh touched Sheetal's shoulder. Heat still radiated from her body. Blisters puffed along her shoulders and down her back in angry, red patches.

"You're lucky they're not third degree." Dr. Pratik closed his medical bag. "In some areas, there's been damage to deeper layers of skin. Obviously, those will take longer to heal."

"Is there anything we should do?"

"Just give her time to heal. Make sure she wears loose, airy clothing. Nandita will be with you for the next week to dress her wounds. For now, a loose bandage is all. And I'll write a prescription for an antibiotic cream. You should expect to see bubbles and pus, typical of second-degree burns, but keep a watch for increased redness and fever. Anything over a hundred and one point five degrees, call me."

"How long will it take to heal?"

"Two to three weeks, is my guess. Provided there is no infection.." Dr. Pratik headed for the bedroom door. "No showers or bath. Nandita will help Mrs. Dhanraj with sponge baths, depending on her recovery. Keep her on her stomach if you can, so the pressure's off her back, and keep her dry. Oh yes, Ibuprofen for pain. I'll give you dosage and instructions."

Rakesh tried to remember the list in his head.

"You have my number. Call me if you need anything." Then he left.

Rakesh knelt on the floor beside Sheetal's bed, his heart thick with grief. This is not what he intended to happen. He had bought the twenty-five paintings to lift her flagging spirits and boost her confidence.

His attention returned to the crumpled orange sari. When he set fire to Sheetal's photograph in the orange sari, did he unknowingly incite doom?

He brushed hair away from her cheek and inhaled the odor of smoke. A few brittle strands snapped on touch, burnt fragments. She lay so deathly still. His throat swelled with a need to cry. He placed two fingers under her nose to feel for breath and exhaled as a wisp of air glided across his skin. She was alive. Barely.

Yash's cries drifted in from the nursery, and a shudder ran through him. What if something happened and she never woke?

He brushed his thumb against her eyelid, willing her eyes to open. He glided his finger down the gentle slope of her nose and across the sharp dip in her upper lip, watching intently for the dimple in her left cheek to appear. Nothing.

What if he lost her like he'd lost Mumma? He imagined raising Yash as a single father, struggling to give the boy both parents' love. First Megha. Now Sheetal. He promised to never remarry, to not let Pushpa raise Yash. He would never condemn Yash to a fate that had been cruel and heartless to him.

He looked to the darkness outside the window. What if Yash one day ran away from him like Megha had? He wrapped his fingers around Sheetal's hand, closed his eyes and lowered his forehead to her wrist. "Come back," he cried into the sheet covering her.

But Sheetal lay as still as the night.

43
PUNARJANAM (REBIRTH)

"Sheetal," someone called out in the darkness.

A halo of white light floated above. Sheetal reached out, touched it, and a kaleidoscope of colors shattered the horizon and disappeared. She spun on her toes. The frilly white dress fanned around her waist. Soft clapping accompanied the jingle of bangles and long, melodious notes that floated in the air.

Warmth enveloped her hand and seeped into her veins. Her finger twitched, and she wiggled her toes as the soft wails of an infant pulled her from the abyss.

44
VARDHAMAN (THE RISING)

"Sheetal?"

Sheetal swam above the drowning tides, surfaced, and took a small breath of air. She opened her eyes to a haze of peach and brown shadows. Familiar faces swam into view as she focused. Mama. Papa. Mummyji. Rakesh.

"Sheetal?" Mama called.

"How are you feeling?" Rakesh asked.

A hand pressed her forehead. "No fever, *Hai Ishwar!*" Mummyji peered at her. "Do you know how worried we've been? I'll phone the doctor right away. Tell him you're awake. Now you stay right where you are. I'll have Janvi bring you some juice." She rushed from the room.

Peach-colored walls and autumn leaves, running in a horizontal border, meant she was in her old bedroom. She tried to move but her body burned. A nurse rushed to her side. What was a nurse doing here? And why was a tube of clear liquid feeding from a drip into her right arm?

"Easy, easy." Rakesh placed a palm on her shoulder and Sheetal winced at his touch.

"Careful," Papa said.

Mama sat on the edge of the mattress. "You're all right. Everything will be fine soon."

Sheetal opened her mouth to say something but her throat felt full of pins and needles. She tried to turn, but a blast of pain seared along her shoulders, her back and enveloped her like a tentacle of fire. "I can't move." Her voice came out a hoarse whisper.

"You caught fire," Rakesh said. "Your sari and..."

Fire. Her attention drifted to the sofa where Rakesh's blazer, marred with holes crusted in gray and black, draped the arm rest. And then it came to her like the ripple on a water's surface. The paintings. The missing necklace.

"You're alive," Rakesh said. "That's what counts."

Dawn at Dusk leaned against the sofa's flank. The top half was intact, but the remainder had charred. The bed of kindling. The paintings. The fire.

"If it hadn't been for Rakeshji," Mama said, "you would have—"

"What were you trying to prove?" Papa intervened. "You almost died. Can you imagine what would..."

Her head throbbed. She had almost died, and Papa was still concerned about everything else. Her heart welled in her throat and she choked back the urge to yell. "Why must everything always be about you? You and Mama lied to save face. Did you ever stop to think what I wanted?"

Papa's eyes widened in shock, and Rakesh inched away from her side.

"All my life, your prestige, honor and integrity burned me alive. You treated me as if I were dead. Invisible. Is this what it takes? For me to almost die to finally matter?"

Papa coughed as if to clear his throat.

Sheetal swallowed. "This is how I am inside. How I've been for a long time."

"Perhaps we should leave, Indu," Papa said. "She needs time to recover."

Sheetal gritted her teeth. "Maybe *you* need time to recover, not me."

Mama looked from her to Papa and back. "We'll come and visit you tomorrow. And...and we'll keep praying that Meghaji returns safe and sound."

Was Megha still missing?

Mama was about to follow Papa out of the room when she turned to Rakesh. "I can stay in case—"

Rakesh followed them. "You have my word, I won't leave her side."

"Where is Yash?" Sheetal asked.

"Moushmi Kaki's with him in the nursery." Rakesh closed the door behind Mama and Papa then sat on the mattress's edge. "What's wrong?"

Sheetal turned to the nurse. "Help me up, please." The nurse and Rakesh slid a palm under her pillow from both sides, and a current of pain, like a short-circuited electric wire, sizzled across her back. They elevated her upright and the pain spread like wildfire across every muscle. The nurse and Rakesh filled the gap between Sheetal and the mattress with pillows and cushions.

Sheetal swallowed and her mouth felt like it was full of sand. "Water."

The nurse brought a cup to Sheetal's lips and gently tipped it. The cool water made its way down Sheetal's throat, flooding more memories. The returned paintings. The delivery. "You bought those paintings behind my back. Making me think I had actually sold them when I—"

"Let's talk later," Rakesh suggested. "We have plenty of time."

"No. Now."

Rakesh gestured for the nurse to leave, and she closed the door on her way out. "Look, I didn't mean for it to happen that way. The paintings weren't supposed to come here," he said. "Only Dawn at Dusk. So you realized how much I cherished that moment and what we had. It's priceless, and I couldn't bear the thought of anyone else putting it on their wall."

"And the other twenty-four?"

"I— That got messed up. I gave Vipul Sahib clear instructions that only Dawn at Dusk should be delivered here. Not—"

"Is that all this is to you? A delivery error? Nothing more? This isn't just about the paintings. It's about us."

He blinked, a blank expression crossing his face. "I was trying to help."

Isn't that what they all said? "How?"

"I wanted to see you happy."

Happy. Sheetal took a small breath. "Buying my work behind my back?"

"There was no demand. People were walking around like it

was a social event or something. I created a need. A market. Didn't you notice? The moment people saw sales, they started buying."

"You can't make our relationship work by buying me out. Or buying me success."

"I wasn't buying you anything. I was making the event successful. Besides, it's not like anyone else knew."

"I do."

"That's not the point."

"This whole thing is about me. Or am I wrong? Is it about you again?"

"It's about how the market works."

"I never asked you for anything except honesty. What you did...made me fall in my own eyes. And where were you planning to hide all twenty-four paintings anyway?"

"I..." He stopped, as if to find the right words. "I don't know, but I was going to eventually tell you."

"Like the time you told me you were at home renovating this room and my studio? And then I found out you had really gone to Amsterdam with someone else? Or the time you claimed to have found me unconscious and it turns out someone else did?"

He turned his back to her. "I had to win back your trust after what happened on your birthday. And your wrecked studio was because of Naina."

"What does Naina have to do with this?"

Rakesh sat on the edge of her bed, near her feet. "Shortly after you left for your mother's place, Naina barged into your studio, destroyed your paintings and wrecked the room. It was beyond simple repair."

Sheetal gulped, absorbing each word. So, the studio had been vandalized and no one had bothered to tell her. Instead, the whole family banded together to hide the event.

"I didn't want to tell you at the time, but...she... I guess you figured she hates you."

"Well, isn't that a surprise?"

"I had your studio renovated before your return so you wouldn't suspect anything."

"Which means you didn't throw away my paintings like you said."

"No."

"Why the lies?"

"Would you have stayed here knowing how much she hates you? She's...she's not normal, but I guess you've figured that out by now."

"I had her medication verified. All of you were hiding things from me." Her throat itched and she swallowed. "Why didn't you just tell me the truth?"

"We had to get her married and settled. We had to somehow convince the Malhotras she was right for Ajay. We tripled the dowry and kept Naina's contact with her in-laws to a minimum so they wouldn't catch on to anything. Imagine the risk to her engagement if anyone outside the family knew."

Her heart fisted in her throat. She'd married into the Dhan-rajs, given birth to one—so, what did that mean? "I'm an outsider then, is that it?"

"You...you were new. What if you leaked the truth?"

"To whom?"

"Anyone."

"I never told anyone a thing, even after I found the Elavils in her room. But look at what all of you have done. You deceived another family."

He raked his fingers through his hair. "It was either that or be stuck with Naina for life."

Bile rose in her throat. She was going to be sick. "So, you basically compensated the Malhotras in cash for taking Naina in."

"It was Pushpa's idea."

"How does it matter? You think no one will know? The Malhotras will find out for sure." She was about to mention Mummyji's recent phone call with Mrs. Malhotra but decided against it. What was the point? "You can't force people into something you want and expect it to work. You have to accept people the way they are. But you've been shoving your will down people's throats. Like that champagne on my birthday. And look how that day ended."

He said nothing.

"It's not about paychecks or profit and loss. It's about relationships. Harmony. Balancing what you have with what you want."

"You don't get it." He lowered his head and cupped his face in his hands. "I had to win you back after I lost you."

"People lose things they own, Rakesh. You never had me to begin with. And how could you after what you did on our first night?"

"I...didn't mean it that way. I—" He rose and crossed to the window. "I wanted to keep you away."

"From what?"

"*Me.* I didn't want to hurt you."

"Hurt?" Sheetal choked on the word. "You raped me on our first night. What could hurt more?"

"Every time I love someone they get hurt. It just happens, and I have no control over it."

"It's not always your doing. Sometimes things happen, like bad coincidences."

"And I'm sick of everything going wrong. How you always find fault in everything I do."

"I don't."

"Say one good thing about me."

The air thickened and her head throbbed. *One good thing. One good thing about him?*

He raised his eyebrows. "Is there anything? Anything, at all, you like about me?"

Her attention fell on a loose thread, snaking from the sheet. Would the truth unravel here? Right now?

"Do you even love me?"

"I..." Her tongue felt like jelly.

"You don't have to say anything."

"How can you blame me? You teamed up with Mummyji against me. Why?"

"What do you mean?"

"I know everything. Your plan to take my inheritance one day."

His expression tightened. "That was her idea. It's all she does, cook things up. I had nothing to do with it. Promise. But you loved someone else before we married, didn't you?"

Sheetal inhaled sharply, and the quick draw of breath made her ribs ache. "He was just a friend."

"You loved him, Sheetal. Admit it."

"It...it's in the past. I gave him up the day we married."

"You still love him. I know."

"He's out of my life."

"I saw you kiss him at the Broken Fort, and I've tried to forget what happened. But I know you still love him, and you want me to be like him."

Was he trying to put words in her mouth? "Why were you spying on me?"

"After lunch that day, at Medit, I followed you and your cousin's home to see where you lived. I saw you slip out the back and I knew something was wrong. How can you hate someone you don't know? Then I understood why. You can't force people into something you want and expect relationships to work. You never accepted me for who I am. When you look at me, it's not at me. It's past me. Like I'm invisible."

Wasn't she the invisible one around here? She turned away and her attention fixed on the clear liquid trickling into her vein, visible only because of the meniscus in the bag.

"It's like you want to find Arvind in me. I'm cold and heartless, aren't I? I see the hatred in your eyes. I somehow knew it would come to this one day. That's why I had someone steal the necklace from your dowry. To bring shame and embarrassment and pressure you and your family to stay put with everything."

"You had thousands of women dying to be Mrs. Dhanraj. Why me?"

"You think they'd put up with Pushpa or Naina?"

The lump tightened in her throat. "You think I can't pick up my bags and leave?"

"I wanted someone who would give me a chance."

"And I tried. But you never gave me a chance. You say you're off to Amsterdam, then you tell me you never went. Then I find out you really did go and...and...a bunch of receipts that meant something else altogether." Her head spun from all the confusion. "Then you shove me off to another room, and I don't know what to believe. My life with you, it's like an illusion. I see you with another woman at Graffiti and I ask you for the truth. I know you're with her. But you lie. You always lie, and I can't take it anymore. And then a baby comes along and now—"

"Let's face it. You were forced into this marriage, like me." He sighed.

"You were so clear at breakfast that morning. You'd never step foot in this house if I went to your office. Clearly, you don't want me in your life. You never wanted this marriage, either. Besides Papa's money, what were you holding on for?" The thought made her sick.

"The—my company's reputation depends on our marriage and this family. I guess you've realized how fucked up we all are. Pushpa and I are stuck together."

"And what about me?"

He turned his back to the window and crossed his arms. "I get it. I was wrong. But there were times, so many times, when it was about us."

"Like when you threw me across the dance floor? When you abandoned me during the pregnancy? Was that us? Or you?" He made for the door, and her stomach went queasy. "What are you going to do about this other woman?"

"Look, I...I was fucking lonely for a long time."

She froze. *Another round of excuses?*

"But it's over now. You were right all along."

For once; it would have been good to be wrong.

He turned the doorknob.

"I was here the whole time, Rakesh. Trying to share my life with you. But you never let me in. You put up walls and you're doing it again."

"Because all you want is Arvind. Look, I'm sorry it didn't work out for you, but that's the truth."

Guilt seeped in with the drips of glucose. Was she equally at fault in signing up for this marriage, determined to hate him? Did she somehow doom this relationship from the start?

"I'll send the nurse in." The door clicked closed.

45
SACHCHAI (TRUTH)

A week later, footsteps thudded along the corridor loud enough to wake Sheetal. She struggled to sit upright. The gauze bandages on her back, like an outer shell, shielded her from the bed linen but did little to ease the scorching pain. Much of the swelling on her shoulders had begun to subside, but when Nandita showed her a reflection of her back, Sheetal was horrified to see a tapestry of welts, swollen patches and pus-filled blisters.

Rakesh threw open the bedroom door, rushed in with a copy of the Sunday edition of *The Raigun Herald* and spread the newspaper on her lap. "You're not going to believe this!"

Naidu Sahib's review of her work in the "Art and Aesthetics" column was circled in red ink. The article used phrases like "deep and meaningful," "able to capture the essence of life with her strokes," and "what it means to be alive." But the title "An Artist Is Born!" and the four-out-of-five-star rating made Sheetal's heart soar.

"He likes my work. He really likes it!"

Rakesh nodded.

Then a thought crossed her mind. "Did you pay Naidu Sahib to write this?"

Rakesh pulled away. "Is that what you think?"

It was hard to trust anything at this point.

"I had nothing to do with this. Honest."

TWO WEEKS LATER, SHEETAL WAS ABLE TO MANAGE SIMPLE TASKS. SHE carried the remains of Dawn at Dusk to her studio and opened the closet door, hoping to find a corner where it might fit. As charred as the painting was, she didn't have the heart to throw it away.

Two cardboard boxes took up the majority of space, and there wasn't much room left in the five-by-seven square foot area, but she didn't want to house the painting anywhere else. She had dragged out the last box when Rakesh walked in.

Rakesh now came home early from work and spent time with Sheetal and Yash before doing anything else. However, Sheetal knew better than to trust this new change.

"Here, let me help you," he said.

"I can do it myself." She looked at Dawn at Dusk and ducked her head. If they were going to live under one roof, the least she could do was be civil. "I was wondering if you knew who this belonged to." She knelt, opened the flap of a box and pulled out the cricket bat, padding gear, and cricket balls.

Rakesh slid a hand along the bat's thin handle then ran a

thumb over a ball's scratched and worn skin. "Where did you find this?"

"I did some clean up before Diwali. They were packed in the closet here."

"I can't believe you found them. Pushpa took these away from me because I'd stopped playing after Mumma died. I searched every cupboard in every room and finally gave up." His expression softened, and Sheetal saw a hint of the chubby little boy in the photographs.

"Why did you stop playing?"

"Mumma used to watch me play on the front lawn. She'd clap and cheer and rally the servants to make two teams. When she died, I couldn't play anymore. I missed her so much. And Pushpa put all this away. She told me she'd thrown it out along with all of Mumma's photos."

Sheetal pulled apart the upper flap of the second box and took out one photo frame at a time.

Rakesh's eyes glazed over and he knelt beside her.

"I didn't know who any of the people were in the photos. I'm guessing that must be your Mumma and Papa. And you." She pointed to the little boy standing beside Ashok and Rashmi outside the Dhanraj mansion.

"I was ten." His voice cracked. "That's Mumma. My beautiful, loving Mumma." He ran his fingers across the glass as if she might come to life at his touch.

"She's so beautiful. I'm sure she must have loved you very much." Sheetal aligned the frames side by side on the carpet, like the missing pieces of his life.

"This was taken outside. And this was taken at someone's

house inauguration." He pointed to the solemn group gathered outside someone's residence.

"I can understand why Megha isn't there. She wasn't born. But where's Naina?"

Rakesh swallowed and the corners of his eyes tightened. "Naina isn't my real sister."

"Oh. She's a cousin then?"

"Pushpa's daughter."

Sheetal stilled. "Mummyji was married to someone else before she— And Naina is her daughter from that first marriage?"

"Pushpa was Papa's mistress before Mumma—" He broke off.

Sheetal took a deep breath and exhaled as reality sank in. "So, Naina is their love child?"

He nodded, his gaze fixed on the carpet.

It all made sense now, why Mummyji favored Naina. Why Naina was so very different. No wonder Megha had been left to the servants' care and Rakesh had assumed the role of a parent at the tender age of thirteen.

"As soon as Mumma died, Papa brought her in. And it's been that way since. Pushpa locked away everything from my past. Like I didn't have one." He ran his fingers over the border of a frame. "And to think, of all the people, you found them." A tear glistened in the corner of his eye.

Sheetal placed a hand on Rakesh's wrist. Maybe now he would find himself.

A WEEK LATER, JANVI'S CRIES FILLED THE MANSION. "MEMSAHIB! Memsahib! She here. She come home."

Megha? Sheetal's heart skipped a beat. She limped down the stairs, followed by Rakesh and Mummyji, and all three halted at the landing.

Ajay and the senior Malhotras stood near the Fulton Whites while Naina lay unmoving on the white cushions. Ajay fished a stack of papers from his briefcase and threw the bundle across the glass coffee table. "Your copy of the divorce papers." He gestured to Naina. "I'm done with her."

Sheetal grabbed the banister for support. The charade was over.

Mummyji turned from Rakesh to Ajay. "Ajayji." She approached him. "I'm sure we can find an alternative to this, I tell you. It's such a small childhood problem, really. And Naina recovers so quickly. I was going to tell you myself, I tell you. Wasn't I, Sheetal?"

"So, this has happened before." Mrs. Malhotra turned to Mummyji. "After the wedding, Sheetal told me the wedding was too much for the girl. That Naina had collapsed from fatigue. Fatigue, my foot!"

Sheetal lowered her gaze to the floor. It was time to reap the rewards of behaving like a Dhanraj, and there was no one to blame but herself.

"Please, listen to me," Pushpa begged. "I'll have Naina's treatment reviewed and—"

"Nonsense. I have nothing more to do with her." Ajay crossed his arms.

"I'll double the dowry," Pushpa pleaded. "I'll—"

"You're paying us to keep her? Is that it?" Ajay barked. "You dump a defective piece on our hands and think you can shut us up with more money? Just you watch, I'll have the entire dowry returned this week and let the media know what you did." Then all three Malhotras turned to leave.

"You can't do this!" Pushpa ran to catch up with them. "Come back. Please, come back."

Two days later, the only thing that came back from the Malhotras was the dowry.

A WEEK LATER, JANVI'S CRIES AGAIN FILLED THE MANSION. "Memsahib! Memsahib! She here. She come home."

Megha? Sheetal descended the stairs, followed by Rakesh and Mummyji, and all three stopped at the landing.

Megha, Raj, and the three Saxenas stood near the Fulton Whites. Dressed in a bridal red and gold salwar suit, Megha held on to Raj's hand.

Rakesh walked toward them, his attention fixed on Megha.

"A copy of our marriage certificate, Sir." Raj handed Rakesh a thin bundle of papers. "We were legally married in court and the temple."

The air escaped Sheetal's lungs and she stood frozen in awe. No dowry. No Swarovski-dotted, silk wedding invitations or colossal golden chariot to mark Megha's wedding. The girl had taken destiny in her own hands. To think, Megha had taken nothing from them, yet had been blessed with everything that wealth, prestige and status couldn't buy: a husband who loved her for who she was.

Rakesh leafed through the papers and swayed like he was about to lose balance. Sheetal advanced and pressed a palm against his back. When the muscles in his back relaxed, she removed her hand.

Rakesh turned to Raj and held out a hand. "Welcome to the family." Then he turned to Megha. "Welcome home."

WITH NAINA BACK, MUMMYJI QUICKLY SETTLED INTO HER PREVIOUS routine, and was even quicker to blame the divorce on the Black Pagoda theme. Plus, she threatened to ostracize Megha from the family for having married a lower-class man of her own choosing. Her remarks, however, had little effect on Sheetal and Rakesh, who pointed out that Naina needed professional therapy and Megha would always be family.

"And what will the world say, I tell you, when they find out Naina's seeing a mental doctor?" Mummyji shook her head.

"That she would have made so much progress by now if you had shown her to a psychiatrist long before instead of worrying about the world's opinions," Sheetal replied.

SITTING BY THE KOI POND ONE AFTERNOON, SHEETAL GENTLY ROCKED Yash in a baby rocker until he fell asleep. The setting sun cast the final rays of sunlight for the day, and Sheetal shifted to block sharp streams from falling across Yash. It was easy to protect him now. He was small and knew nothing of the world. But what would she do as he grew? How would she protect him then? Could she continue to live with Rakesh forever?

The kois darted through the water. One glided up and broke the surface.

The charade had gone on long enough. She had three options. She could easily force three Elavils down the throat of their relationship and live the illusion of happily ever after, or, like Megha, take control of her destiny, which meant seek professional help and get to the root of the problem.

Then, of course, the easiest route involved taking Yash and walking out.

46
PEACE

Rakesh sat alone in the dimly lit den, his attention on the black and white portrait Sheetal had sketched, mounted on the wall. The portrait wasn't just good. It was deep, insightful, and clearly the work of an artist who could see what others didn't.

A sigh escaped his lips and he exhaled. That was the problem. Despite all he'd done, Sheetal had been good to him. She held him up when he was at his weakest. She believed in him when no one else did. She found the missing pieces of his life. She was the one true connection to the real world, the foundation he never had. She was his strength, his peace, and he owed her freedom in order to find his inner peace.

47
HOME

A week later, it was time for Sheetal's annual holiday at Mama's place, but this time she made it clear to Mummyji there would be no time limit and she would decide when to return. "I need time away from all of you," she was firm. "I need to put thought and energy into raising my son now that I'm healing and focus on my career."

Sheetal had received orders and advances from two five-star hotels, three clubs and one convention center, and the requested series of works would easily take two months to complete.

Sheetal walked downstairs, headed to the front door with Rakesh close behind, while servants loaded three Louis Vuitton suitcases into the boot of the black Mercedes.

Rakesh steered her toward the Fulton Whites. "I've been thinking about what you said the other day. You're right. I'm selfish, uncaring, and I'm sorry for everything. My behavior, what I said. And I want you to know, I ended the other relation-ship. It's over. I want us to start afresh."

Was this a joke? Did he expect her to forget and fall lovingly into his arms? "I don't have time for this. I'm getting late."

"And," he went on, "I'm letting you go."

Letting? Sheetal gritted her teeth. *He had the nerve to say that after everything?* "I will decide what I do from now on, with or without permission."

"Don't get me wrong," Rakesh quickly added, "I—"

"I'm tired." Sheetal looked past him to the tessellation of black and white squares spread across the floor like a never-ending maze. Then she looked him in the eye. "Just leave me alone."

Rakesh withdrew a brown envelope from his coat pocket and offered it to her.

"Another timetable? Another list of dos and don'ts? Or am I supposed to follow Dhanraj rules at Mama's house, too?"

Rakesh opened his mouth to say something, but Sheetal grabbed the envelope and rammed it into her handbag. "I'm leaving." Then she walked out the mahogany doors to the waiting car.

"Sheetal!" He followed. "I'll agree to whatever you say. Psychiatric help. A marriage counselor. I'll change. Promise."

Sheetal slid into the back seat beside Moushmi Kaki, who cradled Yash. She sat upright, careful not to press her back against the leather seat. The majority of her burns had healed, but some patches were still swollen with pus. *"Challo, Driverji."*

The driver revved the engine, and Rakesh grabbed the edge of the half-open window and peered in. "Can I come see Yash?"

"You wanted to know what mark I would leave behind in

this world. How people would remember me after I'm gone. Well, look in Yash's eyes and you'll find the answer. And no, you shouldn't, because he needs to get away from you, too."

"But— I'll have all your things shifted back into our room. I'll cut down on my drinking. Smoking. Promise. I— For Yash. I'll do it for Yash."

"If you step back for Yash, that might be better. We don't want to run over your foot."

Rakesh backed away.

"Driverji speed pakro. Late ho rahi hai," Sheetal commanded the driver to pull out and hurry.

48
INSAAF (JUSTICE)

The black Mercedes turned into the driveway at Prasad Bhavan and halted before the main door. Sheetal left the car, climbed the front stairs, and held her breath at the sight of Aunty Hemu standing in the doorway beside two green suitcases. "Are you leaving, Aunty Hemu?"

"Why, *Hambe*. Yes. My job is done for now, and Anjali can manage." Her attention drifted to Sheetal's easel, equipment, and suitcases being carried in. She snorted, and the corner of her lip curled up in a sneer. "*Hambe*, you here to stay?"

"Yes."

"How long?"

"I don't know." Sheetal shrugged. "I'll see."

Aunty Hemu pressed an index finger to her chin. "Doesn't look like anyone's expecting you."

Sheetal took a small breath and held her calm. "I don't care what people expect anymore."

"Problems at the Dhanraj's?"

Sheetal walked past Aunty Hemu and made herself comfortable on a sofa in the living room. Moushmi Kaki, who had followed her, handed Yash over and she propped him on her lap as Aunty Hemu entered the living room. "I thought you were planning on staying forever," Sheetal said. "But you're leaving. Problems at the Prasad's?"

Aunty Hemu brushed the air with a hand. "*Hambe.* It's not right for a woman to spend too much time at her mother's place after marriage. No matter how much it feels like home. A woman's real home is the husband's home."

Sheetal's jaw tightened and she reminded herself to relax. "So true. A woman's real home is the husband's home and in the husband's heart. But she should feel she belongs; otherwise, she is forcing herself where she is not wanted. No?"

Aunty Hemu batted her eyelids and turned away. "Your burns are healed, I suppose. You must be here for rest, then."

"I don't have time to rest. I have several orders I have to start on. I'm here because I want to be here."

"In our days, we didn't—"

"You didn't do a lot of things in your days that women do now. How could you? You didn't have the courage or chance to make yourself heard. You had to do as you were told. But times have changed."

Aunty Hemu spun on her heels and frowned. "We respected our elders. We kept within our limits."

"We keep limits."

"We listened."

Sheetal tightened her grip on Yash. "Listen, Aunty Hemu—"

"Oh Beti!" Mama rushed in. "So good to have you back. And how are the burns now? Healed?"

"Mostly, but a lot of scars and patches still."

"Everything heals and fades with time." Mama sat beside her and took Yash in her arms. "I have some good news."

If Aunty Hemu's plans change, that won't be good news.

"You have your old room back, just the way you wanted."

"Really?"

"Vikram and Anjali have moved into another, bigger one, farther down the hall. And—"

Just then, a car honked.

Aunty Hemu bade them goodbye and left for Vilaspur.

Sheetal lay Yash on her bed and inhaled the comforting scent of lavender. It was good to be home again. She threw open the balcony doors and the fragrance of moist grass flooded the room as Yash cooed and gurgled.

"*Yahaan rakhoon, Choti Sahiba?*" Moushmi Kaki asked if she should put Yash's things in Sheetal's room.

"*Theek hai.*" Sheetal nodded and then asked her to help Mama, who was downstairs, so she could have some privacy. She sat on the edge of the bed, pulled the brown envelope from her handbag, and emptied the contents on the floral-print duvet. A small, white envelope and thin stack of papers slid out. Sheetal unfolded the papers and her chest tightened. Divorce papers. So, that's what Rakesh meant by letting go. She flattened a palm against the duvet. Something hard and bulky pricked her finger-tip. It was the princess-cut diamond ring. She peeled the flap of the white envelope with her thumb and pulled out a white card.

I'm sorry for all the trouble between us. Hope to see you home soon. –Rakesh

Hope and home. Two words she'd carried in her heart for nineteen months. And here they were together in Rakesh's handwriting.

It would be easy, so easy, to shove the ring back into the envelope, sign the divorce papers and return them. She could erase the last year and a half of her life in seconds, pretend it never happened and move on. But there was no pretending. She had lived every moment of those days, weeks and months.

Yash gurgled and laughed, and her attention fell on the curve of his round cheeks and toothless smile. There was no denying any of it. Yash was living proof.

Sheetal held the ring in her right hand and the divorce papers in her left. Yash deserved a family, but how could she give him one without going back? And what was there to return to? Rakesh had lied, cheated and abused her. Going back meant risking everything she had fought for.

The ten-carat diamond sparkled on her palm. Rakesh was guilty of scheming with Mummyji for Papa's fortune behind her back. Laal Bahadur had confessed. But Rakesh had admitted his faults and agreed to therapy, counseling and anything she asked for. He had stood up for her and was willing to give their relationship a shot.

Sheetal slid the ring on the third finger of her left hand where it would cause no interference. Rakesh was willing to make a fresh start. If she agreed to build a future together, it offered Yash the best chance at a normal life. Nothing was more powerful than a mother's love.

After all, Rakesh was the same man, and she was the same woman.

Nothing about them mattered.

Only Yash mattered.

SUGGESTED BOOK CLUB QUESTIONS FOR DYNASTIES

1. How would you describe the relationship between Sheetal and Rakesh?
2. After reading *Dynasties*, what is your opinion of arranged marriages?
3. Has your view of modern India changed after reading *Dynasties*? How?
4. How do you think arranged marriages compare with couples who marry for love and which characters in *Dynasties* amplify the latter?
5. How does the author explore the meaning of love in *Dynasties*? How is the meaning of love different or similar when compared with its meaning in Western society?
6. How does Sheetal's upbringing reflect the values of contemporary Indian society? Which characters contradict those views?

7. Which characters in Sheetal's age group make Sheetal appear conservative and traditional in her viewpoint and actions?

8. How does Sheetal change and grow over the course of the story?

9. Why do you think Rakesh is abusive and uses force to get what he wants? Do you know anyone who behaves in a similar fashion?

10. Is Indu justified in her desires for Sheetal? If you were in Indu's shoes, how would you have handled Sheetal's situation?

11. Do you think Rakesh is a victim of societal pressures? If so, how? How does this affect his behavior and decisions?

12. What issues do Naina and Megha bring to the story? How are they victims of culture and society?

13. How do the numerous aunts in the "Aunty scene" the day after Sheetal's wedding increase tension in the story? What pressure do you think they place on Indu?

14. Who do you see as a villain in *Dynasties*? Which characters reinforce the villain's point of view?

15. How does the birth of Yash affect Sheetal and Rakesh?

16. How do the extremes of wealth and poverty affect the characters' lives and decisions?

17. Several characters in the story struggle to preserve their points of view in *Dynasties*. What are they afraid of losing? Do you know anyone who is dealing with a similar issue?

18. Women's roles in India are shifting and this affects the influence culture and tradition have on their lives. Why do you think some women try to uphold traditional values? Why do others struggle to defeat them? Can you draw a similar parallel in Western society?

19. How does Sheetal struggle to balance the pull toward tradition and culture despite her desire to break from tradition?

20. How is Sheetal trapped between the two families, the Prasads and Dhanrajs? Why doesn't she break free? Do you know anyone else who is similarly trapped?

21. How do Rana, Indu, Pushpa, and Kavita affect Sheetal's decisions in the story?

22. After Sheetal discovers that Arvind has left Raigun, why does she choose to stay in the marriage? How could she have benefited if she had returned to the Prasad's for good?

23. What kind of life do you think Sheetal could have had with Arvind? Considering the wealth and luxuries she's accustomed to, do you think she would have been happier with Arvind than with Rakesh?

24. What examples from other characters' lives give Sheetal insight into the life she could have had with Arvind?

25. What do Rana and Pushpa share in common? Where do they fail as heads of their respective households?

GLOSSARY

Aarti - Hindu ceremony performed to worship the gods.

Agni - Fire

Anand - Happiness

Arrey - Slang for 'hey.'

"Arrey, sambhal ke challo!" - "Hey, look where you're walking!"

Awara - Reckless, vagabond. A person who doesn't care for rules and lives a reckless lifestyle.

Baba - Term of endearment used to address a father or a little boy.

Bachao - Help

Badhi Memsahib - Madame (elderly woman or woman of the house).

Bai - Nanny or maid

Barakh - An edible silver foil used to decorate Indian sweets (mithais).

Behn - Sister

Besharam - Shameless

Beta - Term of affection parents use when addressing sons.

Beti - Term of affection parents use when addressing daughters.

Bhabhiji - Term of respect for an older brother's wife.

Bhaiya - Term of respect used to address an older brother.

Bhavan - A large house or structure built for a specific purpose, e.g. to hold meetings or conferences.

"Bhook lagi hai. Kooch de na." - "I'm hungry. Give us food/something to eat."

Bichari - Poor (an expression of pity or sympathy.)

Bindi - Ornament used by women to decorate the forehead. Tiny, colorful accessories available in different colors and designs and placed between the eyebrows. Bindis were originally worn by married women to show their marital status but are now used as a form of decoration.

Brahma - The Creator of the universe, good and evil, light and dark. The first god in the Hindu triumvirate, or trimurti. The triumvirate consists of three gods who are responsible for the creation, upkeep and destruction of the world. The other two gods are Vishnu and Shiva.

"Bus choot jayegi" - The bus will leave.

Challo - Let's go.

Chana masala - A spicy, tangy and sweet chickpea curry.

Chapati – Whole wheat, circular flatbread cooked on a griddle.

Chikan – Also known as chikankari. A type of white-on-white embroidery that often includes shadow work, used to decorate a variety of lightweight textiles such as muslin, silk, chiffon, organza, net, etc. Modern Chikan embroidery may be worked on pastel-colored fabrics.

Choti Sahiba - Little Madame

Chotte Sahib - Little Master (younger male member in the family).

Churidar - Skin-tight trousers made from cotton and cotton-silk fabrics, cut longer than normal, which allows the fabric to cluster in folds about the ankles.

Dadi - Paternal grandmother

Dal palak – A protein-rich soup of lentils and spinach flavored with spices.

"Dekho, dekho!" - "Look, look!"

Diwali - Hindu festival of Lights occurring anywhere from mid-October to mid-November. The festival involves the lighting of small clay lamps filled with oil to signify the Hindu God Lord Ram's return after fourteen years in exile and his triumph of good over evil.

Diya - A cup-shaped clay lamp with a cotton wick, lit to dispel darkness on religious Indian festivals.

"Doctor ko bulao." - "Call the doctor."

"Driverji speed pakro. Late ho rahi hai." - "Please hurry up, driver. We're running late."

Dupatta - A long scarf that compliments many south Asian women's suits (salwar kameez).

Ganesh - Hindu god with an elephant's head, widely worshipped by most Hindus. He is known as the Remover of Obstacles and Lord of Beginnings and honored at the beginning of rituals and ceremonies.

Ghagra - Woman's clothing which is popular in the northern and western areas of India. The attire consists of a blouse, a full-length skirt and a matching stole. It is usually worn on religious occasions, ceremonies and weddings.

Ghazal - Originating from Arabic and Persian literature, it is a poetic form of expression consisting of rhyming couplets and a refrain, with each line sharing the same meter.

Ghee - Clarified butter

"Hai Ishwar!" - "Oh Lord!"

Halwa - Soft, Indian sweet that is made from a variety of ground nuts, semolina or ground flour. This is cooked in clarified butter and sweetened with sugar.

Harmonium - A type of free-reed organ in the shape of a keyboard that generates sound as air flows past a vibrating piece of thin metal held in a frame.

Hathphool - An Indian bracelet joined to a ring(s) by a chain.

"Hatto Chowkidaar." - "Move aside, security guard."

Havan - A metal vessel that contains a consecrated fire wherein offerings are made to the gods. Used during special occasions such as marriages, births, and home inaugurations.

Hindi - Official language of India, widely spoken in the northern regions.

Insaaf - Justice

"Jaldi jaldi" - Hurry, hurry

"Jaldi karo!" - Hurry up!

Juttis - Silk shoes that fit snugly round the feet and taper to a delicate curl above the toes.

Kaki - A term of respect used to address an older woman.

Karva Chauth - A festival that usually falls in the month of October, 4 days after the full moon, chiefly celebrated by married Hindu women from the northern part of India.

Kesar Barfi - Saffron flavored, dense, milk-based sweet.

Koyal - Cuckoo bird. Glossy, black bird that makes a loud cooing sound.

Krishna - The central figure in Hinduism known as the supreme being and believed to be the eighth and most important avatar of Lord Vishnu. He is usually depicted wearing a yellow, silk dhoti and a crown made from peacock feathers.

Kundan – A traditional form of Indian gemstone jewelry that originates from Rajasthan and Gujrat whereby gems are mounted in gold foil instead of prongs, a technique used most often in the construction of elaborate necklaces.

Kurta - A loose shirt falling either just above or somewhere below the knees of the wearer, traditionally worn by men. Women wear a straight-cut kurta or its shorter version, the kurti.

Lakshmi - The Hindu goddess of wealth, fortune and prosperity. She is the wife and shakti (energy) of Vishnu, one of the principal deities of Hinduism and the Supreme Being in the Vaishnavism Tradition.

"Log kya kahenge?" - "What will people say?"

Maali Kaka - Term of respect used for elderly male gardener.

Maang tikka - A piece of jewelry that consists of a hanging ornament at one end and a hair pin at the other. The pin is attached to the hair in such a way that the ornament dangles at a woman's hairline.

Mahal - Palace

Maji - A term of respect used for mother-in-law (previous generation).

Mandap - A temporary, covered structure with pillars

erected for the purpose of a wedding. The four pillars symbolize the four parents who worked hard to raise the children. The main wedding ceremony takes place under a mandap.

Masala movie – An Indian cinematic production that combines comedy, romance, action, song, and dance in dramatic or melodramatic plots.

Matki - Round earthenware pots that are narrow at the top and bottom with a large middle section, used to hold water.

Megha - Cloud

Mehndi - A form of body art from Ancient India in which decorative designs are created on a person's body using a paste created from the powdered dry leaves of the henna plant. Henna tattoos.

"Mein kholoo, Choti Sahiba?" - "Should I open the door, Little Madame?"

Memsahib - A married or upper-class woman.

"Memsahib, koi aaya hai." - "Madame, someone's here '[to see you]."

"Mera photo aisa hi laina." - "Take my photo like this [in this pose]."

Mithai - Sweet, referring to Indian sweetmeats.

Mogra - Arabian jasmine flowers with a sweet and delicate scent.

Mutter korma - A tangy, creamy curry made with peas and Indian cheese.

Naak - nose

Namaste - Indian form of greeting performed with hands pressed together, palms touching, fingers pointed upward, thumbs close to the chest, and with a slight bow of the head. The equivalent of 'hello' with an element of respect.

Nettipattam - Distinctive golden head covering worn by elephants during temple festivals in the southern regions of India. Meant to symbolize Lord Ganesh in full splendor.

Paan - A preparation combining betel leaf with areca nut and other mouth-freshening condiments, widely consumed in the Indian subcontinent. After chewing, the juice is either spat out or swallowed.

Paisa - A monetary unit in India. One paisa is equivalent to 1/100 of a rupee.

Pallu - The loose end of a sari.

Paneer - Indian cheese

Paneer korma - A spicy, Indian Mughlai curry made with yoghurt, coconut, cashews, and chunks of Indian cheese.

Parajay - Loss

Pashmina - A type of fine Kashmiri wool.

Phera - Wedding vows that constitute seven circumambulations around a sacred fire. The vows are considered unbreakable with the God of Fire held as witness to bless the couple's union.

Phool gobi - Cauliflower

Pithi - A paste made from turmeric, chickpea flour and rosewater and rubbed on the bride and groom's legs, arms, and face to cleanse the skin.

Puja - The act of worship.

Punarjanam - Rebirth

Pundit - A learned sage. In India, the term is used to refer to priests.

Raita - A refreshing side dish made from yoghurt, spices, vegetables and herbs.

Rajasthan - The largest state in India located in the north-western region, comprising most of the wide Thar Desert, also known as the Rajasthan Desert.

Rajkumar - Prince

Rakesh - Lord of the night.

Ram - The seventh avatar of Lord Vishnu, Lord Ram is a major deity in Hindu religion and the central figure of the Hindu epic *Ramayan*.

Ravana - Originally a great devotee of Lord Shiva, Ravana is also the primary antagonist in the ancient Hindu epic *Ramayana* where he is depicted as a Rakshasa, the Great demon king of Lanka with ten heads and twenty arms.

Rupee - The common name for the currency of India. From 1995–1998, the U.S. Dollar to Rupee exchange rate fluctuated from about U.S. $1 = Rs.35 to about U.S. $1 = Rs.42.

Saafa - Turban-like headwear for men, worn by the groom and others at weddings.

Sachchai - Truth

Sahib - A respectful Indian term of address for a man meaning Master/Sir.

Sahiba - Respectful Indian term of address for a woman.

Salwar - A pair of loose trousers with a light fit around the ankles.

Salwar kameez - Popularly known as the Punjabi suit. The traditional dress of women in the Punjab region of north-western India and eastern Pakistan. The outfit comprises a pair of trousers (salwar) and a tunic (kameez) that is usually paired with a scarf (dupatta).

Sanskrit - An ancient Indo-Aryan language of India and the primary language of Hinduism.

Sari - A garment worn by women from the Indian subcontinent that consists of a single drape of fabric, varying from 5–9 yards in length and 2–4 feet in breadth. It is typically wrapped around the waist with one end draped over the shoulder.

Shanti - Peace

Sheetal - Cool/Gentle (wind)

Sherwani - A knee length, full-sleeve coat that buttons to a stand-up collar, worn by men in South Asia.

Shloka - A two-line verse in praise of god.

Sindoor - A red powder (vermilion) used by Indian women to streak the part in their hair to indicate their married status.

Sitar - A plucked string instrument of the lute family that is usually four-feet long and has a gourd-shaped body. The instrument is widely used in Hindustani classical music.

Tabla - A membranophone percussion instrument originating from the Indian subcontinent, consisting of a pair of drums used in traditional, classical, popular, and folk music. One drum is slightly larger than the other. During play, pressure from the heel of the hand is used to vary pitch.

Taiji - Term of respect used to refer to a father's older brother's wife.

Tandoor - A cylindrical clay oven used in cooking and baking.

Thali - A large metal platter with a raised edge used for dining (as plates) and also in rituals and prayers to hold the prayer items.

"Theek hai." - "That's fine."

Tisandhi - The arising

Upma - A thick porridge or soft cake made from dry roasted semolina or coarse rice flour.

Varmala - An Indian wedding garland that is usually strung with flowers and/or rupee notes and exchanged by the bride and groom. The garlanding of flowers ceremony takes place at the commencement of the wedding ceremony.

Vardhaman - Rising

Wallah - Guy

Yaar - Friend/Dude/Mate

"Yahaan rakhoon, Choti Sahiba?" - "Should I keep it here, Little Madame?"

Zardozi - A type of metal embroidery used on Indian textiles and costumes, derived from an ancient Persian artform that predates the Mughal empire. Different shapes of metal and wire (springs, coils, strips, ribbons and discs) are used. Wedding attires are renowned for this type of embroidery.

ACKNOWLEDGMENTS

This book would not have been possible without the support, wisdom and encouragement of talented professionals from all around the world. I am grateful to each one of you for helping to make my dream a reality.

Thank you to my sister, Dr. Shruti Daga MD PhD, UK, for all the medical research, 'homework,' reading and rereading the manuscript until your eyes grew dry. "What happens next?" – Your and Renuka's never-ending enthusiasm for two decades has been like a torch for each book in the series.

Thank you to my soul sister, USA Today Bestseller, Jade Lee (aka Kathy Lyons). You believed in this "Mango in a market of apples and oranges" and forever held my fort. I have come this far because of you. To my Guruji, New York Times Bestseller, Haywood Smith, thank you for teaching me that the art to writing a damn good novel is not to sprint but run a marathon. To USA Today Bestseller Lauren Smith, they say 'Three time's a charm,'. Thanks for being my lucky charm and holding the ropes as I climbed after the landslide. To USA Today Bestseller, Beverly Jenkins, your pioneer strength in today's 'colorful' world of publishing is an inspiration. We fight to be heard in all our colors of diversity.

Sheetal and Rakesh's designer clothes would not have been possible without the incredible advice and expertise of India's leading fashion designers, Ms. Anita Dongre, House of Anita Dongre, and Mr. Arjun Khanna, House of Khanna Classic Couture. I am grateful to you both for your belief and conviction in the characters and this series.

Sheetal's Pilates regiment was carefully orchestrated by Pilates and yoga instructor, Ms. Abbey Brewer, Atlanta, USA. The following authors shared their advice, insightful critiques, and to all of you I am grateful: New York Times Bestseller, Dianna Love, Anna DeStefano, Berta Platas and Carla Fredd.

Warmest thanks to Archana Pai Kulkarni, editor, writer and former Executive Editor, *New Woman* magazine, Mumbai, India. You believed in me and my works over twenty years ago when I was struggling to find my voice. You continue to be an inspiration.

Thanks to my closest friends and cheerleaders, Jayanthi Kanderi, Anshu Chopra and Marilyn Baron–your unrelenting enthusiasm kept me going. To writing organizations: Women's Fiction Writers Association, Georgia Romance Writers, and Atlanta Writers Club–my writing rooms with a hearth— writing is a lonely journey and you helped me find my tribe. To Kathy L Murphy, CEO International Pulpwood Queen and Timber Guys Book Club Reading Nation – thank you for believing in stories of diversity, your unrelenting support and sharing the fan love for Shah Rukh Khan and the Winds of Fire Series. You are a gift to every author.

To my husband, my love, Vivek. I am grateful for your patience and support over the last two decades and many more that lie ahead. I didn't think I would make it this far, but you did. You always said, *"Apna time aayega."* (Our time will come.)

To Vikhyat and Vishesh. My children. Books to an author are like children. You nurture and create the characters with love and dedication hoping each page will shine. Sometimes it takes months or years. Sometimes decades to get a book on its feet. But no book will ever compare or shine like the two of you.

BOOK 2: ONCE AND FOR ALL
TRAPPED

A black Mercedes pulled up to the curb, and a security guard dressed in a black uniform who stood beside Sheetal, opened the passenger door. The boot of the car opened, and the guard gestured for Sheetal's shopping bag. "May I, Madame," he asked in Hindi. "I can store your bags in the boot, so you are more comfortable."

No. She tightened her grip on the bag's handle and the sari tucked inside. She didn't need more room and comfort in the passenger seat. He would never understand how precious the contents of this bag were. It wasn't just any sari, but a designer sari with elaborate red and gold trimmings, the annual *Karva Chauth* gift destined for Megha, to confirm her sister-in-law's marital bliss.

If only she could hold the silk between her fingers and squeeze its promise of love and happiness into her married life so she could reunite with her son. Her heart welled in her throat. Like every other married Hindu woman, she would fast from dawn until moonrise and pray for her husband's welfare, longevity, and prosperity. *Karva Chauth* was intended to bring every couple together and strengthen the foundation of their marriage. It was the tradition of her ancestors.

Sheetal paused on the sidewalk and looked at the traffic flowing toward northern Raigun, the poorer part of town, where Mama and Papa had once lived. But that was in the past, before Papa's business succeeded and he was able to give her away in marriage to a prestigious family.

Her husband, Rakesh, the CEO of Dhanraj & Son, was away on business, as he was most of the time. The extra work hours, late nights and excessive travel were part of his efforts to recoup the three hundred and fifty million rupee debt incurred by her other sister-in-law's wedding.

Rakesh was working hard. Too hard, perhaps? Like she was on her oil paintings and her ten-year marriage. The marriage ensured their son had a family to return to from boarding school. It gave Mama who was battling cancer, reason to endure the chemotherapy and live for another day. It validated that she had done the right thing in marrying the man Mama and Papa had chosen.

Did that mean she was at fault for failing Rakesh when it came to his health and wellbeing?

Sheetal ducked and slid into the car. The door slammed shut behind. She handed the guard a hundred-rupee note through the open window.

"*Dhaniyavad*, Madame," he thanked her and pressed both palms together in namaste, bowing his head several times.

"*Theek hai.*" She told him it was fine.

Was it? Rakesh was the one suffering from weight loss and

fatigue while she was fine. At least, that's what the public thought.

"*Aage kahan?*" The chauffeur, in his crisp, white uniform, asked where she wanted to go next.

"*Hira Moti.*" Diamond Pearl, the jewelry store where the Dhanrajs had their jewelry custom-made.

The car snaked through trucks, black and yellow taxis, private cars and auto rickshaws. Pedestrians rushed along the pavements as diesel from the trucks' tail pipes clouded their bodies, causing them to cough and sneeze. Perhaps if they worked as hard as Papa, they too could rise from the middle class. But what if they weren't blessed for success or had erred in some way, causing the gods to withdraw fate and good luck?

Several pedestrians crossing the road paused between the bumpers of honking traffic, momentarily trapped.

Sheetal sank into the Mercedes' seat, took a deep breath, and exhaled. If she'd married the man she once loved, she could have been trapped like one of those pedestrians. Sheetal bit her lower lip. She had been twenty-two at the time. Any sensible Indian girl would also have chosen wealth and prestige over love.

She ran her right palm over the glossy cover of the October issue of Vogue, India, that she'd been reading on the ride to the sari boutique.

The cover article entitled 'Jump-Start His Engine' was a Top 10 list of guaranteed ways to rake the honeymoon back into stale marriages. Suggestions like keeping open channels of communication, talking, being upfront that you want him, telling him you love him, demanding your man's time and attention, splurging on new lingerie, and transforming dinners into dining with a candle-lit ambience "with you as dessert" had caused Sheetal to cringe. Rakesh wined and dined clients after work. Where was the question of transforming dinners into a dining experience when they hardly ever ate together? On the few occasions when they did, mealtimes included the whole family, and he perpetually turned a deaf ear.

The family. Sheetal bit her lower lip. They were always there. Everywhere. Indian couples rarely expressed affection for one another in public. In private? Sheetal released her lower lip from her teeth. She had spent thousands of rupees on imported lingerie that stuck to her like a second skin by morning. Those who were daring enough to not wait were suggested an alternative. Grab him in the nude and tell him you have to have him. Now.

Sheetal closed the magazine and left it face-down on the seat. Those suggestions worked for western women who were known to be forthright and demanding. Not Indian women who accepted their fate.

There must be another way. Sheetal straightened her posture. A better way.

"*Aa gaye*, Madame." The chauffer eased the Mercedes to a halt in front of the shop with golden pillars and gold and silver letters.

Sheetal entered through the glass doors and was immediately greeted by the store manager, dressed in a suit and tie. Waist-high glass cabinets displaying readymade jewelry ran the shop's perimeter. Salesmen in lime green shirts and gray trousers, and saleswomen in lime green saris with a gray temple-border, were busy attending to several customers. Sheetal followed the manager to the private show room sealed behind a wooden door on the right. Several customers, probably friends shopping together, turned to look, pointed in her direction and whispered to one another.

Sheetal cringed and looked ahead, avoiding their gazes. Her left shoulder covered by the heavily embroidered sari pallu slumped beneath the burden of elite status. Out of habit, she raised a hand to her left earlobe and touch the two-carat diamond solitaire earring. Diamond bangles tinkled along her wrist. More people turned to look in her direction, and Sheetal wished she had kept her hand by her side. It wasn't the expensive pink georgette sari, the diamond earrings, bangles on her wrist or the ten-carat diamond solitaire on the third finger of her left hand that drew everyone's attention. She was a renowned oil-painter, but that wasn't responsible for disturbing the harmony of the shop's rhythm, either. The cause of the disturbance was simple. She was married to a Dhanraj, and the Dhanrajs had a way of making heads turn.

How she longed to be one of the women who stared and talked in hushed whispers. If only she had friends to confide in so she wouldn't have to bear the loneliness of living in a mansion of secrets. She could have lived her dream if she'd married the other man. But she didn't. That decision was in the past. Over.

Sheetal seated herself on a plush swivel chair at a round glass table in the center of the brightly lit private show room and turned to the manager. "Please show me the latest full-set in precious stones and diamonds."

Several salesmen and women rushed back and forth at the manager's call to pull from the vault the latest in designer collections. Rings, bracelets, necklaces and earrings in diamond and gold cascaded before her. Fiery rubies, blue sapphires and green emeralds spilled across beds of plush black velvet, reminding Sheetal of oceans and lands her husband flew across countless times in search of the next business opportunity.

The manager unfolded a dark blue velvet cloth. A necklace with pink diamonds, tiny rubies and white gold trim glittered in the yellow lights. "This one arrived yesterday."

Sheetal's breath caught. "How much is it?"

"Two *crores* for the necklace."

Twenty million rupees? The price of Rakesh's Lamborghini? Sheetal gulped. She couldn't spend that much, even though it matched perfectly with the *Karva Chauth* gift for her sister-in-law.

"The earrings and bracelet are—"

"Just as beautiful, I'm sure," Sheetal cut him short. "But it's for a friend," she lied. "Do you have anything less formal?" He was bound to understand that she meant something less expensive. What he probably wouldn't understand was why a Dhanraj asked for something less expensive. He didn't need to understand. The debt was her business.

A good wife hid the family secrets and lived within her husband's means—even if the husband put the family in debt. Like every good Indian woman from a good Indian family, Sheetal's status at her in-laws', her position in society and her sense of self-worth were measured by the strength of her marriage. Sheetal did everything possible to make her marriage appear intact.

The manager showed her a pendant of mini pearls, rubies and diamonds, and Sheetal laced her fingers through each string of pearls that supported the pendant. The pearls were white like the marble interior of the Dhanraj mansion. The mini palace offered seventy-thousand square feet of living space, but lately Sheetal had been suffocating beneath its sixty-feet-tall ceilings. She ran her thumb over a pearl. Cold. Like the heart of her marriage. "How much is it?"

"Four *lakhs* for the pendant."

Four hundred thousand... Sheetal sat up. The price of the Mercedes. That was better.

"The pearls are..."

Didn't oysters die when a pearl was extracted from its womb? What if she, like the oyster, had died eight years ago when her sari caught on fire? A shudder rippled up her spine. Like Rakesh, her son would have also grown up trapped under the cruel dictatorship of her stepmother-in-law.

She was lucky to be alive. Her marriage? Not so. She released the pendant and it fell onto the bed of plush black. She couldn't let her marriage collapse and risk her son's future.

A good Indian wife didn't give up. She forgave all sins including those of her husband. *Especially* those of her husband because that's what kept the marriage intact. A good Indian wife was loving and caring. If she had needs and desires her husband couldn't fulfill, she forgave him and filled her life with all that he *could* give. Even if he wanted little to do with her.

"This," the manager held up a necklace, "is the latest in Jaipur *Kundan* work. Complete with earrings, rings, bangles..."

Sheetal took the inch-wide necklace constructed in segments and connected by tiny clasps. It, too, would match the sari she had chosen for her sister-in-law. She pulled the band of gold from both sides and tested the minute joints to see if they'd come apart. They didn't. The necklace was sturdy. It would endure and stand the test of time. Rubies. Sapphires. Emeralds. Didn't they weather the wrath of wind, water, earth and fire to sparkle and shine? Her marriage would too. It had to.

Sheetal ran the index finger of her right hand over a single diamond dangling from the necklace's center. It slept in a bezel setting surrounded by an ocean of twenty-two carat gold held in position by four sharp prongs.

It was trapped.

She was trapped.

There was no way out.

ABOUT THE AUTHOR

Fiction author, international freelance journalist, blogger and former newspaper reporter, Anju was born in India but grew up in Hong Kong. She has also lived and been published in Singapore, India, Australia, USA and finally dug her roots in Atlanta, Georgia, with her husband, two dashing boys and a rebel lionhead rabbit. Anju hopes her books will Bridge Cultures and Break Barriers.

Connect with Anju:
www.anjugattani.com
goodreads.com/author/show/5392481.Anju_Gattani

CPSIA information can be obtained
at www.ICGtesting.com
Printed in the USA
LVHW101150110123
736920LV00019B/573/J

9 798986 652405